# The
# Annealing
## of Aliza
# Bennett

## Emma Hartley

Published by Satin Romance
An Imprint of Melange Books, LLC
White Bear Lake, MN 55110
www.satinromance.com

Published in the United States of America.

Cover Design by Fantasia Frog Designs

*For my mother, who inspired my love of writing
and taught me to be strong.*

ANNEAL: *transitive verb*

1: to heat and then cool (as steel or glass) usually for softening and making less brittle; also: to cool slowly usually in a furnace

2: strengthen, toughen

# PART ONE

# ONE

*Sometimes the jeweler starts with a sketch, sometimes only with raw metals, sometimes with stones which may drive the ultimate form, imbuing it with meaning. This time, however, she starts with a word, incubating it in her heart like a fragile humming bird egg, tiny yet brimming with possibility. She rolls it off her tongue during silent moments, like a mantra, allowing it to center her, praying it brings the peace it seems to promise.*

Jesse Black had never experienced a worse flight. Now that he was safely on the ground, he could contemplate with clarity what a true horror the redeye had been. Between the near constant turbulence, intense enough to feel like a roller coaster, and the persistent, borderline obsessive thoughts of his break-up with Grace only hours before, it was all he could do to keep from swearing out loud and muttering to himself like a crazy person. *Wouldn't the tabloids have a field day?*

He had ruminated for hours as he passed over the Rockies, then past the faded patchwork of the Midwest, dawn a distant glimmer on the eastern horizon. Replaying the break-up over and over in his mind, he wondered why he hadn't seen it coming. *Because I'm stupid. All the signs were there.* He couldn't have thought she would move with him, after all. Not Grace, no way. She was LA personified. A little town like Twin Falls would have actually killed her. She would have shriveled up without the smog and bustle and glamour of the city.

Blasting some loud music on his headphones to distract himself hadn't helped. He'd flipped blindly through the airline magazine, but the only thing he saw was her all-American face, blond hair, perfect skin, and the way she glared at him over her water bottle if he'd said something too suggestive. He had to admit, she had become a part of him. A year is a long time when you're young.

Now Jesse was on his way to the smallest town in the universe. Trapped in a limousine with a chatty young driver and self-professed aspiring actor, all he wanted was some peace and quiet. He thought his noncommittal answers and long, reticent silences should have discouraged the guy, but the quieter Jesse was, the more talkative the driver became.

"I was an extra in a movie when I was a kid. Since then, I've had the bug. I want to be in the movies, and I'm saving money so I can move to LA. Is that where you live?"

"Mmm-hmm."

"Gosh, that's got to be the life. I can't imagine how great it is. Perfect weather, gorgeous babes everywhere, ritzy dinners. Is it amazing?"

"Mmm-hmm."

At least he didn't have to elaborate, Jesse thought moodily. *This guy's got the whole picture in his mind. He doesn't need me.* This, however, freed Jesse's mind up to think about Grace and the life he was leaving behind and the horror vacui of the blank slate ahead.

His girlfriend wasn't the only one who couldn't abide a tiny town in the middle of nowhere. His mother had apparently felt the same. Jesse had only been in a couple of commercials and had a few minor roles on TV shows before, all while his mother supported him. She had told him it would be a foot in the door to take the small parts until he landed something bigger. "Be patient," was her mantra. He hated to admit, she had been right. When he was cast in a lead role in a brand new prime-time drama, she was overjoyed for him. Then she found out where it was being shot and decided this time he would have to go on his own. He was old enough, after all, and she wanted her life back.

"Where is Twin Falls, anyway?" she had wondered aloud when he told her the news.

Now, as the limo crested another postcard-perfect New England hill, to his left Jesse's attention refocused on reality as the village unfolded before him. Sunlight glittered on the rooftops of every building in the valley. A lively river wound its way through the center of the town, whitewashed bridges spanning the divide. Trees were full of promiscuous pink and white blossoms, filling the vista with cotton candy colors and a Norman Rockwell sensibility. It was enough to make Jesse's stomach turn. This *would* be painful after LA.

The more positive side of his nature whispered through the angry haze in his mind, *It's work. At least you have a gig.*

Right, his more morose side responded. *It* will *be work living here.* It was no wonder his mother sent him alone and Grace had kicked him to the curb.

Twin Falls appeared to be one of those quintessential old towns, not unlike the one he'd grown up in, where the buildings are all from the late 1800s and there's a town square with a gazebo. Everything looked clean, well-manicured, and perfectly charming. There was very little traffic on the streets, which reinforced the feeling he had stepped back in time.

Jesse vaguely heard the driver's monologue shift to the topic of the "historic village of Twin Falls." The accolades the driver bestowed upon the quaint town cascaded unheard into empty air as Jesse continued to stare out the window in sullen silence.

They wound their way down the hill into the valley and glided onto Main Street. Wow, Jesse mused. *It's actually called Main Street.*

*How friggin' charming is that?* He crossed his arms over his chest moodily. The driver pulled the limo up to a brick building with huge windows overlooking the quiet street. People were walking to and fro, but no one looked real. Steeling himself, Jesse got out, brushed off the driver's best wishes with a backward wave, and shouldered his bag.

A girl came out of the building and approached him. "You must be Jesse." She held out her hand to shake his and said cheerfully, "It's great to meet you."

Rather than shake the hand held out to him, Jesse, looked past her. "I'll take a cup of coffee with cream and sugar. Bring it in as soon as you can. I'm dead tired." He started to brush past her, ignoring the extreme blush coloring the girl's cheeks.

"What in the hell are you talking about?"

"Coffee. C-O-F-F-E-E," he spelled out condescendingly. "Ever heard of it?"

"Wow. You clearly have no idea who I am." She looked thoroughly incensed and hit him a withering glance. "I'm your co-star, you total ass. Welcome to Twin Falls." With a final hard glare, she spun around and strode into the building.

Shame welled up in Jesse's chest, settling in with his other preoccupations, weighing his mood down even more. How had he not realized this was the same girl from every tabloid on the newsstand? Aliza Bennett, child star, struggling actor, ever-troubled love life, and constant fodder for every rag on the market. He hadn't even looked at her. *Great. Could this get any better? What a day.*

Peering through the window before he entered the building, he saw Aliza had started telling a small crowd of people what had happened. She pointed towards the door as he gathered enough courage to step through it. He heard laughter and realized he was being intentionally ignored by the majority of people in the room. *Off to a great start. Lovely.*

Coffee, however, was the priority at the moment. Apologies and introductions could wait. Immediate access to caffeine was of the essence. He sauntered towards a table set with various confections and beverages, tried to look casual, poured a cup of coffee with a splash of milk, and downed it. After his second, he felt almost human again. He took a deep breath and turned to face the crowd, knowing what must be done.

Aliza stood with a group of awkward looking people, clearly techies. She, on the other hand, was quite stunning, now that he could look at her. A certain sort of punk independence electrified the very air around her, intensified by her anger at him. Heavily outlined ice-blue eyes blazed beneath dark lashes. The magazine pictures didn't do her justice. He started towards her, stopping only to pluck a little white flower out of the table arrangement. Of course, she'd noticed him but continued to pretend to ignore him. He stopped just short of her little entourage, knowing his presence was commanding enough to make them turn to face him, even if they weren't aware of the fact.

Silence descended on the group as he approached. Jesse offered her the flower. "Sorry about what happened outside. I'm utterly useless until I've had about a hundred cups of coffee. Please forgive me."

Reluctantly, Aliza accepted the flower, but her expression gave away her lingering annoyance.

He continued, undaunted. "I'm looking forward to working with you, Aliza."

"I hope you're not going to be that kind of rude all the time," she replied fiercely.

"Just before eight, I'm afraid," he responded. His playful smile was usually a powerful mollifier. She remained unmoved, but he enjoyed a challenge.

———

Jesse turned his gaze towards some of the people around them and introduced himself. They were easier to win over, and Aliza resented it. Magnetic or not, Aliza's skepticism won out. His apology was probably an act. She was not convinced of his sincerity, fearing he had showed something of his true nature out there on the sidewalk before he knew they were equals. Her guard was solidly in place. She'd had enough of guys who thought they ruled the world, and she was only twenty-two.

Soon, Rudy, the director, called everyone's attention to the front of the room. Aliza adored this small, charismatic man. He had been a family friend forever. Someone had put out a crate for him to stand on for his speech. Granted, he wasn't very tall, but a box? Really? The more she thought about it, the harder it became to hide her smile. Luckily, he must have been trying out some of his new material. Several of the people in the room were giggling out loud, and most were smiling as the director talked. She stopped holding back and let out a laugh, thankfully blending into the crowd.

She sensed a presence near her, much nearer than she would have preferred. Without looking she knew it was Jesse. She didn't want to move away. To do so would have showed him that he made her uncomfortable. Unable to concentrate on the director's words, they slipped past her, unabsorbed, flickering through the air and out the back door. She resented Jesse's distracting presence. Her conscious mind was fully occupied by assessing Jesse's motives. He took a step closer. One more move on his part and their arms would be touching. How could she let her discomfort show now?

Rudy started calling out names. People raised their hands and introduced themselves, briefly. When it was her turn, Aliza started to tell a little about herself, and in her animation, she knocked right into Jesse's chest with her gesticulating hand.

"Beating me up already? I guess I deserve it." His whisper, although barely audible above her own voice, sent a little jolt of electricity through Aliza.

She continued her speech gracefully. "I feel honored to work with such a talented cast and crew." With those last words, she turned to face Jesse with a cool smile.

Now it was Jesse's turn to introduce himself. He spoke for a shorter time than Aliza had, and ended by looking straight at her.

"Thank you for the warm welcome. I look forward to getting started." He smiled broadly at the room. Everyone smiled back.

Rudy wrapped up his comments and people broke off into groups again, or in some cases, they got back to work. Aliza turned towards Jesse with a fiery expression. "What in the hell was that?"

"What are you talking about?" he replied, nonchalantly.

"Why were you standing so close to me? Were you trying to throw me off my guard?"

"Ah, the direct approach. You don't see much of that anymore, especially with people of our generation. It's refreshing, Aliza." He smiled again. "I'd offer you a cup of coffee, but it looks like you've already had enough."

*I'm going to torture him,* she thought, fuming, as he walked away. As Aliza schemed some dark designs to take him down a peg, her thoughts flickered involuntarily to Jesse's unique eyes, aqua, with a dark green ring around the iris, set off by dark lashes. If she had a weakness, it was light eyes with dark lashes. She gathered herself, put his attractive face out of her mind, and turned to the work ahead.

# TWO

*A fellow on Santa Monica Pier used to write his customer's name on a grain of rice for a couple of dollars. Grandpa had gotten her one, so long ago. She smiles at the memory, allowing it to linger for a moment before passing on. The jeweler writes her word as small as she can on a fine piece of paper and cuts it to fit. Rolling it up into a minuscule scroll, she sets it aside in her desk. The plan in her mind is beginning to coalesce.*

Maryann, the script girl, was insipid—something Aliza couldn't take. Although she went out of her way to be kind to the girl, there was something about the internship-while-mommy-and-daddy-pay-for-college attitude that Aliza couldn't stand. Maybe it was Maryann's khaki pants and white button-down shirts, that made her look as though she had seen a movie about a set intern and decided to copy the part verbatim. The only variation—including her monotone voice-was the color of her silk scarf.

"There have been some changes you might want to look at. I highlighted them in pink for you," Maryann was saying.

Forcing a smile she hoped didn't appear too fake, Aliza thanked the girl and was ready to close the door while Maryann kept talking. "He's cute, isn't he?"

"What?" Aliza sounded impatient, even to herself.

"Jesse Black. He's cute, isn't he? Seems friendly, too," she continued.

Aliza couldn't believe her ears. "If you like that sort of look, I guess."

"It's not one thing or the other. It's the whole package. Great smile, great voice, amazing eyes. Okay, maybe it's the eyes. What do you think?"

"I think I'd better look this over," Aliza said with mock alarm, shaking the script, hoping to end this vapid conversation without incident. "You understand, I'm sure."

"Oh, of course, sorry. See you later," Maryann said absently as she left, monotone intact.

"Bye," Aliza murmured. She tried to close the door of her ready room, only to find a rather expensive and fairly large shoe, of the skater-wanna-be style, planted between the door and the door jam. Annoyed, Aliza was somehow not surprised to see Jesse blocking her progress. He smiled as their eyes met.

"You don't think I'm cute?" he said playfully, giving her his best shocked and hurt puppy dog eyes.

"What are you talking about now?" Aliza released an audible sigh.

"I heard you tell the mouse I'm not your type."

"Don't call her that. Her name is Maryann. Besides, that's not what I said. You should have eavesdropped more closely."

"What did you say?" he said, leaning into the room.

He smelled like spices, cinnamon and nutmeg. "I said, 'If you like that sort of look.' I don't happen to care much for it," she replied curtly, still trying to close the door through his protruding foot. "Now if you don't mind..."

"I do mind. I think *you're* pretty. I assumed you'd want to return the compliment."

"You're cocky, and there's nothing cute about that. Any questions?"

"Yes. Do you want to go over the script together?" He spoke with a little laugh in his voice.

Aliza had to admit it was always better to read with your scene partner. Reluctantly, she agreed. "Fine, but don't act like such an idiot. Okay?"

"I'll try, but I can't help it. I'm not very smart."

"Clearly."

Aliza opened the door for him. Jesse smiled rather victoriously, she thought, as he moved into the room. They both tried to close the door at the same time, their hands meeting unexpectedly. The contact sent an unwelcome thrill of excitement through Aliza, her shock showing on her face. Jerking her hand away, she fixed him with an icy glare.

"Sorry, I was trying to be polite for once," he said and smiled again, more uncertain this time.

"Whatever," she answered, hoping the feeling coursing through her body was some kind of terrible fever, rather than what she suspected it was. Absently, she rubbed the spot where their hands had met as she moved across the room to her chair.

———

Jesse was surprised at how he felt when they touched. He didn't allow himself to become preoccupied by the thought, but every once in a while, when Aliza looked down to read a passage aloud, he snuck a little peek at her and felt increasingly perplexed.

"I'm not going to college this year," she read aloud from the script. "I'm going eventually, but I need to be in town for a while. It's personal." She paused, expecting him to give the next line, but caught him looking at her instead.

Rather than try to hide and pretend he had not been staring at her, he reached out his hand and lifted her chin. He didn't think about this before he did it, but her skin was so inviting he couldn't resist.

She whacked his hand away and exclaimed, "What the hell are you doing now?"

He was stung by her reaction, but only for a moment. Recovering, he said, "Sorry. I wanted to see your face in the light. You really are pretty."

"Is this how you're going to act every time we read together?" she demanded acidly.

"Until you admit I'm cute."

"I don't cave that easily," she replied, a smile tugging at the corners of her mouth.

"Have it your way," he said, focusing back on his script. After a moment, however, he added, "You can't blame a guy for trying."

Jesse caught Aliza smiling behind the dark fringe of her hair as he said the next lines. He couldn't have told you what they were.

———

The following morning, Aliza awoke to a brightening sky. The moon still hung pale and calm, framed by the tips of two majestic pines standing sentry to the town common. As the sun crested the horizon, it slowly transformed the trees from cool greens and browns against the pale blue sky into a warm blaze of reds and golds. The colors intensified for a few moments before the sun was high enough for the light to normalize. *Why don't they ever try to put that sort of moment in a TV show? I bet they'd complain that the light was too intense. What's so wrong with intense?*

Vivid dreams had dogged Aliza, as usual. Colorful cartoon bodies had fallen from the sky while complacent people watched reflections of the scene in tiny circular screens embedded in the rooftop of an old mill building. The thud was heartrending when their squashy forms hit the tar, but the viewers of this bizarre installation could only watch in their little screens. Yellow, blue, red, wearing the primary colors of childhood, these little tiny cartoons plummeted and plopped, each thudding sound reverberating in Aliza's heart, yet hardly affecting the other impotent viewers. This was admittedly one of her crazier dreams. She needed to start writing this stuff down. She finally pulled herself out of bed.

The sun was high enough to signal that Aliza must start her daily routine. Exercise, although she didn't love it, was a given. She had a quality elliptical trainer in her apartment along with some weights, but the morning looked so beautiful she decided to get some fresh air instead. She threw on some old sweats and sneakers, pushed her hair back into a pony tail, and stretched out for a moment before she ran down the stairs and out into the quiet streets of early morning Twin Falls.

It was colder than she had imagined. Puffs of breath hung in front of her as she ran, her eyes tearing up in the cool spring air. She pushed herself hard, trying not to think of the stinging in her thighs or that she'd rather be in bed under her down coverlet. The thought of going back to that crazy dream was worse than running, so she ran even harder.

Rhythmically, her feet hit the pavement, and as she found her groove, it felt like flying. Thankful her trainer had taught her how to run properly, her feet only touched the ground long enough to propel her forward. During her teens, plodding along with heavy footfalls, running had been drudgery. Now she felt agile, graceful, like some wild animal of the African plains.

Running always helped Aliza calm her whirling mind. She only focused on her surroundings to ensure she didn't run out in front of a car or something, unlikely as that appeared to be in tiny Twin Falls. Therefore, she didn't notice when another person sidled up beside her, matching her rhythm as she passed by the gazebo in the town square.

"Good morning," Jesse said, his voice warm and inviting. "Perfect day for a run. I didn't peg you as the type, but you've got great form." He said those last words with a little half-smile on his lips.

To say that Aliza was startled would be a serious understatement. Her heart felt like someone had set off a depth charge, sending shock waves through her entire body. Even moments later, her fingers and toes still tingled with adrenaline. She had no idea whether her extreme surprise had shown its effects on her expression, but judging from Jesse's collected manor, it hadn't. She went with it.

"I'm almost done," she lied. She felt like she could run forever this morning and had been planning to push herself as far as she could go.

"Not me, I like to work up a sweat when I run."

He started to push forward, upping the pace to pass her. Refusing to be outdone, she sped up to match his velocity. He smirked a little and sped up again. She was running faster than she had ever run before, especially after nearly an hour of what she had considered a fairly respectable run. Jesse's smile faded. His expression transformed from playful into determined. He seemed intent on killing her, as he gave it one last blast of power. She would not succumb. Her legs were on fire, her breathing was hard and regular, sweat poured down her face.

"This is a good town for running," she said, trying to sound casual. "No traffic, cool mornings, cute buildings. It's growing on me."

Again, clearly focused on his exertion, Jesse didn't answer.

"Well, I'll see you in a few," Aliza said, and with every ounce of her ability taxed to the very limit, she sprinted forward and turned the corner at her street. Jesse didn't follow.

———

Jesse couldn't do much of anything as Aliza ran away. The second she was out of sight, he let out a terrible groan, slowed his pace to a crawl and eventually to a complete stop. Bending over his knees and panting heavily, he tried to catch his breath. *She's insane. She's completely nuts. How did she do it? Who could have known she could run like a fricking springbok?*

Limping back to his apartment, Jesse prayed this sleepy town was, in fact, still sleeping. It was way after seven. People would soon be going about their days. As he opened his front door, he heard voices, relieved that people actually lived here, proving he hadn't been in some bizarre dream for the past half hour.

He downed half a carton of orange juice, finally caught his breath, and filled his antique tub up with scalding hot water. Some artsy type had painted the base of the tub in metallic blue with silver bubbles. Jesse's tastes leaned towards the stark, so he shook his head involuntarily every time the hand-painted decorations caught his attention. From the inside of the tub, however, it was easy to forget about the overly kitschy design.

Only after a long soak and a few cups of coffee did energy stir within him again. His thoughts, however, continued to swirl, a vortex with Aliza at the center. He had no idea why she captivated him, but she did. While he dressed, he considered her reactions to him and thought about how she played it cool, always looking annoyed. Was it an act? Dwelling on his terrible faux-pas the day before, when he had assumed she had been the gopher, Jesse admitted he had started their relationship off badly. Everything else, her reactions, her distant aloof annoyance, had its roots in that moment. He felt like kicking himself. *Why do people always say they could kick themselves? What would that solve? I want to turn back the clock and undo that one moment. She will never forgive me at this rate.*

Nine o'clock was steadily approaching, and even though it wasn't expected that the talent show up on time, in a town this small, there was nothing else to do. Armed with his courier bag containing a water bottle, his annotated script, and a paperback, Jesse ventured forth.

Hal's Diner stood on the corner of Main Street overlooking the town square. It was a quintessential fifties diner, but Jesse prayed they had decent coffee. Modestly, he introduced himself to the cute waitress when she asked who he was and left her a generous tip on his way out. As he walked out, there Aliza was again, looking fresh and feisty, her punk-rock aura amped up for the long day ahead. He came remarkably close to spilling his coffee on her as he sped out the door.

"More coffee, I see," she said, smiling in a reproachful way. "Don't you get sick of it?"

"Don't you like it?" he asked, eyes wide.

"Of course, I like it. That's why I'm trying to get inside the diner." She looked past him, catching the eye of the server whose attention had been riveted on their exchange. "New fan already, I see," she said, nodding towards the counter.

Jesse turned his head, looking mildly perplexed. "Oh." He realized Aliza meant the waitress.

Aliza didn't wait for an elaboration. She turned back the way she had come. "We'd better go. We're already a couple of minutes late."

Without looking back, the two actors made their way down the street.

"She's cute. Is she your type?" Aliza spoke with genuine interest in her voice.

"What?" Jesse asked, perplexed again. "Is who my type?"

"Really memorable, then. The coffee girl. She definitely seemed to indicate that you're *her* type."

"What does she know about me?" Jesse replied defensively. "How would I be able to tell anything about her from buying a cup of coffee? Anyway, I'm not thinking about that stuff right now."

"Why, don't you like girls?" Aliza said flippantly and looked like she immediately regretted it from the expression on her face. She quickly added, "I mean, whatever. You don't have to tell me."

"It's not that. I like girls. Why are you suddenly so interested in my romantic life?"

"I'm not. I was only wondering about you and the coffee girl."

"There is no me and the coffee girl." Jesse's voice was starting to betray his annoyance at the personal line this conversation seemed hell bent on taking.

17

"Sorry. I don't know why I even asked. Never mind. Let's talk about the weather or something instead. Would that suit you?" Aliza spoke with a dangerous look.

"Looks like a storm brewing," he said coldly, and shouldered past her into the studio.

# THREE

*Days later, the jeweler holds a small piece of silver sheet metal, feeling its weight in her palm, the certainty of her idea as solid as the metal itself. The machine she feeds the silver into is old and smells of grease and rust kept barely at bay. She places the silver between two rollers, gingerly turning the large wheel that drives the gears, compressing the metal inch-by-inch into a thinner sheet. The jeweler appreciates the physicality of this act, of changing something that seems so solid with the simple turning of a wheel. When the plate is ejected from the other side of the machine, it's warm. All of the molecules have been rearranged. They no longer align. The metal is fatigued. If the jeweler is insensitive to this stress, the metal will snap, and she will have to begin again from scratch.*

*What is wrong with me? Now I've taken any leverage I had over the son of a bitch and squandered it on a shit conversation. Lovely. I need to play more chess. My strategy sucks.* Aliza was pissed to the core at allowing herself to get carried away with curiosity and, although she hated to admit it, jealousy. That girl had been smitten, and Aliza had seen that look parlay into bigger things before, even with humble coffee girls.

*Besides, I'm not interested in him. He can do whatever he wants. We're only playing these stupid characters, and that's it. He can live his life however he wants. So, what if he's in love with a coffee girl? He loves coffee. It makes perfect sense.* Aliza reproached herself at the absurdity of her thinking. *Enough. Head back down to earth now, Aliza. Your career is waiting.*

Smiling, she bid a cheerful "Good Morning" to everyone she passed, winding through the room to the drink table. She poured herself a cup of crappy coffee that had been on the heat for the past two years, judging by the acrid odor. The dregs dripped out in a grainy, thick mess into her cup. She added cream hoping it would mask some of the inevitable taste. It didn't. The acidic brew coated her tongue unpleasantly, making her wince.

Jesse laughed across the room, but when she turned to see if he had been watching her, his head was turned towards a different group of people. Despite this, she felt as though his attention was trained on her alone. She had never felt more self-conscious, which only served to enhance her anger. She dared another sip of the coffee and was relieved when Rudy called everyone to attention.

"We're going to pair off this morning to read scripts. You have a few changes to note, and I want everyone to be prepared to film this scene tomorrow. Think about who your characters are. Some are gritty, some refined, some vulnerable. Be them as genuinely as you can. I don't want to see any acting school tricks or bullshit on screen, and I certainly don't want anyone to pull any Diva crap. This town is way too small for big egos. They only impede progress. Besides, this cast was created equal. There is no big star, no lead. You're in it together. Got it, team?"

Despite Rudy's peppy tone, his warning was heard by all. *No egos. Check. We'll see.*

Unable to bear another sip of the science experiment coffee, Aliza tossed the cup gingerly into the trash, hoping Jesse wasn't watching her. Glimpsing herself in the mirrored tea samovar, she checked her teeth, and decided to be the mature one and ask Jesse if he was ready to read. She spun around, and her thighs burned from the morning's exertions. *Why would he do that to me? I'll bet he pays for it too, though.* The thought comforted her slightly. Her long soak had helped temporarily, but she knew this soreness was just the beginning. She'd really pay tomorrow.

Jesse wasn't in the room. She scanned every corner, every lingering group of people, but he had disappeared. Probably went back to the coffee girl, she thought bitterly. Aliza chatted for a moment with a few people she remembered from another project. They were talking about a tiny restaurant on the other side of town, inciting a chuckle from someone about the irony of a town this small even having another side. Aliza mentally noted its location and decided she'd try it some time. She loved cooking, which in turn made her picky about the food she ate at restaurants.

Aliza climbed the stairs, aching with every step, and followed the long corridor to her ready room on the second floor. It was adequately equipped with a small couch and a comfy chair, a mirrored dressing table, and a rolling garment rack. A wide picture window with gauzy drapes that fluttered softly when she opened the window overlooked the town square. This room was a step up from the trailers and backlots she had grown used to in LA. She was starting to appreciate the finer points of being on location. When Aliza opened the door, she found Jesse lounging on her couch, examining the script. There were two cups of coffee on the table before him.

"Double fisting it now?" Aliza asked, smiling in a feisty way.

"I will if you want, but I did get one for you. I ran out and told Maria to put it in high gear this time."

"Maria, eh? So, you're on a first name basis now? Nice. You work fast."

"You were right. She did look all starry-eyed when I walked in again. I had to break it to her that it's never gonna happen. She took it all right. Now we're pals."

"Never gonna happen, huh? Why's that?"

"Man, you ask a lot of questions. Never gonna happen because I'm not interested. I told you, I'm not into that stuff right now."

"What happened?"

"Really?"

"Let's get this topic out of the way and start in on our work."

"My girlfriend broke up with me two nights ago, right before I left LA. She said she didn't want to deal with a small town, a long-distance relationship, or frankly, me, anymore. Are you happy? Now you know."

Feeling stricken, Aliza paused before answering. "Thanks for the coffee. Which one's mine?"

"This one," Jesse said, gesturing to the one on the left.

"I'm sorry about the break-up. Is that why you were in such a foul mood when you got here?"

"I won't make excuses for myself. I was terrible yesterday, and I'm sorry. My behavior was rude and unacceptable."

"I accept the apology. I'm sorry, too. I've been giving you a hard time because of it, and there's no reason for that."

"You're a fists-up kind of girl. I get it. It was cool of you to come out to introduce yourself, though. We might have hit it off right away if I hadn't been such a royal jerk."

"Maybe, but why dwell on sweet could-have-beens? We've got work to do. Thanks again for the coffee. It really is good."

# FOUR

*The process of annealing heats the metal to a high temperature, realigning the molecules, making their bonds strong and flexible again. The flame of her torch is oxygen rich, billowy and orange. She passes the torch over the metal several times, watching it change color beneath the oxidizing flame. The faint glow means the annealing is complete, although the jeweler wonders if the metal is ever as strong afterwards as it was before she began. It is the cost of artistic creation, she supposes, and it's strong enough to continue. With tongs she picks up the hot metal and puts it into a bucket of cool water. It hisses and steams as the water shocks the heat out of the silver.*

Jesse and Aliza read through the script diligently all morning, the wall between them slowly dissolving. They each had their own techniques for memorizing lines, and they made fun of some of the more stilted language. It wasn't what people their age sounded like. For fun, they read in British accents for a while, finally ending in hysterics at each other's efforts.

Around eleven o'clock Rudy came in to see how they were doing. They both smiled a lot, complimented the ready rooms, and asked if they could tweak the script to make the dialogue more natural. He asked for examples, and Jesse read one passage they had hashed out only moments before.

"That's pretty good, guys. Run them by me or one of the writers before you do it. They're easily offended, you know."

"That's natural," Aliza said. "It's their art, after all. No one likes being criticized."

"Criticism is a necessary part of this industry, though. Don't let the small-town setting fool you. This is serious business. Anyway, you two look good," Rudy said, rising. "Keep it up. I expect impressive things tomorrow. Be here at seven for makeup."

"No problem. Thanks," called Jesse as Rudy left the room.

They smiled at each other as he closed the door behind him. "What do you think he meant by 'You two look good'?" Aliza asked.

"Eye candy. Clearly," Jesse answered, laughing a little. "He's right, too."

"Ugh, don't mention candy. I'm starving. My run went on a little long this morning," she said pointedly. "All I had time to eat was an apple."

"Man, you're fast. I was trying to tease you a little, but you schooled me. I mean, I'll be in pain for days."

Aliza laughed. "I didn't know I could run like that. It was amazing. I felt like some creature inside me took over and tried to push through my body. So, thanks, I guess. You showed me something I didn't know I could do."

"I have a feeling you could do anything," Jesse replied, in an uncharacteristically serious sort of way.

"Nah, I can't play guitar," Aliza retorted, keeping it light. "My fingers won't do what they're supposed to do, but everything else? Sure. Why not?" She gave him a smile so natural and warm that he was clearly taken aback. His expression changed from serious to wistful. Aliza thought he looked as though his heart hurt. Her smile faded into unease as she watched his reaction. Insecurity settled in again.

"What did I say?"

"Nothing. Sorry."

"I want to know. You looked like I'd kicked you there for a second. What did I say?"

"You're going to push it again?"

"Yep."

"It's not what you said. It's how you said it. It's weird, but your expression looked familiar for a moment."

"Your old girlfriend?"

"No, it's not that. I don't want to talk about it."

"I didn't mean to make you sad, you know."

"Of course not. You smiled at me. Ordinary people don't dive off cliffs when an attractive girl smiles at them."

"What makes you so out of the ordinary?"

"Absolutely nothing. It felt familiar, but not because of someone I know. More nebulous than that. It's hard to explain. It's sort of like finding a long-lost puzzle piece. Maybe it's a residual familiarity from another lifetime."

"Wow. I guess that is out of the ordinary," Aliza said, smiling again. "Oh, sorry." She quickly changed her expression to an exaggerated frown. "Is that better?"

"You look like Winston Churchill when you make that face. So, yes. Much better."

They rehearsed together for a while longer before interruption came in the form of a very loud rumble from Aliza's stomach.

"Wow," Jesse observed, "I could hear that from way over here. Let's get you something to eat. That is, if you wouldn't mind eating with me."

"Sounds great. One of the gals downstairs was talking about a little restaurant called Neven's. Wanna try that?"

"Okay. Lead the way."

They gathered their things, put their scripts in their bags, and left by the rear staircase, in case someone was keeping an eye on the front. It's an old trick, but, as Aliza explained, it works wonders when you want to escape notice. The backdoor let them out in a service alley lined with dumpsters.

"This is the cleanest, best smelling alley I've ever seen," remarked Jesse.

"Spend a lot of time in alleys in LA?"

"Of course. That's where you find the best hookers."

"Oh, so that's why your girlfriend broke up with you. Too many hookers."

Jesse pretended to stab himself in the heart. "Ah, you sting me to the core."

Aliza was relieved that he hadn't been offended by her joke.

They walked down the alley, knowing they would find a main street. They came out a few blocks away from Neven's, and judging from the ruckus her stomach was making, it was none too soon.

The restaurant was unassuming. From the outside it looked like a tiny shop with curtained windows. Inside, however, was like stepping into the 1940s. Either nothing had changed in ages, or the proprietors had an uncanny knack for accurate recreations. Aliza decided it must be the former. Everything was well-worn and comfortable. The woodwork on the walls was richly toned, the lighting was pleasantly yellowed. Red and white checked tablecloths with scratched glass over the tops were set with a hodgepodge of knickknacks and mismatched silverware.

Jesse smiled broadly, breathed in, and murmured, "Better than home."

"I agree," Aliza whispered next to him, smiling as well.

"Grab a table anywhere you like, kids," said a plump, older woman with antique glasses and an equally antique hairdo.

Scanning the room, they chose a booth by the front windows. They sat down across from each other, still distracted by their surroundings. Signed photographs covered the sunflower-colored walls. Staring out at them from antique frames, people dressed in 1940s clothes were frozen in their glamorous outfits, all hats and dresses and refinement.

"I have no idea who any of these people are, but they're beautiful," Aliza said, wistfully.

"That'll be us, someday," Jesse replied absently, squinting to read one of the signatures. "No one will remember our names, but they'll admire us, frozen in our youthful moment of fame."

Aliza shifted her gaze to Jesse, curious about this pensive side of him. Not wishing to stare at him too long, Aliza let out a little sigh. "Tin ceilings."

"Wow. That's something you don't see too often these days," Jesse added, looking equally impressed. "Not out West, anyway." His gaze floated down from the ceiling and landed on Aliza's face.

The light from the beautiful day outside filtered in through the yellowed lace curtains, making an enchanting pattern on her arm, probably her face as well. She noticed Jesse examining her. Their gazes met, but she was not as self-conscious as she had been before when they had looked at each other.

A flutter of excitement surged through her chest. "What?" she asked.

"I've not met too many people our age who care about antiques, cool old places like this, or tin ceilings in particular. Have you always liked old stuff?"

"I guess so. My Grandpa used to take me to flea markets, garage sales, and the Salvation Army. He told me stories about the things we came across and taught me to see the beauty in each object. Plus, I hate plastic. I hate the feel of it, and I hate the way it falls apart. I don't like new things for that reason. It's all kind of crappy, I guess. Old stuff was built—"

"To last," he interrupted.

"Exactly. To last. Nothing we make today lasts." She looked down at her silverware, dinged up, scratched, and marred. One tine of her fork bent inwards, but the mark on the back indicated that it was old. It was made right and therefore still in service. She smiled at the thought.

She spoke vehemently. "We'll have to start the Good Quality

Revolution, I guess. No more big-box-store-imported garbage. We want good stuff we won't need to replace in five years."

"It will be our generation's Vietnam War protest, only we're protesting waste. How very green of us."

Aliza smiled at him as the waitress brought the menus.

"Today's soup is split pea and ham, and the special sandwich is a Twin Falls hoagie with turkey and gravy. Any questions just holler." She filled up their water glasses and bounded away with more grace than Aliza had expected. It was comforting, somehow.

She smiled again. "How about you? What makes you fond of old things?"

"Grandma's house. It's a treasure trove of crazy old stuff. I could get lost in that place, looking in the nooks and crannies. She collects vintage textiles, antique glassware, old photographs, campy salt and pepper shakers, and she lives in a neat Victorian house, tower room and all."

"In LA?" Aliza was surprised.

"No, not in LA." Jesse replied, laughing. "Not everyone's from LA."

"Where are you from then?"

"I'm from Massachusetts, originally. We moved to LA when I was a kid. My mom thought I was talented and good looking enough to be successful in Hollywood. I think she was about to give up on me for good when I landed this role. We'll see how it goes."

"Do you miss Massachusetts?"

"Sure. I visit every year at Christmas, and it's like stepping back into my past. It's gorgeous there at that time of year. Everything's crystalline, cold, and New England-y, if you know what I mean, and it smells like the sea. That's got to be my favorite smell. It means home to me. Even though LA is coastal, nothing else smells like the sea in the Northeast."

"Sounds lovely. I've never smelled the Northeast until now, to be honest, just seen pictures. New York City is as close as I've come, and it didn't smell particularly memorable. LA is so gross and fake at

Christmas. It's too warm to even pretend. New England at Christmas has always been on my list of things to see, so I can't wait for December. Everything decorated with lights glittering against the snow. It seems so much more authentic, more romantic. Of course, it's probably an idealized vision of reality. I realize that, but a girl can dream."

Jesse smiled, and before Aliza could ask him what he was thinking, the server returned.

"What'll it be, dears?"

Neither one of them had even looked at the menu yet. Jesse ordered the special, and Aliza, scanning quickly, settled on the chicken salad sandwich. After that run, she felt she could afford the extra calories.

"I'll need a cup of coffee as well, when you have a moment," Jesse added.

"Me, too, if you don't mind," Aliza said.

The server smiled at them indulgently and turned back toward the kitchen.

"So," Jesse began again, after a moment. "Have you lived in LA all your life?"

"No, but I don't remember too much of where I lived before that. My mom and dad moved to LA so Dad could write for sitcoms. He's great. You've probably heard of some of the stuff he's done. Growing up around actors and directors, I guess I got the hang of acting early. They started using me as an extra when I was a kid since I was always around, and before long I had speaking roles in various things. I never saw it as a career until recently. I went to college for a couple of years, realized I need the feeling of community that working on a project with like-minded folks brings, and here I am. Coming back was harder than I thought it would be. I mean, I had to audition for this role."

"Imagine that."

"Really. I had always been handed parts for this and that, taking it all for granted. No more of that, but Rudy's great. I know him fairly well. My dad has worked with him, and he's very flexible, cool, and laid back. It's so much better than working with an uptight prick."

Jesse feigned shock at her blunt choice of words, but she continued on, unabashed.

"This one guy I worked with a couple of years back was always screaming, turning purple, and telling the techies to stop eating the donuts, because they were for the 'talent'. Can you picture it? The techies were probably the most talented people on that production. What an ass, but those guys don't last long these days. Everyone has got too much at stake to be a total jerk."

"You never said where you're originally from, though. Don't think I didn't notice."

Aliza smiled coyly, channeling the 1940s glamour girl persona she had always secretly admired. *Maybe a little mystery will do you good, fella.* The food came before she could give into his persuasive gaze. Aliza was so hungry, she ignored him completely as soon as the plate was before her. She ate the sandwich in record time, and she was thrilled it came with a side of cottage cheese and fries. The pickle was the icing on the cake. She giggled a little at her mixed metaphor.

When she came up for air, Jesse was staring at her in disbelief. His sandwich was nearly untouched, the well of gravy in his mashed potatoes remained undisturbed. "Are you all right?"

"You're the one that made me run a marathon this morning. Deal with it. Man, can't a girl even eat anymore? You're worse than the paparazzi." She stuffed a few more fries in her mouth, getting ketchup on her chin in the process.

Jesse reached over and gently wiped it away with his napkin. He smiled at her frozen expression and went back to his lunch.

Now Aliza was torn. She had been dealing with boys like this her whole life. Sometimes they were subtle like Jesse, sometimes forward, but they were all essentially the same, formulaic, like the movies. Her heart squirmed around regardless, making her remember her own very real reasons for keeping her guard up. He *was* cute, though, to use Maryann's prosaic expression. It seemed

Jesse shared Aliza's tastes and interests as well, but he kept on looking at her in *that way*. She didn't know what to make of it. So, by default, she tried to ignore it or play it off with a sarcastic twist. Either way, she had to admit it was getting harder.

With her initial hunger sated, Aliza slowed her pace. She munched her remaining fries absently, sipped her coffee, and watched Jesse eat. His manners were impeccable. He chewed slowly and gracefully, if such a thing were possible. The skin around his eyes was pale lavender. A dusting of barely visible freckles graced his nose and cheeks, a slight contrast to his translucent skin. His dark lashes drove her to distraction. Aliza forced herself to look out the window and take a deep breath.

Jesse chuckled, almost as though he knew what she had been doing, and he had been deliberately giving her a chance to do it.

"Yes, I got a good look," she said acidly, preempting any sarcastic remarks that might come her way.

"Good. I was hoping you would. What do you think?" Jesse said with an innocent expression on his face and in a smooth tone of voice.

He looked so much like a sweet little schoolboy that Aliza couldn't help but smile. "I think guys have it easy. No makeup, no frills, no pretense. What you see is what you get. I mean, don't get me wrong. Makeup is fun to play with, dresses are cute to wear, but a girl is judged by all of those things and taught to judge herself as well. It kind of sucks. You've got a great face, great skin, and stunning eyes. No amount of makeup could enhance that. Is that what you wanted to hear?"

"Why, yes. Yes, it is. By the way, I've heard girls say they'd pay money for these eyelashes," he said, laughing. Aliza shook her head. "I know what you mean though. I've always thought it must be convenient to have something like makeup and long hair to hide behind when you're feeling vulnerable. Guys make masks in different ways, I guess."

"What's yours?" Aliza leaned over her empty plate, fixing Jesse with her most intense stare.

"Sarcasm. I use it when I'm feeling insecure."

"I never would have guessed," Aliza responded, feigning surprise. "Very interesting."

"You do it, too, you know, but your masks are easy to see through, whether you realize it or not."

His words hit her like a kick in the chest. She had always considered herself good at masking her emotions. She was an actress, after all. No one else had ever called her out on it. Then again, who would have bothered? Certainly not her most recent ex. He was too busy being insanely jealous, domineering, and cruel.

Jesse continued. "I mean, you're super feisty and quick-witted all the time, which is probably what makes most people like you, but you never seem to give a genuine response. My guess is it's to guard the soft spot you've got on the inside. You're very defensive."

Aliza cheeks burned. *How could he be so right on?* She was relieved when the server came over to refill their coffee cups.

"How about a piece of chocolate cake or apple pie to share?" she suggested, winking at Aliza.

Flustered, Aliza looked down, and Jesse answered. "Thanks. How about a slice of pie?"

Aliza looked back at him, furious, as the server walked away. "You're going to have to eat it yourself, I'm afraid. I've overdone it already. Look at the time. We should have gotten back ages ago."

She grabbed her bag from the back of her chair and pulled out her wallet. She could feel tears struggling to free themselves behind her eyes. He had gotten under her skin, but she couldn't fathom why.

Jesse reached across the table and put his hand on her arm. She tensed up immediately, leveling him with an intense glare.

"Calm down, Aliza. I'll go tell the server we don't want the pie. It's not a problem. I thought it would be fun is all."

She looked down and fumbled around inside her bag for loose bills.

"What is it?" Jesse said in a serious tone.

"It's nothing. I just want to go."

"Fine. I'll settle at the counter and meet you outside."

"No way. You're not paying for me," she protested, shoving a twenty dollar bill across the table. Without looking back, she breezed out the front door and breathed in the fresh air.

*What in the hell is wrong with me?* Her heart was racing, and she felt like her emotions were ready to burst forth. *Why did honesty and pie put me over the edge?* It dawned on her she wasn't ready to share anything with this guy, let alone secrets or desserts, and his eagerness to do so put her in an uncomfortable position. It sounded crazy, though, when she considered it. He was only thinking out loud when he had unmasked her deeper self. As for the pie, it was only pie, but she also resented that he had taken charge of ordering when the server had asked her specifically.

*Fucking men always think it's okay to take control of everything. Stupid pie.*

Jesse came out as Aliza mastered her emotions. "The server thinks you're a little crazy, but cute. Her words, not mine," he added. "I have to admit I've never seen anyone react so strongly to the concept of dessert before."

*If he keeps it up, I might hit him. Hard.*

"Enough," she growled. "For your own safety."

"Got it."

They didn't speak for a few blocks. Her stomach felt heavy and kind of gross, although she had to admit they probably had salad on the menu. Next time she would exercise more self-control.

"Are you all right?" Jesse spoke after a while.

"Yep, just digesting. Sorry about the dessert thing. I think we should get back."

"Of course. You also don't like guys ordering for you. I've got it. The waitress put us on the spot. I took a risk. I apologize."

Aliza stopped dead in her tracks. "How do you know that? I didn't say anything. You shouldn't be able to know what's in my head. What else am I thinking?"

"I told you I can read through your practiced expressions. They might fool other people, but I'll bet other people don't look at you for *you.* They look at the *you* they expect to see. I, on the other hand, have no such expectations. I see you as you really are. If that makes sense."

"It does, but it's disconcerting. I'm used to keeping my thoughts to myself."

"That gets lonely."

"I guess," she replied, kicking a stone down the sidewalk. "So why did your girlfriend break up with you?"

"I told you already."

"Only partly. Did you think she might be the right person for you, or did you always feel it was temporary?"

"I guess I never thought about it like that. In retrospect, I couldn't have married her. She was very high maintenance and kind of a snob. She would have hated you, for instance."

"What? Why?" Aliza demanded, incensed.

"Because you're real. Seeing other girls be real made her fake qualities show up more. That was my read, anyway."

"Then why did you date her?"

"I don't know. I think it was because she showed interest in me, was attractive, and I didn't know any better. It was LA, after all. We learn as we go."

"Are you still feeling sad about it?"

"The only time I even think about it is when you bring it up. Thanks, by the way. It's great fun to keep hashing it out every five minutes."

"Sorry," she replied, bashfully. "I don't mean to pry. Defense mechanism. Deflect and escape sort of stuff. You understand." She was only half-joking.

"I do," Jesse replied quietly.

Aliza believed him.

# FIVE

*Chaotic designs swirl in her mind before she can etch them onto the metal. A ground will act as a barrier between the metal and the acid, allowing the acid to reach the metal only in its absence. This seems appropriate, somehow, a slow eating away, a controlled violence, a scarification. She applies the ground reverently, allows it to dry, and then uses a variety of tools to scrape it away, exposing the metal in a pattern of cells and veins. Time ebbs away while she works, as though she is meditating. She plots with beauty against this solid surface.*

Once Aliza and Jesse returned to the set, they went to his ready room to finish working on their lines. As if the management had known something of Jesse's personality beforehand, his room was decorated sparsely with an understated, masculine elegance. A chocolate brown sofa with sleek lines dominated the far wall. A matching striped chair, pale gray-blue curtains, and a rug that brought the colors together, completed the space. On top of the rug sat a cool vintage coffee table in the shape of a chevron. Its top was deep blue Formica flecked with gold. An antique desk with a mirror on the wall above it provided his dressing table. No stupid lights, no fancy crap. Just good solid furniture. Jesse had been relieved when he first saw it.

He took the chair, so Aliza could relax on the couch. She kicked off her Converse sneakers and tucked her legs under her. Jesse noticed her socks didn't match, and it made him smile. They started their lines from the beginning, diving in with a serious professionalism.

Somehow, Jesse felt, they were reading with more feeling now, as though the words were genuinely their own. Before, he had felt there was a big clear wall of acrylic between them, mirroring back just enough of themselves to prevent seeing the other clearly. Their words had been mechanical, and he had wondered why he ever chose to take this job. Wouldn't he be happier finishing college like everyone else his age? Now, the lines seemed to take on a new meaning. Two people, a guy named Ken and a girl named Lydia, meet for the first time and are civil to each other. Miraculous. He smiled at the thought.

"What are you smirking about now?" Aliza said to him, as she looked up from the script at that exact moment.

"I was thinking these characters had a better start than we did, is all. It's kind of sweet."

"Sweet? I guess so. Not too interesting though. Maybe it gets more intriguing later. Who knows what these writers have in mind for the following episodes of the show."

"Good point. You lived with a writer. Do they write according to their mood, to the wishes of the director, or what?"

"It depends. Like I said, some directors are insanely controlling. With those, writers don't have any wiggle room for their own feelings about the characters they create. With the cool directors, on the other hand, it's different. Writers get more creative space. My dad always felt the characters were manifestations of people he knew, of feelings he'd had, of times he'd shared with friends or family. It gets personal. I don't have a take on these writers yet, but

I know Rudy is a cool director. This could get interesting. We'll see."

"I don't know. Lydia and Ken seem fine so far. It's like being able to have a normal life through a character. My life has been anything but normal."

"Yeah, but what's a normal life look like, anyway? Is there such a thing? I seriously doubt it. Everyone's screwed up in some way." Aliza fidgeted as she spoke, looking preoccupied.

"Right, but some people handle it better than others. You know, make the best of crappy situations, grow in some way. I wonder if I've grown much."

"You probably can't see yourself objectively." Aliza smiled. "It's like gaining or losing weight. You see yourself in the mirror every day, but changes happen slowly. You don't notice them. The only way to tell is by a standard unit of measurement, like jeans, for instance. They don't change. You do, so either they're too small, too big, or they fit. Then you know how you're doing."

"Or you can get on a scale," Jesse added.

"You know what I mean," Aliza insisted, trying not to show her amusement. "Who would be your constant, your standard unit of measurement for personal growth?"

"Wow. I don't know. My grandma, maybe. She's seen me so sporadically lately I'm sure any changes or growth would be more obvious to her than they are to me. Plus, we were very close when I was a kid. I spent a lot of time with her, like I said. You know, this is a very interesting idea." He paused for a moment looking pensive. "Who's your constant?"

"To be honest, I've never thought about any of this before. I don't know. Give me a minute to think about it." She paused for a moment. "Grandpa. My dad's dad. He was..."

A knock on Jesse's door interrupted their conversation.

"Hello, in there." A blonde head popped through the crack, followed by a perfectly toned body. "Hi. I wanted to introduce myself. I'm Melinda, your mom-in the show." She thrust out her hand in a very peppy, diva way with a smile flooding across her pale, made-up face. She must have been well over fifty, but no one would ever guess it to look at her.

Jesse rose to be polite, took her hand, and shook it. "Great to meet you. I'm Jesse Black, as you seem to have guessed. Have you met Aliza Bennett? She's playing Lydia."

Melinda's haughty gaze shifted to Aliza briefly. "Pleased, I'm sure." She turned back to Jesse with her enthusiasm in full bloom. "We should read our lines together when you have a chance. We don't have too much tomorrow, but we should get to know each other a little before then."

"I'll find you when we're done here. How's that sound?"

Shooting a less enthusiastic look at Aliza, but recovering quickly, Melinda said, "Fine. See you then."

Jesse fully closed the door this time. Turning back to Aliza, they exchanged amused looks. Aliza giggled. "That's awesome. She hates me already."

"Sure looked like it. I'll bet she expected you to say, 'Oh, Melinda, we're done here. Why don't you come sit down, and I'll melt out of sight like the nobody I am?' I don't want to be like that when I'm an aging actor. I hope to have a reserved elegance. Let the whippersnappers come to me."

"They will, I'm sure. You'll be so dapper, they won't know how to stay away. I guess she seems nice enough, despite the fact she dislikes me." Aliza paused for a moment. "Don't be surprised when she says something bad about me in the guise of the *protective mother*."

"You think she will?" he said, shocked.

"You haven't spent enough time around these people. When Rudy mentioned no egos, she's exactly who he meant."

"Do you know her?"

"Only by reputation. She's great as long as she thinks you're equals. Otherwise, good luck. Pure venom."

"Awesome. I've been in a toothpaste commercial. Does that make us equals?" Jesse laughed again.

"Totally. She's going to ask you to relive it, I'm sure. Well, we're prolonging the inevitable. You should go get it over with, don't you think?"

"I guess. Shall we read again tonight?"

"Are you making sure you have plans in order to extricate yourself from Melinda's claws before nightfall?"

"Maybe I am," he responded, amazed she had read the situation so well.

"You can count on me," Aliza responded.

Jesse believed her.

# SIX

*When the ground is laid, and the design is set, the jeweler lays the silver into a bath of acid. The metal is corroded immediately, the savagery of the process is almost hard to watch. She carefully removes the plate from the bath and rinses it to halt the etching. The scars are deep.*

"You called it," Jesse said, a look of reverential amazement on his face.

He had come over to Aliza's apartment as soon as he could leave Melinda. It wasn't even six o'clock yet. Most people would have had more difficulty escaping. Jesse's early arrival attested to his smoothness.

"Tell me everything," Aliza said, her attention rapt.

"We talked for a while. She told me some of the projects she'd been involved with before. Some of them sounded big-league, some not so much. She offered me a drink. I declined. Then she started in on you, like you said she would. If I'd had a drink in my mouth, I would have spit it across the room."

"Man. What did she have to say about me?"

"Do you want to know? It's not great stuff."

"Do your worst, pretty boy," Aliza said with her toughest voice, but feeling very squeamish on the inside.

"Well, she said your dad got you all your jobs, which you explained earlier. Then she said you didn't have much talent, but that's where a pretty face will get you these days."

"She thinks I'm pretty. How nice. Go on."

"She focused on how you've been involved with some naughty boys, one in particular, whose name I didn't recognize, Cameron something, and there were rumors that you had a drinking problem when you were sixteen. Then she got tired of talking about you and talked about herself for the next hour."

A sick feeling in her stomach hit Aliza. She feared Cameron would become the next topic of conversation. "When she said she wanted you guys to get to know each other, she meant she wanted to tell you about herself in a drawn-out monologue. Nice." She kept her expression as level as possible, praying Jesse wouldn't notice anything wrong. She folded her arms across her chest to keep her hands from shaking.

"I left soon after. We only read through the lines once and only because I insisted. She'd had a couple of martinis by that point, and it was relatively amusing."

"Sounds like a blast. Free entertainment."

Jesse, feigning serious concern, said, "Tell me about *your* drinking problem."

"It all began when I was a baby. Instead of milk, my parents put vodka in my bottle. I've had nothing else to drink since. It's a sad story. You'd be a total alcoholic, too, if you grew up like I did." Her tone of voice was very convincing, sad, and plaintive.

"I knew you had some dark, dark secrets. I just knew it."

They both laughed, but Aliza's was forced. Melinda knew about Cameron. It was disconcerting, but she was thankful the actress was so self-absorbed she hadn't revealed all the details. Aliza recovered her manners, jumping off the couch, ready to change the subject.

"I'm so sorry. I'm a terrible hostess. Would you like anything to drink? Vodka martinis, perhaps?"

"Make mine dry."

Aliza went off to pour them some sparkling water with a splash of pomegranate juice, her new favorite drink. She handed it to him and sat down on the other end of the couch from him. They clinked glasses, smiled, and each took a sip.

"I have another prediction to make," Aliza said after a little while.

"Oh, really, Madam Fortuna? Let's hear it."

"When your ex realizes what a hit this show's going to be, and that she let her bright and shining star go off alone to the boondocks, she'll be calling you, saying it was all a mistake. She'll wish she'd never left you. What do you think of that?" She smirked at him.

"You're insane. There's no way. She won't even notice I'm gone. She's already moved to someone else, I'm sure. She's an opportunist."

"Trust me. When she sees this show is a success, she'll be at your doorstep."

"Whatever."

"What would you do? Just out of curiosity."

"Is this your favorite topic? You distract me for hours at a stretch and then bring up these painful memories out of the blue." He put his hand to his forehead, feigning a headache.

Aliza kicked at his leg across the couch, laughing.

"Now you're beating me up. I don't know what I did to deserve this."

"Dork. Are we going to do any more work tonight or not?"

"Why, do you have a date?"

Aliza didn't answer, but she played coy, raising one shoulder and looking away.

"Oh, my gosh, you do."

She looked up at him impishly, enjoying his surprise. Finally, she spoke. "No, I do not have a date. I was going to watch something at nine."

"Let me guess. It's reality TV."

"Nope. I'm not going to tell you. It's embarrassing." Her cheeks grow hot.

"More embarrassing than reality TV?"

"Well, maybe not quite that bad."

"Tell me. I'll be nice."

"Promise not to make fun of me?"

"I promise to try hard not to make fun of you," Jesse said, chuckling.

"*Sherlock Holmes*. I watch it on PBS. There, are you happy? Now you know one of my dark secrets."

"I'm going to be mad at you unless it's the Jeremy Brett series."

"Of course, it is. They say he was completely obsessed with Sherlock Holmes. How could I watch anyone else?"

"May I join you, if it wouldn't be too much trouble?"

"Are you serious? You like it, too?"

"I do," Jesse responded in his most formal British accent.

"Cool. Have you eaten yet?"

"Nope. Melinda sort of stole my appetite. I came directly here."

"Let's cook something. I had an idea for a dish I'd like to try. Are you up for being my guinea pig?"

"Melinda also said you were unstable. You're not going to poison me, are you?" Jesse looked at her with his best frightened expression.

"Slowly over the course of months," she replied. "Don't worry. You won't die tonight."

"I'm in," he said.

They spent almost an hour chopping garlic, chilies, and onions, sautéing them with veggies and shrimp. Aliza made a crazy impromptu sauce and served it over rice noodles. They laughed while they ate and put out the fires in their mouths with copious amounts of water.

"You're not afraid of spicy food. That's for sure." Jesse's cheeks were scarlet, and he looked like he might not have had that much experience with the stuff.

"We had some close friends from India while I was growing up. I loved to watch them cook. The spices were so beautiful, and fragrant, and foreign to me. Now they've become a part of my cooking vernacular."

"That's an eloquent way to put it. You have a lovely way with words. It must come from being in a creative household." Jesse leaned back in the dining room chair, hands folded over his full stomach. He looked pensive.

"I've always felt my upbringing was something rare, yes. Not every kid gets to know famous actors, travel the world, and be on TV by the time she's ten. Like anything, though, it came with its share of problems."

"Like what?"

"Like instability. Like the mercurial temperament of the artist. Like taking on the parental role at a young age. However, when things were good, it was great."

"Do you phrase things like that to hide what wasn't great? Or do you prefer not to share much with me?"

"What do you mean? I'm sharing a lot with you." She was hurt, and realized it showed in her face.

"Sorry. I don't mean to give you a hard time. I guess I like specifics. You know, to build a picture in my mind of what your world was like. When you gloss over things, it only lets people see the top layer. You can't fault me for wanting to know what lies beneath."

"Now who's being eloquent? Besides, we've only known each other for two days. Can't a girl keep some things to herself?"

Jesse smiled in agreement. "Can I do the dishes for you?"

"Now you're talking."

They cleaned up together, chatting idly. Aliza put some water on for tea and brewed a pot of Earl Grey. They sat in the living room, talking and sipping until it was almost time for the show.

"Do you want popcorn? I put my own blend of seasonings on it. It's good."

"Sounds great. I'll help."

They both jumped off the couch, and Aliza led the way.

"Whose job is it to find us places to live? I mean, how do they do such a good job fitting them to our personalities? Mine's amazing, except for this campy painting on the tub. Yours is great, too. It seems so you."

"I don't know. I've never lived on location before. Must be that they get good at guessing what people will like, or maybe they asked your mommy." Aliza smiled coyly.

"What's that supposed to mean?" Jesse's tone was hard, his eyes intense. "Are you seriously making jokes about my mother? Really, now. Grow up."

Aliza froze with the soup pot in her hands and looked at him with wide, horrified eyes. He looked angry. Her eyes grew larger as her tear ducts attempted to betray her again. "Sorry. I was joking, and it was stupid and unnecessary. I'm sure your mom's great."

Aliza turned towards the stove and set down the heavy pot. Holding back tears, she reached for the oil, feeling like she could kick herself, as if that would do any good. She didn't dare look at him, if he was even still in the room.

He was. After a moment, he touched her arm and laughed a little. "Hey, I'm joking. My mom's a sweetheart, and I love her, but she probably did call the set-up people to tell them what I should have."

Aliza turned and looked at him. Jesse was smiling. She whacked him on the arm. "You made me feel terrible. Sometimes I do take it too far," she said. "I've picked up some bad habits over the years. When I was little, I only hung out with grownups, and they are terrible and sarcastic to each other all the time in the name of humor. I try to tone it down most of the time, but I guess I've gotten wired that way. Sorry."

"Wow. This is *toned down*? I'm impressed. Seriously, though, I shouldn't have messed with you. I'm sorry, too. Now where's the popcorn you promised me? Get moving. It's almost nine."

"Crap. You're right." She made the popcorn, seasoned it, and put it in a big blue bowl. She grabbed a couple of napkins, and they headed back to the living room.

Aliza set the bowl down on the coffee table, turned on the TV, and switched it to PBS as the intro song ended. Scenes of Victorian London floated past with yellowed postcard quaintness. She sighed audibly. She loved this show. Jesse, whose attention was rapt, was sitting close enough to smell. Spices and soap. She sighed again.

It was an early episode of *Sherlock Holmes*. Jeremy Brett was in perfect form in a suspenseful story with a tragic ending. However, by that point, Aliza was on the edge of the couch in tears. She could tell Jesse wasn't sure what to do with a crying girl he'd just met from the uncertain look on his face. He settled on tissues. Bringing her a box from the bathroom, he held it out to her and smiled sweetly. Unsure if he was making fun of her, she decided to chance it. She took a couple of tissues and wiped her eyes.

"Thanks. That one always gets to me."

"It's sad, but self-sacrifice usually is. As far as TV shows go, we'll be lucky if ours turns out to be half that good."

"I know. The acting is so perfect. Jeremy Brett managed to channel Sherlock Holmes. It's unreal how convincing he is. There's a rumor that a few seasons in, he started to believe he was actually Sherlock Holmes. Like completely believe it. Like acting the part all the time. Now that's commitment."

"In anything other than acting, that kind of commitment gets you committed." Jesse chuckled a little at his pun.

Aliza regarded him indulgently and shook her head. "Nice."

"Thanks." He looked at her for a moment in silence. "You're tired. You should get some rest. We have a busy day tomorrow."

"I don't have the energy to be offended over you treating me like a little kid. We're the same age, you know. Anyway, you're right. Thanks for hanging out with me. I had fun."

"Maybe next time you won't end up in tears."

"We'll see," she replied, with subdued feistiness.

# SEVEN

*Upon examination, the jeweler decides the depth of the incision is sufficient. She's not satisfied, however. More must be done. She scrapes away another layer of ground, this time with less care, creating a haphazard surface of scars. The acid eats away at the silver once more, biting into the exposed surface. Again, she rinses the metal and surveys the damage. It is perfect. She removes the rest of the ground with a solvent, keeping the remaining silver smooth and intact, a pristine contrast to the wounded lines she has made.*

Jesse went home feeling more like himself than he had in ages. Aliza was cooler than he had expected, and he could let down his guard a little around her now. He marveled over how it had only been two days since they'd met. It seemed like so long ago. The intensive world of acting produced relationships like this at record speed. *It's a crucible. Disparate parts are fused at high temperatures, under intense stress. I wonder what this amalgam will end up looking like.*

*Will it be stronger than its individual parts or brittle and temporary? It could go either way.* He was relieved they seemed to be getting along now. It was a step in the right direction, at the very least.

That night Jesse had wild dreams. He was talking to a faceless friend in a room cluttered with clothes, objects, and furniture, when a stunning kingfisher flew into the room. Its plumage was iridescent royal blue, flashing in the light. The markings on its face were black and white. Its beak was strong. Its tail was stout. The bird circled the room, landing in a pile of clothes on the top shelf of an open closet as though hiding from something.

Jesse and his friend marveled at this rare sight, wondering how it could possibly have found its way into this room. Jesse examined the window and found a kingfisher-sized hole in the screen. When he looked closer, Jesse was confronted with the face of a gigantic, surreal-looking spider staring at him through the hole. It was closing in, fitting its long, spindly, white-tipped legs and strangely segmented head through the space, mere inches from entering the room.

Jesse sensed the kingfisher was endangered by the presence of this spider, and despite his terrible fear of the strange creature, he thought clearly. *Close the window.* His dream body followed the instructions, closing out the spider, who glared at him accusingly. Then it was morning.

*What in the hell could that possibly mean?* Jesse wondered, while the mantle of sleep slowly dissipated, only to be replaced by severely aching muscles. He wished he had spent more time paying attention to what dreams meant back in high school when everyone was interested in that sort of thing. He tried deciphering it anyway for kicks. *Spiders equal danger. That one's easy, but why am I protecting a kingfisher? Not a bird we see too often in LA. Rare for that part of the world, and it was hiding from the spider, even though it was bigger. Am I supposed to be protecting someone from danger?* With an uncomfortable lurch in his stomach, Jesse thought of his mother. She was safe now, but there had been a time when he had sought to protect her. Aliza? Maybe. She acted tougher than she really was, he was sure of that, and she was a rare bird besides.

After a few fruitless minutes, he gingerly got himself out of the bed and made his way to the bathroom. He looked tired. *I got enough sleep. What's the deal?* He hopped in the tub and showered in water cool enough to shock his system into waking up properly. With no steam to cloud up the mirror when he got out, he took another look. *Somewhat better, but not much.* Thankfully, he could smell his coffee brewing in the kitchen and knew it would go a long way toward helping.

It hardly mattered what he wore to the shoot. The costumers would transform him completely. His thoughts wandered to Aliza. Maybe they could get lunch again. He found a thin grey sweater and a favorite pair of jeans, deciding they would do. He was tempted to put some gel in his hair, but the hair and makeup people would hold it against him. Why get anyone else pissed at me, Jesse mused, and skipped the product.

The coffee energized and restored his sense of self with every sip. He murmured his lines to himself quietly to ensure he had them down. Nothing was worse, in his estimation, than actors who felt they were too important to learn their lines. After a quick bowl of cereal, he headed out the door, script and stainless-steel coffee thermos in a courier bag. He also brought along his book with him today, knowing there would be down time.

Jesse arrived on set early, offering a bright hello to whomever he encountered. Some, the morning people, he assumed, returned his perky greeting. Others grunted and kept moving along their predetermined paths. Jesse found his costume in his dressing room. He put it on and hung up his own clothes, thinking they looked an awful lot like the ones he was supposed to wear on set, a comforting coincidence. He headed down to makeup, wondering if he'd ever get used to wearing it.

Aliza was already there, eyes closed, being tended to by a chatty blonde woman with a very tight ponytail. Jesse stayed quiet, wondering if he could sneak up on Aliza with the cooperation of the makeup woman.

His plans were promptly ruined when Aliza said, "I smell spices. Is that you, Jesse?"

The makeup woman looked surprised and stared at Jesse.

"Hi, there. You're here early. Did you sleep well?"

With her eyes still closed, Aliza replied, "Yep. You?"

He sat down in the chair next to her and spun it around. "Yes, I did. Weird dreams though."

"What about?"

"Oh, I had to protect a beautiful bird from a giant spider," he replied nonchalantly. "You know, run of the mill stuff. Are you ready for the big day?"

"Of course, I am. Are you?" Her tone was playful.

"You betcha'."

The makeup woman chimed in, "Jesse, right? I'm Michelle. I'm almost done here. I'll do you in a sec. Okay, hon?"

"No trouble, take your time," Jesse replied in a friendly way.

In a moment, the woman stepped back from Aliza and said, "Okay, open your eyes, please, Aliza."

Jesse was totally stunned. The usual heavy outline around Aliza's pure blue eyes was absent, as was their sardonic edge. She looked utterly captivating, soft and vulnerable. Michelle had gone for a light look, kind of moon-glowy with a warm kiss to it. The eye shadow was the perfect tone of golden brown to make Aliza's eyes appear even bluer, and the mascara was the only dark thing in the whole look. Aliza's eyes appeared gigantic. Striking.

Jesse regained his composure. "Wow. Your eyes look so different. I hope you can make me look that good, Michelle." He didn't say any of the things he felt, but he knew his face said it all.

Aliza blushed a little, enhancing her beauty that much more. "Are you kidding? You don't even need makeup."

Michelle agreed. "You do have perfect skin, my dear. What do you use?"

"Plain old soap and water," Jesse replied with a bashful smile. Now that both women were focused on him, he grew a little self-conscious, positive his blush rivaled Aliza's.

"How cute. We've embarrassed him," Michelle said.

"Cute indeed" Aliza winked at Jesse. "See you on set."

———

*Why did I wink at him? Why? Why? How stupid is that?* She grabbed a lonely apple from a table overflowing with donuts. It was the token healthy thing, but Aliza was glad it was there. She had gotten up late and hardly had time to shower and brush her teeth before she left. Now her stomach was making crazy noises again, and she couldn't abide that during filming. She ate the apple, knowing it wouldn't hold her for long. The donuts were looking better and better.

Jesse snuck up on her, as she was totally absorbed by her hunger. He got right behind her. "Take the jelly one," he whispered. "You know you want it."

Her body jerked forward, and she spun to look at him. "Seriously. Like a three-year old kid hanging out in his mother's dirty laundry basket waiting to strike."

"You obviously speak from experience. I was more of an around-the-corner-terror."

"I can see it. You haven't changed a bit."

"At least, I didn't grab you. I figured you'd never forgive me."

"You do have at least *some* sense," Aliza said darkly, squinting at him. She tossed her apple core into the trash near the table. It was a long shot, but she made it. "Michelle did a good job on you. It doesn't look like you're wearing anything."

"It feels like I am, though. It's the one thing I hate about acting."

"Well, at least there's only one thing you hate."

"Great point."

Rudy called everyone to attention and gave another peppy

speech. He then asked the people in the first scene to gather, and he started giving directions. Knowing it was too late to grab a donut, Aliza followed along when she and Jesse were called to their first set. It took place outside on the green with the gazebo and the town in the background. There was so little background noise Aliza forgot she wasn't on a lot in Hollywood.

They delivered their lines flawlessly, and Rudy said their chemistry was great. "This sets the standard high, ladies and gentlemen. Pay attention." Both actors blushed as they did the spontaneous introduction scene a second time. They were supposed to make their interactions slightly awkward and teenagery at first, but to grow into a sense of comfort with each other as time went on. Eventually, as the plot line was laid out, they were to be lovers, but this scene, with all its strained silences and fumbled words, did not allow the viewer to automatically jump to that conclusion. The characters would have to work for it. As neither was a great communicator, it would take some time. Aliza was incredibly grateful for this. She wasn't ready to jump into a screen romance with this guy, charming as he was. She wanted the time to ease into it, like taking baby steps into a chilly pond.

The pair finished for the day by 12:30, and Aliza couldn't have been more pleased. Her stomach was making itself an obvious nuisance she wouldn't be able to ignore much longer. She would have to remember to pick up some snack bars or fruit, something to have with her from now on. A verbose stomach wasn't acceptable.

Back across the street in her ready room, Aliza caught sight of herself in the mirror. Looking back at her was Lydia. All morning she had felt like her character, of course, but it was kind of a shock to see it in herself so clearly. Studying her face in the mirror she saw the usual pale skin, dark hair, but Jesse had been right earlier when he said Michelle had done something to her eyes. She blinked, she closed her lids as far as she could and still see, trying to solve the mystery of this artful makeup. *So strange. It's not me at all in there, but Lydia's pretty enough, I guess.* How strange the sensation of seeing a different person looking back at her was.

*Enough silliness. I'm starving.*

She whipped off her Lydia outfit, hung it up, and grabbed her skinny jeans and T-shirt, a screen-printed affair she had found in Santa Monica at a funky little shop. The artist had recognized her from one of her previous roles and had given her an extra shirt. It's not one she would have picked herself, but after she wore it the first time, it had become her favorite. Now, with the contrast of the Lydia makeup, it felt very strange. Incompatible. She put her favorite black hoodie on over it and zipped it up most of the way, feeling it was a slight improvement. As she stopped to drink a little water, a light knock sounded on her door.

Before she even opened it, she knew it was Jesse. Who else?

"Come in," she called, setting her water bottle down on the dressing table.

"Hey, there," Jesse said cheerily. "That was great. You *were* Lydia, you know. That made it so easy for me to be Ken. He's kind of a sweet guy, don't you think?"

"I wouldn't know a sweet guy if he were staring me in the face," Aliza answered with unexpected sarcasm.

"Wow. You don't think I'm sweet at all, do you?" Jesse looked crestfallen.

She studied him for a moment, mortified by what she had said. "I don't know why I said that. I'm sorry. You are relatively sweet when you want to be."

"You've had some crappy experiences with guys, haven't you?" Jesse said solemnly.

"Seriously, who hasn't?" she replied, a sharp edge still in her voice. "I don't mean to cut this conversation short, but I'm starving."

"I know. I could hear your stomach on set. I'd be surprised if the mics didn't pick it up. Come eat lunch with me. My treat."

"No, I don't think so." She racked her brain for an adequate excuse.

"I wish you would. I can't force you, of course, but I'd love to talk some more about our characters."

"A working lunch?"

"Sure, if that's what it takes to convince you."

"Fine, but it has to be somewhere close and fast."

"Perfect. Let's go."

He held the door open for her as she grabbed her bag and water. He had washed his makeup off, but he looked nearly the same. *Why does he look the same, and I look so different?* As she brushed past him, her stomach registered something other than hunger with his scent flooding her senses. She scolded herself. *Get a grip.*

It was another iconic spring day, all sunshine and rising temperatures. The deli wasn't far away, and like almost everything else in Twin Falls, it blended in with the buildings around it. They got the last table in the crowded little sandwich shop, and Jesse ordered for them at the counter. Aliza wasn't used to letting a guy pay for her, but desperate times, she thought.

He returned with drinks, two bags of chips, and a number. "The order'll be up soon."

"Thank goodness," Aliza said with genuine relief.

He handed her a bag of chips. "I figured you might want to start on these."

Gratefully, she smiled and accepted it without hesitation. She opened the bag, took one chip out, and savored its greasy goodness. "Mmm. Food. If you hadn't scared the crap out of me earlier, I was on the verge of eating one of those donuts."

"Sorry. I had no idea I'd be facilitating such intense hunger. I'll look for contextual clues next time. If you're eyeing food, I'll let you go. If not, fair game." He winked at her.

"Thanks," she said sarcastically, her mouth full of chips.

"Was your last boyfriend a total asshole or something?" he said cavalierly, out of the blue.

Aliza had forgotten they had started that conversation earlier, and she longed for a way out. None occurred to her. Her blood ran cold in her veins every time she thought about Cameron. She began slowly, looking down at her nearly empty bag of chips. *Why do they make these bags so damn small?*

"It's hard to talk about. I don't know why I let it go on for as long as I did. I know in theory I would never let a guy push me around. I would always stand up for myself, but somehow when you have yourself convinced you're in love, you become more tolerant of all kinds of crap. In retrospect, I was a total idiot, but in the moment, I let him be a jerk."

"How bad of a jerk?"

"Bad enough. It's not something I like to talk about, as you can imagine. I'm embarrassed, for one thing."

"You know you shouldn't be. Lots of smart girls and guys, for that matter, get themselves into shitty situations. I'm glad you got out of it. Don't be embarrassed."

"Thanks. I know all that, but it's still not easy to understand how I let it go so far. I mean dangerously far."

"Melinda's rumors about your wild boyfriends were not that farfetched." His tone was playful, but Aliza's reaction transmuted his expression instantly to regret.

"Everyone knew. Everyone. It was horrible," she whispered vehemently, tears brimming at the corners of her eyes. "I have to go," she said, looking down, feeling desperate.

As she started to rise, Jesse gently caught her hand in both of his. "I'm sorry, Aliza. This is neither the time nor place for this discussion. I am so sorry. Please stay. You're starving. I'll change the subject."

Their lunch came at that moment, looking and smelling so appetizing it overrode Aliza's flight response. She settled herself back into her seat tentatively, looked at Jesse's face, which seemed totally sincere, and decided to stay. "Okay, which one's mine?"

He smiled. "Whichever you want. This one's egg salad, and this one's a turkey bacon melt."

"Let's share them both," she replied, feeling a little more cheerful at the prospect of lunch.

"Great." He divided up the sandwiches, and they ate in near silence.

The food was perfect, despite the nondescript feel of the place. She could forgive a lack of ambiance when the fare made up for it.

After yesterday's record scarfing, she deliberately ate at the most normal pace she could muster, chewing every bite carefully, savoring the quality of the food. Jesse, who finished before her, settled back in his seat, folded his hands over his stomach and smiled at her.

*He's so easy to be with sometimes, and other times so difficult. Or, maybe it's me.* She smiled back anyway.

# EIGHT

*The jeweler draws lines with a thin black marker over the silver's mottled surface. This is where she will pierce shapes out with a saw. The blade of her saw is very fine, creating the thinnest line, as metal is meticulously removed, reduced into a fine powder, which the jeweler catches in a leather pouch below her work area. The piercing proceeds at an interminably slow pace, each turn carefully executed so as not to snap the fragile blade. Even using such care, she must still replace the blade a few times, for the torque is too much to bear. The blade flings itself apart in rebellion.*

Guilt at making Aliza cry gnawed at Jesse. Desperate to make it up to her, he knew he had to take it slow, or he would lose this rare bird forever. The scars of her past ran too deep, of this he was increasingly sure. How badly or in exactly what ways she had been hurt, he didn't dare guess, but it felt disconcertingly familiar. Feelings he'd buried deep within his own psyche bubbled to the surface. He did his best to stuff them down, but even so, it was painful to imagine someone hurting Aliza.

After lunch, Jesse asked her to explore the city with him a little. A walk by the river would do him good. Sensing her hesitation, Jesse appealed to her aesthetic sensibilities.

"Wouldn't you like to see some of the bridges up close? I bet they're pretty."

Aliza appeared ready to bolt, but she softened and relented at his convincing smile. "Fine. It's nice out, at any rate."

After traversing Main Street at the blinking yellow light, and walking for all of three minutes, they quickly passed through the downtown. Within one more block they found themselves in a residential neighborhood lined with old trees. Quintessential New England houses, each with some adorable architectural feature, lined the street.

The fresh air reminded Jesse of his childhood. Spring smelled different on the East Coast than it did out West. It was one of the many things he hadn't realized he'd missed until he visited places like Twin Falls.

They walked at an angle to Main Street on a direct course for the river. It was not more than four blocks before a wide swath of green park opened before them, flanking the river. Dotting the serpentine promenade lay Victorian park benches with ends shaped like swans, all painted in traditional deep green. Swiftly flowing against its banks, the river smelled like it had come directly from melting mountain snow. They stopped and sat on one of the benches facing the water and looked around them.

"It smells so different here than it does in LA," Aliza said, mirroring Jesse's thoughts. "More natural, I guess."

"No smog. It makes a huge difference. I thought I'd lost my sense of smell when I moved there, but it was the smog masking any fragrance nature might try to showcase. It's strange, though, I was thinking about how the river smells when you brought it up."

"Like snow," she said, looking out at it. Her expression was distant, unreadable.

"Yep. Like melted snow." Jesse wondered if she was still upset about what he had said at lunch. He wanted her to know he understood how she felt, but he wasn't sure how to bring it up without upsetting her again.

"Men can be terrible, and before you get mad, or defensive, or try to run away again, I want you to know I truly understand, and I'm sorry."

Aliza stiffened and frowned as Jesse spoke, but when he didn't continue, she relaxed again. "Thanks, Jesse. Sorry for overreacting. I do that, as you've probably guessed. It's like all my emotions are lingering just below the surface, and any little thing is enough to start a deluge. I've got to get myself under control."

"I think you're doing fine. That ability to access real emotion is probably one of the things that makes you such a good actress. You don't have to dig deeply to find a parody of an emotion. You have the real thing. I admire that about you."

"Don't. It's a detriment. I can't have a conversation about anything real or meaningful without bursting at the seams. A little balance would be helpful."

"Artists are never balanced. Balance is boring, and Aliza, you're anything but boring."

The mirror image park on the opposite shore was bathed enticingly in sunlight. Jesse put out his arm for Aliza to take. "Shall we continue our walk?"

She studied him for a moment before replying. "Thank you," she answered quietly, taking his arm and rising.

They strolled across the white stone footbridge, stopping to examine the Victorian era statuary at the ends. "Emotion was okay to display back then, I think. Have you ever seen a Valentine from the 1800s? They're full of flowery language. Hearts on the sleeve, so to speak," Aliza mused aloud. "The sculpture is the same, so romantic and sweet. Do you think things were really like that, or is it an excellent PR job on history?"

Jesse considered the question before answering, staring the statue of a chubby child holding a butterfly in its hands, looking sweet as an angel. "It was probably not all flowers and sentimentality, but people must have interacted differently. I think poor people still suffered and rich people still had everything they wanted, but who knows whether people felt freer with their emotions. I don't know enough about it, one way or the other."

"It still must have been better than it is now. Everyone's hooked up to their phones, listening to their own music in isolation. People used to talk face to face with a friend, and now we spill our guts on the internet for the whole world to see. How much of it's genuine?"

"Like these two guys I saw at a coffee shop in LA before I left. They were sitting together, not saying anything, texting other people in other places. How is that communication?"

A cloud passed in front of the sun as a chilly wind blew over the water. Aliza shivered with an embarrassed smile. She is slight, Jesse thought, a feisty but frail little creature. Jesse put his arm around her shoulder, feeling as he did so that it was the most natural thing in the world. She didn't stiffen or pull away. He held her to him and rubbed her arm to warm her. "Do you want to go back?" he asked reluctantly after a moment.

"No. I don't mind the wind. It makes me feel alive."

Intense desire to kiss her surged up within Jesse, but he hesitated, examining her unreadable expression. Before he could act, she turned and put her hand to his face, gently brushing her fingers along his cheek.

"Your skin is like porcelain," she said, her voice quiet and subdued. Her eyes caught the light, her long lashes fluttered in the breeze.

It was too much. Jesse cupped her face in his free hand, sliding it to the back of her head, and kissed her gently, but with passion. Their lips parted for a moment, as he drew in a sharp breath. He saw what he felt mirrored in her face, surprise mixed with awe. Aliza moved towards him, ever so slightly. Jesse did not hold back this time. He kissed her intensely, fully aware of a powerful attraction. The world closed about them, enveloping them in blissful solitude.

As they parted a second time, Jesse stroked Aliza's hair and pulled her into an embrace, holding her tightly for fear she would try to escape him again. She made no effort to do so. His heart felt so full, he breathed in her scent-vanilla and orange, a creamsicle girl- and hoped she would begin to trust him.

The air turned warm again, and Jesse's initial excuse for holding Aliza dissipated in the strengthening afternoon sunlight. They walked back toward town, hand in hand. Jesse dreaded damaging the bond forming between them. As they approached the downtown, however, he could feel Aliza's discomfort mounting. She probably wasn't ready, he thought, to have everyone talking about the two of them any more than they already were.

Before they were in view of the town square he stopped and took her other hand, facing her. She looked surprised and started to ask why they'd stopped. "I would like to cook dinner for you," he said, "At my place. Tonight. What do you say?"

"At your place?" she replied, looking a little skeptical if not downright concerned.

"Yes. I do know how to cook. Is there anything you don't eat?"

"So far you've seen me scarf down three meals full of meat and cheese and goodness knows what. No, there's very little I don't eat. I've never liked clams outside of a chowder, but I think that's it." She smiled.

"Great. How's six?"

"Fine. What can I bring?"

"Bring yourself. I've got the rest covered." Jesse gave her his address, and they said goodbye. He needed to go grocery shopping. Before he let go of her hands, and just as she was pulling away to leave, he leaned over and kissed her on the cheek.

# NINE

*Once the shapes are cut and the jeweler's trace work pattern peeks through the silver, it is ready to be formed into curved, three-dimensional shapes. The jeweler cuts out ovals and begins the dapping process. Using a hammer and a punch, she pounds the ovals carefully against a die. A thick, protective piece of wool felt over the etched surface protects it from the hammering, although every tool leaves its own marks, unique fingerprints documenting the creative process. Annealing grounds the jeweler, the rhythm repeated often, keeping the metal pliant. Feeling centered she heats the silver again, eager to watch it transform and heal.*

Aliza couldn't believe it had happened. As Jesse kissed her, her emotions had come to life for the first time in ages. Silencing the voice in the back of her mind warning her not to get too close had been hard work. If she was being honest with herself, she would admit she had liked him from day two. Day one was rough, it was true, but by day two, he had been nothing but kind to her. Instinct told her she should keep her guard in place. Actors could be downright liars, as she had seen before. She'd had her heart broken young and often by them and had sworn them off until now. Somehow, though, Jesse didn't seem like the rest. Growing up outside of the business made him more real, but she still couldn't let herself trust him.

Despite Jesse's protestations, she needed to bring something to his place. Her parents had always brought wine or cheese. Maybe cheese. Avoiding the grocery store so as not to run into him again was paramount, lest he should think she was stalking him. She went into Hal's Diner to ask if they knew of a store that would have what she wanted. Of course, she expected them to laugh her out of the place. This wasn't LA, after all. To her surprise, however, there was a tiny boutique of exotic foods with a respectable cheese counter, as the diner manager put it. This wasn't such a hick town after all, she thought, but then decided she was being uncharitable by even using the words "hick town" in the first place.

She found her way to the little store, not surprised that she had walked past it already without realizing it was there. It was microscopic and poorly advertised from the outside, but inside, it was a pure delight. Dried fruits and nuts, spices, teas, imported foods from exotic places, and the glittering gem of a cheese counter exceeded her wildest expectations.

After asking too many questions and tasting more than a few cheeses, Aliza settled on two. One was a soft French blue, the other a nutty sheep's milk cheese from Scotland. They were both delicious. She got some artsy looking crackers to complete the package and was about to leave when something caught her eye. On the newsstand by the door lay the local paper. A full color photo of her with Jesse graced the front page. The photo had been taken of them on the street together the day before with the caption "Hollywood Comes East". She bought a copy and left, horrified at the expression she wore in the picture. She almost forgot her cheese purchase, and the attendant called after her.

Outside the store Aliza stopped and studied the photo. Plenty of tabloid photographers had nagged her over the years, but this was different. Everything she felt about Jesse, from the trepidation to the awe, was obvious in her expression.

The world of tabloid rumors and unflattering paparazzi snapshots was hardly new to her. What threw her was the vulnerability of her emotions, even though she had thought she was tending them so closely. Jesse was right. Her masks were transparent, and this proved it. Her heart sank a bit at the realization. *Crap. If they've been following me around, they probably saw us on the bridge today.* The thought of their first kiss broadcast to the eager public was sickening. Feeling like she'd been hit in the stomach, she hung her head, and walked briskly to her apartment.

When she got in, she made herself a cup of tea. Once her nerves settled, she ate a few dried apricots and some yogurt so her stomach wouldn't be in full-on riot mode when she went to Jesse's. The picture from the paper kept popping back into her thoughts. Jesse looked calm and perfect, of course, the paradigm of composure. She, on the other hand, was an open book. A puppy dog following the star actor around, hanging on his every word. It was downright embarrassing. Nothing could be done about it now. The photo was already out there. Panic rose in Aliza again as she pondered what any new photo of she and Jesse might show. She imagined an image of their intimate kiss on the bridge, printed in black and white for the world to see. She comforted herself with the thought that not too many people lived in this little town, and she was willing to bet most of them couldn't care less about her or Jesse. *Other than the coffee shop girl.* Again, Aliza reprimanded herself for her terrible lack of charity. Maybe they'd get lucky, and the photos wouldn't be picked up by a real tabloid.

By quarter of six, Aliza had cleaned the flat, put on a cute sweater, and done her hair. Cheese in hand, she was almost out the door when her cellphone rang. Hesitating for a second, she decided not to answer it. The number wasn't familiar, and she didn't want to be late. She silenced the ringer, put the phone in her purse, and slipped out the door. Leaving herself fifteen minutes to walk just a few blocks was excessive, she knew, but she'd rather be early than late. Jittery excitement gripped her as she approached his apartment. She found the right building, took a deep breath and rang the buzzer. Jesse's voice crackled out of the intercom.

"Hello?"

"It's Aliza."

"Great. Come up, I'm on the third floor. Number 304." He buzzed open the lock and she headed upstairs.

Heavenly smells greeted her when she reached his already open door. Aliza pushed it open slightly, peering in. Jesse was right. The place suited him perfectly. He appeared at the kitchen doorway wearing an apron and smiled broadly. He had obviously been enjoying himself, and she smiled back warmly. "Hi, I let myself in," she said, realizing how dumb it sounded.

"Good. Sorry for not greeting you more formally, but I'm in the middle of a delicate operation. Make yourself comfortable. I'll be right with you." He disappeared into the kitchen, and she heard the sizzling sound of a pan deglazing. Her stomach rumbled in response.

After a moment, Jesse removed his apron and came over to her. As he kissed her in welcome, little thrills of excitement coursed through her veins at his touch.

"What's this?" he said as he released her, examining the bag she awkwardly handed him. "I thought I told you not to bring anything," he said in a mock-scolding way.

"I couldn't come empty-handed," Aliza replied, trying to get a grip on herself, her heart still racing. "I found a wonderful little epicurean boutique with a cheese counter."

"Thank you, but you shouldn't have," he said, peeking inside the bag. "I'll go put these on a plate, and we can try them out. I love cheese."

While he was out of the room, her gaze wandered from spot to spot, taking in every detail. The high-ceilinged apartment had wide windows in the living room. She went over to the fireplace, wondering if it still worked, and looked at the two photographs arranged on the mantelpiece. The faces looking back at her were warm and open. A woman she assumed was Jesse's mother was in one picture. Her dark hair and light eyes were the same as Jesse's, except with a tinge of sadness or loss. In a small black and white snapshot, a woman Aliza guessed was his grandmother hugged a young Jesse. He was beautiful even then, and his grandmother obviously loved him. That was evident from the joy on her face.

Jesse returned as Aliza continued her examination of the photos. He stood silently behind her, but she felt his presence. "Your grandmother is very kind, isn't she?"

"Yes. She loves me very much. She's one of my favorite people in the world."

"Does she know it?" Aliza said without thinking, regretting it immediately because it sounded accusatory. "I mean..."

"I don't know," Jesse replied, looking at the photograph. "I guess she probably does, but I'm not sure. Maybe I should call her and let her know, although it seems like such a Victorian display of emotion." He smiled slyly, obviously being a little cheeky in referring to their earlier conversation.

"I didn't mean to imply anything. I don't know if the people I love have any idea how I feel about them either. I think I was asking as much for myself as I was for you."

"I get it. No worries, Aliza." Then, he led her by the elbow back to the couch. The cheese plate lay invitingly on the coffee table. "Which one shall we try first?"

"The sheep's milk one. It's nutty, full-flavored, and so good."

"You like cheese as much as I do." Jesse laughed and cut them each a piece. He put them on crackers and handed her one. "Wow, it *is* good," he said with his mouth still full, a true testament to good food.

"When I was a little kid, my parents asked me one morning what I'd dreamed of during the night, and my answer was cheese. I can imagine what a great dream it was."

Jesse laughed. "I can picture how cute you were and how perplexed your parents must have been."

"I don't know if I could keep a straight face if my kid said that to me. Seriously."

"Parents must have special powers to resist that kind of cuteness."

Jesse cut a piece of the blue cheese and put it on a cracker. He handed it to Aliza. It was even better than she remembered it being that afternoon in the store. She closed her eyes and let an involuntary "mmm" escape her lips.

"It's so good."

"Yeah, I was totally thrilled to find the shop. What a gem."

"You'll have to show me where it is."

"No problem. I'd walked by it a couple of times already without giving it a second glance. I wonder how many other things I've been walking by without seeing in this town. In LA everything screams out at you, competing for your attention. Here, all you've got to do is have good cheese, and who needs a sign?"

They both laughed for a moment and then silence descended. Aliza snuck a look at Jesse. He looked happy.

He caught her smiling. "What?"

She looked away embarrassed. "Nothing."

"What were you thinking?"

"I'm embarrassed to say."

He slid closer to her on the couch and took her hand. "You don't need to be embarrassed with me."

She squirmed a little, but there was no room to move. "I was smiling, I guess, because I was thinking you looked happy, and that made me happy." She felt absurdly shy and awkward as a teenager.

Jesse reached across and gently brushed a strand of her hair from her cheek. He gazed at her with intensity. "I am happy."

Aliza smiled as her stomach made an incredulous noise. They both giggled. "You need more cheese," Jesse said.

"I can't say no to that."

They ate a few more slices on crackers, savoring the complex flavors.

"Dinner smells wonderful," Aliza observed, breaking the silence.

"Thanks. Shall we go eat?"

"Definitely."

Even though it was all a part of the same large room, the dining area had its own distinct feel. It was intimate and perfectly proportioned to the size of the space. With its own rug and well-placed furniture, it had a very urban feel.

Jesse pulled out a chair for Aliza and she sat on it. A few moments later he came out with their dinner, a salad of cucumbers, tomatoes, and avocados, and a fragrant chicken dish with apricots and cashews in a thick sauce served over rice.

"This is beautiful," Aliza said, totally impressed. The food looked and smelled delightful. "Thank you so much."

"You haven't tasted it yet, so reserve your thanks," he replied playfully.

Jesse served her some salad in a bowl and took some for himself. "Do you eat your salad before the meal, during, or after?"

"Before, I guess. I never thought about it. Why?"

"We eat ours with the meal where I'm from, but some of my relatives live in upstate New York. They eat theirs after the meal. For you, though, I'll eat mine first tonight."

They ate some salad, and Jesse served them the entrée.

"It's great. You're a good cook. Did your grandmother teach you this, too?"

"In a way. I guess she inspired me to learn to cook. My mom's a prepared food junkie. She never had the time to cook, working two jobs to make ends meet. When we moved to LA, I found I missed well-crafted meals like the ones Grandma used to make, so I started figuring things out for myself. I read cookbooks, practiced sauces, watched old episodes of Julia Child, you know. Now, cooking's second nature. It's enjoyable."

"It's a gift."

They continued with the main course. Aliza could hardly believe how great it was, sweet and fragrant, savory and spicy all at once. The balance was unbelievable. "I'm so embarrassed. This is like five-star gourmet in comparison to the bizarre combination of foods I served you the other night. You must have thought I was a total hack. I guess, I am."

"Your food was great. Unique, but great. It's stuff I'd never think to combine. I like that spontaneity."

"You're being generous."

"No, I'm being honest. Most people can't do that. It speaks to your creativity. You're probably one of those people who could look at the last four ingredients in a cupboard and make something incredible out of them. It's a talent."

They finished their plates, and Aliza offered to wash dishes. Despite Jesse's protestations, she won out, and together they cleaned the kitchen. Neither of them was ready for dessert, so they sat in the living room to relax.

"Did you see us on the front page of the local paper?" Jesse said.

"I did. How totally embarrassing. I look like a star-struck teen. Did you even see that photographer?"

"You looked lovely, and no, I didn't see him at all. I was sort of preoccupied."

Aliza's heart skipped a beat as she thought of their conversation at the time. They'd been talking about his ex-girlfriend. As the realization penetrated, Aliza grew melancholy. In the excitement of the day, she had forgotten about Jesse's recent breakup. "Yeah, I guess you would have been." Before she could stop herself, she continued. "Jesse, I don't want to be a rebound relationship."

"What? What are you talking about?" He sounded surprised and looked genuinely perplexed.

"I'm talking about why you were preoccupied when we were walking together. You were thinking about your ex-girlfriend."

"I was preoccupied with you. The only time I've thought about Grace in the last week is when you've mentioned her. I've been trying to figure you out since we met. It's like a full-time job. I've never met a girl like you. I can't believe you thought I was thinking of her. As for rebounds, I wouldn't do that. I don't do that. It's not who I am."

Aliza felt immediately guilty for the accusation. "I have such a hard time with trust. I'm sorry, I didn't mean to..."

"Please," he said, moving closer to her on the couch. As he took her hand in his, she felt like bursting into tears again. "Don't worry so much."

He pulled her to him and held her tightly. Their embrace filled her with comfort, and her anxiety slowly melted away.

Finally, she pulled away far enough to look him in the eye and whispered, "Thanks."

"For what?"

"Just thanks."

"You know, if you ever want to talk about anything, I'm here."

"I'm fine. Really." Aliza tried her hardest to sound convincing, but she knew Jesse could see right through it. He was so good at that. Then, unbidden, another thought occurred to her. "Oh crap." She startled Jesse with her exclamation. His whole body stiffened.

"What? What's wrong?"

"You and I have been together all day, and never once did we think about tomorrow's lines."

"You're right. What time is it?" They both looked around the room for a clock.

"Jeez, no one thinks of putting clocks anywhere anymore. I thought this was a well-appointed apartment. Where's my cellphone?" She dug it out of her purse and looked at the time. "It's still relatively early. What do you want to do?"

"I've got the script. We'll have to share one. Is that okay?"

"Let's do it."

Jesse jumped up and went to the other room for the script. Aliza gathered her emotions and tried to get herself into a work-frame-of-mind. When he returned, he had a pitcher of water as well as the script. He filled up her glass first and then his own and set the pitcher on the coffee table.

"Where are we?" he asked absently, flipping through the first few pages. "Okay. Here. You start it out."

"You know we set the bar high today. We need to be really good tomorrow."

"I know. Relax," he said and put his arm around her shoulder and kissed her on the forehead. "It's okay."

They read their lines for three hours, perfecting nuances, changing a couple of things here and there that they knew would make the words flow more smoothly. After they had everything down for the next day, Aliza leaned back against the couch. "That was exhausting, but good. I think we've got it. You?"

"Totally. Great stuff. It's late, though, we should probably get some sleep."

"Yeah," Aliza agreed reluctantly. "I guess you're right." She pulled herself off the couch. "Thank you so much for dinner. It was great."

"We never got around to dessert. How about tomorrow?" he said with a wide smile.

Aliza couldn't resist. "Tomorrow it is."

As they walked towards the door, Jesse grabbed his jacket and keys.

"What are you doing?" Aliza said, perplexed.

"I'm walking you home," he replied with a shocked voice, implying she should have assumed that.

"This is not LA, Jesse. Besides, even if it were, you don't have to escort me home."

"Um, yes I do. I invited you here, and now I will see you safely to your door. Any gentleman would do the same."

*Then I've never dated a gentleman before.* It was a sad thought on one hand, but it proved once again how kind Jesse was.

"It isn't necessary."

"This is not up for discussion, Aliza. Let's go."

They walked hand in hand to Aliza's building. Neither of them spoke on the way, settling into a comfortable and familiar silence, the kind of quiet one could nestle into on a brisk evening like this. Little clouds of their breath merged and joined the atmosphere as the stars glistened overhead. At her door, Jesse kissed her goodnight and watched as she let herself into her building. Once she was inside, she looked back at him through the window in the door and smiled wistfully. He really was *good*, and she had no idea what to do.

# TEN

*The hiss of the steam marks another cycle of annealing. The silver is blackened now, and wet, the signs of cutting and hammering and fire obvious. This is why the jeweler fell in love with metalsmithing in the first place. To scar and to heal and ultimately to transform: this is her connection to the process. That in itself gives her hope.*

Relief flooded through Jesse as he returned home and lay on the couch with his feet up. Aliza's revelation about rehearsing lines had seriously saved their asses. He shuddered to think about the consequences otherwise. He needed to make a great impression with this job, but all he'd been able to think about since he arrived was Aliza. *Why does she captivate me so fully? I think about her constantly. It's like an obsession. I need to get a grip.*

Even as he thought these things, a little flip in his stomach reminded him there were more important things in life than work, a lesson his grandma had instilled in him from his youth. He remembered her telling him about how his grandpa had worked so hard for so long and had never gotten to enjoy any of it.

"For what?" she had said sadly. "So that he could see an early grave? That's not a life."

Her love for Grandpa was never so obvious as in her pain at losing him. *I'm lucky to have a person who cares enough for me to teach me that lesson.* Jesse resolved to call his grandma the following day. It was about time.

Jesse's dreams that night were of a vast estate with an enormous swimming pool, all presided over by his fifth-grade teacher. As she put out appetizers for a crowd of people, the pool filled with cheerful, elderly swimmers. Dream Jesse couldn't swim but he stood at the edge of the water anyway, watching light play on the silvered ripples, praying no one started to drown. All the while, a nebulous fear nagged at the back of his mind as he watched the old people frolic like oversized children in the water.

Jesse awoke in surprise to his alarm blaring away on the desk across the room. He shot upright in shock when it went off, crashed back on the bed, and covered his face with a pillow. Exhaustion weighed him down like lead as though he had hardly slept. Remnants of his weird dream lingered and tugged at his emotions. The intense protectiveness that had pervaded his dream clawed at him. Why, for the second night in a row, would he have dreams about fragile lives needing protection? He got up and turned off the alarm. A run was just the thing to clear his mind. He got ready and stretched in his doorway.

As he ran through the sleepy streets, Jesse realized he couldn't avoid Melinda anymore. They would have a scene together tomorrow, and she would want to make a production out of reading together. What he needed was a strategy—a way out. Dessert with Aliza seemed like a flimsy excuse, and this town was too small to have ticketed events for which one would need to leave at a particular time. No, he would have to be strong. In his mind he practiced ways of saying, "I think we're all set. See you tomorrow." Sometimes he said it forcefully, sometimes gently. He had no idea if it would work.

Preoccupied with the problem, he was startled to hear Aliza's voice next to him. "Talking to yourself? Here I thought you were such a normal guy."

Aliza smiled up at him, running in perfect step with his stride, despite being so much smaller. Admiring her good form, he smiled back.

"Did you sleep well?" he asked her.

"Dreamless and dark, like being underwater," she replied. "Just the way I like it."

"Do you usually have weird dreams?"

"Yep. Crazy stuff, but not last night. I think I was too tired to dream. You?"

"I slept terribly. I had strange, unsettling dreams about old people swimming. For some reason I was terrified the whole time. Maybe I thought one of them would drown, and I would have to do something, but in the dream, I couldn't swim. Very weird."

"Sorry. Is that what you were thinking about when I interrupted your thoughts?"

Jesse laughed a little and said, "No. I was thinking about Melinda."

Aliza's step faltered imperceptibly. "Melinda, eh? Fascinating topic, I'm sure."

"At least the dream didn't have her in it. I was wondering how to extricate myself from her clutches. She's going to want to read with me this afternoon, and I need a way out at a specific time."

"Easy enough. Yoga class."

"I don't take yoga."

"Now you do. They have it at the community center, and I'm checking it out at 4:00. Wanna join me?"

"Uh, I don't know. I've never been great at that pretzel stuff."

Aliza laughed. "Better than being tied up with Melinda indefinitely."

"You've got a point. I'm in."

They finished out their run and parted ways at a corner. Jesse went back to his apartment and showered. He got ready quickly, ate a bowl of cereal, and meandered down to the set by way of Hal's for coffee.

It was still early, and Jesse wanted to snag a donut for Aliza. She was such a hummingbird, always needing something to eat. Rudy accosted him the moment he reached the donut table.

"That was some expert work you and Aliza did yesterday."

"Thanks, sir."

"Don't call me sir. Call me Rudy, please. So, are you having a good time so far? Aliza's a spitfire. I've known her since she was so-high," he said, gesturing low.

"She's great, and she's a wonderful actress."

"Troubled life, that one. She never lets it show, though."

"I wouldn't have guessed. What happened to her?" Jesse tried hard to swallow, hiding his shock in his cup of coffee.

"Tough family life. Dad's a great writer—one of the best—but ups and downs like you wouldn't believe. No stability. Mom's a little better but not much. Prozac and white wine kind of took their toll. It's easy to be self-centered in LA. You blend right in. That's hard on a kid. She grew up fast and hard. Tough, I'll tell ya."

"Melinda mentioned she had dated some rotten characters," Jesse said, trying to sound nonchalant. He didn't want Rudy to stop talking or change the subject. It felt important to understand as much about Aliza as he could.

"You haven't heard the worst of it. Poor kid. The last guy knocked her around a little, from what I understand. Very domineering and possessive. Of course, no one in Hollywood presses charges. Too much publicity, but we all knew. Then the tabloids caught wind and the whole country knew. They tortured her almost as much as he had. He's blacklisted now, of course."

"Man, she seems to stay so positive. He's out of her life, though, right?"

"I haven't seen him around. If I do I'll kick his ass," Rudy said, although with his stature it was unconvincing.

"I'll keep my eyes open."

"I'll say this, she needs good guys on her side."

"I'm on it. I like her a lot."

Rudy looked at him quizzically, and Jesse smiled lightly, hoping he hadn't given too much away.

People started coming in and flooding the donut table. Rudy excused himself, and Jesse grabbed a couple of donuts, wrapping them in a napkin. He went to the makeup room, even though he dreaded it, just to get it over with.

Michelle's hair was down and in curls today, and her own makeup was outlandish, like a chameleon in a Miami drag revue. It suited her, somehow. "Good morning, sunshine." She called out to him from her station near the mirrors, putting down a celebrity magazine she'd been reading.

"Hi, Michelle. How's it going?"

"Early, but that's what coffee is for. Sit right down, honey. Let's get 'er done."

She worked quickly and chatted in a friendly way.

"Do you like it here?"

Trying not to move his face too much under Michelle's makeup brush, Jesse answered, "More than I thought I would. It's pretty charming."

"I agree. Although there's nowhere to shop." Michelle's eyes crinkled in good humor. "I also miss all my friends back in LA. You too?"

"I guess. I've been thinking a lot about that, lately. What makes a real friend?"

"Someone with whom you don't mind making a fool of yourself on the dance floor," Michelle replied, laughing.

Jesse was relieved she didn't broach the girlfriend topic. He knew he should keep things with Aliza under wraps for the time being, whether she was in the girlfriend category yet or not.

Michelle was going on about somebody or other she knew in Hollywood who had been involved in yet another scandal when Aliza came in. Jesse realized he had never seen her without makeup. He studied her as she walked toward him. The smile on his face was unconscious, but as usual, she misread it, blushing deeply.

Jesse sensed her unease. "You're even prettier without make-up. Most people aren't. Right, Michelle?"

Michelle looked up at Aliza warmly. "It's true, honey. You're a knockout. Of course, I like a little makeup to enhance nature's work, or in my case, start over completely."

All three of them laughed. "Michelle, you're a work of art," Aliza said.

She sat down, and Jesse asked her how she was doing.

"Just fine. I enjoyed my run this morning and the hot shower afterwards even more, but the apples out on the food table are all gone, and I didn't bring one today."

"Are the donuts gone, too?"

"Yep. Vultures must have descended."

"You've got to be the early bird around here. It's not worth thinking about, otherwise," Michelle added.

"Well, Aliza, I happened to think of you earlier when I saw the impending swarm."

Her face lit up. "Really?"

"Yep. There are two chocolate donuts in my bag, wrapped in napkins, with your name on them." He smiled and glanced sideways at her, under Michelle's powder brush.

"Are you sure?" Aliza was already out of her chair and heading toward the bag.

"I am. That's why I got them."

"Thank you so much. I need to start thinking ahead, I guess, but this is the best."

"No trouble," he replied.

"All done with you, Jesse," Michelle said. "You're next, donut girl. Whenever you're ready."

"Thanks, Michelle. Looks great. You're a wonder." Jesse took one last look at Aliza, who was already partway into the second donut, looking content despite the bit of chocolate on her face. "I'll see you in a few."

"Thanks again, Jesse. These hit the spot."

Jesse left the girls and the donuts behind and headed up to his dressing room. Amusingly enough, his wardrobe had been left with instructions. He wondered how hard it was to put on a shirt and pants. Although, some of the people he'd met in the acting business would need instructions like that. He got dressed and grabbed the script out of his bag, sat on the couch, and went over his lines.

Soon there was a knock on the door. His heart leapt a little thinking it was Aliza. He was a little crestfallen to see Melinda's heavily made-up visage pop through as she opened the door. "Good morning," he cheerfully said.

"Hi there, handsome. Michelle did a good job on you. Are you ready for today? I am. I think the writing for this show is superb so far, don't you? I was thinking we should read together today, what do you think? Would two work?"

She hadn't let him answer any of the questions she had asked in her dizzying staccato pace.

"Two works, but I'll have to be out a little before four. Shall we meet in the coffee shop around the corner or do you want to work here?" He had decided to take a lesson from her book and not give her a chance to tell him that two hours wouldn't be enough. It would be more than enough for him.

"I hate coffee. Let's meet in my ready room. See you then."

"Bye-bye," he called after her, feeling thankful the conversation hadn't lasted any longer and that he'd had the foresight to recommend a short meeting. *Two hours is hardly a short amount of time with Melinda.* He marveled at his own cattiness.

Another knock sounded on his door a moment later. "Come in." It was Maryann the mouse, as Jesse had called her that first day. He thought of Aliza scolding him for it. She was awfully cute when she got feisty.

"Hi, Jesse. I have a few changes to today's script. It's nothing serious. I highlighted the things that affect your dialogue in blue."

"That was thoughtful, Maryann. Thank you so much."

She blushed. "It's no problem, my pleasure." Hesitating, she looked like she couldn't decide whether to stay and chat or to leave immediately. Her curiosity won out, and she turned back to him. "How are you liking it here?"

"I love it. There've been some pleasant surprises. The food is great, and the people are friendly. Even the town is cool. I like it a lot."

"That's great. You'd be amazed at some of the awful things the other actors and crew are saying. They don't appreciate Twin Falls at all. For them, if it's not Hollywood, it's not worth existing."

"That's too bad for them. They're missing out."

"I agree, but I'm keeping you from your script changes. See you later." Maryann looked at him, self-consciously smiling as she left. He suffered a pang of guilt for his nicknaming of her. She was rather amiable, after all. *Shy girls have it so hard.*

Flipping through the script, he laughed aloud. He and Aliza had made the same alteration in the dialogue the evening before. Thankfully, it was nothing serious. He looked at his cellphone for the time. Aliza hadn't come up to see him. *She's probably mad at me for looking at her without makeup this morning. She* would *think the worst.* Feeling wistful, he left his dressing room for the set.

Torn about whether to stop by her room on his way downstairs, he ultimately decided to stop. As he neared her door, which was open a crack, he heard her voice call out, "No, you son of a bitch. Don't you dare. I'm changing this number by the way. Don't call me ever again." There was a loud crash of plastic breaking, which he assumed was her cellphone hitting the wall. Without thinking, he rushed in and found her in tears at her dresser. Her head was hanging down, her hair a glossy fringe hiding her face.

To keep from startling her, he spoke softly. "Aliza."

Undaunted by her fierce expression, Jesse walked across the room to her. Before she shooed him away, which she was clearly about to do from the look on her face, he pulled her into a strong embrace. He held her for several moments until he felt the tension in her small frame release. She let herself be held as though she didn't know what else to do.

Jesse took her shoulders and held her away from him a bit. "Now is the time for those acting skills to assert themselves as never before. We'll deal with this later, okay?"

She nodded her head.

"We'll stop by Michelle for a quick touch-up. We have time. Don't worry. It's my obsessive nature to always be early for things. Let's go."

Taking his outstretched hand, she followed him out of the room.

# ELEVEN

*The jeweler cleans the darkened silver in a heated liquid called the pickle, so named, she assumes, for its piquant aroma. In a few moments, the silver gleams again, bearing no resemblance to the sheet metal with which she began. She examines the form she has created, assessing the curves, the edges, the piercings. It will do.*

Although no one else seemed to notice, Aliza was in a daze. Somehow, she did not let it affect her performance. Jesse masked his deeper emotions as well, knowing he couldn't let them show. All in all, Rudy was pleased with their work and let them go by one.

Jesse escorted Aliza back to her dressing room in silence. He was worried about her but decided not to press. They walked in, and he closed the door behind them. The room was darkened from a passing cloud. He turned on the overhead light, startling Aliza. She jumped a little bit and looked at him. "Sorry. I'm a little out of it."

"No problem. Great job down there, by the way. You didn't let your feelings show at all. Very convincing."

Aliza avoided his gaze, but her sorrow was palpable. "Good," she replied quietly. She noticed the pieces of her cellphone scattered on the floor near the wall and shuddered. "I guess I shouldn't have thrown it. I had everyone's contact info in it. Now what am I gonna do?" She said it like a little girl who had dropped her ice cream cone. Forlorn, she melted into a puddle on the couch.

Jesse's heart ached for her. He sat down and put his arm around her. "It's okay. I'm sure you've got it all backed up on your computer. I can help you if you want me to."

"I don't need help, and I don't need pity," she said acidly, stiffening distinctly, pulling away from his embrace. "This is my problem, my fault, and I'll deal with it."

Startled, Jesse didn't know what to make of her sudden shift to anger. "Sorry. I don't mean to offend you. I care about you, Aliza. That's all."

"Well, don't." She said it firmly, with a bitter edge to her voice, and stood up.

Jesse ached with the sting of it. He knew she was deflecting her feelings, but her words hurt him nevertheless. This was textbook stuff, he only wished he'd paid better attention during his Psychology 101 class. With no idea what else to do, he let it go. He took a deep breath and waited for Aliza to calm down.

It took a couple of minutes of heavy breathing and staring out the window, but she finally came around.

"I don't know why I said that. I'm sorry. You don't deserve it. You've been nothing but kind to me."

"Don't apologize. I'm here because I want to be, because I like you, not because I pity you. Don't forget that. You're a wonderful girl, and you deserve friends and lovers who will respect you."

The tears started flowing again as Aliza listened to his words. "I don't know what I deserve. I am so mad at myself for being so stupid."

"Whatever he did to you wasn't your fault. You are not stupid, by the way. You're one of the sharpest people I've ever met." Jesse smiled at her ever so slightly. "Look forward. Let the past go and learn from it, I guess."

Aliza sat down again, leaving space between herself and Jesse, but she looked into his eyes. "I want to look forward. I want to move forward. I don't want to be bound by a past I never should have let myself become involved in, but the past won't seem to let me go."

"Your ex has been harassing you?"

She hesitated and then acquiesced. "Yes."

"He'd better leave you alone, or he'll have me to deal with." Jesse's tone was protective and hard.

"Thanks, Jesse. I can fight my own battles. But thanks."

They sat in silence for a little while, and Jesse could feel Aliza calming down. Her body was less tense, and she was breathing regularly. He regretted having to leave her.

"Are you going to be okay? I've got to go do lines with Melinda."

"I'm fine. Thanks for sticking around. I appreciate it."

"Are we still on for yoga?" he asked.

"I don't know if I'm up for yoga," she replied, looking a little worn out.

"I understand. We could try to find you a new cellphone. That might be an actual adventure in this town. I haven't seen any big stores or name brands since we got here. Besides, there's nothing quite so the opposite of yoga as shopping."

"I hear there's a mall not far away. I've got a bike, you game?"

"Like a ten-speed?"

"Four."

"Nice. Banana seat and fenders?"

"Fenders, yes." Aliza smiled wickedly, her feisty nature resurfacing for a moment.

"Awesome. I'll swing by your place when I'm done."

"Don't let Melinda get too fresh."

Jesse squinted at Aliza in response. "You are feeling better."

———

When she was alone again, Aliza tried to put the incident on the phone with Cameron out of her mind. He always knew exactly what to say to hurt her the most, and this time was no exception. Shuddering, she recalled his threatening tone. Something was different, more dangerous than before, making her glad she wasn't in LA.

She got changed, touched up her makeup with her own cosmetics, drank some water, and realized she was starving. On her way out, she ran into a techie she had known on other productions. He was a very friendly guy, a little older than her, and well-liked by everyone. They had always been on good terms, and when he saw Aliza he stopped her.

"Hey, Ally Cat," he called out from down the hall.

"What's up, Bertie?" she answered with a smile she tried hard to feel.

"Haven't seen much of you around. It's been busy on our end. Things are shaping up nicely, though, don't you think?"

"I do. You guys always do a bang-up job. Are you liking the crew?"

"Yep. Mostly. There're always some jerks, but people are fairly friendly on the whole. Did you know I'm engaged?"

"No. That's so cool. Who's the lucky lady?"

"Michelle. You know her, right?"

"From makeup? Of course. She's a total sweetheart."

"She is. I couldn't be happier."

"Congratulations. I'm so happy for you both. When's the big day?"

"Not set yet. We've got to figure out where to do it first. We both have huge families that live nowhere near each other."

"Convenient. Sounds like a beach ceremony with just the two of you, and then two big parties later on would do the trick."

"You know, that's not a bad idea. I'll run it by the little lady and see what she has to say."

"I have a feeling she's going to tell you not to call her the little lady." Aliza winked at him.

"I think you're right."

Aliza's telltale stomach interjected loudly enough for Bertie to hear. "I forgot about your sidekick there," he said, pointing to her abdomen and laughing. "Nice to see some things don't change. How's everything in your love life? Last I heard you and Cameron had broken up."

"Yeah, it was a few months ago. He's a jerk," she replied stolidly.

"You said it. I heard the rumors. He was pretty rough on you, wasn't he? What kind of guy would do that?"

"I don't know. I'm glad it's through." Aliza, desperate to change the direction of the conversation said, "Listen, my stomach is eating itself. I have to go find some food."

"I'll join you. I haven't eaten all day, and we're on a break 'til three."

They went for sushi at a little counter down the street. Aliza loved the flag curtain with the sumi-e circle painted on it hanging in the doorway of the shop in the traditional fashion. Somehow, like everything else she had encountered in Twin Falls, the quality of the food was superb. She would have to take Jesse here. *Why am I so attached to him already? We only just met.*

Aliza was thankful Bertie had invited himself along. It was refreshing to talk to someone else for a change. He regaled her with stories about some of the cast members she hadn't gotten to know yet. Everyone had a sordid past. She was no exception. *I wonder if he tells all of them about me and Cameron. Would they care that they're the subject of gossipy techies? Do I care if I am?*

Pondering these things, Aliza ate while Bertie talked through their meal, appreciating that she had to say so little. When they were done, she said goodbye to him and went back to her apartment. A great weight had settled upon her since Cameron's phone call. Feeling terribly tired, she lay down for an hour until Jesse got there. She left her door unlocked for him, settled on the couch, and tucked herself under an afghan her grandmother had made for her many years before. She closed her eyes and was immediately engulfed in a vivid dream.

She was riding with strangers in a convertible across a long bridge spanning a rocky archipelago. The wind whipped her hair into knots as they drove along the road, her companions were hooting and hollering in glee at their speed. The water beyond the bridge was deep azure and the views of the sea beyond were panoramic. Affluent-looking villages carved into the gray stone cliffs dotted the island they headed to. The buildings looked like they'd been there for hundreds of years. Tall cypresses grazed the sky. The driver was going too fast for Aliza to enjoy the details of her exotic surroundings, making her long to slow down.

Pulling up at an elaborate white stone building, a hotel, or a casino, they got out and ventured through wide front doors. She followed the path straight through the building into a vast courtyard. Much darker because of the height of the surrounding walls, it had a depressing, shabby feel in contrast to the opulent facade. Thick upon the lawn, vendors of antique merchandise had set up their wares in stalls. Much of the stuff for sale was Victorian, yellowing lace, early machines, wooden forms, and the cast-iron bones of once-useful objects. One of these booths contained medical antiquities. Sinister glass vials full of strange liquids glimmered, dangerous-looking metal implements Aliza could only guess the original use of were arranged on a table, and a creepy wooden examining table upholstered in cracking leather stood in the center.

The purveyor crept up behind her as she examined the wares. "It all still works, you know," he said in an aged, cracked voice. "I'll show you."

Startled, Aliza spun around and gasped to find the man was Cameron, only a haggard, filthy, ancient Cameron. His squinty, malicious eyes made his intent obvious. He wanted to hurt her. The walls of the courtyard closed in around them as everything else disappeared. Moving towards her, never breaking eye contact, Cameron edged closer, wielding one of the metal instruments from his stall.

There was nowhere to run. As he approached, fear overrode Aliza's survival instincts. When he reached out his hand to grab her, she screamed so loud she woke herself.

Aliza had no idea if the scream had left her lips, but the

pounding on the door and the alarmed voice on the other side of it told her she must have. She staggered up, her mind still foggy, and opened the door.

Jesse burst into the room, looking around for the source of what had made Aliza scream. Finding nothing, "Aliza, are you all right?" he breathlessly demanded. "Someone let me in downstairs. As I came up I heard you screaming."

"God. I'm so embarrassed. I had no idea. I was asleep. It was a terrible, weird dream. I woke up to you banging on the door. What time is it?"

"It's a little after four." He walked past her to the kitchen, poured her a glass of water, and brought it to her. "Here. Drink this. You look like you could use it."

Willingly, Aliza accepted the glass and drank most of the water, feeling a little more in touch with reality. The grasping tentacles of her dream slipped slowly away. "I'm so sorry. I should never take a nap. It's too disorienting, even when I don't have nightmares."

"Tell me about the dream."

Aliza hesitated, but Jesse seemed so solid, so good, she thought it might help to tell him. They sat on the couch, and she explained the dream in detail.

When she was finished, Jesse took a moment to consider it. "You were wandering into your past, I guess. It's like everything was beautiful, you were headed in a good direction, and you entered this place that looked great on the outside, but it was a trick. It's kind of haunting, I guess. You never expected the attack. It ambushed you, but you got away."

"I screamed and did nothing. I want to go back and fight him. I want to grab one of those rusty, sharp metal objects and stand my ground. That's the trouble with dreams. They're over before you can ever do anything."

"I'm convinced they're training exercises for possible scenarios our conscious mind is afraid we'll encounter. In this case, you're preparing yourself for when you see this guy again. The challenge you've presented to yourself is how to handle it."

Aliza thought about this for a moment, amazed at how perceptive Jesse was. "That's a very interesting theory. Like practice makes perfect."

"Exactly."

"I guess I should take some self-defense lessons or something. I was totally powerless in the dream."

"It's not a bad idea, if you think he's dangerous."

"I don't know. I can't tell how far he'd go."

"I wouldn't want to test it."

"Thanks, Jesse. Talking it through helps. I think if I had been alone and had to think about that dream, it would have bothered me more. Your interpretation is better than any of mine would have been."

"Good. I'm glad to help. I took a psychology course once."

"Well, if your acting career goes belly up, you can always be a psychiatrist."

"Thanks for the encouragement, Aliza. You always know what to say," Jesse replied, laughing.

Aliza smiled. "No trouble."

After a few moments in silence, Jesse spoke. "Where's your bicycle?"

Aliza giggled and repeated the word bicycle under her breath derisively. Then, at full volume and with a sly look in her eyes, "I'll show you," she said. "Let's go."

———

They walked hand in hand down to the subterranean garage below her building. Most of the spaces were empty except for a nice vintage motorcycle and a few cars scattered around, but Jesse noted a distinct lack of bicycles.

"Where is it?" he asked her, looking around. As his gaze shifted back toward her direction, he caught the naughty gleam in her eyes and he realized he had been tricked.

"I didn't say bicycle. I said bike, a gorgeous old Indian, to be exact. I hope the extra helmet I have fits you."

As they walked up to the gleaming antique motorcycle, Jesse's eyes widened in disbelief. "This is yours?"

Aliza smiled and nodded.

"It's a beauty. Those lines. The chrome. I love it. How long have you had it?"

"It was my grandfather's, but he hardly ever rode it. When he died seven years ago, my parents were going to sell it. I persuaded them not to and after some cajoling, they agreed I could have it. I've owned it about five years. I've learned a lot since I got it. That's for sure."

"Like what?"

"Like how to fix motorcycles." She laughed and patted the worn leather seat. "It's like an old friend. Ready?"

She took two helmets from the handlebars and tossed him one. The other, lacquered pink with sparkles, she put on. Thankful they weren't both pink, Jesse donned the basic black one.

What a relief her confident driving was to Jesse. He'd never been comfortable on a motorcycle, and his first thought when he saw it was he'd have to decline. He was glad he'd mustered up the courage and very glad he had not shared his initial misgivings with Aliza. They whizzed through the streets, and although it was technically rush hour, the traffic was very light. Up the hilly road leading out of the town, they wended their way to the highway Jesse had traveled on his first day. After a few miles, they saw the vast suburban blight that was the local mall.

They parked and carried their helmets with them. Like every other mall in America, it had been built in the 80's or 90's. With no natural light, it was a vast maze of chain stores which all looked the same. Aliza found one for her cellphone company, and they browsed through the phones. She tested some out by calling Jesse's number and talking to him from across the room. It had both of them in stitches before long, as they pantomimed a real, in-depth conversation. Finally settling on a sleek, pink smart phone, she reasoned "It sounds the best out of all of them." Jesse chuckled under his breath. She shot him a playfully angry glance as she paid, and he pretended he'd done nothing wrong.

"Are you getting hungry?" Jesse said when they left the store.

"I'm always hungry. I think it's a tapeworm. Why? Are you?"

"Yep. It's almost six. I could eat."

"Food court?"

To Jesse, she sounded more exhilarated than any normal person should have at the prospect of eating at a food court. He humored her. "Food court it is. You seem too excited about the idea for me to suggest anything else."

"You are a smart man," she replied, smiling flirtatiously.

The food court was a panoply of the typical fast-food Chinese, Italian, Mexican, and American. Aliza picked Chinese, and Jesse chose an array of tacos and burritos. They sat at a table with an umbrella, despite being indoors with no windows, enjoying the irony.

"We should have stopped at that candle shop and picked up something for a little ambiance," Aliza said, laughing through a mouthful of lo mein.

"Nothing says romance like food court Chinese. I feel like we're teenagers on a first date."

"So, Jimmy, what do you like best about high school?" Aliza said in a ditzy voice.

"Well, Mindy, I like chemistry the best, if you know what I mean." He winked at her in an over-the-top kind of way.

"Why, I don't quite understand," she answered. "Chemistry is so boring."

"Not the way I study it," Jesse replied in an exaggeratedly deep voice and capping off with an intensely suggestive gaze.

They both laughed loudly, and since the court was nearly empty, no one was near enough to care. They continued eating their greasy food and Jesse asked, "What appeals to you about this kind of cuisine?" He spoke the last word with air quotes.

"I don't know. I guess it's kind of like comfort food. It's so predictable, exactly the same on the East Coast as it is on the West, and when I eat it, it's so disgusting, it makes me happy. That sounds crazy, I guess."

"Yeah, a little, but crazy is the new cute." He smiled at her and finished off a taco.

Aliza shook her head and her expression darkened, but Jesse didn't know why.

They finished their food and browsed the shops for a while. When Jesse mentioned he was in the market for a watch, they stopped in a few stores to try some on. Nothing appealed to either one of them.

"I guess I've sort of had this idea in my head that a guy needs a watch, but whenever I try any on, they feel wrong. I don't know why."

"Well, they all look dumb on you," Aliza commented, offhandedly.

"Gee, thanks." Jesse felt a little hurt.

"No, what I mean is they don't look right. Like they don't fit you or something. I don't know. I'm sorry. I mean honestly, you could make anything look good."

"Nice back-peddling."

"Never mind. I can't explain it."

"I'm joking. Maybe for the same reason they feel wrong, they look wrong, but I don't know what the reason is."

"Well, you've managed this long without one. I suppose it won't kill you to go a little longer until you find the right thing."

"You're right. Let's get out of this soul-sucking *monument to consumerism* before I forget my own name."

"*Mallrats?*"

"You caught that. We do have a lot in common."

Outside, the night air was still holding some warmth. Aliza's bike looked inviting to Jesse, now that he knew she could drive it.

"I guess we should head back," Aliza said, swinging her leg over the seat.

Jesse admired how attractive Aliza was sitting there. The mere act of straddling the motorcycle, one hand on the bars, helmet in the other, made her seem so edgy. So sexy. He'd felt that all along, but here she was, a pure enigma, and he didn't want to resist anymore. Her blend of self-assurance and vulnerability, her sharp wit and soft side, her ability to see into him all drew him toward her. Instead of straddling the bike, he moved closer to her, and put his hand on her arm. "I'm not ready to go back. Are you?"

His touch intensified something between them. Aliza swallowed hard and answered in a steady voice. "Not really."

"Let's go for a ride."

As though emboldened and relieved by his request, she smiled wickedly. "You got it. Hop on."

Jesse did as he was told, but this time, when he held on to Aliza's waist he was overly conscious of her body beneath his hands. The bike rumbled to life beneath them, and she tore out of the parking lot. They headed in a random direction, away from the highway. The local road was full of twists and turns and before they knew it, they were flying beneath the countryside's hilly landscape, beneath emerging stars, while scents of spring filled the air.

Their bodies were touching, creating a hyperconscious state in Jesse's mind. Down country roads they sped, scenery whizzing past them on both sides. They passed farms and tiny houses, some dark, some obviously occupied, their yellowy light aglow at the windows. Vast stretches of trees closed in from both sides, creating leafed-in tunnels which suddenly opened up with a heart-filling explosion of sky. When they came upon an ancient looking, decaying metal bridge spanning a wide river gorge, Aliza stopped the bike. She parked at a resting place and took off her helmet. Jesse followed her lead.

"How beautiful." She sighed. Before them, the moonlight reflected off the river's surface, refracting into a splendid jewel necklace. Nearby, picnic tables were scattered about for public enjoyment of the vista. Massive boulders led down to the base of the bridge with a low flat shore at the bottom. They could just make out some lights down the river, but other than that, they were alone.

Aliza hung her helmet from the handlebars and swung around so her legs dangled over one side of the bike. Turning to Jesse, she undid his chinstrap jauntily, a tiny smile playing at her lips. He removed the helmet, and she put it on the other handlebar. When she turned back to him, he couldn't hide his feeling of anguish at her beauty, at her proximity, at the irresistible attraction growing within him. The tension between them was palpable, overwhelming.

Throwing caution to the wind, Jesse cupped Aliza's cheek, pulled her gently towards him, and kissed her. The kiss was gentle at first and then more urgent. He moved his hands down her back, savoring the sensation of closeness, the electricity between them. Resting his hands on her hips, he pulled her as close as he could. Jesse didn't struggle with himself. He wanted this with his whole heart. Impassioned bliss consumed him as he prayed their kiss would never end.

———

The kiss was mesmerizing. Of course, Aliza had wanted Jesse to kiss her, but now she wanted so much more. Energy surged between them as his hands grasped her hips. She desperately wanted to face him, to swing her leg over the bike and straddle him, to pull him close, but she was terrified at the same time. That simple act, coming face to face with this man, wrapping her legs around him, would be the opening of a floodgate she was not ready to handle, but the fight within her was too great. Desire won.

She broke away from him, and in one quick, impulsive movement, she swiveled around to face him. She put her legs over his and pulled herself to him, savoring Jesse's yearning expression. Aliza met his gaze and mirrored his feelings. He grasped her against him in another, more intense kiss. At that moment, she felt their bodies had always waited for this, and fearing it would end too soon, pressed against him as tightly as she could.

Aliza's mind stepped outside of time. The confines of regular dimensional space became too weak to hold her. Her thoughts spun wildly as passion overrode logic, each tearing at the other in a primal clash for supremacy. She never wanted this perfect kiss to end.

It did end, however, as all kisses do. Aliza's eyes burned with emotion. Jesse stroked her cheek lovingly and touched his forehead to hers. Slowly, sounds filtered back to her ears. Water rushed past as the river flowed below, the wind rustled and whispered through new leaves. The moonlit vista glittered before them, but all she wanted to see was Jesse.

"You are beautiful," Jesse whispered.

Aliza's skin blazed under the compliment, and she was thankful the silver light of the evening must have cloaked her embarrassment. "I am human, that's for sure."

"What do you mean?"

"I mean I give in to my own desires too easily."

"Is that wrong?"

"I don't know. It's a struggle. One side of me wants to dive headlong into this, but the other side is terrified of releasing control. It's like there's some little voice cautioning me to wait. Always to wait."

"I'm sorry, I shouldn't have..." Jesse began, looking pained.

"Please don't be. I told you, I'm human. I want this as much as I've ever wanted anything. You didn't do anything wrong." Jesse looked a little relieved, but still worried. "Really," Aliza continued, "if anything, it was too right."

They looked at each other for a moment before she said, "It's been a strange day,"

"Kind of a roller coaster, huh."

"Exactly." Leaning back, she took his hands in hers, and brought them together at her chest. She kissed them one at a time, held them together again, and smiled wistfully.

They held each other for ages, perched upon the cliff's edge. The sky darkened, and the stars came out. Aliza shivered. "It's probably getting late, you know."

"I know," he replied sadly, kissing her once more.

"If you had a watch, we'd know for sure," she teased.

"Time is irrelevant right now. I resent that it always creeps into moments like this."

"Do you have many moments like this?"

"I mean important, seminal moments, and no, I've never experienced anything like this. You are unique, Aliza, and everything we do together is a first for me. You're right, though. We have to be fresh tomorrow. Any idea where we are?"

Aliza looked around to gain her bearings. "No, but I have a feeling if I go west we'll be fine."

"You know which way is west?"

"I do. The moon rose in the east, right? We go the opposite direction, which also happens to be the direction we came from." She laughed and handed him his helmet. "Relax, Jesse. I'll get you home."

After what seemed like a comparatively short ride back to Twin Falls, Aliza dropped Jesse off at his apartment. They said goodnight, fearing to kiss each other goodbye on the street because of any onlookers. She sped back to her building, parked her bike, and climbed the stairs to her apartment. She was so tired her body felt like rubber, but she was wildly exhilarated at the same time. Shockingly, it was nearly one in the morning. Some experiences transcended time, and this was surely one of them.

An ache of longing passed through her as she reviewed the evening's events. They played like a movie in her mind. *I never liked sappy movies. Predictable, cheesy tripe. Living romance, however, is different.*

The accelerated pulse, the sinking feeling of free-fall in the pit of the stomach, the yearning, all these things had Aliza atwitter. The mall scene replayed as she put on her pajamas. She wondered whether Jesse would ever find a watch he liked, and an image of him surrounded by loudly ticking timepieces carried her to sleep the moment she got in bed.

# TWELVE

*Transforming a second oval by dapping it against the die into a half-shell, the jeweler creates a mirror image of the first. They must fit together perfectly, so she takes great care with the hammer this time, measuring her progress. Anneal, cool, pickle, examine. The process continues slowly.*

Aliza dreamed of flying through the streets of her early childhood town. Cookie-cutter post-war homes lay in a silent warren below, the dark rooftops visually blending with the ground as she passed over. She wore a flowing nightgown, like the ones her mother had her wear when she was a kid. When Aliza had outgrown them and switched to comfy old T-shirts instead, her mom was visibly saddened. Her disappointment hadn't fazed Aliza at the time, but it was acutely noticed now in the dream. It was as though her mother had been trying to hold onto the fleeting idylls of childhood, and Aliza, like most young teens, couldn't have cared less.

Now, she embraced the feeling of youth as an old friend, nightgown and all. Flying was easier than she had ever imagined.

She was weightless, unbridled, and free, and her mind felt unencumbered. In her hand she held a basket full of shiny metal pocket watches. They clinked gently against each other as the basket tipped sideways. Understanding she was to deliver these watches to the houses below, she dipped her hand into the midst of the cool metal cases, their chains slithering against each other with an icy sound, and grasped one. The watch was old and yet luminously beautiful in the evening moonlight. She tossed it toward one of the houses where, defying gravity, it gently fluttered down to the porch, landing with a soft thud. Aliza delivered the watches to house after house, all the time aware of the delightful sensation of flight.

When she had a single watch left in her basket, she stopped, floating in mid-air. Examination of the watch revealed it was a pale gold piece, heavier than the rest, with filigreed initials on the front, engraved with an emblem of flowers and birds. The work was exceptionally fine. She did not want to part with this particular watch, for it seemed familiar, and she held onto it tightly. She pressed down on the top and the cover popped open to reveal a pearlescent watch face with delicate gold hands and formal Roman numerals. It was the perfect watch, Aliza decided, as she awoke from the dream.

In reviewing her mind's nightly ramblings, she was relieved she hadn't had to figure out how to land. Flying was one thing. Landing was quite another. Landings had never been her strong suit. What was the significance of the watch? The image of it was fading, but it seemed so very familiar. There was no time to figure it out. Her late night out had robbed her of precious hours of sleep, and she was due on set shortly. *At least I remembered to set the alarm.*

It was going to be a short day for her and Jesse. Their scenes were small and not complicated. Plus, it was Friday. *There's something to be thankful for.*

Aliza ran through her lines one last time before the shoot. She knew she had them down, but she was uneasy anyway. It was unlike her to feel that way, and she wasn't sure what was the root cause. Nor did she have time to resolve it.

Jesse looked fresh, even though he'd been out every bit as late as she had. Her expression must have betrayed her thoughts, because he smiled impishly and winked at her from across the set. She rolled her eyes and shook her head. He'd better be as snappy with his lines as he was with his flirtation. They started the scene, which included a slew of minor characters, some of whom had their first lines today. Rudy was unimpressed. Aliza could tell from his posture he was on the verge of saying something to one of the younger girls Aliza hadn't gotten to know yet. She looked terribly nervous and seemed to realize her performance was being scrutinized by the director, which made it infinitely worse. Aliza felt terrible for her, and before Rudy could intervene, she reached out and took the girl's trembling hand.

"We've all been there," she whispered. "Relax and let the lines come. You're doing fine."

Her sisterly action seemed to put Rudy at bay for the time being, and it gave the girl a chance to catch herself before the scene turned into a disaster. Her final take was passable, and she gave Aliza a grateful smile as she slunk off the set. Aliza and Jesse had yet to finish the scene, the first one their characters touched in. Ken was to take Lydia's arm and pull her back gently to keep her from walking out after a difficult conversation. Aliza was surprised by her body's reaction when Jesse's hand touched her. She tried to jerk her arm away from his hand and looked up into his face with indignance. Then she softened and delivered her line.

He let go, rolling with her new take on the scene, and flawlessly finished his delivery. "I will explain everything as soon as I can," Ken said. Jesse delivered the line with genuine empathy, and Aliza was touched.

Her face must have showed it, because Rudy jumped up and with a smile. "Cut. Perfect. Aliza, where did you get the idea to try to pull away? It was so convincing. I'm so impressed with the two of you. It's like you're meant to be together in this show. Couldn't be happier. Thanks for catching that little girl up to speed. Whatever you said to her worked well enough."

"No trouble, Rudy," Aliza responded. She was still trying to figure out why she had reacted so strangely to Jesse's grabbing her arm. The script had called for it, she had been prepared for it, but it brought up feelings she had not considered, defensive, defiant feelings that were surprisingly primal and intense. "Did you need anything else before the weekend?"

"You're all set. Enjoy it. See you Monday."

Jesse and Aliza mingled a little with some of the other actors before working their way upstairs. The young girl was still there. She'd been watching Aliza and apparently working up the courage to talk to her. Aliza decided to spare her the trouble and initiated the conversation. "You saved it, you know. That's a deciding moment in a young actor's career. Great work."

"Thank you so much. You helped. I was losing it. I knew my lines by heart and suddenly the whole world started to get dim around the edges. I was breathing hard, and I was forgetting everything."

"You recovered. It ended up working out fine."

The girl smiled and reached out her hand. "I'm Kylie."

"Aliza." They shook hands.

"Thanks again, Aliza. See you next time."

The girl took off looking happier, and Jesse came up beside Aliza. "That was kind of you. You're a good role model."

Aliza turned to him to see if there was any sarcasm in his eyes, and to her surprise, there wasn't. She looked down. "We've all been there. A kind word can go a long way and so can a cruel one. I opted for kindness."

"Of course, you did." He patted her on the back and walked away to talk to some other actors.

Aliza watched him from across the room. He was surrounded by a couple of young women, each of whom wore an expression of interest. They hung on Jesse's every word, and with over-the-top attentiveness. Aliza observed the scene for a moment, thinking about how lucky she was to have developed a relationship with him already. He was a great catch. These gals would be envious vipers if they had any idea. Jesse responded politely, but Aliza could tell his heart wasn't in it. He kept up a good show, though, and eventually Aliza turned away. Was that how she looked at him? She shuddered at the thought. *I don't want to be a groupie. That's not my style. I hope that's not what I come off like.* She shook away the disconcerting idea and decided to go change and find some food. Without a backwards glance at Jesse and the groupies, she sauntered away.

———

How could she leave me here in the middle of this, Jesse wondered, as the adoring group of girls fawned around him. *She is* so *going to hear about this.* He kept up his banter with them as long as he could stand it and only managed to extricate himself with a phony excuse. This would never do. The question was how to avoid that kind of situation in the first place. As he made his way up the back staircase, he thought of his ex-girlfriend's demeanor. She never fawned. If anything, she was a little on the calculating side. He didn't like that either, but Aliza, he mused, was perfect. She had the right blend of sarcasm, wit, charm, and intelligence, and she couldn't help but show her true emotions.

Insecurity crept into his thoughts as he pictured her walking away earlier. Maybe she thought it was amusing to leave him in his predicament. He wouldn't put it past her. It did fit with her sardonic sense of humor, but was that it? Somehow, based on her body language, he didn't think so. She didn't want to see him. *Did I say something? Did I offend her?* He thought back on the day so far and decided that wasn't the reason either. *Maybe I'm crowding her. Maybe I've been too in her face. Maybe she needs more space.* It hit him hard to think this, because all he wanted to do was hang out with her. *I don't want to be clingy. I need to step back, I guess.* The thought pained him as he re-imagined their closeness the night before. He wanted more of that, and the idea of stepping back was tough to take.

As he passed her dressing room, he hesitated and continued up to his own. Space was the best thing he could give her. He let himself into his room and changed clothes. His cellphone was lying on the dressing table, and he checked it to make sure he hadn't missed a call from Aliza. Did she even have his number?

Hunger drove Jesse back out onto the street to find some food. He didn't feel like having a long, drawn-out meal, but a cold sandwich didn't appeal to him either. Settling on sushi, he found the tiny place Aliza had told him about, right around the corner. The curtain outside the front door made it feel perfect, a big-city touch in a tiny little town. He was delighted.

The waitress showed him to a seat at the counter, which he graciously accepted with a small bow. He nodded to the sushi chef who nodded back with a calm, enigmatic demeanor. Jesse looked over the menu and settled on a bowl of udon and a spicy tuna roll. Once the waitress had taken his order, he gazed around the little restaurant. There were a couple of businessmen whose plates had been cleared, but they remained engaged in lively conversation on one side of the front door. On the other side sat a young woman reading a book as her remaining noodles steamed away, unnoticed. He thought the image was charming. The steam caught the sunlight streaming through the curtains, dancing and curling enticingly, despite the girl's lack of interest. She was good looking, in an aloof sort of way. A smile tugged at her mouth as she came across an amusing passage. Jesse smiled to himself in an involuntary response and turned back toward the chef before he could get caught staring at a stranger.

Reading a book was a good idea for people eating alone. He didn't have a lot of experience with that. He had been surrounded by people for the past few years and had spent very little time alone. Yet here he was, in a tiny town, without a group of friends to rely on for entertainment at a moment's notice. It felt scary and liberating at the same time, as he settled a little deeper into his new life. When his food came, however, all thought disappeared from his mind, and his stomach took over. The noodles were delicious, and the spicy tuna was perfect.

He had just put a whole piece of sushi in his mouth when he felt a presence by his side. He turned to see who was there and found the girl from the window seat. She had apparently finished her food and was preparing to leave.

Hesitating as Jesse turned to her, she mustered the courage to hand him the book. "I'm done with it. It's good for eating alone."

Jesse accepted the offering, mouth still half-full. "Thanks," he mumbled, as she turned away. It was a well-worn copy of *Cold Comfort Farm* by Stella Gibbons. The girl waved behind her jauntily and left the restaurant.

Jesse felt like she must have read his mind. He flipped through the first few pages and expected her phone number to fall out, scrawled on the wrapper from her chopsticks. It didn't. She had given him the book as an act of kindness. *That would never happen in LA. I can't wait to tell Aliza.*

It occurred to him at that moment that they didn't have any plans together. He didn't know when he would see her next. His stomach squirmed uncomfortably at the idea. Not an hour ago, he had decided to give her some space, and here he was wondering how he could go about making plans without crowding her. *I don't know. I stink at this stuff. If you want to see someone, you should tell them. No games, no mysteries. I'm going to ask her if she wants to do something. If she doesn't, I'll flat out ask her if she wants more space. Then I'll know for sure.* With his resolution intact, he finished his meal, settled the tab, and walked directly towards her place.

The door to her apartment building was propped open, so he climbed up to her floor.

Jesse was prepared to confront this issue head-on, but when he got to her door, her smile was so full of warmth and welcoming and genuine surprise he forgot what he'd planned to say.

"I *so* didn't expect you," she said cheerfully, opening the door. "Come in."

He stepped over the threshold and felt renewed. She had opened all the windows, and the air was cool and faintly lemon-scented. Jesse took a deep breath. "Smells great. You've been busy cleaning, looks like."

"Yeah, I tend to keep a tidy place. I found a new kind of cleaner that doesn't have toxic crap in it and smells like real lemons, not fake ones. I like it a lot."

"It's cheerful," Jesse added. "I like it, too."

"I'll write down the name for you later. Remind me. So, happy Friday."

"Happy Friday indeed. It's like a weight lifted. I can't believe we're done with our first week already."

"It's insane. I feel like it's been going on for months. What do you want to drink?"

"Nothing. I'm fine. You're right, though, it does feel like we've been here for ages. Working in a small environment is like that, I guess."

"Yeah, I have a feeling this is going to turn into a tight cast. People are already forming their friendships. I saw the flock of gals around you earlier trying to pull you into their little group."

"Is that what they were doing?" Jesse said, laughing.

"I think so, but I didn't dare get too close. I value my eyes."

"You think they would have clawed them out?"

"Oh, I wouldn't doubt it. I know how to play my cards right though. I'll have them all eating out of my palm before long."

"They won't like that you and I are dating," Jesse said. As the word dating slipped out of his mouth, he realized they hadn't talked about exactly what they were doing yet. Were they dating?

As though she was reading his mind, Aliza replied with a feisty look in her eyes. "Dating, huh. Is that what we're doing?"

"Um, I don't know. What do you think?" Sweating nervously, Jesse tried his hardest not to show his discomfort.

"I guess that's a term for it. It's weird that we'd go from genuinely disliking each other to dating in a week."

"I never disliked you."

"Well, I disliked you. You deserved it, though."

"I will never live that down, will I?"

"Never. I promise." She smiled naughtily at him.

He slid closer to her on the couch. "I have ways of making you forget," he said seductively. His gaze smoldered, and even though he was joking around, little thrills of attraction shot through his body.

"Your mind tricks won't work on me. Don't even think about it."

He put his hand on her thigh, "We shall see," he whispered and leaned in to kiss her.

Aliza let him.

It was some time before they surfaced for air. The breeze blowing in from the windows had a chill to it, and Aliza shivered. Jesse held her closer as they lounged together on the couch.

"You're not a bad blanket," she said, looking slightly embarrassed.

Jesse held her even closer. He stroked her hair gently and studied the contours of her face and her neck, paying particular attention to the little notch at her collarbone as it disappeared beneath her T-shirt. He ran his finger along the line. She trembled slightly beneath his touch. Hyperaware of the rise and fall of her body as she breathed, he explored her delicate frame with his gaze. "You are perfect. I know you don't like compliments, but I think it's true, and there's nothing you can do about what I think. My thoughts are my own."

Turning her face towards his, mere inches away, Aliza pinned him with a pensive gaze. The sadness in it, made her all the more beautiful to him.

"I can't figure you out," she said softly.

"What do you mean?"

"I mean I can't figure you out. You're so...nice. You're so...gentle. You look through me to the core and see more there than I think is even present."

"You don't give yourself enough credit."

"Even so, you don't know what's in there. How could you?"

"I know you're longing for something. I know you've been hurt, and the pain of it keeps you on guard. I know how happy I am you've credited me with enough trust to lay like this with you." She shifted slightly at these words. "I know having the spotlight on you like this makes you wildly uncomfortable. Which is ironic, mind you, as you're an actress, and the spotlight should suit you, but that's what I find endearing, I think."

Emotion seemed to well up inside Aliza. She closed her eyes and breathed in deeply and evenly, as though trying to quell an inner storm. Jesse held her and watched her patiently.

She had tears in her eyes when she reopened them. "It is so disconcerting to let myself do this. I am two seconds from bolting at any time, yet every part of me wants to be this close to you. It's like I want you to know me without having to tell you everything, and somehow that's exactly what you do. I want you to understand me, the whole me, without having to talk about my past, and you do. Thank you."

Her eyes were so earnest, her expression so genuinely grateful, Jesse's eyes prickled with the possibility of tears. Before they could give him away, though, he cupped her face in his hand once more, and leaned forward to kiss her. Their lips met, their connection reinforcing Jesse's intense desire for Aliza. Instinctively, he knew he must subdue it and take things slow. The kiss ended. Pulling her to his chest, Jesse wrapped his arm around her. They lay silently until sleep insinuated itself.

He awoke half-frozen and totally starved. The sky was nearly dark, as was the room. Jesse felt Aliza's body beneath his hands, the slow, even breathing of the deeply asleep. How close she was, how vulnerable, how soft. Wanting nothing more than to care for this fragile bird he'd been lucky enough to tame, he kissed her on the forehead. She awoke with a start.

"What time is it," she asked sleepily.

"I don't know. It's after sunset."

"I was so asleep," she murmured. "I had a dream I was stuck on a plane for like nine hours. I didn't have my laptop, or a book, or my knitting, or anything. I didn't have a charger for my phone. I was on my way somewhere, but I don't know where or why, and I wasn't prepared to stay. I was so nervous about being without everything I needed, and the plane wasn't going anywhere. It sat there on the tarmac, with the lights of the city flickering in the distance. I just wanted to get out."

"Did you?" he whispered.

"Yeah, I finally got up and demanded to be let off the plane, and here I am." She smiled, but Jesse could only see the faintest traces of her expression in the dim light. "Are you hungry?"

"Yes. Are you?"

"Doesn't that go without saying?"

Jesse laughed softly. "I guess it does. Why does being in the dark automatically make us talk softly?"

"I don't know," she whispered in a forced-quiet way. "It must be human nature. Maybe, in the jungles of our ancestors, talking at night was a dead giveaway for predators. Maybe it's a residual survival instinct. I want pizza. Do you want pizza?"

"That's a good theory, and yes, I want pizza. Let's order for delivery so we don't have to go anywhere."

"Perfect." She twisted off the couch and gave his leg a pat as she stood. She closed the windows and grabbed her sweatshirt from the back of a chair. "What kind do you like?"

"Pepperoni. Is there another kind?"

"Not to my knowledge." They both giggled, still in darkness.

"Close your eyes, I'm turning on the light," Aliza announced. She did, and Jesse pulled himself up off the couch. He was stiff and stood up to stretch. Aliza watched him from across the room, smiling as his shirt lifted, revealing his abs. Red cheeked, she turned around and called the local pizza delivery guys.

She came back to the couch with glasses of sparkling water for them. Jesse thanked her.

"You know," she said wistfully, "I've never slept with someone after just a week. You must be special."

Jesse choked a little on his water. Recovering his composure, he laughed. "No, just easy, I guess."

They hashed out what they should do with the rest of the night, settling on a movie. Aliza had a small collection of black and white films on DVD. She read out the titles, and they chose *The Big Sleep*. Aliza was as big a fan of film noir as Jesse. They talked about Raymond Chandler for a while and about how LA had changed so much since he wrote about it. They agreed it helped romanticize LA for them, making it seem like a place with a history, not only a mecca for boob jobs and tourists. They agreed that Philip Marlow was one of the best characters ever created.

"Every dame falls for him, and he always sabotages it. A happy, stable relationship simply doesn't seem to be in his cards, but you root for him nevertheless," Jesse wondered aloud.

"Yeah, I guess he gets enough out of each tryst to hold him over until the next. Can you imagine him married? Can you picture him with kids or something? Back then, everyone had to have kids."

"Right. They'd be like, 'Dad, take us to the park,' and he'd be like, 'Kids, can't you see I've got this glass of whisky and a big job to do? I don't have time. Besides, don't you know how many people get offed in the park?' Something like that."

"Hilarious. Philip Marlowe. Private Dick and Dick Dad. We should write a new book with him as the main character," Aliza suggested, giggling.

"I don't know. Could you be responsible for your character's eternal happiness or damnation? It's a lot of responsibility."

"I never thought of it like that. I wonder if the screenwriters think of us with that sense of responsibility. Maybe not most of the time, but sometimes a writer will take things very seriously, like they're making it personal. It's almost eerie from the actor's perspective. Like we're puppets or something."

"Some actors do it, too. They don't want anything bad to happen to their character for whatever reason."

"Superstition. I wonder how stuff like that gets started."

"Probably through coincidences that freak people out. They start reading into them, attributing more meaning than is logically possible."

"It's kind of irrational, but then again, people are so emotional. We don't run on logic all the time. Maybe that's why things get so messed up. We don't see issues as they are, but as we think they are."

"Isn't everything a matter of perception, though?" Jesse said. "I mean is the blue I see the same as the blue you see? We're all experiencing the world from our own unique perspective. How can logic always apply to that?"

"I guess it can't. I've let emotions rule my life in the past, and I've felt the consequences acutely. It's awful. You relinquish control when you start thinking things are preordained or that you can't make your own decisions. If we think more logically, though, we're less likely to go off the deep end."

"I wonder why it's called the deep end."

"Because some people can swim, and some people can't," Aliza responded rather wistfully. "If you can't swim, well, think about that weird dream you had with all the old people swimming. It would have been a mess if they were in the deep end without knowing how to swim."

"I guess I'm lucky I learned early."

"It's less traumatic that way, if you ask me."

"There's so many factors, though. It's not only skill that can save you in the deep end. It's adaptability, fitness, and to some degree luck."

"You certainly can't always expect the lifeguard to be there to drag you out, that's for sure."

"That's what I mean. You're lucky if he is. If not, you're—"

The doorbell cut off Jesse's last word. Aliza sprang up at the sound. She answered the door, paid for the pizza, and brought it to the living room table with a greedy smile.

"Mmm. Finally," she cooed. She swiftly retrieved plates and napkins from the kitchen, put the DVD in, and pressed play. "Enough talk. Must eat." She sat down, opened the box, and put three pieces on her plate.

Jesse smiled and followed suit.

They ate contentedly while the film played. They only stopped eating to comment, sometimes with their mouths full, about the lighting, or the different acting styles, or about how glamorous the women were back then. Before long, the pizza was a distant memory, evidence of its existence only revealed by the empty box and plates of crumbs. When they finished eating, they leaned back on the couch, sitting close, and Jesse put his arm around Aliza, holding her to him.

She stiffened at first, as was her usual reaction, but relaxed almost immediately. After a few minutes, she tucked her feet under her, leaned sideways and snuggled into his chest. He kissed the top of her head and smiled to himself. He suddenly thought how different his ex-girlfriend had been from Aliza. Grace was so cold and aloof, so practiced in all her mannerisms. When he had held her, it was as though she had played the part of what he expected a girlfriend to be. Aliza, in contrast, was natural. Her movements, her motives, her quirks were all *her*. It was ironic that Aliza was the actress, and Grace was not. He thanked his lucky stars things had worked out like this. He had not known what he was missing. Contentedly, he kissed Aliza's head again.

She looked up this time. "What was that for?"

"For being you," he answered. It sounded corny, he thought, but he didn't care.

Aliza paused for a moment and then whispered, "Thanks."

———

When the movie ended, they held each other in darkness for a while, listening to each other's breathing. In the distance, Aliza's phone beeped at her, but she barely heard it. She had been ignoring it successfully all day. Why pay attention now? When she finally excused herself to use the restroom, she checked it on her way back. Jesse was lying on the couch. From across the room she could see his form. The dim light filtering in from the streetlamp outside highlighted his contours. His chest rose and fell slightly, and Aliza wondered if he was asleep. She checked her voicemail in the hallway so as not to disturb him if he was. There was one from her mom saying hi and asking how she was getting along out in the "boonies", one from her friend Ashleigh, wondering when Aliza would make it home again, and one from a number she didn't recognize. Aliza's blood ran cold when she heard Cameron's voice. It took her so off-guard. She trembled a little bit as she listened to the message. Fear and old hurt flooded over the calm joy she had been experiencing with Jesse.

"Aliza?" Jesse called out to her with concern in his voice. "Is everything okay?"

She scrambled to put her phone away and restore some semblance of calm, but Jesse had gotten up and turned on a light. He came toward her, and though her back was turned, he caught a glimpse of her reflection in the hall mirror.

"Hey, what's up?" he said with a quiet voice and put his hand on her shoulder.

"Nothing," she lied.

"Tell me. It's him, isn't it. He's got your new number."

She hesitated. She didn't want to draw him into this scene, but he was already there. "Yeah. It doesn't matter. He's being a bully."

"It does matter, Aliza." He gently turned her to face him. "Do you want to call the police?"

"What? No. I mean, there's no reason for that. I'm fine. He's in LA, so it doesn't matter. I can't imagine who gave him the number so fast. I mean, I expected him to fish it out of someone at some point, but in a day? What the hell?"

"It's harassment. It's against the law for him to do this to you. Say the word and I'll help you file a complaint."

"Thanks, but it's not necessary. I'm not going to answer the phone if I don't recognize the number."

"You can't live like that," Jesse cautioned gently. "You shouldn't need to be afraid to answer your phone."

"I am not afraid," she responded vehemently.

"I didn't mean to imply anything," Jesse said, trying to placate her. "I think you're very strong and very brave, but you don't deserve this. Think about it."

Aliza was still holding her phone, and it chimed. She nearly dropped it as her body jumped in alarm. "Sorry," she mumbled in embarrassment. She looked down at the phone and saw there was a text. Jesse saw it over her shoulder as she turned to the side.

"It's from him," she said quietly.

Jesse read the text, and his voice filled with anger and disgust. "Is this the kind of thing he's been saying to you all along or is it getting worse?"

Aliza didn't know how to respond. She wanted to tell him the truth, but what was worse? Knowing she had been putting up with this crap for ages or admitting it was escalating? "It's getting worse," she replied in a small voice.

She walked to the living room, sat down on the couch, and put her head down on her hands. "He was always sarcastic and mean and domineering, and he got increasingly degrading toward the end of our relationship, but this feels more threatening." Unsure whether to continue, she paused again. "This scares me, and it takes a lot for me to admit that. I don't want to be cowed by anyone, particularly someone like Cameron."

"Do you think he's unstable?"

"Yes. When we were first dating, I thought he was unpredictable, a little dangerous, and fun, but it got weird fast. Before I knew it, he was possessive and crazy. He'd go nuts when I talked to other guys, and he..." She stopped talking and swallowed hard. "He got aggressive."

"With you or with them?"

"Both. A few times it even happened in public. That's why people like Melinda know about it. Rumors spread fast back home."

"What did you do about it?"

"I put up with it for way too long. Finally, he went too far and other people, like my family and friends, got involved. It took a lot for them to help me see clearly. Eventually I did, and I broke up with him."

"Wow. It took a lot of courage to do that, you know."

"Courage? I don't think so," Aliza said. "I was stupid from the very beginning. Thank goodness people who cared about me could see the situation objectively. I owe them a lot."

"He had been leaving you alone for a while, but now he's started back up, and it's worse. Is that right?" Jesse asked in a matter-of-fact way that Aliza appreciated. It helped her stay objective rather than emotional.

"Yeah, it was like when I moved, he couldn't keep track of me anymore. We had some friends in common, and they helped him keep tabs on me at home. He knew I wasn't dating anyone else, and I think that's all he cared about. Now I'm out of his immediate influence. He can't handle it. I don't know what he's capable of."

"It's impossible to say." Jesse put his arm around Aliza, but she did not relax this time. She felt a pang at her own defensiveness, not wanting her feelings about Cameron to infect her new relationship with Jesse.

"I'm sorry to take up your time with this crap," she said suddenly, turning to face him. He slid his hand from her shoulder down her arm to her hand and held it. "It isn't fair to you, and I was afraid I'd be *your* rebound relationship. You're too nice for all this seedy business."

"Seedy, huh," Jesse replied, squinting sideways at her. "Don't you worry your pretty little head about it, sweetheart," he replied in his best Bogart impersonation.

Aliza couldn't help but laugh. She leaned forward and kissed him. "Thanks," she said.

"For what?"

"For being you. For being here." She knew it was silly, but she was so glad to have him with her. What would she have done or felt if he wasn't? She hardly dared to imagine. The last time she went through this, she'd come close to cracking. Jesse was distracting her, at the very least. She didn't feel quite so desperate, but the fear she would end up losing Jesse because of Cameron nagged at the back of her mind, mingling with all the other fears that had been resurrected over the past couple of days. She mustered all of her concentration to squash those negative thoughts down, far from sight.

They talked and held hands until well past midnight, until Jesse noticed how tired Aliza was. "I think we'd better get some sleep," he told her.

Aliza was crestfallen. It must have shown on her face. "Do you want me to stay here? I can sleep on the couch. It might make you feel better."

"I'm fine. You should go home," she replied, halfheartedly.

"I'd like to stay, if you don't mind."

Aliza looked at this beautiful man before her and considered how kind he truly was. It had always been hard for her to ask for help, but in this case, she didn't need to. He was offering it and not making her feel weak for needing him. She agreed.

Aliza knew she shouldn't check her messages for the rest of the night, so she left her phone in the living room, to avoid being tempted. After a goodnight kiss, Aliza tucked Jesse in on the couch under the afghan and her soft, old quilt.

Jesse held it close, breathed it in and murmured, "It even smells like you. Goodnight, Aliza."

"Goodnight, Jesse." Before she had even left the room, Aliza could hear his breathing change as he drifted peacefully into sleep.

Aliza, on the other hand, lay awake for some time. Her fearful thoughts crept back in without Jesse's presence to distract her. Knowing he was right there on the other side of her door was a comfort, but now that she was alone, Cameron's words reverberated in her mind. He had been cruel and degrading, but that was not the part that bothered her. It was a reference he made to her "new life" that struck her as odd. Turning it around in her mind, she tried to dissect its meaning, unsure if it was as foreboding as she felt it was. It seemed to whisper a threat that her new life was not her own, but rather his to manipulate. The feeling that she was endangered was hardly new to her. Shuddering, she flipped to her other side, and closed her eyes.

Aliza tried to focus her thoughts on the positive. She was starting a new relationship with a guy who genuinely seemed to like her. The writing for the show was fantastic. Twin Falls was thousands of miles from LA. It was time to move forward, and even if it took a restraining order, she would do it. *After all, I am a strong, independent woman. I should not live in fear.*

Theoretically, she knew this was true. Though she repeated it to herself over and over, Cameron had damaged something deep within her subconscious. Try as she might, she could not forget. Not totally. Like a bird with a mended wing, she could fly, but she was not as strong as she had been before him.

When sleep finally washed over her, she was sucked into a current of swirling images and conflicting emotions. The characters in her dreams were twisted, fragments of people she had known all her life, but they were grotesquely transformed, not so much physically as from deep within. Aliza spoke to them, but they stared at her dully. Aliza pleaded with them, but they looked through her without seeing, unresponsive. Her panic mounted as she tried to engage her aunts and uncles, her friends from childhood, actors she had known from other projects, all of whom disregarded her presence, lobotomized shells of once-vibrant people. Then, the voice she dreaded more than any other sound called out, "Next." Aliza screamed as she realized he referred to her.

Jesse was at her side before she knew where she was. She was slick with perspiration, twisted in her sheet, and struggling like a wounded animal. He pulled her up to a seated position and held her close as she resurfaced from the dream. Finally, Jesse's comforting words filtered down to her sleep-drenched consciousness. There was a little light filtering through the windows. This was the second time he had come to her after a nightmare about Cameron. She needed to get a grip, for tears streamed down her face.

"I'm so sorry," she whimpered.

"Shh. It's okay. It's okay," Jesse repeated. He kissed her on the forehead, laid her back down, and adjusted the sheets and blankets around her. Her breathing was still fast, and her body still trembled a bit. He lay down next to her, outside the little cocoon he had made for her, and held her tightly. Soon, her breathing slowed, she succumbed to the calm he brought her, and she drifted back into sleep. It was mercifully dreamless.

Aliza awoke to the smell of coffee and eggs. It was like a childhood memory come alive, full of comfort and the promise of a good start to the day. She smiled, eyes still closed, enjoying the nebulous ground between sleeping and wakefulness. The smells were too tempting, however, and her stomach acknowledged her hunger with a weak groan. She got out of bed and padded quietly to the kitchen, hardly giving a thought to the wreck she must look after just waking.

There stood Jesse, clad in her favorite flowered apron. It was her mom's. Aliza had stolen it when she left. The bold flowers shone in bright 70's colors, unfaded by time. Jesse looked perfect. Whatever else she might have going on in her life, she could not have dreamed of something as sweet as this sight, and it was all hers. She moved forward into the kitchen and kissed him. He had a spatula in one hand, but he embraced her with the other.

"Good morning," he chirped as she let him go.

"Indeed," she replied, smiling. "This is awesome."

"Coffee?"

"Do you need to ask?"

He poured her a mug full, to which she added milk. She sipped it smiling.

"I hope you like scrambled eggs with cheese."

"The word like doesn't go far enough. Thanks."

They ate their breakfast in a pleasant near-silence, each lost in thought and distracted by eggs. Aliza thoroughly enjoyed every bite, and somehow Jesse's coffee tasted better than hers ever did, even though he had used the same grounds and pot to make it. She shook her head.

"What?" he said. "Is there something wrong with the eggs?"

"No, I was thinking about the coffee. Sort of as a metaphor for other things."

"You're going to have to explain that. For me, coffee is just coffee. If I have it, I'm fine. If not, well, you've seen the outcome."

They both laughed, remembering his surly behavior on the day they met.

"Well," she began, "two people can take the same ingredients and the same tools and end up with far different outcomes. It's like art, I guess. Same paints, same canvas, infinite combinations, yet some paintings are great, and some are crap."

"And..."

"And..." She hesitated before admitting, "...your coffee is better than mine."

He laughed out loud. "I appreciate the compliment. You know, I think you're right."

"Modesty at its finest," Aliza said sarcastically, rolling her eyes.

"No. Not about the coffee necessarily. I haven't had the pleasure of sampling yours yet. What I meant was you're right about art and cooking, but isn't the judgment still a matter of perception? Maybe some people out there would like your coffee better. Maybe you only like mine better because it's different from yours. Do you see what I mean?"

"I do. You're very modest after all." She smiled at him slyly.

He kicked her playfully under the table, and they both started laughing again.

"Really," she went on, "this is interesting. Like with the eggs, I happen to have a thing for cheese. When combined with eggs, another favorite, sparks fly, but someone who hasn't developed a taste for exotic cheeses would taste these eggs and be revolted. No offense. Is it a matter of wiring or experience that gives us such a wide variety of opinions regarding taste?"

"Good question, Jesse responded. "It's a dichotomy. Maybe the answer is as simple as both. If you're brought up never tasting spicy foods, chances are you're only going to experience the heat, not the nuances of flavor in a spicy dish. Whereas, if you're weaned on the stuff, you've got a better shot at appreciating it."

"Or, if you discover Indian curries on a date with a person you're very attracted to, maybe your opinion would be different than if you were force-fed chilies in solitary confinement."

"It's experience *and* wiring. Truly, an extreme experience can hard-wire our brains. That's been proven. It's why we vividly remember the very good things and the very bad things that happen to us, whereas all the day-to-day stuff sort of blurs together in our memories."

"I can vouch for that," Aliza said without thinking, immediately regretting it. She looked down at her almost empty plate.

A few moments passed in silence. Jesse sipped his coffee pensively while Aliza tried to decide what to say next. He must have sensed she wanted to talk and waited patiently. Finally, she spoke.

"I know I keep apologizing for my freak-outs after the fact, but it doesn't change the reality that you don't deserve to be involved in my mess. I don't want you to have to keep picking up the pieces. It's not fair to you. You hardly know me. You should start over with this cast and crew before the social lines are drawn too deep. Get in good with those girls you were talking to. They'll take good care of you. I'm too much of a disaster to waste your time with. I appreciate all the care you've shown me, but it's not fair to you."

"Aliza," he began slowly but vehemently, "I am not here because I feel obligated. I'm here because I want to be. There is something very special about you that I'm attached to already, and the thought of leaving you so I can go hang out with a bunch of vapid party-girls doesn't appeal. Do you think I have conversations like this with everyone I meet? There have been precious few other people I can talk with like I can talk with you. Get this through your sweet, thick skull. I like you, and I want to be with you. Deal with it. You're not getting rid of me that easily."

Jesse's diatribe brought tears to her eyes. "I can't promise you anything right now. Cameron's behavior is getting worse, and I don't think it's fair to involve you."

"Tough. I'm involved."

"I don't know what he's capable of."

"We'll see. In the meantime, can you accept the fact that I like you and want to be with you, regardless?"

Aliza's mind reeled with a mixture of relief, regret, and guilt. She agreed out of her selfish desire to be with Jesse, but she still felt in her heart it was unfair to him. "Okay," she said. "Don't forget I tried to stop you, though. I don't want you to get hurt."

"Don't worry about me," he replied brazenly. "Now, we should do something fun with the day. I'm going to go home to take a shower, and I'll pick you up in an hour. Does that sound good?"

"Fine. Thanks for breakfast."

"My pleasure."

# THIRTEEN

*Piercing has left jagged places along all the open edges, as well as along each tiny avenue of trace work, so the jeweler begins to file everything smooth. She does this with the patience of a mother, relishing the transformation from raw material into art. Jagged edges fall away beneath the files, the surface is refined.*

"I hope you have a swimsuit."

Jesse walked into Aliza's apartment looking excited. She had left the door open for him and emerged from the bedroom perplexed.

"I'm not swimming in May."

"Just wait. You're going to love this. It's a place upstream from here called, get this, *The Gorge*. It's a narrowing in the river where the water rushes by like a natural waterslide. We visited some gorges in Maine when I was a kid. They're absolutely beautiful. Can you swim?"

"Yeah, I'm pretty good, but like I said, I'm not insane. Are you sure we're allowed there? It's not private property? Rudy would be fully pissed if we got arrested." Aliza was of a practical nature when it impacted her career.

"It's totally fine. I asked at the diner, and they even drew me a map." Jesse showed it to her. His enthusiasm was infectious. "I love hand-drawn maps. They're just so, I don't know, personal. So specific, so subjective. I can't wait. Besides, it's going to be hot today. Maybe you'll change your mind."

"Well, okay then. Let me get my things."

Aliza disappeared for a few minutes while Jesse examined his map. "We'll need food," he called. "And water. And towels." His voice was full of excitement.

"Okay, okay," she replied, feigning annoyance. "Almost ready."

She emerged feeling fresh. She hadn't put on much makeup, but she didn't mind being around Jesse without it anymore. She carried out a medium-sized bag.

"I've brought sunblock too," she said proudly. "We can't let our skin color change too much, you know. How funny would it look for me to be ghostly pale in one scene and a sunburned wreck in the next?" She giggled.

"Talk about Rudy freaking out." He smiled at her. "You look great, as usual. Are you ready?"

"Yep, and thanks. Not so bad yourself."

"Thanks. Let's stop and grab some sandwiches or something to take with us. I don't know what's around the gorge."

"Great idea. You know me."

"No swimming on a full tummy, though."

"Okay, Dad."

They gathered their provisions, disinterred Aliza's bike, and headed out of town. The gorge was about half an hour from Twin Falls, and the road they followed diminished in size and quality, which was a feat considering the roads had started out small. Eventually, they ended up at the landmark the map had noted. They parked and hiked toward the river, following a path through underbrush and thicket. The sun blazed overhead and the temperature had started to spike when the gorge appeared before them. To the left were two swift channels carved into solid rock, polished and surreal. To the right were some large boulders, a huge pool, and high cliffs behind. Everything was hemmed in by tall, old trees, edged with ferns and moss. The smell was of dewy arboreal forests just waking up in the dappled sunlight. It was an entrancing view, and it seemed even more magical to Aliza because they were alone for the time being.

"Where should we set up our stuff?" Aliza looked at the scene, dazzled by the view.

"How about over there?" Jesse pointed to a wide, flat rock. They'd have to get across a broad section of the gorge where water was flowing swiftly. Someone had placed a rock in the middle for what appeared to be this exact reason. Jesse hopped onto the rock and leapt across the divide. Aliza felt unsure. She stood on the edge, contemplating how to cross.

"Here, catch," she said, tossing her bag to Jesse. She took a deep breath and mustered the courage to jump to the rock. Her concern mounted, for she'd only just landed on the rock. The second half of the crossing was noticeably wider than the first. Jesse watched from the other side with interest and mild apprehension playing across his features.

"You can do it. I've seen you run."

"Running has nothing to do with this. It's wider than my widest leap."

"The only obstacle is in your mind."

"What is this, *The Matrix*?"

Jesse laughed. "I am sure you can do it. I'll catch you if you're short."

She was breathing heavily, and her palms were sweating. She took a step back as far as she could go and thrust herself forward in a grand balletic leap. Jesse caught her as she narrowly missed the edge of the rock. Her sneaker got wet, but she wasn't hurt.

"I'm impressed," he said, letting go of her arms. "I wasn't sure if it was too far. You're not that tall, you know."

Aliza looked up at him in disbelief and whacked him on the arm. "Jerk. I can't believe you let me do that. It was dangerous."

"But you did it." He smiled at her.

She reciprocated, feeling a little proud of herself for having the courage.

———

They laid out the towels Aliza brought and undressed in the sunlight. Aliza stripped off one article at a time, ending with her T-shirt. Her crimson bikini contrasted beautifully with her pale skin. Jesse was so enthralled he forgot to pretend not to look. She was so lovely. Her body was very lean, perfectly toned, but not sickly skinny. She was exactly right. Her skin was the color of the full moon, and she shone as brightly against the saturated colors around her. Applying her sunscreen with extreme care, she paid special attention to her face and neck. She tossed him the tube, and he followed suit.

They basked quietly on their rock like lizards waking up from a long hibernation. The sun warmed them from the top, and the heat coming from the rock was very therapeutic. Aliza sighed with pleasure. Jesse turned on his side, so he could look at her. He was desperate to run his fingers along her midriff, to explore her reaches, to pull her closer to him, to kiss every inch of her body. The fantasy about what it would feel like to make love to her, right here, against the rock drove Jesse crazy. A plunge in the icy water of the gorge would have to be his next move if he wasn't careful. He flipped over onto his stomach, leaning on his elbows, still greedily drinking her in.

She opened her eyes and shielded them with her hand, turning her head to look at him. She must have caught the slightly pained expression on his face before he had a chance to conceal it, for hers mirrored it.

He knew he'd been caught and turned away, feeling guilty. *Why do we feel guilty for natural emotions? I admit it. I want her, but why shouldn't I? It's only human, and she's very attractive, after all.* Uncomfortable, he sat up and faced the rushing river. Aliza sat up as well and moved closer, leaning her cheek against his bare back, tracing his pale freckles with her fingers.

"Your shoulders are frecklier than the rest of you. How come?"

"Sun damage," he replied. "Who knew the sun was bad for you when we were kids? I was out in it all the time."

"It's so cute," she said softly, still gliding her fingers from freckle to freckle, her soft skin against his back. "It's like looking at the stars. You start to see constellations. I'm going to call this one The Apple and this one is Isis. Her wings are stretched out protectively. You're very lucky to have her. I've always admired her."

"Why? Who is she?"

"In ancient Egyptian mythology, she was a loyal wife and a good mother, but she was also powerful. Her magic brought her husband Osiris back from the dead. Pretty romantic." She kissed Jesse's shoulder blade and retraced the newly discovered constellation. She kissed him again, a little farther on, and again near his neck.

The sensation that surged through Jesse at feeling her lips on his back nearly overwhelmed his self-control. He stood up abruptly. "It's time for a swim."

Aliza watched with an expression of surprise and mild hurt as he adeptly slipped into the icy water. The shock of it helped to divert his attention from what his body desperately wanted. He knew this was neither the time nor the place to let feelings like that take over. Aliza was only being playful, after all. He knew better than to ascribe more meaning to her fond actions than was really there. She was not ready to move any further physically. He knew it, and he could deal with it.

After a few minutes of diving under the water and swimming from side to side in the swirling, glittering pool, Jesse climbed out of the water and walked back to Aliza who had been watching him the whole time.

He smiled broadly. "Sorry—I just needed to cool down."

"I understand," she replied. "Maybe I should too." She looked away bashfully. "How's the water?"

"Insanely cold. Here, feel." He went closer and shook out his hair, showering her with tiny drops of icy water.

"Hey," she yelled, giggling, shielding her face.

"Are you hungry? I'm hungry."

"It's a first. You beat me to it. Must be the swim. What do you want? A full lunch or a snack?"

"Full lunch. Roll out the banquet."

"Yes, sir," she replied, with a salute.

Aliza laid out the food on her towel, and they enjoyed sandwiches and apples and sparkling water. They talked a little while they ate, keeping the conversation light.

A family had found their way to the gorge, the mother helped a boy and a girl who looked to be around 3 and 5 years old navigate the rocks. The father scouted out a spot upstream, across the divide. The kids bickered and chased each other as their mom set up their blankets and unpacked their things. Aliza and Jesse glanced up out of curiosity, then resumed their lunch, too enthralled with each other's company to care about much else.

Moments later, a scream rent the air, startling Aliza. The little girl seemed to have cut her foot on a rock and was hysterical. Both parents attended to her, one held her while the other examined her foot.

"Jeez, I hope she's okay. She sure is screaming loud enough," Jesse said.

"Don't you remember? Everything's a huge deal when you're little. You've got no perspective. Too few former experiences to draw on for comparison. One little cut and bang, freak-out city."

"I guess so. It seems like a long time ago, though," Jesse replied.

Aliza's expression changed as she watched the family. "Weren't there two kids over there?"

"Oh, you're totally right."

Aliza sprang to her feet and ran to the edge of the pool. Jesse's heart raced in terror as they scanned the water. "There," Aliza shouted, pointing at a bright color floating on the surface of the water. Without hesitating, she dove in and swam. Jesse had already jumped back over the gorge, hollering to the parents, and running towards them. Once he had gotten their attention, he turned back towards Aliza who had hold of the little kid. The child's eyes were closed, and his skin had a horrible pallor to it. He was unresponsive, but Aliza swam swiftly, supporting his head above water. With her efficient action, it couldn't have been more than thirty seconds since she had first noticed the boy was gone to when she hoisted him out of the water onto the rock ledge and started performing compressions. Fully focused on the little boy's small body, she whispered, "Come on. Please, wake up."

Sound filtered back into Jesse's consciousness. The mother and the daughter were both screaming. The father had run to the edge of the pool and stood over Aliza and his son with mounting horror playing across his features. Aliza, intent in her actions, did not look up from the child's face. She had started mouth-to-mouth when the boy finally opened his eyes and coughed up a huge amount of water. She rolled him on his side and slapped his back. He sputtered and coughed, threw up, and started screaming.

The father scooped him up, tears streaming down his face. "It's okay, Danny, it's okay. You're all right now."

The mother and daughter had joined the crowd and were suddenly very calm and quiet. The mother was clearly in shock, unable to absorb the gravity of what had just happened.

It took a few moments for Danny to calm down, all the while Aliza and Jesse stood watching, motionless observers, waiting to be sure the child was okay. Finally, the father looked up at them. Jesse took Aliza's hand automatically.

"Thank God you were here. You moved so fast, you saved his life," the father said, his voice cracking with those last few words. "Thank you, thank you so much."

"It was only by chance that we noticed he was missing. Is he okay, do you think?"

"I think so. We'll get him to the hospital just in case, but I think he'll be fine. I don't know how to thank you. You were like his guardian angel. I can't even think what would have happened."

"George," the mother finally spoke, "Don't think about what could have happened. It's too horrible." She turned to face Aliza. Her face wore a mystifying, unreadable expression. She moved toward the couple and hugged Aliza. Tears streamed down her face once more as she whispered in Aliza's ear. "Someday, when you're a mother, you will remember this moment. Only then will you know how much you've done here today, and how utterly grateful we are. Thank you. Thank you." Sobbing, she released Aliza, turned back toward her family, and ushered them away.

Jesse and Aliza were left stunned. They watched the family swiftly gather their things and leave. A deep silence followed. Aliza shivered, her sopping wet hair hung limp down her pale back, rivulets of water tracking their way back to the river. Jesse turned to her and gathered her into his arms. Her skin was icy to the touch.

"You're amazing, Aliza. You saved that kid's life. You truly are incredible. I've never seen anything like it."

She shivered again, and this time she didn't stop. "I did what anyone would have done. I'm so glad we were here. The mom was right. It's too horrible to think about what would have happened. It wasn't their fault, either. It all happened so fast. Imagine the guilt they would have felt for the rest of their lives if he had..." She couldn't even finish the sentence.

"Shh. Don't say it." Jesse's hands were on Aliza's skin, which was covered with goose bumps. She was deathly pale. "We need to get you warm. I'll jump back over and bring our things, so you don't have to swim back across or try jumping it again. I'll be right back."

Aliza stood in a sunny patch trying to warm herself, but she was shivering uncontrollably now.

Jesse brought over their stuff and wrapped her in a towel. He rubbed her arms and her hair while she stood still, allowing him to baby her a little bit.

"Did you bring a change of under things?" he asked her, trying to be delicate. "I think you should get out of the swimsuit. It's keeping you cold."

"I did. I don't know where to change."

"I won't look, I promise."

As the cold set in, Aliza's speech became more abstruse, almost like she had been drinking. "It seems so stupid, doesn't it, to hide from each other? Life is so fragile, so temporary. Why do we hide?"

Her teeth chattered, and her voice was unsteady. She reached into her bag with a trembling hand and dug out her clothes. She laid them on the ground and, instead of turning away, she untied her bikini top and let it fall to the rock below. She did the same with the bottoms. "See, here I am. Just another human, full of frailty and fears and faults. Filled with potential for good or ill, misled into thinking I have much of a choice in the course of my life. Here we are, Jesse."

Jesse was a ball of mixed emotions. He was enthralled by her beauty, this Venus of the Gorge, and wanted nothing more than to watch her standing nude in the sunlight against this fairyland backdrop, some Pre-Raphaelite painting come to life. On the other hand, he was deeply concerned she was hypothermic. It would explain her obscure thinking and her rash choice to stand there before him so brazenly, beautifully nude. In a split second, his chivalrous nature won, and he moved to wrap her in her towel again. She swiped the towel from his hands, took a step forward, and pressed her body to his, wrapping her arms around him tightly. He held her closely, letting his heat transfer through her pale, cold skin, hoping it would help warm her sufficiently.

A few moments passed, and they heard voices again. Jesse wasted no time. He grabbed the towel and held it up. "Get dressed."

Aliza followed his instructions. In a moment, the place was flooded with raucous teenagers staking claim on the rocks. Jesse and Aliza put on their shoes and hiked back to her bike. By the time they got to it, Jesse could tell Aliza was feeling more like herself. The exertion of climbing the hill had raised her body temperature.

"Are you okay to drive?" he said.

"Thanks, I'm fine now." She smiled sweetly at him and handed him a helmet.

By the time they returned to Twin Falls, it was after four. It was the first time the town had looked inhabited all week. The village green was full of people, some hanging out under the gazebo, some playing games on the grass, and some feeding pigeons from park benches. The picturesque scene struck Jesse as surreal, compared to the events at the gorge.

Aliza parked the bike on the street. They took off their helmets and looked around. Jesse was having a hard time processing it and was deliberating whether he could embrace the quaint vision before him when Aliza spoke. "This too-good-to-be-true, small-town life is starting to grow on me," The disbelief was obvious in her voice.

"How could this be real?" Jesse muttered, not expecting an answer. He turned to face her. "How could any of it be real? A week ago, I was living what I thought was a normal life in LA, full of action and people, lights and chaos, but it turns out LA is a facsimile of life and being there isn't really living. I wasn't doing or experiencing anything real, and now I realize I've never felt more alive than I do here." He hesitated and then added, "With you."

"I want to know how it can happen so fast. I always thought this kind of change of heart took months, or years, or something. Now, in a matter of days, my entire perception has changed. Just like the little girl who hurt her foot—maybe I've had no perspective. Maybe I've been living the only life I knew, assuming it was the best. You're right, though. I've done more living here than I've done in years, and it is because of you."

They kissed, forgetting they were in public, forgetting that people could see them, forgetting that one photograph could hit the tabloids and precipitate an absolute storm. In that very moment, Aliza and Jesse embraced the new life they had discovered together and dove in wholeheartedly.

# PART TWO

# ONE

*Hinges are a delicate operation. In order for the piece to open and close as the jeweler has envisioned, hinges are necessary, but she wants to keep them hidden. She cuts short lengths of silver tubing to go along the edges of her two shapes, which together create a small, hollow egg. Marking out where the knuckles of the hinge will go, the jeweler carefully pierces a little mortise on each piece of the shell. The hinge will nestle in, flush with the edge.*

Weeks passed as Aliza and Jesse established a routine of rehearsals, shooting scenes, and exploring their new life together. They were still captivated by each other, still enjoying the quiet moments during which they could lay beneath the stars or share a pizza. Photographs of them together started appearing in various magazines, from the sordid rags to the comparatively truthful tabloids. Neither of them cared. Their relationship was in the open now. They had nothing to hide.

The nasty phone calls and texts from Cameron escalated in direct proportion to the media coverage of their budding relationship. At first, Aliza seemed less fazed than she had with the previous calls. She tried to maintain a stolid front, but with each successive call, she seemed to lose a little more of her composure. Just as granite can be eroded eventually, Aliza's facade of strength began to crumble. Jesse started keeping her phone with him to screen her from the worsening emotional roller coaster each episode seemed to evoke.

They consulted the police who took a very laissez faire approach to the matter. Jesse tried to convince them and Aliza that a restraining order was the best option, but they were noncommittal.

"That kind of stuff doesn't happen in Twin Falls," the officer had said, looking perplexed. "He'll get bored and stop bugging her. I'm sure of it."

Seeing their faces on the front pages of magazines and reading the headlines, however, had intensified Cameron's cruelty until the words he used bordered on criminal threatening. Though Jesse tried to downplay his distress over each new attack, his concern was mounting. Aliza had been right when she'd said she wasn't sure what Cameron was capable of. Jesse wasn't sure, either.

It depressed him to have what was otherwise the happiest time in his life marred by worry and fear. How does one protect another from such an ambiguous enemy? Jesse was reminded often of the strange dreams he'd had when he and Aliza had first started seeing each other. His protective instinct had become very pronounced. Ultimately, he decided to take action. He answered Aliza's phone one night, ready to confront the monster on the other end. He was surprised at how calm the other man seemed. Unlike in his messages, his voice was suave, collected, and mocking.

"I wondered when you'd answer her phone for her," said the voice on the other line.

"She's not getting any of your messages. I'm making sure of it."

"You're her big protector now. She likes them big, take that from me," Cameron said with a cruel laugh.

"You're disgusting, but you're not going to get me worked up. Stop calling her, stop texting her, leave her alone, or you're going to have a restraining order placed on you. Got it?" Jesse said in a calm, authoritative voice.

"Got it. You can't handle it, and you're calling in the police. Nice. Very manly."

"Oh, it's manly to terrorize a woman simply because she doesn't want you anymore?"

"She wants me." Cameron's voice grew menacing, full of hatred and anger. "You know she does, and she always will."

"Leave her alone, Cameron. I mean it. Goodbye."

Jesse was polite and calm all the way to the end of the call, despite his intense feelings of dislike for the guy. He did not raise his voice, but he was left with serious doubts as to how effective his words would prove to be. Cameron was clearly a total psychopath, and the conversation had not reduced any of Jesse's fears. Praying his intervention had not inadvertently made matters worse, he tried to put it from his mind.

He didn't tell Aliza of the interaction, fearing she would be cross with him. Nightmares still plagued her, often she would wake up screaming or in tears. Sometimes, Jesse would catch her staring off into space, startled to find herself in the present, as though she were expecting to be somewhere else. She had still not shared the extent of Cameron's abuse with him, and he couldn't bring himself to ask her directly.

If Cameron continued to exert his power over her, Jesse feared matters would escalate. How this might happen, Jesse couldn't guess, but he felt powerless. Vigilance seemed his only option as he bided his time.

Filming was going well. Rudy seemed increasingly excited about the project, as though at the beginning he'd held some of his enthusiasm back so as not to be premature. Now, he had let go of his reservations, and his daily comments were borderline outlandish. The cast and crew clearly loved him, and his gusto was infectious.

The actors had all formed their groups of friends, and once Aliza and Jesse opened up about their relationship, they'd made friends with the other actors. Jesse thought it was nice to belong to community. People went out together in larger groups for dinner, had each other over for cocktails, the usual sort of superficial but entertaining stuff.

None of these friendships seemed particularly strong to Jesse, but he reminded himself, that relative to his feelings for Aliza, little could compare. She continued to fascinate him. He wanted to do something special for her, to take her out someplace fancy or find her a meaningful gift. They had been together for exactly a month, and although it felt a little high-schoolish, he wanted to celebrate. After scenes were done, Jesse stopped by a little jewelry store he'd noticed. Every store in Twin Falls was locally owned and independent. Jesse loved that aspect of the place. There were no chain stores except for the gas station on the way into town.

He walked into the jewelry store, expecting to see typical mass-produced-looking jewelry, despite its being a local place. He couldn't have been more surprised. Everything was a handmade creation, and each was one of a kind. The proprietor, a middle-aged woman with horn rim glasses, greeted him warmly.

"Hi, there. How are you today?"

"Great," Jesse replied, smiling.

"Are you looking for anything in particular?"

"I'm looking for a special piece of jewelry for my girlfriend. Your work is beautiful. Are you the jeweler?"

"I am. Thank you for asking. All the designs are my own, the silver is mostly recycled, and all the stones are local. I don't believe in mining for precious stones. What's the difference between a naturally polished piece of granite with garnet inclusions and a diamond? No one dies for the granite."

"You've sold me. I love that they're local rocks. We've fallen in love with this place over the last month. I think it would be very meaningful."

"You're in the TV show, right? Jesse Black?"

"I fear I'll never be anonymous again." He stretched his hand out to shake hers. "Jesse Black, indeed."

"Karen McDonald. Pleased to meet you. Look around. Ask questions. I'll be right here."

"Thanks, Karen."

Jesse examined the cases carefully. Her work did not have the heavy-handed quality he'd noticed in other handmade jewelry. Each of Karen's pieces was delicate but solid, the forms worked perfectly with each other, the metal and stone complementing each other beautifully.

"Your work is remarkable. How do you get your ideas?"

"They come to me as I work sometimes. Making jewelry is like an act of meditation. The time it takes to make a piece is significant, but it feels like a dream while you are doing it. Three hours can go by without my even feeling it sometimes. I'll look up and have no memory of time passing. Being so focused is a very freeing experience."

"How so? I would have thought the opposite. Metal work seems so laborious and rigid to me."

"Until you master it, it can be, but like anything you love doing, once you get to a high level of proficiency, you're freed by the work, and the act of creation is the focus. It allows me to let go of any worries or fears that have been eating away at me. I clear out all the garbage and focus on the creation, and in that focus is the freedom. I guess it's not easy to explain, but the phenomenon is known as flow. People don't usually ask me about the work. They either like it or not. Then, they buy something or not. Anyway, I'll stop talking and let you look some more."

They smiled at each other, and Jesse continued looking through the cases. After a moment, one particular piece caught his eye. It was a silver pendant containing a striking, incredibly smooth, black stone in the center. Next to the piece lay a notecard describing a labyrinth, and Jesse wondered how the two things related to each other. He looked up to find Karen watching him with an enigmatic smile.

"It's my favorite piece, too. Let me show you the back."

She removed the pendant from the case and laid it on a black velvet mat. Jesse picked it up and turned it over, admiring it. The stone was as smooth as it looked, perfectly oval, jet black, and was set with a fine silver band around the edge. The back was a delicately pierced silver labyrinth like the one on the card. The work was so fine it bordered on filigree. He followed the curving and backtracking lines all the way to the heart-shaped center. Through the pierced lines you could see the black of the stone.

"The labyrinth is an ancient idea, and this particular one is known as a unicursal labyrinth. It is basically a maze in which there is only one, single way to the middle. The path is long and complex, full of twists and turns. It may seem like you're lost inside it, but ultimately it leads you to the center. That's why it's become a symbol for use in meditation. Life leads us astray, but our hearts know the way."

"What's at the center?" Jesse spoke pensively.

"That depends on who you are, but isn't it a comfort to know that there *is* a center?"

Jesse looked up from the piece to find Karen smiling at him. He smiled back. "I love it. Where is this particular stone from?"

"The gorge, about 30 miles from here. It is a naturally tumbled stone, meaning I did not alter the shape of it. I found it as it is, perfect, like a gift. I polished it, and it spoke to me. I can see it's speaking to you as well. For every creation a home, I say."

"The gorge. Amazing. It's perfect. I'll take it."

"The path is long and complicated, Jesse. Have faith."

"It's worth it in the end," Jesse replied, still looking at the smooth black stone. "Some of us just need a little more help getting there."

# TWO

*Keeping the minuscule bits of tubing in place while she solders them to the silver shell is the most difficult thing the jeweler has had to do so far. She paints the surface with flux, which allows the solder to flow into the space between the tubing and the egg. It has to be done carefully. If she overheats the metal, the tubing will melt and collapse. If something shifts, the parts won't fit together properly. If the solder doesn't flow, there will be structural weaknesses. She sets everything up using stands with clips on them, praying her hands stay steady. She takes a drink of water, lights her torch, adjusts the flame, and gently solders the tubes in place.*

Aliza worried she had counted incorrectly. She looked at the calendar again to make sure. It was true. She had been in Twin Falls for exactly a month and two days, which meant she and Jesse had been together for a month already. On one hand, it didn't feel like that much time had passed. On the other, she felt like she and Jesse had known each other since birth. They had spent nearly every waking-and most non-waking-hours together, working, playing, staying together. It had forged their friendship and their relationship intensely. She knew the actual amount of time didn't matter after all, but she wanted to celebrate it anyway.

A few days earlier, she had come across a little box of things her mom had given her when her grandfather had passed away. At the time, too sad to look through it, she had closed it and put it away, although she'd carried it with her wherever she'd moved. Lately, though, something had been nagging at her to look in the box. When she did, she found something remarkable. It had been there all along, yet she had totally forgotten its existence. Now, as she thought about what to give Jesse to celebrate their time together, the answer was obvious, Grandpa's pocket watch.

Jesse was not a wristwatch person, as evidenced by their first trip to the mall together. Relying solely on his cellphone to tell the time always seemed to annoy him. He liked watches, especially old-school mechanical ones, but he looked weird wearing one. A pocket watch, however, was perfect. Aliza examined it for the hundredth time in two days. This pocket watch was especially perfect. It was from the late 1800s, made of gold, and it had the most beautiful engraving on it. It was very manly, even though the engraving had some swallows carrying a very Victorian-looking banner between them. On the banner was the inscription: "Time is the wisest counselor of all." - Pericles

Grandpa had shown it to her many times, always reading the quote before he opened the watch. It was as though he was proving its point, for he was the wisest person she had ever known. She missed him keenly. Her eyes misted as she popped open the case and examined the face. Its mother of pearl surface was luminous in contrast with the shining, delicate gold Roman numerals and ornate gold hands. She opened the back as well and read the inscription. The watch had been someone else's before it was her grandpa's, and it had a series of initials, lastly his own, engraved in the back. She wondered if she could get the watch engraved with Jesse's initials and the date. As late as it was on a Friday afternoon, she hoped she could get it done.

She looked on the internet to see what there was available. It listed two jewelry stores in Twin Falls, one of which was very close by. Aliza called and asked if they could engrave something on such short notice, and they told her to bring it by. She sped out of the apartment and completed her errand in little less than half an hour. Upon returning, she made a little card to go with the gift. Then, on a whim, she snipped off a lock of her hair and tied it with a bit of baker's string, winding it into the space between the back cover and the engraved area. *I hope this isn't too foolish, but it is a very Victorian thing to do.* Lastly, she embroidered some scrap corduroy with the symbol for eternity using her remaining baker's twine and sewed a little pouch for the watch. *All in all, not bad.*

Jesse had made plans for a dinner out, so Aliza focused on getting ready. Usually jeans and a T-shirt would suffice, but not tonight. Even in childhood, Aliza had steadfastly refused to wear a dress unless it was for a job. She wasn't the dress-up type, but she did have a few outfits that would do.

Aliza pawed through the contents of her closet until she found the item she wanted, a vintage, beaded top made from sheer crepe with a fitted silk underlay. It was a pale, dusty rose color, nearly the same tone as her skin. When she wore it, it was as though the shimmering beads floated upon her very body. It fit her perfectly. The beading, which was very art deco, always made her happy to look at. Recalling an early conversation with Jesse about starting the "Good Quality Revolution," she smiled, deciding it was not a bad idea. How many shirts had she owned over the past couple of years that had fallen apart after a few months of wear? Yet this top, almost a hundred years old, held together beautifully. *What are we doing wrong? It's like we're unlearning a long heritage of craftsmanship and replacing it with completely disposable crap.*

She finished off her outfit with a black pencil skirt and some cute heels, touched up her makeup, and as she wondered what to do with her hair, Jesse knocked. "Good enough," she muttered as she scurried to the door.

Jesse stood before her looking like a catalog model, as usual. Even so, he had stepped up his game, wearing what appeared to be a fifties tie with his sleek suit. She was relieved she had not opted for jeans this evening.

She greeted him with a kiss.

"Hi, there. You look amazing. Is that top vintage?"

"You know it." She spun around in her best imitation of a model on a catwalk. Jesse laughed and so did she. "Happy one-month anniversary. I don't dress up for any old occasion, you know." She smiled slyly.

"Happy anniversary." He took both of her hands in his as he spoke, and there was sincerity in his eyes and in his voice. "It doesn't seem like that much time has passed by, but on the other hand, it seems as though we've been together for ages. I'm not sure what to make of it, but I'm very thankful."

"I'm thankful too," she replied, full of emotion. "I don't know how I could possibly deserve a man as kind, and tender, and intelligent as you. You have restored a piece of me I thought was broken. Thank you."

Jesse kissed her tenderly. "We have a few minutes before we need to leave for dinner. Come sit with me, I have something for you."

"You didn't need to get me a present." Aliza said, leading Jesse to the couch.

"I wanted to."

Jesse took a tiny gift wrapped in magazine paper from his breast pocket. Before he handed it to her, he looked in her eyes. "This has been the happiest month of my life. I love being with you, Aliza." He handed her the box. "I hope you like it. When I saw this, it was as though it had your name on it."

She accepted the box. "I don't deserve it."

"That's where you're wrong, my dear. You deserve the world. This is one tiny thing."

Carefully, she opened the wrapping, revealing a jewelry box. She removed the lid of the box and examined the contents.

"This is stunning," she said quietly. "Absolutely stunning. I'm amazed. This stone. Where is it from?"

"It's from our gorge. The artist takes local materials and uses them in her work. Flip it over."

Doing as she was told, Aliza took the necklace from its nest of velvet. She studied the trace-work on the back, immediately recognizing the symbol. "A labyrinth," she said, feeling awed.

"There is only one path. It's not an easy path to follow, but have faith, and it will lead you to the center. It reminded me so much of you. You've struggled, you've fought, you've persevered, and you are still you. Maybe when you're feeling overwhelmed or lost, this will be a reminder that your heart knows the way."

Aliza was stunned. The lovely, poignant gift touched her deeply. She looked up at Jesse whose face was expectant and reserved at the same time. "You are amazing, Jesse. You really are. This is so perfect and so beautiful. I will cherish it." She ran her finger over the lines of the labyrinth. "I could use a reminder sometimes, especially lately. You're right when you say this is the happiest time in our lives, but it's also been one of the hardest. I try to focus on what is truly important, but it isn't always easy. Thank you so much." She leaned over and took his face in her free hand and kissed him. "Will you put it on me?"

"Of course."

The pendant nestled perfectly into the space above the V-neck of her top and the black stone lay in striking contrast against her pale skin. She touched the stone with her finger, feeling its smoothness. "Thank you, Jesse. I love it. I can't believe the stone is from our gorge."

"I couldn't believe it, either. It was so perfect. The jeweler was cool. She said there's a perfect home for every one of her creations. I believe for this piece, at least, it's true."

"Thank you so much." She paused, holding the necklace for a moment, looking pensive. "Do you want your present now?"

"You know you didn't have to get me anything," Jesse said softly.

"I didn't get you anything. It's something I've had all along and want you to have it. Here." She handed him the little corduroy pouch.

"Did you make the pouch?" Jesse examined it.

"Yep."

"I love it." He traced the infinity symbol with his finger before he undid the top of the pouch. Slowly, he withdrew the pocket watch and examined it, his eyes wide with wonder. He ran his finger over the front cover, reading the quote. The ornate engraving on the back cover held his attention for a long while. "This is too much. This is way too much."

"I told you I didn't buy it. It was my grandpa's, and before you scold me for parting with a family heirloom, I want you to know something. Grandpa was the most honest, steadfast, and wisest person I have ever known. You have reminded me of him since our first real conversation. He would have loved you, you know. When I came across this piece the other day, I knew it was meant for you. Objects have destinies too. This one was destined for you. Open it."

Jesse did as he was told. The face glittered. "It's so serene. So perfect. Like a full moon with numbers on it."

"It is, isn't it? Now you won't have to check your phone every five-seconds or wear a watch that doesn't fit you. It's like this one was made with you in mind."

Jesse opened the back cover as well and found where Aliza had concealed the lock of hair and engraved his initials. "Thank you so much. This is very Victorian, you know."

"I know. That's why I did it. I hope you don't think it's stupid."

"Stupid? Really? You must know me better than that. It's one of the most intimate gestures anyone's ever shown me. I love it, and I will cherish it. Thank you for having it engraved. It means so much to me. This is truly a precious gift."

"I'm glad you like it. I think the inscription is apt. 'Time *is* the wisest councilor of all.' Grandpa agreed."

"I'm overwhelmed, Aliza. Thank you so much." Taking her face in his hand, he kissed her, pulled back to regard her for a moment, and kissed her again. "I never expected to feel so strongly about another person, particularly after only a month. Somehow this feels different from other relationships I've been in. It feels right. I thanked my lucky stars you gave me a second chance after I was such an ass to you the day we met. I've been thanking them ever since."

Aliza patted his hand. "I couldn't agree more. It's like the song from *The Sound of Music*." She sang it clearly. "'Somewhere in my youth or childhood, I must have done something good.'"

"I've always loved that one. See what I mean? How many people our age love that movie? Or antiques? Or nature? It's *incredible*."

Aliza's stomach made its intentions known loudly and they both cracked up. "You don't even need to look at the watch. My stomach knows what time it is."

"Shall we?" Jesse stood and held out his hand. Aliza took it, and they left together happily.

They dined at a high-end boutique restaurant whose clientele contained a mix of locals and TV people. Aliza and Jesse waved at the people they recognized but were then seated in a cozy private alcove booth in the window. The world around them disappeared. They ate well, enjoyed the romantic ambiance, and were almost sad when dessert came. They tasted it, agreeing it was sumptuous. The candle on their table had burned low. They had been there for hours by the time they finished with their coffee. As they left, Aliza looked back to watch as the flame flickered and burned out. Somehow, it gave her a pang of regret to see it, although she didn't stop to contemplate why.

Jesse suggested a stroll through the green. Fewer people were out than there had been earlier in the evening, but a scattering of couples and a stray loner or two stood out in silhouette against the streetlamp light. Jesse led Aliza up the stairs of the gazebo, which was lit by tiny Christmas lights, all strung around the beams and up to the pinnacle.

"I've got to admit, I'm a fan of these lights," Aliza said, looking up.

Jesse nodded in agreement. "I'm glad they don't make us take them down after filming every day. That would be a pain."

"I think the locals like them, too, you know. It's like they're meant to be here, and everyone knows it. I bet that long after our show is over, and the crew has packed it all up, the lights will stay. They'll be here in a hundred years, and no one will even remember why."

Jesse pulled Aliza in close and kissed the top of her head. Gazing up at him, she allowed herself to feel the emotion of the moment. She had let her guard down almost completely with him. She trusted him and felt deeply that he shared her feelings. They kissed passionately, forgetting their surroundings. It had been the perfect night.

# THREE

*The jeweler baptizes the hot metal in the tub of water once more, relishing the release of steam as though it is her own breath, exhaled in relief. The solder job was good, the gaps have filled with silver completely, which is the best she could ask for.*

The next morning Jesse left Aliza's apartment feeling joyful. It was a sunny Sunday morning, he had the greatest girlfriend in the world, and he couldn't have been happier. As he pushed open the front door of her building, a man reached out for the door as it started to close. Jesse held it open for the guy.

"Thanks, man."

Jesse continued down the street with a growing sense of unease. He got all the way to his own apartment before he realized why the interaction with the stranger had unsettled him. That voice, so cold and suave. He knew it from somewhere. As it hit him, he broke into a cold sweat. The voice was Cameron's. He recognized it from the brief phone call they had shared not a week before.

Jesse panicked, realizing that Aliza was in immediate danger. He spun around and sprinted back towards her apartment, calling the police on his way. He got there ahead of them, let himself into the building with a key Aliza had made for him, and ran up the stairs. His heart froze as he heard Aliza crying from the hallway, her wild scream, and then silence. Bursting through Aliza's door, Jesse was horrified to find Cameron balanced over her. Dishes lay scattered and broken on the floor, the dining room chairs and table were upturned. Aliza had clearly fought him, but Cameron was a big guy. Jesse flashed back to his childhood, seeing his mother terribly hurt by his stepfather, and adrenaline spiked through his body. Pushing the memories aside, he assessed the situation.

Aliza lay unconscious, twisted into a terrible contortion on the couch. Cameron was positioned aggressively against her, his belt unbuckled, and Jesse knew exactly what would have happened next if he hadn't interrupted.

Cameron spun around when the door burst open, and he fixed Jesse with a hard, hateful glare. Breathing heavily, he held Aliza's limp body with one hand. He let go and faced Jesse.

Jesse struggled to control his emotions. His fury at Cameron and his concern for Aliza nearly overwhelmed him, but he moved forward as calmly as he could.

"Get away from her," Jesse ordered in a commanding voice. "Get away from her right now."

"From our pretty little doll? She was so happy to see me. She missed me." His mocking tone baited Jesse. Leering, he slid his hand down one of Aliza's legs.

"Get away from her, Cameron. You're fucked up, and you need some major help." He edged forward.

"Stop, don't come any closer, Black," Cameron yelled. "I'm taking back what's mine, and if I can't have her, I'm not going to let anyone else have her, either." He reached for Aliza's exposed neck, still holding Jesse's gaze.

The words chilled Jesse. He froze, unsure what to do next. A police siren sounded faintly outside, growing louder. Relief flooded his veins. He boldly took another step forward. "Do you hear that?" he shouted. "The game is up. It's over. Get away from her."

Cameron's expression changed when he heard the sirens. His face was red, his expression crazed.

Footsteps thudded down the hall. A voice yelled, "Freeze!" From behind Jesse, the police filled the doorway, weapons drawn. One cop shouldered Jesse aside. "Step away from the girl and raise your hands."

Cameron laughed a thin, cruel laugh. "You guys are a joke compared to the LAPD. What, are you going to shoot me? No way."

He kept laughing, but he complied with their orders, relaxing his stance and stepping away from Aliza. One cop moved forward and handcuffed him while another kept Cameron at gunpoint. Still another had gotten on his radio and called for an ambulance.

Jesse's head spun as they dragged Cameron out of the apartment door. "This isn't over, Black," he yelled over his shoulder.

Jesse hardly heard him as he pushed through the chaos. At Aliza's side, he checked her pulse, found where she was bleeding and applied pressure. He stroked her hair with his other hand, even though it was thick and matted with blood. Shaking and sick to his stomach at the sight of this beautiful girl laying there helpless and hurt, he realized how deeply he loved her. Tears streamed down his face as he kissed her pale cheek.

"Don't worry sweetheart, an ambulance is on the way. You're safe now. I'm so sorry this happened."

As he said the words, another realization hit him. If only he hadn't let Cameron in the front door Aliza would still be safe. Jesse agonized over this, and his heart felt like it would burst with guilt. *How could I be so careless?* The scene of himself holding the door for Aliza's worst nightmare played over and over in his mind until his better sense resurfaced and reminded him that someone else would inevitably have let Cameron in, it was a small town after all. No matter what, he would have found a way to get to her. Knowing this, however, didn't alleviate Jesse's raging remorse.

It felt like eons until the ambulance arrived, and all he could do was whisper, "You're going to be okay, Aliza. You're safe now."

The bruises on her face were starting to redden and swell. She was still unconscious and hadn't stirred at all. Jesse could only imagine what had happened in those few terrible minutes before he had gotten back to her.

When the medics came, they put Aliza on a stretcher, hooked up some oxygen, and rushed her out of the room. Jesse followed and stayed with her through the trip to the hospital and was ushered into a waiting room when they arrived. He watched as they wheeled her quickly through a set of double doors marked "No Admittance".

All feeling seemed to flood out of his body as he watched her disappear. The world spun around, his senses dimmed, his ears filled with a buzzing noise. Shadows edged in around his sight. Somehow, he managed to find a chair and to sit down before he blacked out completely.

His breathing was rapid and shallow, and his color must have been terrible. He was leaning forward with his head in his hands when an orderly brought him a bottle of water and said, "Drink this, sir." Jesse did as he was told. Consciousness ebbed back to him slowly with each sip of the cold water. "You gonna be okay?" The orderly's voice sounded far off, like it was coming through a league of water. When Jesse had finally processed the words, he nodded his head and the guy left him.

"Thanks for the water," Jesse called weakly after him.

"No problem."

It was over an hour before someone came out to talk to Jesse about Aliza's condition. The doctor was female looked disgusted as she described Aliza's injuries.

"I understand this was done by someone she knows," the doctor said.

"Yes," replied Jesse, struggling to find his voice through the emotion consuming him. "Her ex-boyfriend."

"You called the police?"

"Yes, doctor."

"You may have saved her life. The police tell me the assault was still in progress when they arrived."

"He would have killed her. He wanted to," Jesse said, emotion finally getting the best of him.

"You aren't family. I can't discuss her condition with you in detail."

"Her family is in Los Angeles. I'm her boyfriend and the closest thing to family she has in Twin Falls." His voice was shaking.

The doctor patted his shoulder. "She's going to recover. I don't doubt that, but she should see a counselor. This was a terrible assault. The concussion alone could have caused a brain injury had she not gotten here in time. The other contusions and the amount of bruising tells me that this was no ordinary beating. I mean, he cracked her ribs. This was passion and insanity mixed in a terrible combination. I hope the guy stays behind bars where he belongs. Anyway, you can see her now. She's unconscious, on a heavy dose of painkillers, and she may be foggy for a while."

"Thank you so much, doctor. Is there anything I can do for her?"

"Call her family, I guess. They should know what happened."

"Okay, I will."

Jesse followed the doctor through the double doors and into the ICU. There was a quiet hustle and bustle, punctuated by the beeping of countless monitors and machines, and the antiseptic smell hit Jesse hard. He pulled himself together, keeping pace with the doctor. She pointed to a room and kept walking. Jesse stopped outside the room and peered in. It was dimly lit, and a thin curtain was partly drawn, obscuring Aliza's figure from immediate view. Entering slowly, he pulled the curtain aside and stood still, watching her. It was very hard for him to keep a level mindset, but he mustered his strength for her. He approached the bed, drew a chair to its side, and held her hand.

She looked worse than she had when he had found her, minus the blood. They had cleaned her up, but the bruising on her face and arms was alarming, heartrending. Cameron had hit her forcefully and repeatedly. *No wonder the doctor had looked so disgusted. How could anyone do this to someone else? How?*

He lay his head down by her side, still holding her hand, and he wept for her pain.

For the next several hours, Jesse stayed steadfastly by Aliza. He only left to let the nurses do their checks. As the hours ticked by, he became more concerned that she hadn't woken up yet, although some part of him knew it was probably better this way. She would have to face the pain and the reality soon enough. Sleep was a gift.

He made phone calls from a chair by the window. First, he called Rudy, but he only got his voicemail. This wasn't something Jesse could leave on a message. He told the director to call him as soon as he could. Aliza's parents were a different story, though. He didn't want to upset them, but he needed to inform them of her condition. He called his mom first to ask her what she thought.

She knew of his relationship with Aliza and had been happy for him. She answered cheerfully. "Hi, Jesse."

"Hi, Mom."

"What's wrong, honey?" She could always tell from his voice when things weren't quite right.

"I need your advice. Something happened to Aliza, and she's in the hospital. She's unconscious, but the doctors say she'll recover. I need to tell her parents, but I don't want to alarm them unnecessarily. Should I wait until she wakes up or should I call them now?"

"What happened to her?" His mom's voice waivered, revealing her concern.

"Do you genuinely want to know?" Jesse said protectively, not wanting to bring back horrible memories for his mother but seeing no choice.

"Of course, I do."

He took a moment to breathe, knowing he was on the verge of losing his composure. "She was attacked by her insanely jealous ex-boyfriend. He beat the hell out of her and probably would have killed her had I not stopped him. Luckily the injuries were not as bad as they could have been."

His mom took a deep breath, too, and then, in an empathetic

voice, she replied, "Oh, sweetheart. I'm so sorry. Is there anything I can do?"

"No, but what should I say to her parents?"

"You should call them now and tell them everything. They will want to know immediately. Maybe they'll fly out or something. I'd want to know right away if, God forbid, something happened to you."

"I'm sure you're right. Thanks, Mom. I'll call you soon to let you know how Aliza is."

"Jesse," his mom said urgently.

"Yes?"

"You take good care of her now. You hear? She will need your strength." His mom's voice cracked a little. He knew why. She had been in Aliza's position, as Jesse remembered all too well.

"I will, Mom. I love you."

"Love you, too."

Usually, Jesse tried hard not to think about his abusive stepfather, but the memories were vividly impressed upon his psyche. He felt like he was six again. He and his mom had lived at his grandmother's house after his mom had left his stepdad. His stepfather showed up one night and created a scene, breaking things and yelling, rampaging, terrorizing. Jesse's grandmother grabbed Jesse out of the way and ran up the stairs with him. She locked them in a bedroom and called the police. This course of action had unfortunately left Jesse's mother defenseless and alone with a drunken madman. Before the police showed up to intervene, his mom had sustained some serious injuries. What, Jesse had wondered even then, could drive a man to such hateful actions?

Afternoon sun filtered through the drawn blinds of the hospital room, creating abstract patterns on the blue and white tiled floor. Little pools of sunlight separated by expanses of shadow, they crept slowly across the room as the sun completed its daily arc. Jesse took a deep breath and mustered the courage to call Aliza's parents. It would not be easy, but it was the right thing to do.

He took her phone out of his pocket and dialed their home

number quickly before he lost his nerve. A woman's voice answered. It reminded him of Aliza in its lithe and cheerful tone.

"Is this Ms. Bennett, Aliza's mom?"

"Yes, who is this?" she said, still in a friendly tone but slightly more guarded.

"This is Jesse Black. I'm a friend of Aliza's."

"Of course, Jesse. I've heard Aliza mention you. What can I do for you, dear?"

Jesse cleared his throat and took a deep breath. "I need to tell you something, ma'am, but I don't want to alarm you. Aliza is okay, but she's in the hospital. I am here with her."

"What happened?" Her voice tensed slightly. "Is she all right?"

"Yes, the doctors agree she'll be all right. Cameron attacked her and beat her up pretty badly." Jesse's voice broke. He had to swallow a couple of times in order to continue. "The police have arrested him for assault."

"That bastard. I told Aliza he was bad news. Is she conscious?"

"She's sleeping at the moment. The doctors have her on painkillers. They assure me she will be all right, though. I wanted you to know what happened. I promise I will have Aliza call you as soon as she is able."

"Thank you, young man. You sound like a kind person, and I appreciate your candor. You care for Aliza a great deal, don't you?"

"Yes, ma'am, I truly do. I'm sorry I didn't protect her better." Jesse's voice waivered, tears fell silently. Trying to maintain some semblance of composure, he kept talking, but it was difficult. "Cameron had been harassing Aliza on the phone for weeks. I was trying to keep him from hurting her emotionally. I never thought he would come after her like this."

"It's hardly your fault, Jesse. Thank you for doing what you've done. She has always run with the wrong crowd of guys, but it sounds to me like she's turned that around with you. I'm so glad. Thank you."

The conversation ended with Jesse's reiterated promise to keep Aliza's mom informed of her progress. He took a deep breath when he hung up, feeling thankful that things had gone so well. After a few moments, however, he started to wonder why Mrs. Bennett hadn't freaked out. He knew his mom would have gone into a hysterical state if something like this had happened to him. Aliza's mom, however, had sounded somewhat surprised, but not wildly alarmed and certainly not frantic. Maybe she would feel differently if she saw how helpless and hurt Aliza was. Maybe it would take a little while to sink in. He was a stranger to her, after all, but Jesse's unease did not abate.

Aliza's slight frame looked even smaller beneath the hospital covers. It was so hard to see her like this, so frail when she was usually so feisty. Sharing information about her family life was not something Aliza had done much of. She was guarded and elusive whenever they talked about their childhoods. Once in a while, she would tell a funny story about her father's friends or her mother's cooking, but none of them were substantial or deeply illuminating. Now, after talking to her mother, he wondered why. Were they detached and preoccupied with themselves? Didn't they care about Aliza the way his mother cared about him?

Aliza stirred slightly, shifted her arm, and turned her head. Still she slept. Jesse replayed the incident with Cameron and tried to keep himself from picturing what had happened in the seconds before he had burst in. Jesse slid his chair closer to Aliza's bed and took her hand gently in his own. Bruises bloomed around her wrists, showing where Cameron had grabbed her. Thinking about it made Jesse's stomach turn.

Cameron was obsessed with Aliza. He wanted to possess her. He wanted her to yield to him, and her refusal had turned him violent. The man would have forced himself on her, that much was evident by the undone belt buckle and the way he'd positioned himself against her. It hurt to think about that, but it made him wonder what Cameron's relationship with Aliza had been like before. Aliza was elusive about that, too. They had never talked about sex. He had no idea whether Cameron and she had been together but judging from the jealous rage Cameron displayed at the prospect of anyone else being with her, he assumed they had. Now that the question presented itself, Jesse wondered whether it was because she wanted to or because he'd pressured her into it. The more Jesse thought about it, the more upsetting he found the possibilities. He knew he shouldn't speculate. Cameron was clearly a psychopath, but there was another layer here concerning Aliza that Jesse didn't understand.

He closed his eyes to try to clear his head. Aliza stirred again, moaning a little. He squeezed her hand gently to let her know he was with her. She started murmuring. "No, go away." Her slurred words were foggy, but clear enough to understand, like she was reliving what had happened earlier. Jesse couldn't bear it, so he spoke gently in her ear. "Aliza, it's Jesse. I'm here, and you're safe. Aliza, can you hear me? I'm here, and you're safe."

She opened her eyes slightly but didn't see him. She squeezed them shut and opened them to try focusing on him again.

"Hi," she finally managed to squeak out. Her voice was dry and cracked. He placed a cup with a tippy straw to her lips for her to drink.

"Hi, sweetheart. I'm so glad you're awake. You had me worried, but the doctors assured me you'll be fine.

"Where am I?" she said weakly, sounding dazed. "What happened?"

"We can talk about it later when you feel stronger. Aliza, I want you to know you're safe now. I'm so sorry I didn't protect you better."

"Aliza?" She murmured her own name with uncertainty, as though she didn't recognize it, closed her eyes and fell back to sleep.

Jesse felt a chilling discomfort at her reaction. He reported the waking up to the nurses and asked them to call for the doctor. Sometime later, the same doctor he'd met earlier showed up. "Hi, there," she said to Jesse, but she was looking at Aliza. She moved to the bedside, checked Aliza's pulse, and said, "I hear our friend woke up for a minute."

"Yes," Jesse replied. "She didn't seem to recognize her name."

"That's not unheard of. It's possible that it's a combination of the painkillers and the concussion. Like I said, he hit her very hard. It may take a little while for her to be herself again. Thanks for letting me know."

The doctor lifted Aliza's eyelids and flashed a light in to check her pupils. They dilated just as Jesse expected them to. He was relieved, despite the fact that he had no idea what it meant.

Finally, the doctor looked at him squarely. "Have you eaten?"

"No," he replied, remembering his corporeal self for the first time in hours.

"You should. The cafeteria is terrible but, nevertheless, you need to eat."

"Doctor's orders?"

She smiled. "Doctor's orders."

Jesse hated leaving until Aliza had gained full consciousness. He wanted to be with her. He didn't want her to wake up alone and scared.

Sometime later, a police detective showed up with an officer Jesse recognized from earlier. They stood in the doorway, and the officer whispered to the detective, "Yes, that's the guy."

The detective knocked on the doorframe and looked at Aliza respectfully before addressing Jesse. "Mr. Black?" he said in a quiet voice.

"Yes, sir," Jesse replied.

"Do you mind if I ask you about the incident earlier?"

"Not at all, sir. Cameron is still in custody, right?"

"Yes, he'll be with us for a while, judging by the looks of this poor little one here."

"Good. He is dangerous and totally insane."

"I'm going to take your statement. Start from the beginning."

Jesse told the detective all about the texts and phone calls, about the harassment and the constant threat Cameron had been for the past month. He described the day's situation exactly as it happened, from recognizing Cameron's voice to calling the police to interrupting the violence. He gave a verbatim account of Cameron's words.

"When I got there, he was standing over her unconscious body with his belt buckle undone and his hands on her. He had murder in his eyes. He would have raped and killed her if no one had stopped him."

"You think so?"

"Absolutely. He stood over her with such dominance and hatred, and I can't describe the look he gave me when I entered. It was pure madness. He said if he couldn't have her, then no one would. He went for her neck, as though to strangle her. The sirens startled him into pausing, thank God. I'm only sorry I didn't stop him sooner."

"He did a number on her, that's obvious. How long do you think you were gone?"

"Not more than ten minutes all together. It's about a five-minute walk to my apartment from hers, and I had gotten all the way to my door. I called you guys while I sprinted back."

"Amazing, isn't it? It doesn't take long to do some serious damage. What did the doctors say, if you don't mind me asking?"

Jesse smiled wanly, thankful for the detective's concern. "They tell me she should be okay, but I'm worried nonetheless. I wanted to thank you for your prompt response today. I don't know what he would have done if he hadn't heard the sirens. I certainly hadn't gotten him to back down."

"You made the right choice, son. I'm glad you didn't get physically involved. That always complicates things, despite people's best intentions." He looked down at Aliza again. "I have a daughter, you know. I'd go insane if anyone did this to her. I'm glad you kept your cool. I'll keep you posted."

"Thank you."

"No problem."

When Jesse was alone, he stood and stretched. Leaning his forehead against the window, he watched the clouds change color for a while as the sun set. The skies in this part of the country were beautiful, all pinks and oranges and purples when the sun went down. Maybe it was the smog, but Jesse didn't remember sunsets in LA being so pretty. Maybe they were, and he'd been too self-absorbed to notice. Melancholy set in once the sun was gone, and Jesse sat back down. Aliza hadn't moved or made a sound in what felt like ages.

Jesse's phone buzzed. He answered quickly and quietly. It was Rudy. Jesse explained the situation as succinctly as he could. Rudy was clearly upset by the news, and Jesse was sure that it was for more than professional reasons. He said he'd be by sometime that evening to check on Aliza. Rudy had a wife and kids, and Jesse was sure Rudy was thinking about how angry he'd be if anything like this happened to them.

Perhaps Jesse's childhood had prepared him to deal with this horrible situation. It was difficult to keep his emotions under control, but he understood more intimately than the others what this would mean for Aliza. She would be shattered, as his mother had been. She would cope in unpredictable ways. He worried that fear would manifest itself in her psyche, and she would not be the same after this. From helping his mom through her troubles, however, Jesse was also aware that the spirit is strong and that recovery, though it may be slow, is possible. The fact his mom had gone on to be happy and productive was proof of this. Jesse felt a glimmer of hope in his heart for the first time all day.

Rudy showed up with a small pizza around 7:30 that evening. Jesse had dozed off in the chair, still holding Aliza's hand. He awoke to the rumblings of his stomach in clear response to the smell of food. Ignoring the doctor's advice, he had stayed with Aliza, but he was wildly grateful for Rudy's thoughtfulness.

Rudy stood at the end of Aliza's bed, his expression dark. His intense concern for Aliza was obvious. Gone was the jocund man of their on-set pep talks.

Examining Aliza's injuries in the low light, he could not hide his feelings. "Wow. She looks worse than I imagined."

"Cameron was brutal. Absolutely insane. I should have been there faster, Rudy," Jesse said, emotion finally getting the best of him. He stood and turned away, trying to master himself, but it had been a long, taxing day.

"You intervened. You stopped him before he killed her. Don't feel bad about not being there sooner. Cameron is an opportunist. He would have found a way to hurt her regardless of your vigilance. You probably saved her life. Thank you. You know this kid means a lot to me."

"I know."

"Did you call her parents?"

"Yeah, I did. I talked to her mom."

"And?"

"She was concerned and wanted updates, but she didn't sound really upset or anything. She thanked me for looking after Aliza."

"That's all?"

"That's all. I told her I'd ask Aliza to call them when she woke up."

"Well, that's about typical. Her mom's on massive doses of Prozac and white wine these days. It doesn't surprise me that she didn't react more. I don't know how you grew up, but my parents weren't self-absorbed zombies. They honestly cared about how I felt, how I acted, who I hung out with. All the typical things parents should care about. Aliza, on the other hand, has had a different experience."

"It seems like Hollywood is a tough place to grow up, even with parents who care. I guess I was lucky to start out in a normal place and to come to LA with a mom who looked after me. She still looks after me. I guess we looked after each other, in a way. My dad passed away when I was young. Mom remarried, and the guy was a colossal jerk. He terrorized and assaulted her until she divorced him. I don't know if he gave up on us after that or switched his attentions to some other poor woman or what, but the experience forged a bond between Mom and me that we still have to this day. You should have heard her when I told her what happened. I think she cared more than Aliza's mom."

"Getting through the haze of drugs to reach a genuine emotion is nearly impossible. It's not fair to compare, I guess. Different people, different worlds. Carolyn Bennett is a prisoner in her own jail."

"You guys were all friends when Aliza was a kid?"

"Yeah. Carolyn and Paul were entertaining, in the right circles, and they could throw a wicked bash. Aliza was such a smart and witty child. She was delightful. They used her as a party trick, though. I don't know what effect that has on a kid, but I wasn't surprised when she started running with the wrong crowd a few years ago. I gave her this job because she's talented, Jesse. Very talented, but she was also pretty lost, and it was taking its toll. She has been more like the old Aliza-the child I knew-with you during the last month than she has been for years. I don't know what effect this is going to have on her, but I am going to ask you again, please look after her."

"You don't have to ask, Rudy. I'm in love with her." As the words came out, he knew it was the truth. It was a relief to say them. "I care more deeply for her than I have for anyone else I've known. She means the world to me."

"Good. She deserves that. You're a great guy, Jesse. I'm glad you're here. Enjoy the pizza. I figured you wouldn't leave her side, even to eat."

"Man, that smells good," Jesse said, gratefully accepting the box.


It wasn't until ten in the evening when Aliza finally woke up. She was fuzzy, foggy, and clearly in pain. Jesse pressed the button for the nurse who came in quickly. She checked Aliza's vitals and asked her how she felt.

"It hurts," was Aliza's muffled response.

"I know, sweetheart. I'll get you some more medication."

The nurse left to find the doctor who ordered a morphine drip. Aliza drifted back into a fog. Jesse knew it was better this way. The pain would be too much for her, after everything else.

# FOUR

*Eagerly, the jeweler takes the cooled metal from the water, and with a keen eye she checks her work. It is sturdy and well aligned. She marks where the tubing will fit on the second piece of the shell, double checks that it is in the right place, and sets up her soldering station again. Flux, clips, torch, heat, solder, flow, cool, exhale. Now, will they fit together?*

Aliza's dreams were more real than reality. Bright images intensified, with startling clarity, set against familiar backdrops, making them all the more terrifying. She was caught in a strange loop, a hated song on repeat, an endless cycling vision, with one solid terror at the center. Cameron. His gravity held her in a harrowing orbit as she struggled in vain to escape. Cold eyes locked with hers, his grip an iron shackle encircling her fragile wrist. He had taken so much, and he continued to take so much. He would consume her if he could.

The endless loop begins the same way, a light knock on the door, unwarily answered. Fear drains the life from her body, replacing it with ice. She trembles, steps backwards. He follows, a predator, stalking her, mimicking her moves, mocking her obvious fear. The words he speaks are a nightmare within a nightmare, a threat so deeply felt it's as though she is violated with each new word he utters.

"You are mine. Your body is mine. Your soul is mine."

He wears his power like a second skin. She stumbles backward. He pounces, grasps her wrists, twisting and crushing like a vice. Pulling her to him, his ravenous, malicious eyes bore into her. She struggles to free herself. She kicks and writhes. Laughing, he holds fast, all the while saying the words she knows he will act out next. His voice drowns out her own which is crying to be heard. Or is it? Is the voice able to escape when the body can't? She cannot hear herself either way, so her voice is rendered unreal. Making good on his threat, he licks the side of her neck and face, tasting her collarbone, pausing at her pulsing veins. He repeats the same words now, again and again, "You know you've missed me. You know you want me. You know what I am going to do to you, and you know you like it."

Drenched with sweat and tears, she is still struggling, a bird caught in a hunter's net. His body is pressed against hers. Her heart is racing so fast she may expire at any moment. She starts to collapse, and he makes his mistake. Her single moment of reprieve. He lets go of one wrist to catch her. She does not hesitate. She lashes out and punches him in the face as hard as she can. He staggers. She is strong for her size. She moves away but he follows, enraged, and flies at her with fierce brutality, unlike anything she has ever imagined.

Table and chairs are overturned, dishes crack on the floor. She kicks. He sidesteps, and then he has her. Blow upon blow, a cracking sound, a hot wound deep in her chest. A final massive crack to the head and everything fragments. Colors intensify, jagged black lines edge her vision as her own voice becomes an echo in the wilderness. An earthquake in her mind shifts the solid forms of reality into monstrous new creations. She lifts from her body. Below, Aliza is pale and covered in beads of sweat like tiny pearls. Rivulets of blood thickly stream from her wounds, crimson against her pale skin. The last vestiges of her true self call out as though from behind a thick veil of water. She sees herself from outside, collapsing against the arm of the sofa. She sinks beneath a swelling tide. A last tear escapes her eye, a lone mark of despair before the darkness. She is lost.

A new voice yells, "Stop."

It begins again. And again. Endless purgatory.

Then, a variation.

A new voice rings out like a bell in a far-off monastery. It echoes too many times to decipher. It filters down through layers of darkness, bounces off a deep well of smooth stone. Aliza floats at the bottom of the well, so far away she can't see even a pinpoint of light at the surface that might be hope. Though she knows the voice, it reaches her too vaguely. She cannot call out in answer. She sinks again beneath the black enveloping waters. Suspended, she floats far beneath the surface while furious dreams wash like waves through darkened sleep, ebbing and flowing in time with her pulse, holding her fast in their prison. Her anger is subdued, frozen like a pale figment of what it was, a wildness quenched by the pressure of the water on all sides. She longs for quiet dreams where light filters down through the depths, patterning her skin like some ancient creature of the deep. Her lungs are a flood. She has no voice, but she responds to the bell above with projected thoughts, swirling with the water, words she cannot utter and that come like a prayer to her mind. *Please, find me.*

# FIVE

*Fitting a hinge is painstaking to get right, but it is such an integral part of making jewelry that it is not a feat of engineering as much as an exercise in one's craft. In this case, everything fits together perfectly. The hinge will work well, the jeweler thinks, with a feeling of pride. Very well indeed.*

Jesse slept fitfully in the uncomfortable hospital chair. The darkness outside overwhelmed him in his brief awakenings, filling him with terrible sadness and a sense of loss. The terror he felt as a child, helplessly watching his stepfather's cruelty toward his mother, rushed through him, intensifying his feeling of helplessness now with Aliza. All he had wanted to do was protect the women he loved, and he had been unable to in either case.

Jesse had not seen his stepfather in many years. The man's physical appearance had faded in his memory over time, but the cruelty in his eyes was unforgettable. He should have recognized it in Cameron's as he passed him outside the apartment building, for it was the same. Again and again, Jesse tried to sleep, but each time he was awakened by terrible images, like a horror movie on repeat in his mind.

The dawn finally took pity on him. Jesse took the first glimmer of sunlight at the horizon as a cue to go get coffee. He patted Aliza's hand, smoothed a strand of hair on her forehead.

"I'll be right back," he whispered.

Stepping outside the hospital, he breathed in the fresh cold morning air. It filled him with an energy he would have hardly thought possible considering how long he had gone without real sleep. The air braced him, he moved forward onto the sidewalk and began his search for a quality cup of coffee. If all else failed, the diner was within walking distance, and it should be open by the time he arrived on its doorstep. The thought of stopping by his apartment was appealing as well. A fresh shirt would be nice. With a plan in place, Jesse felt more hopeful than he had in two days. Maybe Aliza would grow more alert today. Maybe.


Armed with a thermos of diner coffee, a shower, and a fresh change of clothes, Jesse headed back to the hospital. He stopped at the bakery to buy muffins for the nurses, just to show his gratitude for their work. Their dedication, spinning in their orbits of service to the sick, inspired him. They were thrilled with his offering.

He had also picked up the local newspaper where he found the story of Aliza's attack had been leaked. It showed a headshot of her looking totally beautiful. The story lacked depth or detail, but it was there in print nevertheless. It disturbed him to know no one had asked her permission to print it. Now, the next issue of every tabloid would have exaggerated, inaccurate, accounts of Cameron's attack. They would dredge up interviews with all Aliza's old friends in LA, and create a thorough bastardization of the truth, all while completely invading her privacy. It was infuriating, but Jesse didn't have the energy or wherewithal to deal with it. He recycled the newspaper before he got into Aliza's room to keep her from seeing the article.

Aliza had been tended to in his absence but had not regained full consciousness. The nurse in charge told him she'd mumbled a bit while her sheets were being changed and her IV was replaced, but that she had sunk back into her torpor soon after.

Jesse resumed his vigil. Holding Aliza's hand, he settled into the armchair and read a paperback.

Around eleven AM, Aliza stirred. Clearly frustrated by being held captive for so many hours, her body was restless, and she couldn't seem to get comfortable. When she woke up fully, Jesse put down his book, his heart frozen in anticipation. Would she be alert or forgetful? Would she be in a drug-induced haze or would she be clear minded?

Still holding her hand, he slid to the edge of his seat and leaned closer to her. "Aliza," he said quietly and with a smile. "Good morning, Aliza."

She turned to look at him and for a moment fear seized him as her eyes seemed unfocused and lost, but in a moment, she seemed to regain some clarity. "Hi," she said weakly. "What's going on?"

"You're in the hospital. You've been asleep for quite a while. How are you feeling? Does it hurt a lot, or are you okay?"

"I had the worst dreams imaginable, and they wouldn't stop. It was like I was a prisoner in a deep well at the same time as I was watching a movie of horrible things happening to me. I felt like I kept drowning and coming up for air, drowning again, and the water was so cold."

"It's okay. They were only dreams. You're here, and I'm with you, sweetheart. I'm not going anywhere."

"Okay. Thank you for not leaving." She closed her eyes again for a moment and then opened them and looked at him strangely. "You know, maybe they weren't dreams."

"What do you mean?" Jesse tried hard to disguise the alarm in his voice.

"I mean how did I get here? Tell me the truth." The fierceness of her spirit shone through despite the condition of her body.

"What do you remember?" he said to stay on the safe side.

"I remember the dream. Only the dream. It was Cameron. He came after me, and then everything sort of shattered, and I was at the bottom of the well." Tears filled her eyes, and her heart rate increased.

"There was no well, but the Cameron part is true. He found you, and he knocked you around. You're okay, though. The police arrested him. He won't hurt you anymore."

"I remember pieces of it. Who called the police?"

"I did. It took me a minute, but I recognized Cameron's voice as I passed him. I'm sorry I didn't realize it sooner."

"Then what happened?"

"As soon as I realized who it was, I ran back to your place, but you were already unconscious. You did a good job fighting him, though, from what the police told me. Do you remember that?"

"Yeah. It's coming back to me. He scared the crap out of me. I thought..." She let out a little cry and tried to stifle it at the same time.

Jesse's heart was breaking. He squeezed her hand tighter, both to give himself strength and to give strength to her as well.

"He said the most awful things. He was planning on—I can't even say it, but I did fight him. Then he got crazy vicious. After that it's all black."

"I think that's when I came in and stopped him. As I came up, I heard you cry out. The police got there a minute or two later. As bad as this is, it could have been so much worse," Jesse stated gently. "I'm so sorry I didn't recognize him sooner, Aliza. I could have spared you all of this pain. I am so sorry."

"You have nothing to be sorry about. I got myself into this, and it has nothing to do with you. Thank you for stopping him when you did."

Jesse's eyes filled with tears, and he couldn't bear to look at her. He kept his head down and held her hand tightly. The guilt of not doing enough, not doing more, was agonizing.

Aliza's breathing was rapid, and her heart rate raced. The nurse entered, having been alerted by a monitor at her station. "Oh. We're awake." Her voice was respectfully low, but cheerful. "It's wonderful to see you so alert, dear."

Aliza took a deep breath and winced.

"Oh, that must hurt, doesn't it? Cracked ribs are a horrible pain."

"Cracked ribs?" Aliza's soft voice sounded grave.

Jesse looked up at the nurse. He hadn't told Aliza the extent of her injuries. He was working through the information slowly, only sharing what he thought she could handle. Revealing exactly how close she had come to dying at Cameron's hands wasn't wise.

The nurse glanced at Jesse and then back at Aliza. "That man almost killed you, but you're a fighter, aren't you, sweetheart. You'll be right as rain in a few short weeks. Don't worry."

The nurse fussed around with various things, raising the angle of the bed, and fluffing the pillows. Aliza closed her eyes. Jesse's alarm mounted. This revelation could undo the progress they had gained in their conversation. He couldn't predict what affect the knowledge of the entire assault, as well as Cameron's intention to kill her, would have.

After a few minutes the nurse asked about Aliza's pain level and if she felt she needed more medication.

"I don't know," Aliza replied, eyes still closed.

"Well, let me know if you need more relief. I'm just outside your door."

The nurse left them alone, closing the door behind her.

After a few silent moments of watching her blank expression, Jesse spoke. "Aliza? Are you okay?"

She took a breath, not too deeply this time, and answered quietly. "Just the tiniest difference between creating misery and putting me out of it. Why does he always know exactly where that line is?" She turned her head to the side, shutting Jesse out for the time being. Soon he could tell by her breathing she was sleeping again, but tears tracked her cheeks.

Had he made a mistake? Should he have told her the full truth right away? He couldn't be mad at the nurse for telling Aliza everything, but he'd wanted to be the one. He wanted someone to blame. Then he remembered Cameron's hateful eyes. There was only one person to blame, and it was him. Jesse prayed that Cameron would be charged with attempted rape and murder. That was the only way he would stay in jail for a while, and the only way Aliza would be safe.

At least she seemed to know her name. The confusion she had expressed the day before was absent, but her mind was on fragile footing. The nurse had shaken the foundation a little. Jesse hoped that with time all of this damage would be undone.

While Aliza slept, and Jesse read, time passed slowly. The nurse came in a few hours later to tell Jesse that Aliza had visitors. She was still sleeping, and he didn't want to wake her. He followed the nurse into the hallway to see who it was and was astounded to see the family from the gorge.

"Hello," the man said "We weren't properly introduced the last time we met. I'm George Anders, this is my wife Natalie and our two children. We recognized Miss Bennett's photo in the paper and were shocked to hear she'd been hurt. We never properly thanked her, but we had no idea who she was or where she'd gone. Is she going to be okay?"

Jesse recovered his composure and shook Mr. Anders' hand. "She is going to recover. The attack was terrible, though. She's very out of it at the moment, but she will be so happy to know that you were here."

Natalie Anders reached forward to hand Jesse the flowers she was holding. "Bad things shouldn't happen to good people. I know Miss Bennett is a good person. She saved our baby's life, and for that we will be forever in her debt."

"Here is my card. Please make sure to tell Aliza if she needs anything, she has family here in Twin Falls."

———

Aliza fell back into her dreams seamlessly. This time, however, she seemed more equipped. Instead of reliving the experiences in an endless spiral, she was more objectively aware of them happening, as though watching a film of the events. She still felt a separation from reality, from her own identity. If she had allowed this to happen to herself, then she was not strong enough. Who was strong? Her mother? Her dad? What other role models did she even have? Someone nagged at her subconscious, but the movie playing out in her mind distracted her attention.

She was acting the part of the victim and the fighter at the same time, and both parts showed in her eyes. Who would she be when she surfaced again? Would Aliza know Aliza? Would she be someone else? A fragmented Aliza set on a dusty shelf in the back of her mind to be replaced by someone more capable? By someone like her TV character Lydia, perhaps? Lydia was strong and feisty in the way that Aliza always pretended to be. Beneath it all, she knew she was a marshmallow. Lydia was steel in comparison. It would be so much better. So much safer. So much easier. Why go through this ever again?

As she watched the events play out again and again, a mere spectator becoming ever more detached, she felt both empathy for and anger towards this lifeless rag doll being thrown around. She analyzed the girl's reaction, from the moment the brute stepped through her door until the moment the scene went black, as she collapsed on the couch. She fought, it was true, but she fought poorly. She was hindered by fear, and fear was what vanquished her in the end.

The spectator decided then and there never to be in that position again.

# SIX

*How to suspend the glass phial inside the egg is the jeweler's next challenge. Wondering what the best approach is, she tries some possibilities out in brass. Silver is expensive and is not the best material for testing a theory. Satisfied that she understands her next steps, she readies her tools.*

Over the next few days, Jesse stayed with Aliza for as long as he could, leaving only to shower and change clothes and to check in on set, shooting a few scenes with other actors. Aliza's absence had caused a ripple effect in the shooting schedule. Jesse hated to think of what it must have cost the production, but everyone worked around it empathetically. According to the doctors, the bruises would be nearly gone in another week or so.

People from the production came to visit, bringing flowers or balloons, curious about the details of her attack but too courteous to ask outright. Jesse was sure the news had spread rapidly because Michelle and Bertie seemed well informed. They were the closest thing Aliza had to old friends on set, besides Rudy, and they stopped by often.

Aliza was recovering physically, but she was still very spacey and lost when she awoke. The hospital staff kept her well medicated, which seemed to be confusing her. She kept mixing up personal experiences with pieces of the plot line of their TV show, blending her character and herself up in a frightful jumble. It was disconcerting enough to drive most visitors away rather quickly.

The Anders family came back once more, but Aliza was asleep. When Jesse told her about their second visit, she lit up for a moment, but then got cloudy again. It was as though she recalled them and then lost the memory as quickly as it had come.

Jesse missed Aliza's quippy, witty banter. Seeing her languish in a confused torpor for days on end was pure torture, he only longed for her to be well again. Steadfast in his attentions, Jesse's faith never wavered, even when Aliza looked at him as though she didn't recognize him. He simply waited, and loved her, and hoped it would be enough.

The cracked ribs took the longest to heal. It was painful for Aliza to breathe and worse to move. Once, while the nurses changed her bandages, Jesse had accidentally caught sight of the worst cuts and bruises Aliza had sustained as she had struggled against the attack. He had walked back into the room after being gone a while and glimpsed Aliza's milky skin, her perfect body, marred by livid wounds only now starting to heal. The acute physical pain it caused him was unexpected. These scars would stay with her forever, deep, daily, physical reminders of what she had suffered.

The doctors assured him she was healing on track, her progress was good, and she would be out of the hospital in no time. They said she could go home by the end of the week. She could even start working again, if she took it easy. Jesse was unsure. He listened to her sleep-talk and questioned her gently when she was awake. Based on her words and her tone, he knew something was wrong, psychologically speaking. It would manifest itself more clearly when the drugs wore off. Slowly, they did, proving Jesse's concern was not unfounded.

On the fourth day after the attack, Aliza awoke from a vivid nightmare and looked at him with strangely fevered eyes. "I had the worst dream," she murmured. "This poor girl got beaten up badly by her terrible ex-boyfriend. Poor thing." She paused and looked around. "Oh, Ken, I must have fallen asleep. Sorry. Where were we?"

"What do you mean?" he said, masking his concern. "We're in the hospital."

"Right. The hospital scene. Where's Rudy?"

"He was here earlier. He had to go."

"Oh. Well, I'm ready to shoot, whenever, so let him know. Wanna go for a walk in the meantime?"

"Oh, sure, I guess we could do that. It's easier now that you're off the IV, after all."

Aliza laughed. "IV. Good one, Ken." She swung her legs around the edge of the bed and sat up quickly and then pain contorted her face as she grabbed her chest. She bent forward, breathing heavily and looked at him in an accusatory way. "What's going on? Did I get hurt?"

"I think we need to get the doctor, Aliza." Jesse tried to maintain his even tone of voice, but it was getting harder.

"What doctor? Why do you keep calling me Aliza? That's my character's name, not mine. What's going on? I don't understand." She was fierce, her eyes were livid. She directed her anger at Jesse and he tried very hard not to take it personally.

"It's going to be okay. We're going to sort out everything. Aliza is your name. Lydia is your character's name in our TV show. You're from LA. We live in Twin Falls where we're shooting the show, and my name is Jesse. I love you, and I promise it will all be okay."

The ferocity of her gaze bored into him. "It is not okay, and I am not Aliza. I don't know why you'd say I am."

"You need to remember the truth, Aliza. Cameron came after you. Your nightmare was real. That happened. He assaulted you. The police arrested him."

"No. No. That's just the script. That's just the dream. No." She started to cry.

Jesse pressed the call button for the nurses. When they came, he quietly asked them to send for the doctor.

When the doctor came, Jesse released Aliza's hand, left her on the side of the bed crying, and took the doctor outside her door. "She's totally confused. She's mixing up reality with the plot of our TV show. She needs to see a psychologist, right now."

"She's reacting to the trauma. It's going to take a while for things to get back to normal, Mr. Black. She's been through a lot."

"I know she's been through a lot," he snapped. "This is a break with reality. This is not Aliza. This is not the strong, feisty girl I know. Something is going on, and she needs help."

"I'll call the psychiatrist on duty and ask him to come down. In the meantime, I can give her something to calm her down."

"She doesn't need more drugs. She needs help."

"Thank you for your medical opinion, Mr. Black," the doctor replied sharply and turned away.

Jesse managed to calm Aliza. He sat by her, stroked her hair, and put his arm around her. She eventually stopped crying, but she still had a dazed, far-off look in her eyes. He could tell she couldn't make sense of what her mind was telling her, couldn't sort out the fact from the fiction. He did not want to risk alarming her again and refrained from saying her name.

Eventually, the psychologist came. Aliza looked up at him with confused eyes and looked away again, uninterested. Jesse stood and whispered to her that he'd be right back. He led the doctor out into the hallway to confer with him.

"I'm Jesse Black. I'm Aliza's boyfriend."

"Not the one who beat her up, I assume," the doctor said, sardonically.

"No. That is the ex-boyfriend," Jesse replied coldly, finding the doctor's manor distasteful.

"So, what's going on?"

"She is very confused about who she is. She is mixing up reality with the characters of our TV show."

"That is probably her mind trying to protect itself from the trauma of her experiences. She has subsumed the personality of the stronger character, feeling safer that way. The subconscious works in interesting ways."

"How do we help her back to herself again?"

"Give it time, Mr. Black. She'll be fine."

"Please don't dismiss this as routine. I'm telling you, she's in trouble. There's something deeply disturbing about this switch, and I'm terribly worried. Aliza has been through so much. It wouldn't be fair to her to play along with her fantasy. I owe her more than that."

The doctor paused for a moment, measuring his reply. "I'll interview her, and we'll go from there. However, since you're not next of kin, I won't be able to discuss her condition with you." He said this last bit with an air of condescension that Jesse couldn't stomach.

"I understand, but her family is not here. They're in California."

"Are any of them planning to come?"

"I don't know." Jesse lowered his eyes to the floor, feeling totally helpless. "I care about her so much, Doctor. Please understand that. I only want what's best for Aliza. She's the most amazing person, and this guy has shattered her."

"I understand. I'll do what I can." Softening slightly, he patted Jesse on the arm and went in to see Aliza.

Feeling frustrated and helpless, Jesse left the hospital and went for a walk. He hated the doctor's smug manner, and he doubted whether his attentions would help Aliza's condition. How else could Jesse help her, though?

Memories kept flooding back to him. Scenes from his own early life played back in his mind, the protective bearing of his grandmother, the way his mother had clung to Jesse so strongly after each encounter with his stepfather, as though Jesse were a talisman to keep the madman away. Maybe she had also been clinging to what she had thought to be the good in the man, however slight and fleeting that part must have been. For it must have been there, even in a minute quantity, for his mother to have married him. Either that or he had been an even better actor than Jesse.

His mother had overcome the abuse. How had she done it? She had been a good mother to him all along, despite the trauma she had experienced. She was the only mother he knew, the only parent, for that matter. Objectivity was not afforded him on this point. He thought of her dimly lit bedroom, of the thin shafts of winter light filtering through careless gaps in the curtains, creating little glowing patterned pools, haphazardly crisscrossing her bed. Rocking back and forth, crying silently she would lay there, caught between her desire for Jesse not to know that she cried and her wish for his comfort. Ultimately, he would comfort her. He would snuggle up behind her and hold her, telling her it would be okay. As long as he believed it, it seemed like enough. In the end, maybe it was.

The afternoon was gloomy and overcast. A cool wind blew ahead of a storm, and it stung his eyes as it mixed with the tears streaming down his face as he walked. He snapped back into the present, unaware he'd been crying. These old wounds, these traumatic memories of a childhood marred by cruelty, malice, and abuse were set deeper into his psyche than he had ever imagined. It had been so many years since he'd even thought of his stepfather. Of his childhood. Of any of it.

He stopped at a park bench near the river and sat watching the young mothers run with their strollers up and down the path. They all wore headphones, were all insulated in their own worlds, their children either asleep or content, with glazed expressions playing across their innocent faces. In all the pictures of him as a child, he, too, had that innocent expression. He had no idea, no frame of reference to compare his life to anyone else's.

*That is the amazing part of childhood. We can get through anything because we don't know any better. Our minds are infinitely flexible. We can adapt to our situations. When does it fall apart?*

Just as he had with his mother, Jesse would find the strength to help Aliza regain her sense of self. After all, he thought, that is what those barbarians were trying to steal with their jealousy and their violence. They wanted to eradicate the spark that made a woman special. To snuff it out, to subdue it, to dominate it, made those men feel powerful. He had watched the glimmer in his stepfather's drunken eyes as he closed in on his mother and knew it had been the same with Cameron. Was it a question of wiring? Of soul? Of conscience?

Cameron, and a million heartless bastards just like him, had acted this way since the beginning of human evolution and would continue until the end came. It was that simple. Aliza was caught in the web of dependence and abuse. It had nothing to do with intelligence or will. It was not a flaw in her personality that left her vulnerable. Jesse did not know why these men picked certain women to target. He only wished to revere Aliza's unique nature, not dominate it.

It was all too much to think about, and he could not afford to let himself become overwhelmed. Breathing cleared his head, allowing him to focus on the soothing rush of the river below. It occurred to him that he hadn't talked to his grandmother about Aliza's attack yet. Thinking about his past so vividly had made him miss her even more than usual. He called her.

Charlotte Black was a strong woman, to say the least. The moment he heard her reassuring voice on the phone, Jesse felt calmer. She knew what was wrong. Jesse's mom had told her.

"You know she's going to be all right, Jesse," she reminded him.

"I know, Grandma. It's just been so hard to watch her go through this."

"You're strong enough for both of you, just like you were when you were a kid. You'll come through it together."

"I love you, Grandma. I hope you know how much."

"Oh, Jesse. Don't you make an old woman cry. I love you, too. Come see me soon."

When he got up and started back to the hospital, he felt a renewed strength and a sense of purpose well up from deep within him. He didn't know what to expect, but he felt ready, at the very least, to give it his best.

On his way back, Jesse stopped by Aliza's apartment. He thought if he could take some of her things to her, she might have an easier time staying tied to reality. Her comfort was important to him, and the hospital gown was so horrible and demeaning. Maybe some clothes would help. It did not occur to him that he was going back to a crime scene until he saw the police tape across the open door.

Inside were the last remnants of an investigation. The two detectives were packing up their tools and putting their coats on when Jesse caught their attention.

"This is a crime scene, sir. Can we help you?" The investigator was not much older than Jesse and of slight build. The other investigator watched Jesse with intense interest obvious on her face.

"I know. I was the witness to the assault and called the police. My girlfriend was the victim." Jesse swallowed hard at that word. "I was hoping to take some of Aliza's personal things to the hospital."

"Sure, sir. We're done here anyway and were about to take the tape down, but I am going to need to verify your identity."

"No problem." Jesse fished his ID out of his wallet. "I've got her keys, if that makes you feel better about letting me stay. I can wait until you leave and let myself in, if it would help."

"That's okay. I recognize you from the newspapers anyway, Mr. Black."

Jesse was invited into the apartment and until the moment he stepped through the doorway he didn't realize what "crime scene" implied. Aliza's blood was everywhere. It took Jesse by such surprise that his face turned white, and his ears filled up with noise.

"Are you okay? Here, sit down. Get him a glass of water, Sid," said the detective who had been silent until now. "It is not easy to return to the place of a crime, especially when it was someone you care about that got hurt. How is she?"

Jesse recovered somewhat. "She's healing physically. I think it's going to take some time for the emotional healing, though. Thank you for asking."

He managed a weak smile.

She handed him a card with a cleaner's name and number on it. "These guys will clean this place up in no time. Give them a call and say Dianne referred you to them. They'll treat you right. Stains like this are near impossible for normal people to get out, but these guys are magicians."

"I never thought about it. I mean, until I saw the police tape, I had not even thought about what the place would look like. There's so much blood. Her blood."

Dianne took a look at Jesse. "You seem like a good guy. Don't worry. She'll be okay."

"Thank you. I think I'm going to get her things together and get out of here. I appreciate your help."

"Please, call the number on the card. You shouldn't have to deal with this on top of everything else." Dianne had a kind voice under her official facade.

"Oh, I found this under the couch when we were fishing around," Sid said, handing something to Jesse. "It looks like it might have been what she was wearing during the attack. She might like it back." He handed Jesse the labyrinth necklace. "We were going to take it to the lab, but it's not necessary. We all know what happened."

Jesse took the pendant in his hand, feeling its weight. It was such a beautiful piece. Its chain was broken at the clasp, and Jesse shivered as he imagined Cameron yanking the necklace from Aliza's neck. It explained the marks on the back of her neck that he had noticed before.

He looked up at Sid. "Thank you. I appreciate it. I gave this to her. He must have ripped it off her neck. I..." He lost the ability to speak and looked at the pendant in his hand. He flipped it over and traced the labyrinth with his finger. He remembered the jeweler's words when he had bought the necklace. "A long road to the center," he murmured. "A long road home."

Aliza was alone when he returned to her room. Before he could even speak, she put up her hand and stopped him in his tracks. "I am so sorry, Jesse." She spoke slowly and deliberately. "I can't explain why I had things mixed up. I'm okay now. The doctor and I had a talk, and he told me it was my mind compensating for the trauma.

Whatever that means." She put her hand down and looked up at him with tired, unfathomable blue eyes.

He moved forward and sat next to her on the bed. Taking her hand in both of his he saw how the bruises encircling her wrists were already fading. Absently, he traced the brownish-yellow lines with his fingers. "You have nothing, nothing, to be sorry for." He brought her hand to his lips and kissed it gently. She looked down at the floor, long lashes moistened with tears. "In a few days, they're going to let you out of here, and I guarantee you'll feel better. You'll be yourself, your strong and feisty self, in no time."

"Will I?" she said quietly. "I don't know anymore. I just don't know."

"You absolutely will. You will recover. You will feel better, and you will be an even stronger person because of it."

"It's so much easier to let go. I don't want to be this weak little girl. I don't feel like I can ever be my true self again, if I ever even had a true self. Who am I, Jesse?" She looked at him like a bewildered child.

His heart was torn apart at the sight of her sadness, her helplessness. "You are a fighter. You are the strongest woman I know, aside from my mother and my grandmother. You fought Cameron. You will keep fighting him, until he's put away for good, and you will regain your sense of self. I know it. I've seen it happen, and I know it's possible. Besides, we have a show to film. They need us."

He managed a smile. She looked up and met his eyes. Her expression was full of sadness, but he did not see the bewilderment as before. He was relieved beyond imagining. He smiled again, this time for real.

# SEVEN

*The jeweler snips a length of heavy gauge silver wire. Tapering the end into a crude point using a hammer, she then fits it into a plate with different sized and shaped holes in it. Choosing the square, she will draw the silver down into a long rectangle rather than a cylinder. She tightens the plate into a vice and grasps the end of the wire with pliers. Using all her strength, she pulls the wire through the plate in one steady swipe, so no marks of hesitation will be left. Everything leaves a mark if you're not careful.*

During one of the few times Jesse left Aliza's side over the next few days, he brought the broken necklace back to the jeweler. She did not look surprised to see him, and Jesse assumed she knew what had happened. It was a small town, after all.

"Jesse Black," she greeted him, with a nod of the head. "How is your friend doing?"

"She's doing better, Karen. Thank you for asking. She is getting stronger and more herself every day."

"Sid told me I'd be seeing you soon enough. Let me see the chain."

Jesse pulled the necklace out of his pocket and handed it to Karen.

Her expression darkened. "This was a very strong chain. Most jewelers don't bother to make their own chains anymore. It's tons of work, and you can get good quality ones from overseas. This one, however, I made myself, and I know for a fact that it must have taken a lot of force to break it." She fixed him with an intense stare. "I hope that guy pays for what he did to her." Her voice caught a little as she spoke.

"They have him in jail, and I'm told he won't get out for a good long while. He tried to kill her. They won't take that lightly."

"I'm so glad she's okay." Karen flipped the pendant over in her hand and examined the labyrinth for a moment. "We can never tell what lies around each bend. All we can do is pray for the strength to find a way through it. Who could have known something like this would happen to her? Like I told you when you bought this, every piece has its owner. I can fix this while you wait."

Karen disappeared into the back for a few moments, giving Jesse a chance to look around. Karen fascinated him, for she seemed to see more deeply than other people. *Perhaps that's what makes her a great artist.*

When she reappeared after a while she was carrying the necklace gently. She took Jesse's outstretched hand and poured out the chain like water into his palm. This gesture of significance revealed some solidarity Karen must have felt with Aliza.

"What do I owe you for the repair?" Jesse asked.

"Nothing," she said, still grasping his hand. "Don't lose patience with her on this long road back to herself. You must be steadfast. You are the rock at the center of it all, even though you may not have asked to be there."

Jesse's stomach felt tight, his throat closed with unexpected emotion. "Thank you. I promise I will do all I can for her."

"Of course, you will," she said and smiled at him.

When Jesse presented Aliza with the necklace for the second time, she teared up. "I hadn't forgotten about it, Jesse. I didn't know what happened to it. I thought it got lost in the apartment after Cameron grabbed it." Her voice got quieter as she said Cameron's name.

"I understand. The police found it when they were working in your apartment. The chain was broken, but I had it fixed for you. The jeweler's name is Karen, and she sends you her best."

"I suppose everyone in the world knows what happened, by now," she said sadly.

"It's a small town, Aliza. I guess that's how it works."

"Will you put it on me?"

"I'd be happy to."

Aliza held up her hair as he put the necklace around her slender neck. The marks from where Cameron had torn it off were fading and did not look as painful as they had at first. "There. We should go back to the gorge sometime soon. It was beautiful."

"Everyone on set knows, right?"

Jesse shifted uncomfortably and hesitated before answering, hoping to phrase things so as not to upset her. "I think everyone we work with knows by now, yes."

Aliza didn't comment. Instead, she picked up the pendant and ran her fingers over the smooth stone again and again. She was lost in thought, and Jesse didn't want to be overbearing.

"I can't seem to find my way to the center of this maze I'm in," she finally said. "I'm blindly groping smooth walls. Everything appears the same in all directions." Continuing after a moment, her voice like that of a lost child, she asked, "There is a center, right? I will find my way back to some semblance of normalcy, don't you think?"

"I know it. I have never doubted it. You are more like yourself with each passing day."

"Myself..." Aliza's voice trailed off as she considered the word.

Later, Aliza and Jesse went for walks through the hospital halls, and each day she seemed stronger, but she was still very subdued and quiet. Jesse had to support any conversation they had. He did not despair, nor did he waver. Steadfast in his devotion to her recovery, he was thrilled when they decided to release her from the hospital.

Jesse had seen to it that Aliza's apartment was cleaned and restored. He had even gone in and rearranged the furniture, so she would not be confronted with the images of that horrible morning with Cameron. Aliza was terrified. She stalled getting ready to leave, broke down in tears as she said goodbye to the nurses, and snapped at Jesse when he tried to help her into a taxi. Elated at taking her home, he was determined not to take it personally.

"Don't worry, Aliza. I know you're nervous about going home, but..."

She interrupted him, "This is not my home. I don't even know what home is." She looked out the window at the familiar sights of Twin Falls as they passed them by. Jesse's heart started to sink.

"Sometimes home isn't a place. It's who we're with. I was hoping you felt at home with me."

Aliza was silent for a moment. "I'm sorry. I don't mean to be short-tempered or emotional. I'm just scared. I don't know what I'll feel when I walk into that place."

Jesse reached for Aliza's hand, and she withdrew it. His heart sank a little more. She was pulling away, and he didn't know what to do. They arrived at her apartment building before panic could seize him. By the time he got to her side of the car to open it, she was already standing by the cab. "Take your time," he said gently.

"I'm fine," she said, but with an edge. She strode forward. He paid the cabbie and followed her into her apartment building and up the stairs. She hesitated outside her door, realizing she didn't have the keys. Jesse unlocked the door and let Aliza open it. She did so slowly. She wasn't breathing. Putting his hand on her shoulder made her flinch. He let his hand remain, however, as a reminder that she was not alone. She stepped forward into the apartment.

"Who rearranged everything?" Her voice was edgy, and Jesse was suddenly unsure whether he had made the right decision.

"I did. I had everything cleaned up, and I rearranged the furniture a little, so it would be like coming to a new apartment. I'm sorry if it's not what you expected. I can always put it all back."

Walking forward slowly, Aliza took everything in. She was breathing again, at least. She spun to face him. "Thanks for cleaning. I almost expected to see a big pool of blood or broken dishes. It's weird to have it like this. I don't know."

For a time, Jesse was uncertain what to say. Remaining silent, he watched Aliza move around her place like it was a foreign country to explore. She touched objects, ran her hand along the back of the couch, hesitated before a family picture, picked it up, and put it down again.

Jesse walked to the kitchen and poured two glasses of water. He brought one to her and drank half of the other in a few swallows. The tension between them was awkward and unexpected. Jesse didn't know how to fix it.

"Do you want me to stay?"

"You don't have to," she replied.

"I know I don't have to. I want to, but only if you want me here."

She moved to the front window and looked through it. "I don't know what I want right now. I don't want to hurt you. You've been kinder to me than anyone in my adult life. I don't deserve it."

"Yes, you do," he corrected her with vehemence.

"I don't know. Maybe someday I will, but right now, I don't know."

"I understand."

"No, you don't," she yelled, turning to face him with a fierce look in her eyes. "You don't understand this at all."

He was stunned into silence for a moment. "Let me know when you're ready for company. You know where to find me."

Jesse turned around and headed for the door. He was still holding his glass of water. He turned back to set it on the dining table. As he did so, he caught the glint of tears on the edge of Aliza's cheek. She was still staring out the window, her fingers absently tracing the circlet of silver surrounding the stone on her pendant.

He mustered his courage, knowing he was strong enough to handle one last rebuff if she should shout at him again. He crossed the room and pulled Aliza into a tight embrace. She sobbed and sobbed against his chest, her whole body shaking with the weight of her pain. He kissed the top of her head and held her tightly until she was still and silent again.

That afternoon, Rudy came by to check on them. Jesse and he had prearranged this meeting so that Jesse could go out and get some clothes and provisions. Jesse excused himself and walked outside into the blinding sunshine. He basked in it for a moment before heading to his place.

The difficult couple of moments with Aliza popped back into his head. Of course, she would snap at him. Although he understood it theoretically, it didn't keep him from feeling sad about it. Everything would be different now. Jesse had been there with her through the entire ordeal, and he would persist. Considering what she had been through some changes in her demeanor were to be expected. *People who go through trauma have personality shifts. She'll get back to normal before long.* Deep inside, however, he knew he was in for a struggle, and he lamented the loss, albeit temporary, of the Aliza he knew and loved.

When he returned, Aliza was smiling. Rudy was regaling her with stories about the people they knew back in LA. She asked questions. He gave answers, used goofy voices, and generally took her mind off the present circumstances. By the time Rudy left, Aliza had a spark in her eyes again and seemed to be more herself. Jesse knew better than to place any real stock in these changes, but he was thankful for them nevertheless.

He made them a simple dinner of chicken and rice with broccoli in a tarragon-butter-white wine sauce. Aliza marveled at its elegance and ate with aplomb. She had lost some weight during her hospital stay, and Jesse was determined to make sure she didn't lose any more. The doctor had been right. The food there was terrible.

As the night progressed, Jesse began to worry about whether Aliza would want him to stay, what her state would be, and if the mostly pleasant tone of the day so far could possibly continue. His fears were unfounded. Aliza got so tired so fast, he had to assist her off the couch and put her to bed. He decided to stay, dug out some of her old movies, and fell asleep on the couch while watching them.

In the middle of the night, it was as he expected. Aliza woke up screaming, tangled in sheets, absolute terror masking her lovely face. He got to her in an instant and wrapped her in his arms. She fought him, scratching his arm, and writhed around to get away before she woke enough to understand it was him.

He whispered comforting things while rocking her gently, and as she fell back asleep she murmured, "Thank you."

He stayed in the bed with her, stroking her hair as she slept. Adrenaline had spiked through him as he calmed Aliza down and he couldn't fall back to sleep. Aliza's journey to recovery was going to be a long one, and he prayed that he could help her find her center again.

The following morning, they visited the set, where Aliza was politely mobbed by everyone. They were tactful enough not to bring up the details or ask personal questions, but their attention was overwhelming. Aliza's default Hollywood nature took over, and she hugged and talked to and charmed everyone who came to her, assuring them that she was fine and would be back to work soon. It was easy for Jesse to believe her when she was in this context, and he wondered if work wouldn't be her best medicine. He and Rudy were reluctant to push her too far too fast but seeing her in her element was a reminder of exactly how strong her spirit was.

# EIGHT

*Once the jeweler achieves the shape she desires, she anneals the metal and cools it. She cuts it into short lengths, bends two of the skinny rectangles into rings by pounding them around a ring form. Testing the fit of her glass phial within them, she gets the exact measurement of the phial, solders the rings closed, cools, and pickles them. The glass slides into the rings with no room to spare.*

The writers had scripted reasons into the show to explain Aliza's absence. Vacation, illness, trite stuff, but necessary. Rudy told them to ease her back into the story, starting out slowly so she could acclimate without feeling overwhelmed. Monday, when Jesse and Aliza showed up for their scenes, Aliza looked more like herself than she had since the attack weeks before.

When Michelle saw her, she squealed with delight and hugged Aliza vigorously. "I am so happy to see you, Aliza. Your bruises are almost gone."

"I never doubted you could do magic on them, though," Aliza replied, trying to sound cheerful. She shifted uncomfortably under Michelle's scrutiny.

"Let's get to work," Michelle said.

Aliza hardly recognized herself when Michelle finished, reminding Aliza of when Michelle had done her "Lydia" makeup the first time. Now, it was a relief to get to be someone else for a little while. She thanked Michelle and found her way to the set. Shooting went well. She opened up in the scene, feeling her way through the emotion of it, and reveling in her craft.

Jesse had extra scenes to do with other characters and plot lines that had been developed while she was gone, leaving Aliza on her own for a while afterwards. Thankful for a little space, she changed her clothes, leaving her makeup as it was, and took a walk by the river. The weather had ripened into summer without her realizing it. *I've been so out of it.*

The walk did her good. As her mind cleared, she walked to the bridge where she and Jesse had had their first kiss. Crossing to the middle, she hopped up on the thick stone railing. Sitting there, staring into the water, with her back against one of the sculptures, she tried hard to remember the last time she'd been free of fear. It was certainly before she had met Cameron, but even then, was she without fear? She had always feared being unsuccessful, being ugly, being lonely. These were average fears.

The kind of fear she had experienced with Cameron was different altogether. He had tapped into her deepest insecurities and exploited them, turning her against herself and making her depend on him for validation. Then he would twist her thoughts around, making her think she needed him for any positive feelings of self-worth. It was sick, but it had happened so slowly, so subtly, she hadn't felt her independence slipping away. He had somehow exerted his dominance over her in a way that made her think it was her own doing. She was finally starting to realize it was all a part of his sick game. He was purposeful in all his moves, a master chess player thinking out his strategy well in advance, trapping innocent pawns in his web.

She thought back to how he had finally gotten her to bed, manipulating her emotions until she was the one asking *him* to take her virginity. She shuddered at the thought and berated herself for being so stupid. *At least it's not the 1800s or I'd be jumping into this river right now for the shame of it.* Then she heard Jesse's voice in her mind, clear and decisive, "You are not stupid, Aliza. He is sick, and this was his way of dominating you. This was not your fault." *But it is my fault. If it's not my fault, how did I let it go so far? I couldn't see him for what he was. I didn't even know I was being manipulated.*

Cameron had taken her, just as she had asked, and he did it in a hard, forceful way that made her feel sick afterwards. She had regretted it instantly, but that regret was mixed with a new dependence on him she couldn't explain. The swift water of the river flowed below her as she wondered if she would ever feel like herself again.

During the past two months with Jesse, she had felt more like the real Aliza than she had since she was a child. Even so, the shadow of her past was always there, looming over their relationship, and all while Cameron had plotted against her. She was right to fear him. She knew it, but what now?

She felt impure, sullied, disconnected, distanced from her family in a profound way. The precious few friends that did not connect back to Cameron seemed so far away. She had nothing. She felt like a child's balloon, let go by accident, left to find its way through branches and storms, only to deflate and disintegrate in the end. Not a very happy fate.

What about Jesse? Should she rely on him to tether her back to the ground? Back to reality? Could she trust him? Did she want that? Shouldn't she avoid reliance on anyone else after what had happened with Cameron? She felt she should perhaps harden herself, become self-reliant and let go of all of her dependent tendencies. On the other hand, Jesse loved her. How could she throw that away simply to make a point to herself? Did she love Jesse? She needed time to sort it out.

Looking up over the bridge, she saw a form that sent a wave of fear and panic over her body. It was Cameron walking towards her. Her eyes fixed on him. Her breathing stopped, and her body froze.

As the man walked closer she realized it wasn't Cameron, but not before the man saw her expression.

"Are you okay, Miss?" Concern was evident in his expression.

Tears ran down her face, and she trembled. Managing a weak nod, she was thankful he kept walking. She scolded herself. *Pull yourself together.* Instead, she buried her head in her hands and sobbed.

She had snapped at Jesse often since returning home. He handled her outbursts with the patience of a loving parent, but it just made her angrier. Everything he said was too kind, too loving, too good. She didn't want to hear it. All she wanted to hear was how this mess was entirely her fault and that she was lucky to be alive. Being short tempered and knowing he didn't deserve it made her feel incredibly guilty.

Rudy invited Aliza over for dinner with his family. She accepted, feeling he was a connection to a positive part of her past, however distant, that she needed to reestablish ties with it. Saying he was thrilled she felt well enough to be out, Jesse sent her on her way.

When she and Rudy were alone, the conversation inevitably turned to Jesse.

"That guy cares for you, Aliza. He's been so devoted."

"Yeah, tell me about it," she replied with a cavalier tone she hadn't expected to hear come from her own voice.

"Why do you sound so skeptical?"

"I don't know. He's just too good." She couldn't believe she was saying these things aloud.

Rudy took a pause before responding. He measured his words. "Jesse is good, Aliza. Good for you. You don't see it. Good is good for you."

"Yeah, I guess." She looked out the window into the darkening sky. "It's just that his good makes me feel worse about how bad I am."

"What are you talking about? You're not bad. You've been terribly mistreated, you've had shitty role models for relationships all your life, and you fell into a trap millions of other women and men, mind you, have fallen into throughout the ages. It's the cycle of dominance. Cameron did that to you intentionally and with calculated cruelty. Don't you dare blame yourself."

"I do blame myself, Rudy," she yelled, surprised at the harsh sound of her own voice. "You don't get it, and neither does Jesse, even though he pretends he does."

"What do you mean?"

"Oh, like he gets it. He says stuff like 'I understand, Aliza,' in this dopey way. How could he? How could he possibly understand?"

"Actually, he does," Rudy said quietly, looking down at his drink.

"What?"

"He does understand, Aliza. He didn't tell you about his childhood?"

Aliza felt a sharp pain deep in her gut. "No."

"Maybe you should ask him before you go jumping to conclusions." Rudy's tone wasn't harsh, but she felt like a scolded child, anyway. The shame was too much. *I am horrible.* What had he been through?

"Come on, Aliza. It smells like dinner is ready." Any shred of an appetite had deserted her, but she followed Rudy to the dining room anyway. They spent the remainder of the evening talking about light topics, and Aliza left early.

Before she left, she took Rudy aside. "I'm sorry about before. I didn't mean to act like such a brat. I don't know what's gotten into me. I don't even recognize myself anymore, and I don't like the person I've become."

"Listen to me, my dear. I care very much about you. You've been like a part of my family for many years but healing only comes with forgiveness. On that one, you need to start with yourself." He hugged her and sent her on her way, his words settling like a stone in her heart.

# NINE

*What is the best way to attach the rings to the shell, the jeweler wonders. Should she suspend the circles from the rear, so the phial appears to float? Or should she bind the phial with obvious restraints protruding from the sides? Considering her word, the simple word that has been her muse all along, she decides it is a word that shouldn't be restrained. She cuts and files two rectangles of silver, fitting the pieces together perfectly. She shapes the edge where the rectangle will meet the shell. She solders the rings to the stays and the stays to the shell, praying everything will fit.*

"Rudy told me you had a tough childhood. Why didn't you ever tell me?"

She hadn't even set her bag down before she faced Jesse with the question.

He was taken aback at first, stood, and walked to her, kissing her on the cheek in greeting. Then he stood back and looked into her eyes. Her expression was a blend of accusation and pleading. He couldn't decide what to do.

"Well, first of all, my childhood was, for the most part, quite idyllic. There was only one aspect of my experience that I would classify as tough. What do you want to know?"

"I want to know whether you meant it when you said you understand how I feel after this whole experience with Cameron." She tripped over the name as she said it.

"You know me well enough by now to know I don't lie."

"Then tell me what happened to you." Her tone was still hard, and she must have realized it. "Please?" she continued more softly. "I need to know."

Jesse led her to the couch and told her the story of his life from the beginning. He left out no detail, painting a picture of loving women plagued by one crazy, domineering man, his stepfather.

"I'm so sorry," she said when he finished his story. "I had no idea what you'd been through. I've been so awful to you."

Jesse looked down and was shocked to see blood where Aliza had dug her fingernails into her arm, her knuckles white with strain. He took her hand in his and it relaxed. She looked down at her own arm as though it belonged to someone else. She looked back up at Jesse with an expression of horror and pain written on her features. Without speaking, he led her to the sink to clean the wounds.

"I know it hurts. It gets better, and now you know I speak from experience."

"I'm slipping."

"No, you're not. You're stronger than that."

"Everything shattered inside me that day. I felt myself... fragment. Reality hasn't seemed quite so real ever since. Like I'm swimming through some dream I can't control. The colors are skewed. I don't know who I am or who I'm supposed to be. I catch myself at the same time wanting to rely on you for everything and wanting to scream in your face because you're too kind, and you're giving me so much more than I deserve."

As she delivered this diatribe, her voice had gotten louder and louder. Tears were streaming down her face and an angry expression twisted with pain contorted her face.

Jesse took her forcefully by the arms and looked her in the eyes with such intensity that she froze in his grasp. "Now you listen to me. You will get through this, and you will be more yourself in the end than you have ever imagined. I'm not promising easy. I'm promising that with patience and hard work you will regain everything you've lost, and you will be stronger for it, if that's even possible. You *deserve* love and happiness. Have faith. You are such a good person, Aliza. One of the best I've met. What happened with Cameron wasn't your fault, just like what my stepfather did to my mother wasn't her fault or mine. Some guys are sick bastards, and your loving nature left you open to his cruelty. Now you know how to avoid that kind of trap."

After a few moments of silence Aliza asked, "Is your mom happy?"

Jesse hesitated, still looking her in her eyes. "I believe she is. She was in a different set of circumstances, though. She was trying to be a mother at the time and to preserve something of a relationship for me with my stepfather, since he was the only father figure I had ever known. In the end, it proved impossible, and I don't know if she's ever let that go. She blames herself for finding the wrong man to fill that role."

"What did you do? How did you cope with watching your mom go through this? Did he hurt you, too?"

"I was so young when it started. I remember him hitting her and me wanting to protect her, When I tried once, he knocked me across the room. My grandmother wasn't there that time. The next time he got violent, grandma sheltered me, and had the wherewithal to call the police. My mom wouldn't have."

"Cameron would have done far worse damage to me if you hadn't come in when you did."

"I know. I saw it in his eyes. We're going to work through this, Aliza. Together."

"You deserve better, Jesse." She turned her head away. "I was so caught in his web of manipulation that I let him..." She started crying again, softly this time.

"The past is dead and gone, Aliza. Don't let it rule your present or your future. We learn from the past. We do not let ourselves be controlled by it."

"But he..."

"No. It doesn't matter. This begins the long process of letting go."

"You deserve better."

"I want you and only you. Cameron and his sick, twisted ways have nothing to do with that, nor does any action of your past. You need to know this. When I walked through your door and saw you lying limp, I thought he'd killed you, and my heart stopped. I thought I had died with you. It was at that very moment that I realized how much I love you."

Aliza could not look him in the eyes. Her emotions and her haywire reactions restrained her. In a raw, barely audible, voice she continued. "I was falling in love with you before this happened. I felt closer to you than I had to anyone in my life. Now... I don't know anymore."

"Now you need time to heal. I get it. I have all the time in the world to give you. Promise me you'll be honest with yourself and with me. Tell me how you feel even if you think it will hurt me. It's all I ask."

"I'll do my best," Aliza promised.

# TEN

*The jeweler examines her work so far, fighting her own impatient desire to polish the outside of the shell. She still has work to do that could damage the finish if she polishes it now. That's why they call it a finish, she thinks, chuckling to herself.*

Jesse desperately needed a vacation. Shooting had gone on for two months without interruption, and although the cast and crew had gotten closer during that time, Jesse thought a change of scenery might give Aliza the perspective she needed. Cameron's trial would happen eventually. The judge had not let him post bail because of the brutality of his crime, affording Aliza at least some assurance of her present safety. Concerned that the trial would bring all of Aliza's memories of the attack to the surface, Jesse hatched a plan to take her somewhere.

Some days, the old, self-reliant, feisty girl he had fallen for was back. Other days, Aliza withdrew dangerously into her own mind. Nothing could pull her back. These were the days Jesse had to steel himself to face her outbursts. She would lash out at him with words that were difficult to hear. Although he knew she didn't mean what she was saying, it hurt him nevertheless.

Jesse sought the advice of his grandmother's best friend, a semi-retired psychologist. Christopher Mason was kindhearted and brilliant, humble, and wise. Jesse had always liked him a great deal. He was the also closest thing Jesse had to a grandfather, or to a father for that matter, and he had always welcomed Jesse's calls for advice. This time was no different. He greeted Jesse as an old friend, listening patiently while Jesse described Aliza's troubled mindset.

"Aliza is suffering from Post-Traumatic Stress Disorder, or PTSD," Christopher explained. "It's the same thing soldiers experience after living through the trauma of war. Aliza's experience certainly qualifies as traumatic."

"That's true. She's been through hell," Jesse agreed. "I just don't know how to help her."

"Be patient. She's bound to go through phases where her attack and all the events leading up to it will seem more real to Aliza than the present. During these episodes, she could become abusive or withdrawn. She might try to lash out or lay blame on others, but this behavior is her mind's way of managing the experience."

"I guess that makes sense. It's just hard to deal with. What can I do to help her other than stay patient?"

"She needs counseling, Jesse. It's vital to her recovery. Drugs don't touch PTSD because it's not caused by a chemical imbalance. She needs to talk to someone who has experience with this particular disorder," Christopher warned.

"She won't talk to anyone about any of it. She's trying to pretend it never happened."

"That won't work, and it will only make things worse. She needs counseling."

"She's not going to be easy to convince."

"Most people resist until they hit rock bottom, and by then the road back to wellness has become doubly hard."

"Can you talk to her if we visit Marblehead? I was thinking of taking her on a vacation to meet Grandma."

"It depends. She'll resent it if you try to trick her into talking with me. She'll feel manipulated. From what it sounds like, this girl has been manipulated by the men in her life. Lying to her is the last thing she needs. Be honest with her and I'll consider it. If she comes to me freely, we can talk, although it would need to be informally. I can't take on friends and family as patients for ethical reasons."

"That's fair. It would be such a help. Thank you."

"In the meantime, do some research. It might help you through the rough spots."

"I will. Thank you, Christopher. I'll be in touch soon."

Jesse was relieved to have a plan. Now, he needed Aliza to get on board. That would be the hard part. He didn't waste any time and asked her at dinner that evening.

"How would you like to meet my grandmother? She's invited us up for vacation week. She wants to meet you."

Aliza was in one of her brighter moods and was obviously giving the matter some thought. Jesse waited hopefully as she considered his proposal.

Before she could answer, he added, "You'll love Massachusetts. The area Grandma is in is very New England-y. Lots of cute old houses and shady streets, town squares, colonial accents, and a fabulous coastline. A great family friend, Christopher Mason, is there, too. He's the closest thing I've got to a grandpa, or a dad, for that matter. He's a semi-retired psychologist and one of the smartest people I know. Oh, Aliza, I want you to meet them, and they want to meet you."

She hesitated again before answering. "Is he going to analyze me?"

Jesse marveled at how sharp she was. "I don't think analyze is the word. He was distressed to hear about your ordeal, and he has offered to talk with you, if you want, but only with your consent and interest. He's got a lot of experience helping people who have experienced things similar to what you've been through. He's first and foremost my great friend. Anything else that comes of our visit is up to you to decide."

Aliza's expression darkened for a moment before she regained her control. "Okay, but I'm not a headcase, Jesse. I'm not interested in talking to a shrink."

"I know. Trust me, Christopher is no LA shrink. Besides, I think I need to talk to him, too. I admit, the past two months have put me face to face with feelings I had buried so deeply I'm surprised by how intense they still are. Watching the women you love go through these terrible things, while you sit idly by is not a picnic."

"You've hardly been idle, Jesse. You're a great friend, and you've helped me a lot. I do want to meet your grandma. She sounds like a lovely person. Besides, I could use a change of scenery."

"It's settled, then. I'm excited, Aliza. You're going to love each other, you and Grandma."

The final week leading up to vacation was the most difficult yet for Aliza. Whether it was the pressure of meeting his grandmother or that she was feeling overwhelmed, Jesse didn't know. Jesse and Rudy tried their best to support her with patience and kindness. With two days to go before their vacation, Aliza had a very disturbing moment on set, right in the middle of her lines. The scene was a romantic one with Ken and Lydia's first moments of intimacy. Aliza was in Jesse's arms and she froze, staring at Jesse blankly right before he was supposed to kiss her.

Rudy, who had assumed she had forgotten her lines, called cut and started instructing Aliza on the next few words. He must have caught sight of Jesse's alarmed expression and changed his tack. "Let's break here," Rudy said. "I have to make a phone call in a minute. Jesse, Aliza, be back in fifteen."

He shot Jesse a meaningful glance, and Jesse steered the unresponsive Aliza out through the back door and into an empty ready room.

Rudy met them there and studied Aliza.

Holding her hands, Jesse looked into Aliza's eyes. "She stopped talking and looked sort of through me," Jesse said quietly, as Rudy looked on. "Her eyes got all unfocused, and she started trembling a little. Thank you for noticing and not calling attention to it."

"What do you think it is?" Rudy spoke with unmasked alarm.

"She has done something similar a few other times, like she'll get real spaced out and stops talking. Then she asks what she'd been saying. Stuff like that. Nothing lasting this long and nothing quite so weird. Aliza, can you hear me?" Jesse spoke these last few words louder and directly into Aliza's face.

She flinched, blinking back tears. "Why would you yell my name like that? You startled me," she cried angrily. "Seriously. What are you trying to do? Why are you looking at me like that, Rudy?"

"Aliza, do you feel all right?" Rudy said in a hushed voice.

Aliza looked from one man to the other and back before she answered. "I..." She faltered. "I...feel...so sad. I don't know why." The tears escaped now, streaming down her face. "Why are we in this room? What about the scene?"

"Don't worry about the scene. We just want you to feel better," Jesse said softly.

"Don't treat me like a kid, Jesse."

Rudy and Jesse stiffened as her voice rose, exchanging worried glances.

"I hate it when you do this. You treat me like I'm some sort of invalid." She stood and backed away like a cornered animal, her voice even louder. "Just stop it. Stop looking at each other like I'm crazy. I'm not crazy. I'm not."

"We don't think you're crazy," crooned Rudy. "You had a little moment on set where you forgot your lines. We wanted to give you a chance to practice them and finish the scene later. Do you think you can do that?"

Aliza's breathing calmed a little, her eyes grew wide, and she slumped. "I forgot my lines? I'm so sorry." Her tone shifted from anger to contrition, and her tears continued to flow. "It won't happen again, Rudy. I'm so sorry."

"Aliza, Jesse and I want you to be happy. Don't worry about the lines. Is there anything we can do to help you feel like yourself again?"

"I'm fine, Rudy. I really am," Aliza replied quietly. "Maybe I'm tired. I didn't sleep well again."

"More nightmares?" Jesse said warily.

Aliza looked away and didn't answer. She brushed off the front of her shirt with her hands and turned to look in a mirror. "Oh, great," she said after a glimpse of her tear-streaked visage. "If we're going to continue with this scene, I need to go see Michelle. I hope she can work miracles."

————

Aliza left the two men in the ready room and wandered off to find Michelle. The makeup room was empty, so Aliza sat in one of the chairs to wait. She spun around to face a lighted mirror. Aliza studied her reflection. Puffy blue eyes stared back at her, and some of the brown eyeliner Michelle used to transform her into Lydia had smudged.

Leaning towards the mirror, she looked more closely. *Whose skin is that? Whose lips?* They didn't look like her own. She touched her lips, and it felt like touching a stranger's face. Aliza's heart raced, her head felt distanced from her body. *Who am I? I don't look like myself. I don't feel like myself. What is a self, anyway? Just a bunch of electrochemical signals firing from one side of my brain to the other. Something is jumbled up. Wires are crossed, crisscrossed, crisscrossed. Lydia is prettier than me and nicer, too. I think I hate her.*

Aliza snatched some lipstick from Michelle's supplies which lay scattered beneath the mirror. She drew a crimson line through her reflection on the glass. "Fuck you, Lydia." With a black eyeliner Aliza scribbled back and forth across her reflected face, trying to cross it out.

"Why do you have to show me up?" Aliza demanded with asperity.

She stabbed at the obscured reflection with another lipstick. It crumbled and squashed beneath the force. "I can't be like you. I don't want to be like you. You're too perfect. You don't understand anything."

Surging to her feet, she threw an open jar of powder against the desecrated mirror. It shattered, cracking the mirror in the process. Still, Aliza could see her face, contorted in rage, shattered in the damaged glass. The sound of Michelle's shriek behind her startled Aliza.

The shock in Michelle's expression had a sobering effect on Aliza. She examined the aftermath of her rage with openmouthed awe. She looked down at her hands, now covered in a mixture of cosmetics, and then up at Michelle again. "I...I'm sorry, Michelle. I will pay for all the damage I did. I didn't mean to..."

Michelle rushed over and pulled Aliza to her in a tight hug. "It's okay, sweetie. It's okay. It'll be all right."

For the first time since the attack, Aliza felt deeply comforted. Michelle held her in a motherly way, and Aliza who had been tense and full of adrenaline, relaxed and went limp in the older woman's arms. She began to cry again. Michelle comforted her, sat her down in a different chair away from the destruction, and started to clean Aliza's hands and face with cold cream. "You've been through too much. You're a good girl, my dear. You honestly are. That son-of-a-bitch should rot in jail for what he's done to you."

"It was all my fault, Michelle," Aliza said, stifling a sob.

"You think so?"

"I know it was. I let him into my head. I let him into my heart. I let him into my body." Her voice cracked at the last word, and she leaned over with her arms wrapped tight over her stomach.

"We all make mistakes. You were looking for something real, for a loving person, and a good boyfriend. Instead you found a liar and a psychopath. He lied to you and sucked you into his world. That is not your fault, Aliza. You are only guilty of wanting to be loved. We're all guilty of that. You just got mixed up with the wrong guy, is all, but it's over."

Once more, Michelle leaned forward and wrapped her arms around Aliza, patting her on the back and soothing her.

"I feel so stupid, Michelle. How did I let it happen? Why didn't I see him for what he was sooner?"

"Because that is his art. He is a deceiver, and he was damn good at it. He had a lot of people fooled."

"I hate myself for being so dumb."

"Don't." Michelle's voice was forceful now. She took Aliza by the shoulders and looked into her eyes. "Don't you ever say that. You are a beautiful, kind, and vivacious woman. You have inner strength you don't even know about yet. You will get through this, but don't you *ever* say you hate yourself. You are Aliza Bennett, an excellent actress and a charming woman who made one mistake. There is no room for hate, here, my dear. You are loved by so many people. You need to learn to love yourself as well."

Aliza wasn't fully convinced, but she felt a shift within her. She wanted to believe what Michelle was saying. She wanted to forgive herself, but she didn't know how.

Michelle's forceful voice interrupted Aliza's inner turmoil. "Now, we will clean you up and you will finish these scenes. You can do this, my dear. Are you ready?"

Aliza felt younger and more vulnerable than ever. "Yes. I'm ready," she answered in a subdued voice.

Michelle could work wonders, because in under ten minutes, Aliza was back on set like nothing had happened. She finished the scene, left the set with Jesse, and went back to her apartment for dinner. After dinner, she and Jesse watched a movie and went to bed. It was the first good night's sleep she had gotten in ages.

# ELEVEN

*The egg shape requires a closing mechanism. She fabricates a concealed friction clasp just inside the shell. The jeweler solders a tiny silver pin with a ball on the end and daps a tiny matching indentation directly across from it so that when closed they snap together and stay shut. All one has to do to open the piece is to gently pry it open, like a locket. It's a simple system, but she thinks it will work.*

"Should we drive my bike to Marblehead?" Aliza asked as they packed for the trip.

"Are you crazy?" Jesse said. "My ass hurts just thinking about it. It's a five-hour drive."

Aliza laughed at his comment. It also made her feel self-conscious. Beneath her lighthearted tone, Aliza was secretly terrified to meet Jesse's grandmother and Christopher Mason. What would they think of her? Was Dr. Mason going to psychoanalyze her and then tell Jesse she was crazy? The way things had been going lately, it was likely she was, indeed, crazy. The thought made her sad to her core.

*I don't want to be crazy. I want to feel right again.*

Although she was afraid to meet them, she had to admit a change of scenery would do her good. Somehow, even though Cameron was locked up, his presence close by in jail had cast an inescapable shadow. It angered her that he could still hold such power over her, despite his incarceration. That was what he wanted, after all. *When will it end?*

The day they left for Marblehead, Massachusetts was lovely. They borrowed Michelle's car, bought a road atlas, rather than use GPS, and set out by scenic back roads. They decided it would be more relaxing not to take the highways, if possible, even though it would take longer. They loaded up the car with snacks and sifted through Michelle's music, settling on some classic punk.

"It feels good to get out of town," Aliza confided, as they crested one of the hills on the outskirts of Twin Falls.

"Couldn't be a better day to travel, either. We needed a little vacation. We've earned it, wouldn't you say?"

"And then some," Aliza agreed. "I felt like time stood still there for a while. It's moving again, and I feel a little better."

Jesse nodded his head.

Aliza was afraid she had already said something irrational and was beginning to doubt herself when Jesse said, "Time did stand still. I didn't want to talk about this unless you brought it up, but when I was in the hospital waiting for word of your condition, I swear that's how I felt. When they told me you'd be all right, it was like reality caught up and synched with my brain."

"It's so strange." She hesitated, wondering if she could speak honestly. Deciding she had nothing left to lose she continued. "I feel like I'm not quite synched up yet. It's taking a while, and sometimes it scares me. The feeling catches me off guard, and suddenly I'm not sure where or when or who I am. I relive some of what happened and reality slips away for a while. It's a relief to hear you felt that way too, even for a short time. It feels kind of like I'm losing it when that happens. I try so hard to hang on to the present, but his face slips in between me and what I'm looking at or doing, at the oddest moments, and I'm paralyzed. Sometimes it's his face, sometimes I relive the violence. I only recently remembered the whole thing. Up until then, it was just fragments."

She stared out the window, leaned against the door, and held the labyrinth necklace absently as she spoke. Jesse reached over and took her hand, causing her to jump. She recovered, looked over at him, and smiled wanly. "I didn't mean to bring this all up, either, but I guess I'm ready to admit that something rotten happened to me, and I'm ready to get over it. Talking about it might help, but I'm not sure."

"You know I'm here. I want to hear everything. There's been a wall between us since this happened. I understand why, but I think you're right, talking about it will help."

"There's things from before, with him, that I can't talk about. They're such a big part of what happened. You only have half the picture, but I can't let myself go there. I can't forgive myself for ever caring about him."

"Forgiving yourself is the first step. You have to know it wasn't your fault. Any of it."

"I know, theoretically, but it doesn't help. I was so stupid. All the stuff in the tabloids, the stuff that sounded too stupid to be true, is *all* true. I'm disgusted with myself. Before the attack, I had deluded myself into thinking that I could start over, that I deserved to start over. With you." Her voice was almost a whisper.

"It means everything to me to hear you say you wanted to start over with me. Now that he's in jail, you can start over. We can be free of him and the negativity he infected your life with. You do deserve to start over. Clean slate."

"There is no such thing in Hollywood, and there is no such thing in real life. We move on, but we don't start over."

"Plenty of people start over," Jesse said with authority in his voice.

"Yeah, like who?"

Jesse swallowed. "Like my mother," he replied. "She had the courage to leave town, to travel with her son across the country, and to make a new life for herself. She succeeded. She is happy, you know. She has a meaningful life and great friends. She's even dating someone. She moved on, but she started over as well. She reinvented herself as the strong, independent woman she had always been before my stepfather got a hold of her."

Aliza thought for a long while about what Jesse said. His mom sounded like an amazing woman. "I don't know if I have that kind of courage," she said quietly.

"Of course, you do." Jesse squeezed her hand.

They drove on for a while, listening to the music. They both started singing to "Rock the Casbah" at the same time, and it made them laugh, which in turn upped the mood of the journey significantly.

They arrived at Marblehead late in the day and slowly made their way through the narrow, winding streets. Eagerly, Aliza sat up and took everything in. With the windows down, they breathed the sea air deeply. "I see what you mean about the smell. It's phenomenal," she said smiling.

"It is very distinctive."

The storefronts lining the main street were antique but full of fashionable boutiques and artist's galleries. Every building and street lamp was covered in stars and stripes bunting for Independence Day, lending a quaint feel to the small downtown. They headed south with the ocean on their left. They drove past colonial houses and ancient graveyards, until they reached a quiet residential street. The view of the water beyond was commanding. Aliza was nervous when they pulled up to a quaint, old Victorian home, well cared for and beautifully painted in blues and greens, like the landscape itself.

"This is it," exclaimed Jesse.

He looks excited, Aliza thought. *He genuinely loves his grandmother.*

They got out, and Aliza took a deep breath, as much to steady her nerves as to smell the fresh, salt air. They grabbed their bags and crunched down a crushed shell path surrounded on both sides by lavender and shrub roses. Clematis vines and climbing roses scrambled over the front porch, the blooms gleamed bright in the afternoon sun.

Jesse's grandmother saw them coming. She rushed from her front door and ran down the steps to meet them with a seemingly endless stream of welcoming words. Aliza's first thought was, she didn't look like a grandma. Charlotte Black had short, curly, steel grey hair and a great tan. She was trim and fit. Her clothes were very current in style, and a broad smile graced her very attractive, exuberant face. She looked at them both happily, hugged Jesse for a long moment before she turned to Aliza.

Aliza's heart beat erratically as she said, "Thank you so much for inviting us to stay, Mrs. Black."

She took hold of Aliza's hands. "So wonderful to meet you. You are even prettier in person than your pictures in all the magazines, my dear, and that's saying something. Welcome to Marblehead, and *please* call me Charlotte. We're all adults, no need for formalities." She kissed Aliza on the cheek and, only releasing one of her hands, led them up the steps and into the house.

It happened so fast Aliza could only mutter, "Thanks." She was overwhelmed, but not uncomfortably so. Charlotte seemed so genuine and so loving, it was impossible to feel anything but contentment in her presence.

"I made Lime Rickeys. Let's put your stuff away and have a refreshing drink on the patio." She led them upstairs to the bedrooms. "I don't know what your sleeping arrangement preferences are. I'll leave it all up to you, but if you want separate rooms, here is one for you, Aliza, and Jesse, you can have your usual. I'll let you get settled and see you downstairs."

She smiled again as she left them in the hallway. As she went downstairs she called, "Oh, Jesse, show Aliza where the bathroom is. I forgot."

"She is so cute," Aliza said. "She has an amazing amount of energy, and she doesn't seem like a grandma."

"That's the truth. The grandmotherly thing shows up in how she takes care of everyone, though. It's not in her physical bearing, more in her heart, if you know what I mean."

"I do. She seems so progressive. She'd let us share a room?"

"Yep."

"We can't. I'd be too embarrassed, but I love that she doesn't mind. Let me put my things away. See you in a minute."

"Wait, let me show you where the bathroom is, or I'll get scolded."

Jesse gave Aliza a brief tour of the upstairs, showing her the bathroom and his childhood room, which he said had changed very little. It was perfect. The faded blue and red calico quilt on the bed, light blue gingham curtains on the windows, and pure white walls with sweet paintings of animals and framed needlework were perfect for a kid's room. That Jesse had never changed it was a testament to his tender heart. Most guys would have torn all that stuff down when they became teenagers. Instead, Jesse seemed to consider it part of the room's history, as well as his own.

The guest room, on the other hand, was all about the sea. It had a view of the ocean Aliza wished she could look at all day long. The walls were the palest shade of robin's egg blue with dazzlingly white trim. The brass bed was painted white and covered in fluffy, white linens. To Aliza's astonishment, there was even a fireplace that appeared to be functional. It was set for the summer with some birch logs, their peeling white paper bark a perfect complement to the rest of the room. Shell-covered frames with pictures of Jesse and Charlotte and a woman Aliza recognized as Jesse's mother, Victoria, decorated the mantle. The bed stand had a milk glass vase with fresh lavender in it, and there was a purity to everything that Aliza found refreshing. The window was open, and a gentle breeze stirred the curtains. *I can heal here.* Immediately her heart felt lighter than it had in months.

A light tap on the door brought Aliza out of her reverie. Framed in the doorway, Jesse stood smiling at her. There was such a resemblance between him and his grandmother that for a moment

Aliza thought she might giggle. In the depths of her imagination, a quippy comment started to surface. It fizzled away before she could fully take hold of it, but the familiar desire to banter with him instilled some hope of recovering her old self.

"This place is perfect," she said instead. She turned to look back out the window. "I can't believe how fresh and beautiful it is. I could live here forever."

"So could I. When Mom and I first left for LA I didn't think I would survive. The colors there are different—too vivid, somehow. The noise is unbelievable, the smog is unbearable, and the people, no offense, were so fake. I hated school, I hated acting, and I just wanted to come back here. After a while, though, I forgot. It wasn't until Twin Falls, and frankly, meeting you, that I was jarred back into a sense of who I used to be, and maybe who I want to be. That's why I was so anxious to show you this place. It's such a part of me and a part I had lost for so long. I'm so glad I can share it with you."

"I'm glad, too. There is no place I would rather be right now than right here with you."

They kissed, really kissed, for the first time in ages. The glimmer of attraction rekindled in her as Aliza's spirit grew stronger. She let herself feel the love Jesse had for her, the way love should be.

They eventually found their way downstairs and walked through the large living room into the dining room, which adjoined the kitchen. From there, they went through two open French doors leading out to the patio. The view was breathtaking. Aliza didn't know where to look first. The house was situated high up on a cliff overlooking the sea crashing on rocks below. The yard was not huge but so well planted and private it felt like an oasis. The bluestone patio was set with mismatched antique garden furniture, all painted with glossy white enamel, set under a canopy of white sailcloth.

Charlotte was waiting for them in a cushioned antique glider. Sitting comfortably with her feet tucked under her, she was reading a novel. When she saw them, she hopped up and poured them Lime Rickeys from a crystal pitcher, adorning the drinks with a couple of frilly paper umbrellas. She handed them over with a smile, "Are you both comfortable upstairs? Is there anything you need?"

"It's all perfect, Mrs. Black. Sorry, I mean Charlotte. Thank you so much," Aliza replied earnestly. "You are so kind."

"It's my pleasure. I never get to see my grandson, so this is the best kind of treat. I can't wait to spoil you two rotten. Wait until you see what I have planned for dinner. I made chocolate mousse."

"That's my favorite dessert of all time," Aliza replied with genuine excitement, any trace of her former nervousness dissipating rapidly. "How do you make yours?"

They all sat down and discussed the various methods of making a traditional French-style chocolate mousse. Jesse was visibly happy to be with his grandmother, and it made Aliza smile.

"Your house is incredible," Aliza said after the topic of mousse had been thoroughly discussed. "It's like a dream home. Everything is perfect, from the paint colors to the landscaping. You're a real designer."

"Thank you," Charlotte replied with obvious pleasure. "It's not a house someone like me could afford to buy these days, not in this neighborhood. I couldn't afford it even if my husband was alive, God rest his soul. We bought it in 1966 when we were first married, back when no one wanted to live in a drafty old Victorian by the sea. Imagine that."

"I can't," Aliza said.

"Me, neither. I never understood it. The ranch house was big back then, sprawling places right out of magazines, all on one level. You know the type. Now, suddenly, this property is worth something again. I'm sitting on a few million dollars' worth of history, here, but I wouldn't sell it for anything. I've put so much love and care into the old place, and she deserves it. Franklin, my late husband, and I were always antique buffs. When we were dating, we'd go to garage sales and barn sales where people were practically giving things away because they had a little dust or wear on them. We knew what they were parting with was treasure. We snapped it all up for a song, cleaned it off, and displayed it proudly. People didn't understand.

Back then, they wanted everything to have a modern sensibility, all chrome and Formica. Give me brass or wood any day. That's why these things have all held up, even right next to the salt water like this."

"Everything in LA is made of plastic. It's all a big facade covered in sparkly lights, masking a pretty seedy world underneath." Aliza kind of surprised herself with the vehemence of her description. "Compared to this town, or to Twin Falls even, it is fake. This, on the other hand, feels like a real place. It has history and architecture. It's lovely. I can't imagine living anywhere better."

"Thank you. I'm glad you feel that way. Love at first sight, eh?" Charlotte winked playfully.

Aliza blushed, remembering that with Jesse, it had been love at *second* sight. She hadn't wanted to admit it at the time, but she was thinking more clearly now than she had in ages. As though Jesse could read her thoughts, he took her hand, smiling.

"Speaking of love at first sight, it might sound crazy, but the first moment I saw you, Aliza-I mean really saw you-I think I did fall in love with you," he said. "Of course, I was sleep deprived and had just broken up with my ex-girlfriend, so I didn't *see* you when I first saw you, if you know what I mean."

Aliza turned to Charlotte. "He was terribly rude to me when we first met. He brushed me off thinking I was a lowly set gopher, but he has been a perfect gentleman ever since. I forgave him within 24 hours."

"Jesse, you didn't tell me you had been rude to this dear girl. I thought we brought you up better than that."

"Sorry, Grandma. I won't let it happen again," Jesse said with played-up contrition. "In reality, though, getting out of LA was the best thing that ever happened to me. I think I was starting to lose myself. That kind of rude, dismissive behavior is de rigueur. At first, it seems shocking, but after a while, it rubs off on you. Before you know it, you're not looking waiters in the eye when you order, you're bossing people around, and wearing very expensive jeans. Twin

Falls was a wake-up call, and Aliza was a breath of fresh air, exactly what I needed."

"A kick in your pricy pants, in other words?"

His grandma was more accurate than she could have known. Aliza remembered their first exchanges and smiled. "I gave him a very hard time, at first, but he grew on me."

"I'm so glad," interjected Charlotte. "You are a lovely girl, and it sounds like Jesse here needed someone who could help him be himself again."

"He has also done that for me. It's like together we've been able to find our better natures, however deeply they were hidden. In my case, pretty deep."

"Don't say that, Aliza," Jesse said vehemently. "You have been genuine since I met you."

"I guess that's not what I mean. I mean I've put up some serious walls inside. I'm not usually rude or mean, but I've been out of touch. I was hurting myself for a long time without knowing why. It's all part of what I need to figure out, and for the first time in recent memory, I feel I am thinking clearly about all of it. I think it's this place."

Talking quickly, Aliza wanted to get it all out before she lost the thread of her thoughts. "Charlotte, I don't know how much Jesse has told you about what happened to me, but we might as well be honest from the start. For whatever deep-rooted psychological reasons, I allowed myself to become entangled with a very abusive and cruel man. He abused me, and I allowed it for a long time before I ended our relationship. When I did finally end it, he still wanted to exercise control over me by calling me constantly, texting me, saying terrible things about me to my friends and to the press, and ultimately..." Aliza took a deep breath before continuing, "... ultimately, he tried to kill me, and Jesse stopped him." She had made it through without crying, panicking, or having terrible flashbacks. A sense of strength and pride welled up in her for this small accomplishment.

"Thank you for thinking enough of me to share your

experiences. Jesse had given me the gist of the matter already, but hearing your story brings back some very difficult memories. I'm sure you know about Victoria's experience with Jesse's stepfather."

"Yes, ma'am. He has shared his stories with me. I'm so sorry you all had to go through that."

"Do you think she was stupid for letting herself get involved with such a madman?"

"No!" Aliza was shocked at the question. "Of course not. People misjudge. People make mistakes, and sometimes don't realize until they're in the middle of it."

"Do you think it's because I raised her badly?"

"My goodness, no."

"Those are important points. Victoria was a feisty, strong-willed girl. She was beautiful and kind, but she was lost and needy. She had just lost Jesse's father and that man saw an opportunity to take terrible advantage. He wanted to destroy something pure. He almost did. If she bears any fault, it is having loved him unconditionally, right up to the last. Trust me, she was far from stupid, and her upbringing was as solid as any." She fixed Aliza with a steady, loving gaze. "It's easy to blame yourself. It's easy to blame your upbringing, but who deserves the blame?"

"I don't know. In my case, I should have known better. The blame does rest with me," replied Aliza, starting to lose her composure.

"That is your only mistake. Only one person deserves the blame, my dear, and that is the man who hurt you. *He* is responsible, Aliza. Only him. You are smart. You are beautiful, and you are kind, and those are the qualities he sought to destroy. He is to blame. Not you."

Charlotte stood up and walked over to where Aliza sat trembling slightly. Sitting down on the low patio table so she could face Aliza at eye level, she took Aliza's hands in her own. The contrast was striking, the older woman's skin was sun-darkened, papery and veined, whereas Aliza's was nearly white, and her youth showed in the resilience of her skin.

Aliza looked into Charlotte's grey-blue eyes and found, not the judgment she expected, but tears, kindness, and deep affection. It struck her intensely as tears welled up in her own eyes.

"You have been through the hardest part," Charlotte continued. "Now is the time for letting go, for healing, for forgiving, moving on, but not for forgetting. That is how we grow." She kissed Aliza on the forehead in such a motherly way Aliza reached forward and hugged her, sobbing on her shoulder. "It's okay, my dear. Cry all you need. I'll cry with you. I'll cry for all of the poor girls in this world who have been hurt by such horrible men."

And cry they did.

———

Jesse was astounded and touched, astounded that Aliza had been so open and touched that his grandmother cared so much. For him to sit there unmoved, watching this scene of solidarity, would have been impossible. All the pain of his experiences with his stepfather and Cameron flooded him with sadness. He turned to face the sea. The sky was streaked with pink and purple clouds as the sun receded. The water reflected this riot of colors, scattering and regrouping them as countless waves crested and broke. The sea always calmed him, and this time was no exception. When he faced the women again, they had ended their embrace but were still holding hands. They turned towards him with their tear-streaked faces, so full of the sadness. He felt fortified and resolved not to wallow in his past hurts. He would be strong for Aliza as he had been strong for his mother.

"I love you two very much," he said. "We will get through this. We are strong, happy people, and we can move on with our lives."

At that moment, Aliza's stomach reasserted itself like never before. The growl it made was somehow amplified by the gravity of the moment. This was like the return of a long-lost friend to Jesse and Aliza, who giggled a little.

"Well, I think that says it all," Charlotte said. "Give me ten minutes and dinner will be on the table." With that, she entered the house, leaving Jesse and Aliza still smiling.

They went for a walk to the edge of the cliffs to get a closer look at the ocean. The air had a noticeable nip in it, despite the fact it was July. The breezes coming off the water blew stronger, and Aliza's hair flew around her, making her look like some kind of wild sea-goddess, or so Jesse mused. He put his arm around her when he noticed her shiver.

"I'm okay," she said, although she didn't pull away. "I love the wind, remember? This is some very nice wind." She breathed in deeply. "I wasn't joking. I could live here."

"Maybe we should," Jesse replied absently. "Who needs LA?" As he considered what was at first a flippant remark, it settled into a spot in his mind and took root. After a few moments he asked, "Why not, Aliza? Why shouldn't we live here?"

"What could we do for money?"

"Sign autographs at the coffee shop until people forget who we are."

"Or we could start our own talent agency. For a local market, you know, commercials and stuff."

"Or we could write a tell-all book about why we left Hollywood. It would be a best seller, and we could live off the royalties."

"That's a good idea. It would be so great. We could live next door to your grandma."

"Wait until you taste her cooking, and you'll mean that."

They laughed and hugged, and Jesse felt light enough to be swept away by the ocean breeze.

"Well, who knows how the show will do, anyway. We might be looking for jobs come fall. Most TV shows don't make it to a second season."

"What makes you say that?" Jesse sobered with concern. He liked being on the show and wasn't ready to say goodbye to it.

"It's the truth. Sometimes the characters don't have enough depth, or the plot is too similar to other things that have been done. I don't know, but don't worry. We have a backup plan now."

"The coffee shop autograph business?"
"You know it."


Jesse drove his concern about the show out of his mind. The elation he felt at having what he considered an "old-Aliza" kind of conversation was all consuming. They went in for dinner, hand in hand, smiling and feeling refreshed.

Charlotte served a lavish strawberry and spinach salad with toasted pine nuts and goat cheese. The main dish was slow-roasted beef with a savory pan sauce, sautéed mushrooms with brown butter and fresh sage from her garden, and roasted fingerling potatoes with garlic and fresh herbs.

Aliza ate with much of her old aplomb, never forgetting her manners. The conversation remained light and friendly, as though the dark topics of earlier had already forged a close bond. Aliza seemed totally calm, smiling and laughing easily, absently fingering her labyrinth necklace sometimes, as though it was a talisman. She even offered to do the dishes, a job Jesse knew she despised. She washed, and he dried. By the time they were done the kitchen was spotless.

She mentioned how excited she was about the chocolate mousse no less than four times between the start of dinner and the last of the cleaning. Charlotte couldn't help but laugh when Aliza brought it up again, and she blushed profusely.

"I think it's wonderful. Too many girls your age skip dessert."

"That seems crazy to me. Have the dessert tonight, go running in the morning. It couldn't work out better."

Jesse was astounded at Aliza's mention of running as well. She hadn't run much since the attack, and neither had he.

"That sounds perfect," he interjected. "It's been way too long since I exercised."

Aliza went quiet after his remark, and he instantly regretted referring to her convalescence.

"Is there a powder room down here or should I go upstairs," Aliza said after an awkward moment.

"Down the hall to your right, under the stairs. It's a funny little space, very New England. I'm sure you'll enjoy the novelty." Charlotte pointed the way with a smile.

While Aliza was out of the room, Charlotte turned to face her grandson. "That has got to be one of the sweetest girls on God's green earth, Jesse. What an angel. I like her, in case you were wondering, but her fragility is so familiar. She will get better with time, but it would help her to talk with a counselor."

"I asked Christopher. He agreed that if she comes of her own accord, he will talk with her. I think she will, Gram. She doesn't deny she could use a little help."

The older woman took Jesse's hand and stroked it gently. "Life is hard on some folks, and then there are others who slide on through. I don't get it. I never have, and I've frankly stopped trying. I'll tell you this, my dear, she will be stronger for it, in the end."

Jesse hugged his grandmother tightly, kissed her on the forehead, which was conveniently at chin-level. "I love you, Gram."

"I know, and I love you. I'm so glad you came."

"I am, too. I missed you."

"You missed my cooking. By the way, there are no houses for sale next door. Someday you will be ready to leave the spotlight, Jesse, but don't rush out too soon, not after you've worked so hard to get there."

"You heard us?"

"The windows are wide open, my dear. It was hard not to hear."

"Sometimes I do wonder what I'm doing in Hollywood. I love acting, but I slipped away from my better self for a while. I don't want that place to suck the goodness out of me over time. I'd rather leave while I'm still me."

"You don't have to worry, Jesse. I don't think it will happen again."

"How do you know, Gram?"

"Because now that you are concerned about it, you'll be vigilant.

Besides, that little girl of yours isn't about to let you turn into some jerk."

"No way," Aliza said from the doorway as she returned to the kitchen. "Jesse has watched out for me, and I will watch out for him." She put her arms around Jesse's waist from behind and hugged him.

Jesse turned and hugged her back. "I should have done a better job, you know."

"Not this again, Jesse. Cameron would have come after me no matter what you did. He could have sweet-talked his way through a 24-hour police guard. That's his way. If I have to stop blaming myself, so do you."

"Well said, my dear. It's time for chocolate mousse, anyway. Grab a sweater and let's have dessert out on the patio."

The evening had set in and fairy lights twinkled in the tall hedgerow separating the property from the neighbors. A string of lanterns hanging from poles gave off a soft glow, and Jesse lit candles to keep any mosquitoes away. Aliza and Jesse huddled together on a glider under a throw blanket and Charlotte sat in an old metal rocking chair. They enjoyed their chocolate mousse in reverent silence, the only sounds were the crash of the ocean and the high-pitched tinkle of silver spoons against crystal dishes. Aliza managed to scrape up and eat every bit of mousse.

"That was officially the best dessert in history," Aliza exclaimed when she finally relinquished her bowl. "I had a hard time not licking the bowl clean."

"Seriously, Grandma. You've outdone yourself. Again."

"You're too kind. It was tasty, though. I made some coffee too. Would you like some?"

"Definitely," answered Jesse.

"His body is ninety-eight percent coffee," Aliza said, turning to Charlotte. "He can't survive without it. I'd like some too. Thanks."

"I'll go get it," said Jesse, taking the dirty dishes with him back into the house.

"I blame myself," said Charlotte. "When he was a little thing, I used to sit him on my lap and let him have sips of my coffee when his mother wasn't looking."

"So funny."

"He'd get all wired and run around like a crazy person for a while and then he'd crash. I got such a big kick out of it. He was such a cute little boy. I'll have to dig out the albums while you're here. Embarrass him a little."

"I'd like to see them," Aliza said earnestly. "I bet he was the sweetest little person. He still is."

"I'm glad you think so."

"I do. I told myself after I left Cameron, I wouldn't rely on another guy again, but Jesse wants to take care of me rather than make me think I need him. It's not the bad kind of dependence, I don't think. I fought it for a while, though, before I realized the distinction."

"It's wise of you to understand that at such a young age. Many people don't."

"Many people are unhappy, too," replied Aliza pensively. "I am tired of being unhappy. I don't know exactly how, but I think that is my new quest. I'm going to strive for happiness."

"I can't think of a worthier goal, save one."

"What's that?"

"Love," replied Charlotte. "Only love. Love is the root of all happiness. Striving for love in all you do begins with learning to love yourself, assets and faults alike. If you love openly and with abandon, something starts to happen in your life."

"What do you mean?"

"Your heart opens up to all the good of the world. It's like a channel to God, I guess. You find you're able to deal with the negative things life throws at you more gracefully. You become a cornerstone for the people in your life. You throw down roots and reach to the sky all at once."

"Sounds like inner peace is what you're talking about," Aliza said wistfully.

"I am, and from peace springs the happiness you desire. Let me ask you this, what makes people happy, Aliza?"

"Not money and not fame, that's for sure."

"No. Definitely not. Although those things can be good sometimes, in the right hands. Love and peace make people happy. Don't forget that. Being right with yourself is being right with the world."

"Right on." Jesse came out bearing coffee and smiling. "Are we having a philosophical moment, ladies?"

"Too deep for you, I'm afraid," said his grandmother jokingly.

"Mud puddles are too deep for me, Grandma," Jesse said in return, grinning. He set down the serving tray and handed a cup of coffee to his grandmother and another to Aliza. They served themselves sugar and cream in comfortable silence.

"What a lovely serving set, Charlotte," Aliza said, examining the silver creamer after she had poured her cream. "And the cups are bone china. You have great taste."

"Thank you, my dear. I've always been of the mind that you don't need a huge collection of everything, but the things you do have can be spectacular. The silver is early American, and the china is from England. When you're finished with the coffee, hold the cup up to the light and look through the bottom. There's a surprise."

"So cool," Aliza said, smiling. "Remember our plan for the Good Quality Revolution, Jesse?"

"I do. That was right after we first met. We were eating in this cute little place in Twin Falls and decided we're done with crappy plastic stuff. We demand more."

"Why not?" Charlotte interjected. "It's like we've unlearned centuries of craftsmanship in under fifty years."

"I know. My uncles built my grandmother's house, back in the 1950s. Who would know how to build a house these days? Even the people who build houses for a living do a crappy job compared to someplace like this." Aliza gestured to the darkened Victorian facade. "Nothing compares. It makes me want to make things," she said with finality, absently holding onto her necklace with one hand and her coffee cup with the other.

"What would you make?" Jesse asked.

"I don't know. I've been wondering about it. I don't think I'm a woodworker at heart, and ceramics are too breakable for me to deal with. Maybe metals. I guess jewelry would be great to make. It's fine, detailed work with elements from the earth itself. Like my necklace. Did you see this Charlotte? Jesse got it for me for our one-month anniversary. It is amazing how one object can take on such significance in your life. I find myself holding it or touching it often, most of the time without thinking. It always helps me center again, or at least it makes me feel a little better. The jeweler told Jesse that the necklace was meant for me, and that every piece she creates has a specific owner out there somewhere."

Charlotte studied the necklace. She held it in a stream of light coming from the kitchen window behind her. She felt the smooth stone, and the satiny metal, and then she turned it over. "It is very fine workmanship indeed. This is a beautiful object. Tell me the significance of the design on the back. It looks like a maze."

"It is." Aliza explained the labyrinth. "I'm still searching for my center, but I know it's there."

As they carried their dishes inside, Aliza remembered that Charlotte had told her to hold the cup up to the light. After she rinsed it out she held it up, curious to discover its hidden secret. Carved into the porcelain was a portrait of a beautiful young girl. The china was so thin and delicate Aliza was amazed it held together. "That is so cool," Aliza murmured.

"It's called lithophane china. I couldn't believe I found the whole set at a garage sale for a song. I don't know what made me hold them up to the light, just instinct, I guess. I was very excited. So was Franklin."

"I can see why. They are unique."

Jesse yawned, and his grandmother, in a very protective and motherly way, informed them that it was time they all went to sleep. No one argued. It had been a very long day.

Jesse and Aliza brushed their teeth together, and Jesse came into her room to say good night. They lay in each other's arms for a little while, reluctant to relinquish the happiest day they had had in recent memory to sleep.

"Did I ever tell you about Karen McDonald?" Jesse said after a few moments.

"Ex-girlfriend?" Aliza suggested impishly.

"No. Jeweler. She's the person who made your necklace."

"Right, I'd forgotten her name."

"Your idea about wanting to make jewelry reminded me of what she told me when I bought the necklace. She said once you master the art of metalsmithing, it becomes like an act of meditation. You lose all sense of time and place, and it frees your mind of-how did she put it-all the garbage. I hadn't given much thought to those words until tonight."

"I'm serious about it. I think I'd like to learn."

"Maybe she would teach you. She's very cool. You guys would get along, I know it."

"Maybe I'll go see her when we get back to Twin Falls."

"You should. I bet she'd like that."

"What do you want to make?" Aliza's eyes were starting to close, and her breathing was getting deeper.

Before she nodded off she heard Jesse say, "I want to make people happy."

"You already do," she whispered.

He kissed her on the forehead and left the room as she fell into the waiting arms of sleep.

# TWELVE

*In order for this little shell or egg shape to be a pendant, it must have a bail for the chain to go through. The jeweler fabricates a small, flattened circle. She solders it closed and then solders it to the back half of the shell. The jeweler files down the extra solder. She is almost ready to polish, and she is antsy to do so. She pickles the piece for a while until the silver reclaims the color of the full moon in winter.*

Aliza's sleep was not dreamless, but it was certainly deep. Her thoughts swirled from face to face and from time to time. Memories of her earliest childhood mixed together in a bizarre alchemy with movies she had been in, the recent events with Cameron fought with fantasies she had harbored silently in her heart.

The most vivid of her dreams, and the one she remembered the most clearly in the morning, had to do with the drowning child at the gorge. The colors were over-saturated, the midday sun flooding everything with intense light. Aliza felt the sickening realization that the boy was not with his family. She ran to the edge of the eddying pool, spotting his lifeless form she dove into that frigid water only to be caught in a swift current pulling her away from him. She swam as hard as she could, gasping for air, spray from the white water stinging her eyes. Rocks scraped against her skin and the current pulled her farther and farther away from saving him. Jesse dragged her out of the undertow as she gasped for air. She fought him, screaming, to let her back in the water to help the boy.

"It's too late," he said over and over, holding her with a binding grip. "It's too late."

Aliza woke up gasping for air as though she had been underwater. Disconcerted by her surroundings, she whimpered aloud. She tried to catch her breath, but her heart felt like it would dive through her chest. As the realization of her location came into focus, Aliza desperately tried to master her fear. The image of Natalie Anders' face came to her mind, but instead of the woman's grief or fear or panic, Aliza focused on Natalie's gratitude. *I saved her son. He's okay.* Aliza repeated these words to herself. *This was a dream. The little boy lived. He is okay.*

Her breathing finally normalized and her racing heart calmed down. From the quality of the light, she guessed it was just before dawn. She couldn't imagine going back to sleep with so much adrenaline coursing through her body. She put on the same clothes she had worn the day before, crept quietly downstairs, and out the back door. Somehow, she was not surprised to find it unlocked. She loved the trust people had in each other in a small town.

The early morning air was very cold, even though it was summer. It was so wildly unlike LA, Aliza thought she might as well be in a different country all together. She breathed in the salty scent of the sea and the sweetness of the hedge roses. She shivered, but it felt so good to be awake and in this magical place. Feeling lighter and freer than she had since she was a kid, Aliza twirled across the dewy grass. She laughed a little at her own capriciousness, then laughed at the fact that she had laughed aloud. Before long, she was frolicking in the predawn light and scampering along the jagged rocks at the water's edge. The incessant crashing of the waves drowned out the sound of her laughter.

The happiness asserting itself in her, she realized, was all because of that terrifying dream. Now, as she stood staring at the glowing horizon, waiting breathlessly for the sun to make its grand appearance, she understood that the dream was meaningless. She had saved the child's life, no ifs, ands, or buts about it. She had delivered that sopping, sputtering child to his parents alive and, although she hadn't appreciated the gravity of it at the time, only wanting to dry off and get warm, it had rooted in her mind somewhere and was now flowering into the most spectacular sensation. She, Aliza Bennett, broken and misused, insecure and fragile, strong and feisty, unique in all humanity, had saved another person's life, and in doing so, had saved a family from terrible tragedy. She had given this little boy a chance to become something great someday. *Maybe he'll find a cure for cancer. Maybe he will be a president, or fix global warming, or crusade against domestic violence. Whatever happens, he has a chance to become whatever he wants.*

Then a miraculous thing happened. Aliza realized she, too, could be whatever she wanted. *I am that child. I survived, and I can grow up to be whatever I want to be. Do I want to find a cure for cancer? I've always sucked at science. Do I want to be president? No. Too much pressure. Do I want to be an actress anymore? It's never brought me much happiness, but I am good at it. What do I want? I want to live right here and make jewelry. Simple and perfect. That's what I want.*

The sun broke free and blazed over the ocean, its light glittering and dancing on the waves in a spectacle of oranges, pinks, and blues. It was the happiest sight Aliza had ever seen. She sat down on a rock and watched the ever-changing light show. She even spotted a dolphin or a seal splashing in the water a few hundred yards from shore. It was delightful. She had found the way to her center, and now she wanted to hunker down and dig her heels in and never ever leave. So many things must be done before she could be a jewelry maker living in the relative obscurity of a tiny Massachusetts town, though. She would need a plan, but she could deal with that later. She wanted to relish this spectacular moment in the now.

She stood up and hopped along the rocks towards a pebble beach she'd spotted. Before long, she had taken off her shoes and socks, rolled up her jeans, and waded in the frigid water. The tide was receding, leaving a clear delineation between wet and dry. The pebbles were smooth beneath her feet, and she found herself studying them as she walked, their colors more varied than she would have assumed. She put a few of the special ones in her pocket. As she stooped to examine one, something greenish caught her eye. Closer examination revealed a smooth, almost velvety piece of sea-tumbled glass. Brushing the grains of sand from the glass, she held it to the light and studied it, realizing at once that this was no ordinary object. Indeed, it was part of an antique, mold-blown bottle. Aliza stared in disbelief at this rare gift from the sea. Tears came to her eyes as she accepted it with gratitude.

# THIRTEEN

*The jeweler polishes the outside of her work with special care. She works from a fine grit to an ultra-fine grit up to a polish. The surface shines like a mirror. There are only a few tiny scars to buff out because she has been extremely careful. When the pieces gleam and shine, she adds the wire to the inside of the knuckles, finishing the hinge. She tests it out for a while, enjoying the satisfying sound the clasp makes when the two halves meet.*

Jesse woke to a sweet ocean breeze and the light of early morning streaming in through his childhood curtains. It was wonderful to wake up in a place he loved as much as this. It was like a great gift he could enjoy all day. He stretched and lounged in his bed for a while until the lure of a good cup of coffee was finally too much. His grandma always put the coffee maker on a timer in the morning, and he was ready to drink at least half of that first pot by himself.

Putting on his robe, he tiptoed out of his room, and crept down the hall. As he passed Aliza's door, he noticed it was ajar. He couldn't resist a glimpse of her lovely face in perfect repose. He was startled to find she was not in her bed. Nor, upon further observation, was she in the room at all. He continued his search through the house finding only the French doors out to the patio slightly ajar. *Has she gone for a walk to see the sunrise?* It seemed unlikely. She liked to sleep in a little when she could. Still, it was possible. If that was the case, maybe she'd like some time alone. Unsure how to proceed, he was standing in the open doorway when his grandma found him.

"Taking the sea air?" she said with her characteristic good humor.

"I'm wondering where Aliza is," he replied. He faced back into the kitchen and noticed his grandmother was pouring two cups of coffee. He took it as a sign he should give Aliza some space and pulled the door closed behind him as he came back into the kitchen.

His grandmother handed him one of the oversized coffee mugs, so different from the delicate china they had indulged in the previous night.

"These mugs are cool," he said, trying to mask his obvious concern over Aliza's whereabouts.

"She's fine, Jesse. I saw her from my balcony just now. She's on Pebble Beach looking at the rocks. She had her socks and shoes off."

Jesse smiled. It was a good sign. "I didn't ask, Grandma."

"No, but you were wondering. The mugs are from a local potter. I liked the fact you could fit nearly half a pot of coffee in each one. Seemed better than going back and forth over and over all morning."

"Very practical. I like the glaze."

"So do I. Silvery tones on an orange background. Who would have thought. I guess it's from taking all the oxygen out of the kiln when they fire it, although I know very little about pottery. It's called a reduction firing."

"Cool," Jesse responded, holding the rounded mug with both hands to absorb its warmth.

"Yes. Very cool," his Grandmother replied, winking at him. "Come sit with me in the sunroom."

"Okay."

They went through the living room and into the sunroom, where windows on three sides let in loads of light. Charlotte's house plants seemed to appreciate it. A morning sea breeze floated in through the open windows, so Charlotte sat on the couch and pulled a throw blanket over her knees. "There's plenty to share," she said, gesturing to the blanket.

"Thanks, Gram. Don't mind if I do." Like a little kid, Jesse snuggled under the blanket with his grandma.

"How have you been, my dear?"

"Life is more complicated than I ever imagined, but I love it. I've wanted to visit you for ages, you know. Sorry it took us so long to get here."

"It's not like you've been sitting around drinking martinis by the pool. You've had a lot on your plate these past few months, Jesse. I understand."

"I know you do, Grandma. Thank you. How have you been? What's new?"

"Christopher asked me to marry him."

"What?" Jesse's reaction startled her, almost spilling her coffee. "Oh, sorry. I'm so excited for you."

"I haven't said yes."

"Oh." Jesse was surprised by her response. He loved Christopher and couldn't imagine why his grandma would hesitate. "Is everything all right between you?"

"Yes. Of course, it is. We've never been happier together, but I don't know. I'm not in my twenties. I don't need a wedding to tell me I love another person."

"That's not the whole point," Jesse responded. "He's got to make an honest woman out of you. It's about time."

She turned to face him with a stunned expression, her mouth open. He was smiling broadly. "You think you're funny, Jesse. You really do."

"No, Gram. I know it, but that's beside the point. Why on earth don't you just say yes?"

"Why? So, I can decide whether to make him move or move myself to his place? I can't leave this house." She got a little choked up. "I think Franklin would understand I've moved on, but somehow this place has kept us connected, even beyond death, if you understand me. However, leaving it? I can't bear the thought of leaving it and certainly not of selling it. It would feel so wrong."

"Sell it to me," Jesse said impulsively. "I love this place. This is my true home. I think you only ever know that once you leave a place and then return to it. When I drove up, I was overwhelmed with the desire to be here for the rest of my life. That way Grandpa's legacy lives on, you can visit any time you like, and we'll be neighbors. It's not a big town. Besides, Christopher's house is amazing."

"Yes, it is. I don't know, Jesse. Let me think about it. You're too young to know what you want. Besides, a house is a big responsibility."

"I know it is, but it's one I'm ready to assume."

"I couldn't sell it to you."

"Why not?" Jesse demanded, indignant.

"I would just give it to you. You're my grandson. I would have willed it to you, anyway. This way, I'd get to see you enjoy it."

"Sounds like you're coming closer to a decision."

"Don't you pressure me, young man." They both laughed.

"I'm glad Christopher asked you to marry him. You're good for each other. Besides, marriage is not only for young people anymore," Jesse said, winking at her.

"Thanks for the tip," she said sarcastically, rolling her eyes.

———

Aliza made her way back into the house. Finding Jesse and Charlotte in the sunroom, she bounded in with a huge smile, windswept hair, and a palm full of sea glass.

"You look like a little kid who was told school is cancelled for the rest of the year," Charlotte said to her.

"I hope I'm not interrupting," Aliza said.

"Of course not. Now, what did you find?"

"It's so pretty. I've never seen anything like it. What is it? I mean, it's obviously glass, but, why does it look like this?"

"It's sea glass," Jesse answered. "For hundreds of years, people dumped their garbage into the ocean, and the glass would break and then get tumbled against sand and rocks on the ocean floor. Sea glass is the result. It washes up on beaches after storms."

"That is so cool. How come I've never heard of it before?"

"I don't know. Maybe they don't have it out West."

"I've been collecting sea glass for many years," Charlotte said. "I'll show you my collection later if you'd like. Now let's see what you've found."

Aliza spilled out the colorful bits of glass onto the coffee table. They shone in the morning light like a fragmented rainbow, colors ranging from deep green and aqua to purple and brown. They tinkled as the three observers moved the pieces around on the table. Each picked up a piece to examine more closely now and then, and Charlotte described the types of vessels that each used to be.

Aliza had never been more fascinated. "These would make a great pendant together, don't you think?" She held up a large, oblong piece of aqua and a smaller, rounded bit of pale purple. "Can you make them into jewelry?"

"Yes, of course," Charlotte said. "Lots of jewelers around here use sea glass in their work. Some of it is better than others, mind you, but I've seen some gorgeous pieces with silver edging, made so you can still see through the glass."

"Like a frame."

"Yes, and it works very well, visually. You can also drill tiny holes in the glass and use it like beads."

"I love it. Where can I find some more?"

"How about breakfast first," Jesse suggested. "I'm too hungry for words."

"Eggs, then a true sea glass hunt. Sounds like a plan for the day," Charlotte responded, looking happy. "Maybe I'll call Christopher and see if he'd like to join us." She winked at Jesse. He beamed back at her as she left the room.

Aliza played with her new-found treasure, thinking about how such a violent process as broken glass scraping against stones for a hundred years could produce something so beautiful. *I guess that's how a lot of beautiful things are made. Glass is made through intense heat, diamonds are made through intense pressure. What will I become?*

Eventually, Aliza noticed Jesse watching her. "Hi," she said happily. "Sorry, I've been a little absorbed by this glass. It's so fascinating."

"People get obsessed with it around here. Wait until you see Grandma's collection. You look really happy, by the way."

"I am. I woke up in the strangest way, not knowing where I was. It was like I had passed out of my old life somehow in the night, then woke with the sound of the ocean and the fluttering curtains in the pre-dawn light. I felt renewed, I guess. I left the house and played around on the rocks for a while and watched the sunrise. Then I found this stuff."

"Sounds like the perfect morning."

"It is now," she said, smiling shyly at him. She stood, sat on his lap, and kissed him, giving herself over to the intense attraction she had buried deeply for so long. After a long series of kisses, she put her forehead against his. "Thank you for being patient with me."

"You don't need to thank me," he replied earnestly, looking into her eyes.

"Yes, I do," she said quietly. "Not many people would have stuck by me during all of this, but I appreciate it more than I can say."

"Aliza." He paused, taking her face in his hand and gazing into her eyes. "I love you. I have loved you from the very beginning."

She swallowed hard, her mouth feeling suddenly very dry. She mustered the courage to answer. "I love you, too, Jesse."

———

The sea glass hunt was very productive. Although Christopher couldn't join them for their beach walk, he asked them over for dinner. Aliza was nervous about meeting him. She had been feeling so much more like her old self since her arrival in Marblehead that she had quite forgotten she'd promised Jesse she would speak with Christopher about her troubles. Anxiety curdled her stomach whenever she thought about meeting Christopher.

Being at the water's edge searching for bits of colored glass distracted her for long stretches, but then anxiety would sneak up on her. A dark and queasy feeling would pass through her for a moment. The very fact she was having such a difficult time mastering her emotions told her she still needed counseling. She tried not to resent the realization because she wanted to be truly well.

When they arrived at Christopher's that evening, Aliza's first thought was holy crap. The facade greeting them as they strode up the path was like something out of *Architectural Digest*. It was very modern, but not ugly modern. The house seemed to be made primarily of glass, and you could see all the way through it at a few points to the sea beyond. The grounds were well-manicured but not that chemical-green Aliza hated. It all had a sort of relaxed yet luxurious feel, and Aliza entirely forgot her fear.

Christopher opened the front door before they were even on the wide granite stoop, greeting them with a warm smile. He hugged and kissed Charlotte and then hugged Jesse, all with enthusiastic words of greeting. Then he turned to face Aliza.

"Ms. Bennett. A true pleasure. I've seen your work, and it is great. You're a very talented actress." He held out his hand to shake hers.

She took it and smiled demurely. "Thank you so much, Dr. Mason, but please call me Aliza."

He smiled. "Thank you, Aliza, and please, call me Christopher. Welcome to my home."

"It's incredible." Aliza spoke before she could stop herself. "The architect who built this place understood how to incorporate the surroundings without making the building feel intrusive. It must be all the glass."

"I worked very closely with her to design every aspect of this place. It was a real labor of love. She thought I was crazy when we first started our collaboration. Some of my suggestions were a little off the wall, but I'm thrilled with how it turned out."

"They used local materials where they could, too." Jesse's animated explanation tickled Aliza. "I'm a big fan of the ocean pebble floor in the master bathroom."

Christopher gave them a tour of the house. Everywhere Aliza found examples of good craftsmanship gleaming back at her.

"This banister was carved by a local shipbuilder. There was so little demand for his skills during his later years that he switched over to custom work like this. I think he did a remarkable job."

Aliza examined the satiny, serpentine banister. "It's exquisite. Everything is so well made. This house, and everything in it, represents the lost art of craftsmanship, but with a modern sensibility. The stonework, the woodwork, even the paintings are lovely."

She was drawn to one painting in particular hanging above the stone fireplace, a modern landscape, full of active, thick brush strokes, without the amateurish quality so many paintings in that style seemed to have. The colors were balanced and realistic. Warm light drenched the canvas, and the waves seemed playful.

"Thank you. You have a discerning eye, Aliza. The paintings are very contemporary, but they have more artistic merit than a lot of work I see lately. This artist is local as well, and I love how the scenes mirror what you see out of the windows. I framed them simply, so it's almost a deception if you aren't paying attention. That, however, I do not perceive to be one of your flaws. You notice everything."

Aliza blushed, looking down, her hair falling across her face. Suddenly, she felt very young and very exposed.

Christopher must have noticed her unease, for he changed the subject and led them into a wide-open room with high windows on three sides and a step down onto a flag stone floor. It was set with very comfortable looking furniture and a breathtaking view of the ocean beyond. Forgetting her unease, she moved to the open French doors leading out onto a patio made of the same stone and overlooking a yard lined with lush blue hydrangeas. Lavender edged the patio, and steppingstones led out to the cliffs beyond. The bird feeders were full of tiny golden birds, and butterflies swirled through the air over the lavender. *Wow, this is incredible. I can't believe what a draw this ocean seems to have on me. Every time I see it, I want to jump in. I'll bet it's cold, though.*

Jesse broke her reverie a few moments later. He came up and put his arm around her. She started, not having heard him approach, then she felt bad she was so jumpy. "Sorry, I'm just absorbed with the view."

"It's great, isn't it?"

"It is great. I'd live here. Although I still prefer your grandmother's house. You know I like the old places better."

Jesse squeezed her to him in a way that seemed to contain a lot of emotion. Then he kissed her on the head.

Jesse's grandmother entered the room carrying a tray of appetizers, followed by Christopher who was carrying a bottle of champagne in one hand and a tray of flutes in the other. Both wore enormous smiles. Aliza looked at Jesse who was looking quizzically at his grandmother. His expression changed into a wide grin. "Really?"

Aliza was still in the dark but judging from the excited smiles on Christopher and Charlotte's faces, she could see there was something major happening.

"Really," Charlotte replied, looking like an overjoyed child. She hugged Jesse with exuberance.

"I'm missing something," Aliza said.

"Not for long," Christopher replied, pouring champagne into the glasses. He handed them out. "I would like to make a toast to the most wonderful woman I know. Charlotte has finally agreed to marry me. I am the luckiest man in the world. To love." He raised his glass, and everyone followed.

"To love."

A deluge of congratulations followed.

Jesse proposed another toast. "I have seldom known a more wonderful couple. Christopher, I am glad you asked her to marry you. Grandma, I'm so glad you said yes. Here's to following what makes you happy."

"Here, here."

Aliza was elated and totally surprised by this news. Although she had only known Charlotte for one day and Christopher for under an hour, she already felt like they were a part of her family. She hugged Charlotte, whose eyes were teary. "I'm so happy for you."

"Thank you," Charlotte replied. "I've been torturing him for a while."

"It's true," Christopher said. "I was not expecting this tonight. What did you say to her, Jesse?"

"Grandmother-grandson privilege prevents me from disclosing such information, I'm afraid." Jesse winked at his grandmother, and she beamed back.

"You've always been a good boy. Christopher, I've finally said yes. Isn't that enough?"

"Never. I have a naturally curious mind. For weeks I think you're going to tell me to take a hike, then suddenly we're engaged. I must ask why. Of course, it hardly matters. The answer is the one I've wanted. I suppose I should let it rest."

"Yes, you should. Now I want to try one of these lovely appetizers we've been ignoring. Your cooking, by the way, is why I've consented to marry you. I will be working up a contract for you to sign that says you'll cook me at least three top-of-the-line meals a week."

"You have my word. I will be your private chef, on call 24 hours a day, my dear."

Aliza watched this exchange feeling giddy. *They're so comfortable with each other and with themselves. It's wonderful to see. They're so real, so genuine. That is what I want to be.* She took Jesse's hand in hers and leaned her head on his shoulder, content.

Christopher, as it turned out, was a fantastic cook. Aliza was impressed. They ate their meal on the terrace, enjoying the fresh sea breeze and the scenic view in addition to the gourmet meal. He had grilled gigantic scallops wrapped in prosciutto and had made a summery, yet rich, sauce out of caramelized peaches, fresh ginger, and bourbon to top them. The jasmine rice was fragrant and fluffy, and the grilled asparagus was garnished with crumbled farmer's cheese and garlic infused olive oil. They had a cherry cheesecake for dessert. It was pure bliss.

The conversation was light and friendly all evening. Christopher was very open and seemed interested in everything she and Jesse had to say. It was hard not to like him. Yet, in the back of Aliza's mind, her guard was creeping back up. She knew at some point soon, she would have to face his scrutiny and his judgment, or so she felt, and she was truly dreading it.

Charlotte sent Aliza and Jesse on their way, so she and Christopher could celebrate alone. Blushing at Charlotte's openness, Aliza tried to put the idea out of her head. Their goodbyes were full of exuberant thanks for the wonderful meal and wishes for a pleasant evening. When Jesse and Aliza stepped out of the front door at the end of the evening, she had a sudden burst of giddiness. Her worst fears about Christopher psychoanalyzing her at dinner had been unfounded, and it felt like a narrow escape.

"That was great," she exclaimed, skipping a little. "What now?"

"What do you mean?"

"Let's do something fun. Something a little wild or outrageous."

"What, like go to the Golden Banana?"

"I don't even want to know what that is."

"No, you don't. Believe me."

"I'm serious. I'm feeling reckless. If I had my bike here, we'd be screaming through every tiny town from here to Maine by now."

"Okay, okay. Let me think." Jesse scratched his head in a mock-thinking gesture, and Aliza elbowed him in the ribs. "Ouch. Okay. I've got it. It's a surprise."

They got in the car. The windows were down, and the wind

whipped her hair around. She closed her eyes, faced the rush of fresh air, and smiled.

"What brought on this wild mood, huh?"

She opened her eyes again and watched the landscape speed past. "I don't know. Like I said, I feel better here, and to be honest, I half thought Christopher was going to psychoanalyze me at the dinner table. When he didn't, it's like a pall was lifted. I feel great."

"You don't need to talk to him, you know. It was only a suggestion."

"I know. Let's not talk about this right now. I want to feel the wind on my face and not think so much."

"No trouble. It's a perfect night, isn't it?"

"Mmm," Aliza replied, closing her eyes again.

After a short while, they pulled into a deserted parking lot by some train tracks. The quaint, minuscule train station from the 1800s looked more like part of a period movie set than a real building.

"Where are we?" Aliza looked around.

"You'll see."

Jesse led her around some buildings, equally deserted, and down a wooded path that looked unofficial at best. The path through the thicket widened and before them was an expanse of white sand beach. The water glittered in the moonlight and the surf foamed invitingly.

"Oh, so pretty," Aliza said. She kicked off her shoes and walked with Jesse onto the sand. After a few steps, she stopped. "What is that humming?"

"It's the sand."

"What?" She was so surprised, she looked down expecting to see tiny little creatures humming at her.

"Yeah. I've heard it's got a high quartz content so that it hums when you walk on it. The granules rub together and create that sound. It's called Singing Beach."

"That is so cool." Aliza took off running, delighting in the crazy sound the sand made beneath her feet.

Jesse took off after her, only catching her when they had crossed half the length of the beach. He caught her around the middle, lifted her up, and swung her around. She squealed playfully. Aliza kicked her legs, and Jesse finally put her down, only to have Aliza tackle him in a pitiful wrestling move. Before long, they were play-wrestling on the beach, laughing hysterically.

When they were both exhausted, they lay in the cool sand, drenched in sweat and moonlight. Aliza's head rested on Jesse's shoulder. Nestling against him, she was absorbed by the sound of his breathing mixing with the crash of the surf. She wanted more than to lie next to him. She wanted to make love to him, right there on the beach, with the moon as their witness. She wanted to roll around, covered in sand, and let herself be free to love, with her body as well as with her heart, but she couldn't bring herself to allow it yet. As she admitted this to herself, her emotions started to spiral out of control again. She thought she would burst with the intensity of the sadness. Why had Cameron ruined her? Here she was, in the most perfect place with the most perfect man, who happened to love her more than anybody ever had, and she couldn't let herself love him back. She sobbed into Jesse's shirt.

He sat up with her in his arms, pulled her into his lap and rocked her like a child. "Whoa, Aliza. It's going to be okay. You're okay," he whispered.

"No, I'm not okay. I'll never be whole again. All I want is to love you, to give myself to you with complete abandon, and instead I ruin every perfect moment just like Cameron ruined me." She sobbed even harder.

"No one can ruin you, Aliza. You are made of tougher stuff than that."

"I let him do things to me, back when we were dating. Really bad things. I felt so dirty and wrong afterwards, but I *let* him. He didn't force me to. I *let* him. You deserve someone pure and perfect, and flawless and clean, and I'm none of those things anymore."

"I never want to have to tell you this again. I don't care about any of that. I don't care if you guys had sex in front of a room of people or tried every position in the book. It doesn't matter to me. What matters is that you are *you*, Aliza. Nothing, *nothing,* can change that unless you let it. I love you, and you are perfect. This is not Victorian England, Aliza. People have sex all the time. This may shock you," he said, his voice dead serious. "I am not a virgin."

"Jesse," she said, trying to stay serious.

"I know. I should have saved myself for you."

"Are you making fun of me?"

"I am trying to explain this to you using my own body as an example. I'm not ashamed of having been with other women. Why should I be? It sounds like Cameron convinced you to do things that made you uncomfortable. Hell, I'm surprised he didn't film you guys and put it on the internet. That seems like something he'd do."

Aliza laughed a short, non-committal laugh. "Yeah. I guess he's not that creative. He's in the film world and everything."

Jesse laughed. "There. You see? You are *you,* and nothing can change your sense of humor, your bravery, your creativity, your drive, your wit. These are the things that make you *you.* Not your purity. Not your cleanliness, although you do smell like lavender soap most of the time, so that one you don't have to sweat."

Aliza pressed her face against his chest and let herself be held. "For a moment, a little while ago, I wanted very badly to make love to you."

"Now, I've become thoroughly unattractive. I understand."

"You're so silly. I don't know. Every time I start feeling that way about you all the Cameron crap starts getting in the way." She paused, not wanting to say what she knew needed to be said. Finally, mustering the courage she whispered. "Tomorrow, I will talk to Christopher. This has got to stop."

"Good. Very good, my love. I'm so proud of you. See what courage you have?"

"It's not out of courage. It's out of desperation. I want to be me again. While I've been here, I've gotten better and better glimpses of the real me I remember being, like a thick fog lifts, every once in a while, to reveal a rich landscape beneath, but then settles back in.

Maybe now that I know there's hope, that the old me isn't totally lost, I can see how counseling will help. I want it to so badly."

"I have faith. It will help, and you'll be more and more yourself as time goes on."

"Boy, I hope so. I'm getting so sick of this emotional roller coaster I've been dragging you on with me. I want to be able to lay with you in happy, cloudless bliss. No more shadows of the past haunting me every time I feel an ounce of joy."

"You deserve happiness, and now that it's your goal, you can achieve it."

"Are you sure you weren't a cheerleader in high school?"

"You're feeling better already. It takes courage to say that to a guy, by the way."

"You want to see courage? Let's dive into that ice-cold water."

"No. That's not courage. That's insanity."

"Great, now you're calling me crazy."

"That's not what I meant." His tone was tentative and defensive.

"I guess maybe I am. I'll race you to the water. First one with their clothes off wins." With that, she was off, her shirt flying over her head before Jesse could even stand up.

The water was indeed frigid, but they frolicked anyway. Aliza was unabashed to be in front of Jesse without her clothes. It was, after all, not the first time. She recalled standing before him at the gorge and how she'd felt the shame of nudity slip from her like silk, leaving her pale and goose-bumped flesh to breathe in the warm spring air. Now, she was liquid in liquid, a slippery fish at home in its element. She dove into each oncoming wave, surfacing in the darkness of the water, wet skin silver in the moon's glow.

Jesse was beautiful. Her heart raced to see him so near her, his muscular body an invitation she wanted desperately to accept. In the back of her mind she felt a hesitation, the past tugging at her through the new layers of happiness that were forming like the luster on a pearl. She raged against the hesitation, all the guilt, sadness, torment, and self-doubt that it represented, fighting it with her very soul. As Jesse dove under a wave, she followed, her body slippery against his skin. When they resurfaced, they embraced with ferocity and kissed with abandon. The water washed away Aliza's guilt and loss, at least for the time being, and bliss took its place.

Admitting they were half-frozen with no hope of a towel in sight, they left the water. They had scattered their clothes in a shocking radius. Retrieval was a nightmare in the dark. Even with the moon's light, they kept mistaking piles of seaweed for shirts and pants, running over to a dark mound on the sand and finding only smelly detritus, laughing hysterically every time.

When they were eventually re-clothed, still wet and covered in sand, they made their way to the car. Jesse's arm draped over Aliza's shoulder as they walked. Neither of them spoke. Aliza did not want to mar a perfect moment with words. They drove home hand in hand and took a shower together, since Charlotte wasn't home yet. They crawled into Jesse's bed exhausted and content.

Waves and glittering moonlight filled Aliza's dreams, but instead of the idyllic scene she and Jesse had shared earlier, a foreboding, enhanced by the impenetrable darkness of the water, haunted her. Aliza got in anyway but hesitated to dive beneath a wave. It seemed to triple in size and speed as it approached, crashing down upon her with unbelievable force. Underwater and disoriented, a strong undercurrent grasped at her ankles and calves. She struggled to find the surface as she ran out of air.

*This is the end.* All because of her reckless decision to swim in unfamiliar waters at night; all because of her wish to wash away countless past transgressions. That is why she was here, wasn't it? A midnight baptism in frigid waters, a naive attempt to cleanse away the fear, loss, and regret that had become so tangible, like the seawater flooding her lungs.

In the morning, they would find her naked, bloated, fish-bitten body on the shoals, miles from here, and only Jesse would lament her death. The thought of his sadness filled her with remorse, for she had never wanted him to feel sorrow like this. *Can you cry underwater? What happens to the tears? Salt water to salt water, dust to dust.*

Everything cut to black.

Aliza opened her eyes, half-expecting to be in the water, or washed up on some beach somewhere. Instead, she saw Jesse's calm, sleeping face, a sliver of pale morning sunlight streaming through the curtains, highlighting his perfect features. She took a moment to absorb the scene, awash in relief, and thankful that it had only been a dream.

Jesse's chest rose and fell with each breath. His serenity was palpable and contagious. She started breathing deeply, in synch with Jesse. The moments passed out of time. Aliza wanted the image of him in repose, in this perfect place of happiness and peace, to become fixed in her mind. *Why is it only the worst things we remember so vividly later? Why can't it be things like this? I don't want to lose this image. This memory. This instant.*

She strained her mind to preserve the moment in her memory, then she relaxed again and lay watching the face she loved most until Jesse finally stirred. How much time went by, she didn't know. She had viscerally noted the path of a sunny spot as it passed gently over Jesse's features, but didn't try to assess what it meant in terms of the actual time.

Jesse woke to Aliza intently gazing at him. The recognition that she had watched him while he slept glittered across his face as he asked, "Did you get a good look?"

"That's the second time you've caught me staring at you."

"I remember. Any changes?"

"None to speak of, except the slight tan from being outside all day yesterday. I hope Michelle can fix it for you."

"If anyone could, it's Michelle."

"So true."

"Did you sleep well, sweetheart?"

"Yes. Well, no. Weird dreams again."

"Anything you want to share?"

"Not right now, Jesse. I have a feeling I'm going to be sharing a lot with Christopher whenever we can arrange a time. Right now, I'd like to enjoy breathing deeply and looking at you."

"Here I am. Look to your heart's content." He made a very model-esque facial expression.

Aliza giggled. "Did you use that one in your toothpaste commercial?" she asked playfully.

"Cheap shot, and here I was just about to get up and make you some breakfast."

"Sorry. You know I love your face no matter what you do with it."

"Thanks. You're in a feisty mood. That will come in handy."

Aliza knew he was referring to her inevitable meeting with Christopher. The thought of it was like ice water being poured down her spine. Their relaxing moment was over. No more reveling in the early-morning quiet. Real life had burst open the door again, arms full of demands, fears, doubts, and difficulties, dampening Aliza's budding feisty mood.

She wasn't sure what to say. She settled on, "Breakfast sounds good." She kissed him on the forehead, swung her legs over the side of the bed, and was across the room before Jesse could so much as stir. "I think I'll go for a quick run first, if that's okay."

"Enjoy."

She put on her clothes and left, deciding she should continue this day with a clear head, and running always helped that. She was terribly out of shape since the attack. Her rib injury still bothered her a little when she started to push hard on a hill, for instance, but the doctors assured her she could do no further harm. *Why does it still hurt so much, then?* No one seemed able to tell her. She had an eccentric idea that negative energy was lingering in the site of the wound, but how she was supposed to deal with that, she didn't know.

The run made her feel much better. She showered, dressed quickly and met Jesse on the patio. He was reading the local morning paper and The New York Times at the same time. Aliza, for some reason, thought it was funny.

"Are you cross-referencing the local articles against the big boys?" she said playfully.

"Just keeping current. You look happy. The run was good, I take it?"

"Yes. Perfectly refreshing. I love it here. Anything new in the world?"

"Same-old, same-old, I'm afraid. War, ecological disasters, the local softball team lost again, you get the picture."

"I do," Aliza said. "After breakfast, can you call Christopher and see if he has time to see me today?"

"I've already spoken with him."

"What?" The fact that Jesse had done this without talking it over with her first filled her with anger and anxiety. It must have shown on her blazing cheeks.

"Simmer down, Aliza. He called here this morning to say that he had time open if you wanted it. I did not call him. You need to have a little more faith in me than that."

Jesse's reprimand was gentle, but Aliza still felt ashamed for assuming the worst. "Sorry. I guess there's one more thing for him and me to talk about, my unbelievably short fuse."

"It's okay. No worries. You must be hungry after your run. Let me get you some food. I made a very low calorie baked French toast you'll probably hate." He winked at her and headed inside. He turned back for a moment. "Oh, it's at eleven, if you still want to go."

"Thanks," she called halfheartedly.

*Only a few more hours.* Dread crept back into her consciousness and settled right in. Luckily Jesse's French toast was a natural palliative. She felt passably better after two helpings and three cups of coffee.

"He's going to think I'm crazy when I have to go to the bathroom every five minutes during our talk," she stated, pouring out her fourth cup. "But, this is great coffee. I'll make breakfast tomorrow. How about that?"

"Sounds like a perfect plan."

They took off a little before eleven and got to Christopher's office right on time. Jesse entered with Aliza, greeted the secretary, whom he recognized, and sat next to Aliza whose leg bounced up and down.

"Don't be nervous," he whispered encouragingly. "You had dinner with the man last night. You discussed early-American crafts. He likes you. You like him. It will all be okay. Like talking to a friend."

"I know, Jesse. I don't know why I feel like this. My heart is racing."

"Breathe deeply, sweetheart. Muster your courage. You can do it."

The secretary called for Aliza. She jumped a little in her seat then sprang out of it. Jesse stood and kissed her. "I love you."

All Aliza could do was offer back a feeble smile before she turned and faced the inevitable.

Christopher's office was airy and full of light with high ceilings. The windows were floor to ceiling with French doors that led out to a balcony overlooking the sea. There was no leather couch, which was a great relief.

She had pictured a dark, wood-paneled office with a massive desk and the iconic leather couch. Instead, there was no desk in sight, there were two love seat sized couches facing each other over a beautiful, simple mahogany table. The colors in the room were grayed blues and greens, and everything offered an air of serenity. It even smelled good, like lavender. Christopher entered from another door. She noticed now that there were three doors to this room and she wondered why.

"Good morning, Aliza."

"Good morning, Dr. Mason."

"Really? After our lovely conversation last night, you're going to call me Dr. Mason?"

"Sorry. I'm terribly nervous."

"I understand completely. Please, sit down. I wanted to explain something before we talk. As a psychologist, I'm not technically allowed to take you on as a patient. This conversation will be just that—a conversation. I'll let you know if I think you need to see someone else professionally, and I've got a long list of recommendations. I'm going to have a cup of tea. Would you like one?"

"Yes, please." Aliza wasn't sure why she had agreed to the tea. It really wasn't her cup of tea. She laughed to herself at the stupid pun. *Now I look like a real lunatic, sitting here giggling to myself. Lord help me.*

"Something I'm missing?"

"Too silly to share. Sorry."

"Don't apologize. I still, after all these years, think that laughter truly is the best medicine. Many of the people I've seen have lost even their ability to laugh. I am glad to see you have not experienced that terrible fate."

"I've been getting better recently. After the attack, though, well, I felt completely detached from myself. Nothing seemed funny or interesting at all."

"Perfectly natural, after what you've been through."

"Can I ask you a question?"

"Of course. This is a two-way street."

"Why are there three doors in this room? I assume the one you came through leads to your office, and I know the one I came through, but where does that one go?"

"I prefer to have my clients leave from a different direction than the one by which they entered. That way they don't encounter anyone they know in the waiting room as they leave. It is a simple courtesy. I have some high-profile clients who would be embarrassed if others knew they were seeking counseling, although I have never understood the stigma. You'd get help immediately for a broken bone. Much more long-term damage can be done if people don't seek help for problems with their mental state. To that effect, I am glad you're here."

"Thank you for seeing me. I'm ashamed I was hesitant to talk to you. I haven't wanted to admit I need help, but I do. It's like sometimes I feel I'm headed in the right direction, like I've got myself under control and my emotions are mastered. Then something sets me off and before I know it, I've done or said something I regret. Or, there's moments when I hardly even know where I am. Like a break with reality. That's the terrifying thing. It sneaks up on me, and before I know it, I've lost ten minutes of my life. This must all sound wild and crazy."

"Nope. This is totally normal stuff. You are recovering from a trauma. This is called Post Traumatic Stress Disorder, or PTSD for short. You might have heard about it in the news lately. A lot of soldiers return from conflict with it. Those can be sad and severe cases. A lot of the homeless veterans you see have it, and unfortunately the mind is only so pliable. In the most extreme instances, something vital snaps, and they relive the worst moment of their life over and over in perpetuity."

"God, that is so sad."

"It is, and at that level, it becomes hard-wired in the brain and much more difficult to help. You, on the other hand, have a very mild case. Your trauma, although intense, was not sustained over a long length of time. Drugs don't touch this, by the way. The only thing that has been proven to help is counseling."

"Why?"

"We're going to unpack your memories, so to speak, unraveling them one by one, and hanging them out in the light of day. With help, in time, you will be able to retrain your mind to deal with the memories more gracefully. You will feel more at peace with yourself, and you will learn to manage the emotions that spring up without lashing out."

"In other words, we'll break the cycle I'm stuck in."

"Exactly. I anticipate great success, Aliza. You have a strong will and a solid personality, but it will take some hard work and diligence on your part."

"I want to be better so badly, I'm willing to work at it night and day."

"Good. Very good. Then let's start with whatever you want to tell me about your experience. You can include as much or as little detail as you like. You can skip things if you want to, but just like airing out dirty laundry, one piece held back makes the whole batch smelly. Be honest with yourself."

"You're going to think I'm the worst person. That's part of why this is so hard. I am guilty of doing stupid things and of allowing Cameron to manipulate me. I've had a hard time admitting any of this to anyone. I feel so wrong. So contaminated."

"I do not sit here to judge you. That's not my job. I'm here as a friend to help you work through your experiences and to come out the other side a whole and happy person."

"Okay. How much time do you have?"

Christopher smiled. "I have hours. I'm semi-retired, you know. I usually don't work much in the afternoons."

"Are you sure you sure it's okay for me to take up your personal time?"

"It is my pleasure. Besides, you have come a long way, and you don't live here. We have a lot to accomplish in a short amount of time."

"Thank you. Okay. Here goes."

Aliza shared every detail of her relationship with Cameron. She told Christopher how Cameron had manipulated her into being his submissive sex toy, berated her in public, made her feel terrible about herself, and how he'd convinced her she needed him because no one else would want her after what she had done with him. She told Christopher how she had believed Cameron's lies and had thought she loved him. She was honest about the depth of Cameron's depravity and cruelty for the first time. With each detail she revealed a fresh layer of the abuse, not pausing to analyze or lay blame on herself like she ordinarily did. She gave the facts in an unemotional monologue, for some part of her knew she would never make it through if she stopped for breath.

Christopher listened patiently, sometimes looking at her, sometimes shaking his head and looking pensively out the windows. Whether he found solace in the view or simply didn't want to stare at her, Aliza didn't know. When she was finished, she was in a sweat from head to toe. She felt like she had run a hundred miles without stopping. She was even a little out of breath. She looked down and at the tea Christopher had gotten her ages ago, knowing it had gotten cold, and drank it down anyway. Her hand trembled as she replaced the cup on its saucer.

"Thank you for trusting me enough to share your story. I know it wasn't easy. Most people wouldn't have made it through the whole thing without stopping. You are a strong woman. I admire your courage."

"Don't," Aliza said acidly. "It isn't courage. It is the opposite. I didn't want to cry and have to stop and start over and over. I wanted to get it out there. Now what?"

"Now I would like to ask you to do something. It's like a protocol or rules of engagement, however you would like to think of it. This is my only request. Do not berate yourself. Accept a compliment when one is given, trusting that the person who gave it meant it. Do you agree to that?"

"What if I disagree about the compliment?"

"You are entitled to your own opinion, of course. All I ask is that you open your mind and heart to believe that you may appear differently to an objective observer than you do to yourself."

Aliza blushed. Christopher sounded exactly like Jesse. She had always assumed Jesse had been trying to make her feel better about herself and that his compliments were unfounded. Now Christopher was saying the same kinds of things and challenging her, if not to believe them, at least not to negate them outright. "Okay. I can agree to that rule."

"Do you have any rules you would like me to follow as we proceed?"

Aliza considered Christopher. He was not what she had expected which was such a relief. "Yeah, just don't say 'So, how does that make you feel?'"

Christopher looked at her, his eyes widening a little, and she smiled slyly to show she was joking. "Jesse was right. You are a spitfire."

"In all seriousness, I trust you, and I know I need to talk to someone, so, no, no rules. Do what you have to do to help me get better."

Christopher smiled. "That I can agree to." He paused and then, in a German accent spoke. "So, tell me about your mother."

Aliza laughed genuinely, and Christopher joined. He seemed glad that she appreciated his joke. She enjoyed this man's company, if nothing else. He had a lively spirit and a very down to earth sense of humor.

When they had settled down, Christopher spoke again. "It would actually help me to know a little about your family. Sometimes there are clues that provide a window into why you are who you are."

*Who is that? Should I tell him I thought that question? Is it important?* She decided to ask him. "Before we talk about my family, can I ask you a question?"

"Of course."

"Should I say all the things that come to my mind? Like the unbidden commentary the sarcastic *me* always has running alongside my regular thought pattern?"

"Such as?"

"Such as when you said you're looking for clues to help you understand who I am, my sidekick there demanded, 'Who is that?'"

"Right. The internal dialogue. Sure. Share it. Unscrew the filter. Let the whole truth pour out unadulterated. It is all you, after all. The good, the bad, and the otherwise."

"Okay. I guess I'll refer to that little voice as my sidekick, then, if that's okay. It doesn't sound too crazy?"

"Trust me. You don't come close."

Hearing these words from a doctor Aliza was growing to trust and respect was the best news she could have imagined. "Really? Do you mean that? Because for the longest time I have felt like I was going crazy. My emotions are haywire. I have the shortest fuse in history. I can't look in the mirror without experiencing varying degrees of self-loathing. Even my deepest emotions were sort of shut down for a while there, like I was watching myself from across the room. None of this means I'm crazy?"

"PTSD is very different from what I think you're referring to as crazy. Although I admit, that is not a word people in my profession use anymore. The connotations are too reminiscent of Bedlam. We prefer terms like suffering from bipolar disorder, or schizophrenia. They are more specific, less derisive, and they're more PC. However, like I said. You're none of those things, so you're not, as you say, crazy."

"I feel like you've given me part of my life back. I can't tell you how happy that makes me."

"I am glad, but just because you are not suffering from one of the more physical mental illnesses doesn't mean your road to recovery will not be a rigorous one. Part of getting better will include some serious homework in retraining your mind. This kind of thing is not easy, it doesn't come naturally to most people, and if you don't commit yourself wholeheartedly it won't work."

"I intend to work as hard as I can to recover myself. I have to."

"Good. Your family is as good a place to start as any."

"Okay. I grew up in Hollywood, for the most part. Anything before that is hardly memorable at all. From the time I can remember I was always involved in the acting scene. My dad's a writer for TV, and he's done a couple of movies over the years. We would see a lot of famous people all the time, and they all thought I was funny and charming as a little kid. My parents would let me stay up late and hang out at their parties. I guess people got a kick out of me, and I ate it up. I got more attention from these acquaintances than I did from my parents most of the time.

"My parents were mercurial. Sometimes Dad would go into long silences, emerging only to eat, use the bathroom, or sleep. Other times, he'd be so excited about his work he'd talk constantly. His sense of humor is great, and I think it shows up in his writing. As far as being a dad, though, he has never been very available in the typical ways a kid might expect. Same with Mom. She's like two people. In our personal lives she is quiet and has always seemed more like a transparency of a person than a mother. She was indirect, distant and, come to find out, high most of the time. When she had company, though, it's like she was totally engaging, a great conversationalist, and a very funny person. We're even more distant now.

"My grandpa was different from both my parents. He loved me more than anything, and I loved him. I spent a lot of time with him. He taught me everything I know, I think. Everything worth knowing, that is. He encouraged my talent as well. He knew acting was easy for me, and he made sure I wasn't overlooked. We did everything together, and my parents were probably very thankful for that. I didn't get in their way. I still don't.

"Anyway, Grandpa passed away a few years ago." Aliza stopped talking and looked out the windows for a moment.

"You must have been bereft."

"I still am. I admit I haven't gotten over losing him. I think I closed off a little bit of my heart after that. It was too much."

"Was that when you started getting into some trouble?"

"Yeah. You know, it's crazy to have your whole adolescence broadcast in every stupid tabloid, online fan site, and entertainment show. For years, every flaw, every mistake, every poor choice, the whole nation gets to see. You sort of stop caring, and caring is what tethers us to a moral life."

"Well put. I'm sorry you had to go through all that. I wouldn't want every mistake I've ever made read about by millions of people, I know that."

"You tell yourself it's no big thing, that it doesn't matter, but it eats away at you anyway. Before you know it, you're a different person." She hung her head a little bit, and for the first time in front of Christopher, her eyes teared up. "I doubt my sweet grandpa would even recognize me anymore." She tried to hold back the tears, but it had been so long since she'd thought about him, really thought about her love for him, that she couldn't hold back. "He raised me to be so much smarter than I've been," she sobbed. "He would be so disappointed."

"Life is a continuum, Aliza. When you are older, these short years will pale in respect to your life as a whole. The wild transgressions of youth pass into mere reflections in a pool, looked back upon with less and less clarity, as the winds of time ripple the waters."

"Do you write poetry, too?" Aliza said with a little laugh and a genuine smile through her tears.

"Why? Do you think I should?"

"You have a way with words, Christopher. You are an eloquent man."

"Here's a tissue." He handed her a box. "How's that for poetry?"

They both giggled a little, and Aliza wiped her tear-streaked face. "I love him so much."

"Your grandpa?"

"Yeah. He's the only one, until Jesse, that is, who loved me for me. I miss him terribly."

"It sounds like you never let yourself process that loss. How old were you?"

"Sixteen. Old enough to know what I had lost."

"Sixteen is a difficult enough age to manage without losing your best friend and role model."

"Yeah."

"I have your first bit of homework for you, then. Tonight, write a letter to your grandpa. Tell him everything. Open the lines of communication with him again. I'll bet he misses you as much as you miss him."

Aliza burst into tears again. "Do you think so? You don't think he's mad at me or disappointed in me?"

"I can say with complete confidence and some experience, mind you, that he loves you unconditionally. Even from the great beyond. We cannot let our lost loved ones go, you know. I believe that we maintain the connections we forged in love in this life forever. Write him a letter."

"Okay, I will."

"Do you think that's enough for today?"

"Yeah, I do. I'm wiped out," she said, blowing her nose and dabbing her eyes.

"Would tomorrow be too soon to talk again?"

"No. It would be perfect. Do you have the time?"

"Of course, I do. I will see you at eleven again."

"You don't think I need to see someone else?"

"Do you want to?"

"No. I like talking with you. I'm comfortable with you."

"I think we can accomplish a lot together informally, Aliza. You will be okay. I have every confidence in you."

"Thank you, Christopher." Aliza stood to leave. "Thank you so much." She rushed forward and hugged him.

If he was taken aback, he didn't let it show. "It is my honor. See you tomorrow."

Jesse was waiting for Aliza in the cafe down the street, as they had planned. She greeted him wordlessly, with a long embrace. He kissed her on the forehead and hugged her again for good measure.

"Do you want something?"

"Not yet," Aliza said. "I'm still sort of getting my bearings."

"Let me know." He paused and seemed at a loss for words.

"It's okay, Jesse. It all went well."

"You look a little shell-shocked, to be honest."

"That's exactly how I feel. It's like bloodletting, I think. I feel totally drained, but purer, somehow."

"Christopher is good."

"He is good. In all ways. We are all lucky to have him." She paused for a moment. "I promise to tell you everything someday, but I don't have the energy right now."

"I don't expect you to tell me anything, sweetheart. Please know that. Whatever you and Christopher say to each other is between the two of you. You don't have to include me in this process unless you want to."

"Someday I think I'll want to. We'll see."

"Okay. Do you feel like resting or did you want to do something today?"

"It's only twelve-thirty. Let's do something but something relaxing."

"Want to drive up the coast? I can show you a little of Maine. There's a gem of a museum in Portland I know you'd love."

"As long as you have me back by eleven tomorrow. Let's go."

The weather was perfect again, and Jesse got them to the museum in record time. They saw great paintings by Winslow Homer, and Aliza fell in love with one called *Weatherbeaten*. It was something she could stare at for hours. Waves crashed against rocky cliffs, the water was luminous green beneath the crest of white sea spray, all set against a deep gray sky. The water looked as though it could fly off the canvas and soak the viewer.

Aliza asked to see some more of the coast, so Jesse took her to a lighthouse that also looked like it should be in a painting. He told her that in fact, it was in several. She stared out over the sparkling water, wondering about the islands that seemed so close and yet so distant, examining the passing boats, and commenting generally about how much she liked Maine already. "It's the opposite of California in every way," she said.

Jesse agreed.

They ate dinner in Portland, and the food was wonderful. For a city, it was a good sized one, just big enough to have a museum and some great restaurants, while not so big it was overwhelming. She wondered what winters would be like but decided not to ask. Some things were better left undiscussed, and she had a feeling Maine winters were just such a topic. Instead, she reveled in the perfect sunshine of the day and took everything in with a light heart.

They headed back to Marblehead after eight. Aliza was sleepy and content when they returned. Charlotte had brought out her collection of sea glass for Aliza to examine.

"This is quite a collection," Aliza observed, examining the color-coordinated glass jars. "I like how you have them arranged by color. It's like a portable rainbow."

"I know a lot of people who collect sea glass and then put it into wooden shadow boxes. I prefer how the glass containers bring light to the pieces. Light is what makes sea glass special. Each piece interacts with the light in its own way."

Aliza examined the contents of the red jar, which was much smaller than the others. "Not too many of these, I see."

"Nope. Red is the rarest color. I think there was very little red glass, and it was only used for signal lights and such, but every once in a while, you get lucky and find one. Amber is pretty rare, too. Cobalt blue is a little more common, but it's still exciting to find. My favorite, though, rarity aside, has to be the aqua range. I adore them."

Aliza took the jar Charlotte handed her and poured it out on the table. The bits of glass were the calmest of aqua blues. "I think I agree, Charlotte. These are lovely. So serene. Oh." Aliza had suddenly realized why the color was so familiar. "This is what inspired the color of my bedroom upstairs, isn't it?"

"Yes. Like I said, it's my favorite. It's like the glass is part of the ocean itself rather than something manmade."

"Totally," Jesse agreed.

They both smiled at him, Aliza took his hand and kissed the top of it.

"What time is it getting to be," Charlotte asked. "I told Christopher I'd call him, and I don't want to call too late."

Jesse withdrew Aliza's grandfather's watch from his pocket. "It's nine-twenty-five."

The sight of the pocket watch reminded Aliza that she had homework to do. "Do you mind if I go to bed early tonight? Christopher gave me some homework to do, and I think I'll want to go to sleep right afterwards."

"You're not actually asking permission to go to bed, are you?" Jesse joked.

Aliza paused before answering. She looked long and hard at Jesse, who started to look alarmed, like maybe he had said the wrong thing. She smiled. "Politeness. It's all part of the new and improved me." Aliza stood up and noticing how relieved he looked, kissed him. She hugged Charlotte. "Thanks again for sharing your sea glass collection with me. It's lovely."

"My pleasure. Good luck with your homework."

"Thanks. Can I take some paper from the desk in the living room?" She had noticed it earlier.

"Take all you need. Sweet dreams."

Aliza left them, took some paper, a nice pen, and a glass of water. As she brushed her teeth and put her pajamas on, she thought hard about what to say to Grandpa. She wasn't sure where to start or whether the exercise would accomplish anything, but she was committed to getting better and she trusted Christopher's judgment.

She finally sat down to write, stared out the window for a moment at the dark sea beyond, took a deep breath, and wrote.

*Dear Grandpa,*

*I know it's been ages since I've talked to you. I'm so sorry. Hopefully time goes by in a different way for you than it does for me. It seems like a lifetime ago when you held my hand and told me you adored me. I miss you so much, and I hope I told you how much I love you when you were alive.*

*I guess I'm writing this letter because I have confessions to make. I have not been the virtuous and good person I know you raised me to be. For that, I am sorry. I don't know what happened, exactly, and I won't try to make excuses for myself. I hope you are not too disappointed in me, and I hope you still love me. My new friend Christopher says that love is unconditional and transcends death. I hope that's true. Somehow, I feel it might be. You're with me, I know, but maybe I forgot it for a while. I promise, I won't forget again.*

*Let me tell you about what has happened lately. Please don't judge me too harshly.*

Aliza wrote page after page of details, tears stained the paper from time to time. It was after eleven by the time she turned off the light. She was drained and so tired she fell immediately into a dark and dreamless sleep.

———

Jesse basked in the glow of his wonderful day with Aliza. Her mood had improved so dramatically since they had gotten to Marblehead he was simply elated. At the same time, however, he was terrified that this was just another up-cycle on the roller coaster, albeit a longer lasting one. Was the crash coming? Would everything get blown apart again when he said the wrong thing, or something set her off? He could hardly bear to think about that possibility. He would have to wait and see.

Being aware of what he was saying and doing at all times in relation to the human land mine sitting next to him was exhausting. So many things he said had set her off, and he was never sure when his words might trigger her next outburst. He missed being able to interact with Aliza without so much self-editing.

He had faith in her, though, especially now that Christopher was talking with her. If she hadn't agreed to see him, well, Jesse couldn't even bring himself to think of the possibilities. Things might have eventually fallen apart. It broke his heart to consider. Now, maybe she could piece herself back together, and like a broken Ming vase, the scars would be there, but she would be every bit as beautiful, for scars tell stories. Who on this earth was without scars, anyway? Aliza's were just a little deeper than average.

He started analyzing what it meant to be scarred. Even with Aliza's sad and violent history with Cameron, her experience didn't compare with what some people in the world had to deal with. He thought about war and famine and corruption and rape. *Those people were scarred*, he thought sadly. *How on earth do you put yourself back together after living through something like that?* The answer was embedded in the question. *Living through.* If you could live through it, you could live through anything. There must be some terrific strength in that and in knowing you are not alone. *There is a community of suffering in war-torn countries. Maybe what Aliza needs is a community of people who have experienced what she has been through.* Jesse was enticed by the thought. What kind of support groups there were in Twin Falls?

All this thinking got him thirsty. He went to the kitchen and found his grandmother saying goodbye to Christopher on the phone and Jesse thought she looked like a coy teenager.

"Why didn't you go over there to talk? It's like three minutes away. You were on the phone for ages."

"It's like we're dating. We ask each other silly questions and talk about things we'd never dream of discussing in person. It's cute. We don't do it often, but sometimes the space is nice. There's a lot to space. Room to wiggle. Room to stretch. I like space, Jesse. It's why I was so reluctant to say yes to Christopher for so long. I didn't want to lose my space. When I was younger, for a woman, space meant autonomy. I guess it's not like that, anymore. Not with someone like Christopher, anyway. I've had my own identity for so long it's kind of a heartbreaker to suddenly find myself in jeopardy of losing it."

"That would never happen, Gram. Never. You're so, I don't know, so *you*. No one else compares."

"Thank you, dear. You're too sweet. Now, speaking of sweet, I'm going to have a little sorbet. I made it this afternoon, and it should be ready."

"Mmm. What kind is it?"

"Raspberry-Rose."

"What? Why would you eat flowers?"

"Just taste it, Jesse. Then let me know what you think."

She scooped small portions of the sorbet into crystal ice cream dishes and returned the rest to the freezer. Jesse looked at it skeptically.

"Wait," Charlotte added. "I forgot the finishing touch."

From inside a cabinet she pulled out some fancy looking chocolate-dipped cookies. "These were a splurge the other day. I think they'll go well with the flavors. Dig in."

Jesse looked at the livid hot pink sorbet. It smelled like the garden. He looked up at Charlotte who was watching him expectantly.

"Okay. Here goes." He tasted the sorbet and was instantly overcome with excitement. "Oh, seriously. That is so good."

"I know. I got the idea from a little ice cream shop in Paris. I walked around the outside of Notre Dame while I ate a tiny little raspberry rose flavored ice cream cone. Each bite of this is like being back there."

"Let's eat it out on the terrace. That way, raspberry rose will always remind me of sitting with you on the terrace rather than standing in the kitchen."

Charlotte laughed. "Great idea."

They enjoyed their sorbet in the cool evening breeze. The scent of the rugosa roses mixed with the confection, amplifying the *rosiness* of it. Jesse was surprised how enjoyable eating flowers could be. "I had no idea you could eat roses. It's so cool. What other flowers can you eat?"

This sudden interest in flowers, a topic he had never found fascinating before, amused him. Their culinary potential had gripped his imagination.

"There are many poisonous flowers, but there are plenty of edible ones, too. Violets, some orchids, roses, squash blossoms, chive flowers, lavender, anything that grows out of an herb, pretty much. You didn't know?"

"No. This is very cool. I bet they'd be great in salads. They would look fantastic."

"You can crystalize them too," Charlotte added. "Egg white and sugar. It's very simple and they are stunning. The sugar makes them a little sparkly. I'm a big fan."

"I'll bet you are," Jesse said, laughing.

They were quiet for a little while, their spoons tinkling against the crystal as they tried to scrape every last bit of flavor up.

"Can I ask you something, Grandma?"

"Anything, dear."

"I was wondering about what you did to help Mom back when I was a kid when my stepfather was hurting her. How long did it take her to get better?"

"I've been wondering when you'd want to talk about this. I'm surprised it took you this long." Charlotte smiled sadly, looking down at her hands.

Unlike her face, they showed her age. Against her translucent skin, her raised veins looked vulnerable. Jesse felt a surge of deep affection for this woman who had been through so much and had still not forgotten how to love. He took her hand and held it as she continued.

"It was hard for a while. She became very jumpy and short tempered. She would fly off the handle at the slightest thing. I was patient. I kept you with me as much as I could, so you didn't have to see her in that state. It went on for several months, even after he was gone. She finally started talking to other battered women at a special group and eventually she healed. I think moving to LA helped the most. It was a change of scenery, and it helped her start her life over."

"That's what I thought. I think a support group would help Aliza, too, but I don't know."

"She is healing already, Jesse. I can sense that. She is a wonderful person."

"I know, but before we came here, she was a real mess. She would space out, get super angry, say horrible things... I don't know. She is so much more herself since we got here that I never want to leave."

"I understand, but you have responsibilities. Running away is not a choice right now."

"Yeah, but it would be so nice."

"I'm sure it would."

"I'm scared to go back to Twin Falls. I'm scared she'll have a relapse and that all this progress is only a vacation from the real problems. At some point, we'll also have to face the trial against the guy who hurt her. I don't know."

"You are strong and so is Aliza. Be brave, Jesse. It's not over yet, but you've reached a turning point, I think. It's not going to be smooth sailing, but since when has life been smooth? She will still have outbursts, but they will lesson in severity. She remembers who she is again. That is deeply important, and it will help guide her, like her labyrinth. She remembers there's a center and she'll have the faith to find her way there."

"Thank you, Gram." Jesse leaned over and hugged her. She smelled the same as he remembered her smelling when he was a kid. "I've missed you."

"Well, don't wait so damn long to visit next time."

# FOURTEEN

*Sliding her minuscule scroll, upon which is written her mantra word, into the glass phial is very satisfying. She caps it with a tiny cork. She slides the phial into the silver rings inside the pendant, fastening it in place with a discrete dab of glue. The jeweler smiles as she snaps the pendant closed. Choosing a medium length, thick silver chain, she slips it through the bail. She lays her finished work upon a piece of black velvet to examine in the light.*

The next few days went by too fast for Aliza's liking. Her talks with Christopher had seen her through some very rough spots, but on the whole, she felt like a renewed version of herself. Most importantly, she could look at herself in the mirror without turning away in disgust. That was a distinct improvement.

She had also gotten her "sidekick" under control. Christopher was teaching her how to redirect her negative thoughts, how to give them less purchase in her mind.

"If a seed can't take root," he said, "then it is just another bit of matter. Only those with roots blossom into weeds or flowers. It's important to figure out which one it is, before you allow it to settle."

"You should write poetry, Christopher," she responded.

He laughed, as he did the first time she'd said it, but a new expression blossomed on his face, as though he were now taking the idea more seriously.

"I want to keep talking on the phone regularly when you get back to Twin Falls. Being in the place where the attack took place will bring back painful memories of the assault. Do not be afraid to let yourself experience whatever emotions come but let them pass by like water in a stream."

"I'd rather just stay here," Aliza said sadly.

He laughed. "It's a very picturesque little town. Don't worry, Aliza. You're going to be okay. You know, Jesse is probably feeling just as nervous as you are."

"I guess so," she responded. "I hadn't thought about it. I should have. I was very hard to deal with before we left."

"Your healing has come a long way. Have faith."


On their last evening at Charlotte's house, Jesse and Aliza made dinner for her and Christopher. They bought food at the farmer's market and spent the afternoon preparing a meal together. They were natural, happy, and so much themselves that when Aliza thought about it, it suddenly broke the spell. She got quiet, went to the French doors, and looked out at the ocean.

Jesse went over to her and put his arms around her from behind. She turned in his arms and embraced him, tears flowing down her face.

"I don't want this to end. I want to stay here forever. I'm so scared to go back."

Jesse held her close. "I know. I'm scared, too. I don't remember ever being this happy."

"Me, neither," Aliza agreed. "Can't we stay?"

"Someday, sweetheart. Someday."

"I'm going to hold you to that." She laughed a little.

"I would expect nothing less. You know you're going to be fine, right?"

"I do. Christopher has helped so much."

"You know what he would say to that?"

"No."

"That you've helped yourself, that you allowed him to help you help yourself. The power to heal was within you all the time."

"I'm not sure about that."

"Then you've got more work to do. I'm with you, and Christopher is with you, and Gram. We all love you and believe in you. I think you're starting to love and believe in yourself again. Then you'll be truly happy."

"Thanks, Jesse. You're talking like a new-age guru again, but I like it." He frowned at her, and she laughed. They hugged for a minute and then got back to cooking.

They put on a gourmet meal that genuinely impressed Christopher and Charlotte. They'd made fresh mozzarella and basil crostini, roasted pork loin with a blueberry sage sauce and tiny, fingerling potatoes baked with olive oil, parmesan, garlic, and Herbs de Provence. Aliza wanted something simple for dessert, so she made homemade chocolate chip cookies with her family's secret recipe. When Charlotte pressed her to share the recipe, she laughed and said it was on the bag of chocolate chips. Everyone laughed until they were teary as Aliza regaled them with the story of her mother tricking a whole host of movie stars with her "secret" cookie recipe.

"Whoever would have thought a corporate recipe could be so wonderful," Charlotte asked.

"Seriously. They're like Mom's chocolate chip cookies, except my mom never made them," added Christopher.

"That was a great meal, kids. Thank you so much," Charlotte said.

"Ditto," said Christopher.

"We wanted to thank you both for everything," Aliza started. "I can't tell you how much your hospitality and help have meant to me. You have allowed me to regain a sense of myself I thought I'd lost.

Cameron shattered me. He tried to destroy my faith in other people and my love for myself, but even shattered people can be glued back together. Thank you so much."

"You're a wonderful girl. We care very much about you, and I hope you will consider us your East Coast family from now on. You're always welcome here." Charlotte hugged her.

"You know what you need to do from here on out," Christopher added. "Your work will continue, but never be afraid to ask for help. We're here for you. May our new love for you help you find a new love for yourself, because you deserve it."

Tears streamed down Aliza's face, but she was not ashamed. "Thank you so much. I appreciate it."

Jesse leaned over and put his arm around her and held her tight.

She smiled and started to laugh. "No more tears. Let's have a fun last night together."

"Agreed. I'll get another bottle of champagne," Charlotte chirped, hopping off the couch. She kissed Aliza on the head as she walked by and winked at Jesse.

They shared another bottle of wine, played Scrabble on the terrace until they couldn't see their letters by candlelight, and resisted the persistent call of sleep until well past one. They finally straggled off to their rooms, wishing each other a bleary goodnight.

Jesse slept in Aliza's room for the first time since they had gotten to Marblehead. Reluctant to leave her, he didn't even ask. He followed her after they brushed their teeth together. Aliza didn't object. She took his hand and led him to her comfy white bed. They kissed and held each other until their eyes closed. They slept soundly, nestled together, each warding off the other's nightmares, and awoke to the sound of sea birds calling to each other in the distance.

Aliza's first thought was, Heaven. *This is pure heaven.* She nuzzled into the still sleeping Jesse's chest, closing her eyes again for a moment. When she opened them once more, she drank in the pale turquoise walls, the fresh white curtains fluttering in the sea breeze, the scent of salt air, and beach roses. She wanted this moment to etch itself into her memory, for if the center of her labyrinth could be an actual place, this was it. She was fully content, even if it was for one last moment before reality set in. The thought that they would be leaving this magical place in a matter of hours barged in on her reverie. Instead of letting sadness shatter her perfect contentment and replace it with anxiety, she held happiness. Like a mother holds her child, close to her breast, breathing it in, Aliza loved this tender moment with all her soul.

Jesse stirred, and Aliza's focus shifted from her thoughts of leaving to thoughts of Jesse. She observed the pale lavender skin around his eyes and the way his milky skin set off his freckles. He was every girl's dream guy, and here he was, in her bed, loving her despite her frailties and failures. Her happiness deepened, and she allowed herself to focus on him instead of herself, dwelling on each hair on his head and every breath he took. He was part of the center of her labyrinth as well. Without him, she would not have maintained even a shred of perspective and self-worth. Not to mention, she loved him.

As she thought it, the purest love welled up within her. She loved him. She loved him because he cared so deeply for her. She loved him because he had so steadfastly believed in her ability to recover. She loved him for the sweet, gentle, attractive, intelligent, sarcastic, charming man he was. With this deep love came some peace. It swept aside the anxiety she felt about leaving. She was only leaving the place, after all, not the person she loved.

She nuzzled into him again overjoyed to love someone so much. Christopher was right. She needed to love herself before she could love Jesse, and this proved she was getting there. In her contentment, Aliza fell asleep again until Jesse woke her with a kiss.

Propped up on his elbow, he looked at her, and she could still feel the sensation of his lips on hers from a moment ago. Aliza remembered the feelings of love and contentment that had ushered her to sleep as they swept back into her consciousness. They must have settled around her like an aura, because Jesse looked quizzical.

"You look like an angle," he said. "Like a peaceful angel in a renaissance painting."

"That's funny," she returned, "because I feel more like a frolicking wood nymph."

She tickled him in the spot right above his ribs and under his arms that drove him to distraction. He jerked himself away, laughing as she swung herself on top of him, pinning him down by the wrists.

The tension between their bodies sobered both of them into silence. Aliza was extremely conscious of her breathing, wondering if she always breathed this loud. Jesse seemed hyper-aware, too. His eyes sparkled brightly, and his breathing was erratic. She felt him come alive beneath her, and it was thrilling. Wanting him now more than ever she asked herself a simple question. *Why not? Everyone else gets to enjoy their relationships. Why not me?*

With that liberating thought, she pressed her body against his, still holding his wrists, and kissed him deeply.

She was about to whisper her deepest desires to him when there was a knock on the door. Aliza sprang out of the bed, horror-struck, and ran to the door. "Yes," she called out in a shaky voice.

"Don't mean to disturb the lovebirds, but Jesse left his cellphone downstairs. It just rang. I thought he'd want to know." Charlotte's voice sounded totally amused.

Aliza opened the door to show Charlotte they were innocent of her suspicions, at least for the time being. "I'll tell him to go down."

Charlotte winked at her, and Aliza blushed deeply. She shut the door and went over to Jesse who looked like he was about to burst with laughter.

"You jumped out of bed so fast. I've never seen a wild animal move with speed like that."

Aliza gave him a playful smack on the arm. "I'm mortified. The only night we stayed together in here, and she has to find us in the morning? Uh."

"That's Charlotte Black for you. Don't kid yourself. She's been checking every morning. I think she's been waiting to give me the safe sex speech."

Aliza hid her face in her hands and shook her head. "Oh, goodness. I'm so embarrassed."

"Don't be. It's not like we were going at it or anything."

Aliza looked at Jesse with a tortured expression and then turned away. "You have a phone call, Jesse."

"You wanted to, didn't you?"

"Just go down. We can talk later."

"You know I did too, right? That I've wanted to for ages? Like since the moment I met you?"

"Why have you waited to tell me that?"

"Because love is more than just sex. Besides. I'm kind of a glutton for punishment." He kissed her on the cheek. "I'll see you downstairs. I love you."


Aliza tried to put the fiasco out of her mind. She took a shower, got dressed, and went down only to hear the last moments of Jesse's phone conversation. She suddenly wished she'd taken a much longer shower.

"You need to go to sleep. It's like four in the morning there. Sober up." He paused, obviously listening to the person on the other line. "I told you, we're over...I've been seeing someone else for months...Yes. I love her...No, I didn't love you..."

Jesse fiddled with the objects around the living room as he paced. He picked up a paperweight made of glass. "I'm sorry you feel that way. Well, you should have thought about that before I left LA...I'm sorry, Grace. It's too late for that...Yes, I had a great time with you...Sure. You know that...No, it doesn't matter...I don't know, maybe. I mean it, Grace."

He continued pacing, pausing to lean his arm across the mantelpiece, looking exasperated. "Go to bed. You'll forget all about this in the morning...Well, there's not much that can be done about it now. I've moved on. I hope you feel better. Good bye."

Aliza's stomach knotted. Her eavesdropping was totally unintentional, but she had heard so much. Grace. She hadn't thought about Grace in months. Maybe Jesse still loved her after all. She was super beautiful. Aliza had seen pictures. What would Jesse say? Would he tell her the truth about who was on the phone? Would he try to lie? What did she want, anyway? It sounded like she wanted him back. Aliza groaned. Jesse turned around. She came down the stairs, hoping she didn't look as stricken as she felt.

"You look great," Jesse said, despite her expression. He kissed her, but he seemed distracted.

"Thanks. Who was that on the phone?"

Jesse hesitated. "Do you really want to know?"

"Yes, but only if you want to tell me."

"It was Grace. She was wasted and was drunk dialing people. I guess I'm still on her phone list."

"She still has a thing for you."

"Apparently. I didn't know, though, until just now. I guess honesty was never her strong suit."

"Do you want to go back to her? You can, you know. There is nothing tying you to me."

"You mean other than the undying devotion anchoring my soul to yours? No, you're right. That's hardly worth mentioning." He gave Aliza a playful kiss on the head.

"I mean it. You don't have to stay with me. You could go back to her."

"Why on earth would I do that? Your memory must not be very good, but I remember that the moment I met you, I forgot all about Grace. You were all I could think about. You still are."

"Really?" Aliza said miserably.

"Really. I love you, Aliza. You mean the world to me. I'm sure there's a cheesy song I could sing you right now, but I value my shins too much."

"I would kick you. You're right." They both laughed and went into the kitchen to make coffee.

"I'm going to miss this place like crazy," Aliza said as they sat huddled together under a blanket on the terrace. The air was cool and dewy. The coffee warmed them from the inside.

"I will too. I don't know how it happened, but I think I had forgotten how much I love it here until this visit."

"What's going to happen to this place when your grandma and Christopher get married?"

"I don't know. She should sell it and live in Christopher's house, but I don't think she will. She knows I love it here, but that shouldn't affect her decision."

"Gosh, I hope she doesn't sell it. I want to come back. I know that's pure selfishness, but I want to come back."

"We'll see what happens, I guess. I've already told her I don't want her to let it go, and she said she was having a hard time even thinking about leaving. It means too much."

"Good."

"Are you ready for the drive?"

"No. I don't want to leave so I didn't pack."

"That's one way of dealing with it."

"I don't want to face the crew and the cast back in Twin Falls. I just don't. The thought makes me a little sick to my stomach."

"Why? Everyone loves you. They're all rooting for you."

"That's the problem. I want to be normal, live a normal life, blend in. You know."

"You'll always stand out. For starters, you're a knockout. Then there's your personality. Over the top."

"Yeah, yeah. You know what I mean."

"Sure, I do. Instead of having everyone look at you as Aliza Bennett, Child Star, you want them to see Aliza. Who you are and what you are. As is."

"Like a broken, mis-matched set of china sold in a junk shop. As is."

"Exactly."

They both giggled again, then drifted into a comfortable silence, watching the sea.

Charlotte and Christopher eventually joined them, and Aliza knew that the goodbyes were imminent. It gave her the butterflies to think of leaving Marblehead. She had grown to love Charlotte and

Christopher as though they were her own family and Marblehead as if it was her home.

When they got the car packed and had eaten some eggs and had drank what amounted to three pots of coffee, it was finally time to say goodbye.

"I hope you'll come back for the wedding," Charlotte said to Aliza as she hugged her for the third time.

"Of course. Let us know when you set a date."

"Done deal," Christopher interjected. "I'm not going to let this lovely woman have a chance to change her mind. We're aiming for somewhere near Christmas."

"Perfect. I love a holiday wedding," Jesse said.

Everyone looked at him like he was crazy. He got defensive. "What? A guy can't like the idea of a holiday wedding? Geez."

They all giggled and laughed.

When it was Christopher's turn to hug Aliza, he slipped her a card. "This has my private number on it. I want you to call me any time, day or night."

"Thank you. You've already done so much for me."

"I mean it, Aliza. Use the number. I want you to be well, understand?"

"Yes."

"You've come a long way in a short amount of time. You will recover, my dear. You will be whole. Believe it."

"I do believe it, Christopher. Thank you so much." Aliza hugged him fiercely.

Jesse and Charlotte watched them say goodbye from a few paces away. Jesse's arm was around his grandmother and tears were streaming down her cheeks. Charlotte snuck one more hug in for each of them before they left, wishing them a safe trip.

They didn't talk for a while, but they held hands as they drove. It was enough. As they left Massachusetts, they finally managed some small talk, but neither of them wanted to bring up what they were thinking about, their imminent return to Twin Falls. It would be upon them soon enough without discussing it.

They pulled into the town in the late afternoon and stopped at Neven's Restaurant for dinner. Aliza thought it was funny to be back in the first restaurant they had ever eaten at together. It was like starting over. She ordered a slice of apple pie for old time's sake.

"Damn, that's good," Jesse exclaimed after the first bite.

"I can't believe this is what we missed out on that day because I couldn't deal with you reading my mind."

"You just didn't like me ordering for you."

"That was definitely part of it," Aliza agreed, smiling. "The waitress thought I was nuts. Maybe I was."

"Nuts are for squirrels, Aliza. You're just you. Simple as that."

"If I didn't love you so much, I would kick you under the table for that one, but I love you, so I won't." Aliza's eyes glittered wickedly.

Jesse rolled his eyes. "Fine. I won't say trite things, but you can't stop me from thinking them." He smiled at her warmly and she shook her head, thinking about how lucky she felt to have him.


Evening fell as they made their way up to Aliza's apartment. Jesse had asked if she wanted to stay at his place that night, but she insisted on going back to her own place. "It will be fine. I've been living there for months. It's okay."

"I have to go to my place and get some things together."

"Clean underwear, you mean."

Jesse blushed, which gave away how nervous he was about being back. "Yes, if you must know. I've recycled two pair already," he said sheepishly.

"I'm usually such a big fan of recycling, too." Aliza went over to Jesse and hugged him.

"What was that for?" he said to her in surprise.

"You are wonderful, and I'm lucky to have you. Go home, underwear boy. I'll see you in a little while. We can watch old movies and fall asleep on the couch."

"Sounds like a plan. But 'underwear boy?'"

Aliza winked and pushed him out the door. She locked it behind him and took a deep breath before turning around. *I can do this.* She spun around to face the empty room, half expecting to see the specter of her memory manifest itself before her, but nothing happened. She hesitated and then gingerly padded across the room. Sitting in the armchair, she realized she wasn't sure what to expect anymore. She nearly hit the ceiling when her phone rang in her pocket. She laughed at herself for being so jumpy and answered it.

It was Rudy checking in on her.

"Tell me all about your vacation," the director said to her.

"It was incredible. The ocean was breathtaking, much quainter than LA, and Jesse's grandmother is the kindest woman I've ever met."

"That's wonderful. My vacation, in contrast, was a disaster."

Rudy gave her a detailed account of his inauspicious trip to see his cousins in New York City. Wires had gotten crossed. They weren't expecting him until the following week. He left no moment unaccounted for.

By the time Aliza got off the phone with him Jesse was back. She accused him immediately. "Did you tell Rudy to call me?"

"What? No. Why would I do that?"

"Because you didn't want me to be by myself while you were gone."

Jesse shifted uncomfortably. "Okay, yes. I did. I told him to talk to you until he couldn't talk any more. I'm sorry. I was only thinking about your feelings."

"Well, he talked incessantly. I was wondering what was wrong with him, then it hit me. You did it."

"Yes. I did, and I'd do it again." Jesse was using a playful tone, but he seemed guarded never the less.

"Come here. You need punishment for that near hour of torture."

"What exactly do you have in mind?

"I'm sure I'll think of something." Instead of being mad at Jesse for being so overprotective, Aliza was grateful, a departure from her personality the past couple of months. It was like finally seeing a window where there had always been a brick wall.

He walked over to her, kneeled, and put his head in her lap. Aliza felt the warmth of his face against her thigh as she stroked his hair. Then, she took his face in her hands and gently lifted it up to meet hers. She leaned in and kissed him.

"Just don't do it again," she said in a mock- reprimanding tone. "Get me a pizza and all is forgiven."

"Pepperoni?"

"Do you have to ask?"

They spent what Aliza deemed to be a perfect evening, eating pizza and watching Sherlock Holmes. Aliza had finally broken down and bought the Jeremy Brett versions on DVD. Jesse was now as big a fan as Aliza.

"I looked him up, you know," she said as she put in the DVD.

"Really? What did you find?"

"Jeremy Brett led an interesting life, but it was very sad towards the end. He lost his wife to cancer and his manic-depressive tendencies took hold. He started obsessing over his role as Sherlock Holmes, sometimes forgetting himself completely. The tragedy seemed to have put him over the edge. His friends tried to help him get better, but he stayed committed to his role of Sherlock Holmes until the very end."

"Wow. You'd never know by watching him act that there was anything wrong. He is so perfect."

"Yeah, I know. He embodies his role. I guess maybe it's because of his illness. It's hard to know. People go through a lot, don't they?"

"Yep. I was thinking about that recently. People who face war or famine or genocide must go through so much emotional and physical pain, but they can still recover. Humans are so resilient. The spirit can spring back after even the most amazingly difficult experiences."

"I know where you're going with this," Aliza murmured, looking away.

"Well, your assault was awful. You could have died. It's not as terrible seeing a war all around you or being starved half to death, but it's still rotten, and you are recovering."

"It's not a fair comparison. What I went through doesn't even come close to what tortured people endure, I know it. It's part of why I won't cut myself any slack, Jesse. I need to suck it up and plow ahead."

"See, that's where I think you're wrong. I hope you don't mind me talking frankly with you. I've been thinking a lot about it lately because of your work with Christopher. You need to know you were hurt, that it's okay to be sad, angry, or scared, or all of the above. You need to know that you are not alone in your experiences."

"Are you talking about a support group?"

"Maybe. I don't know. I think Christopher is a great first step, but maybe you'll want to use your experience to help other people."

Aliza paused, thinking about what Jesse was saying. She'd had thoughts along those lines before, but she was unsure whether she was fit to help anyone. Lately, though, she was feeling stronger. *Maybe.*

"I'll think about it," she said. "You think if Jeremy Brett had joined a support group after his wife died then he wouldn't have gone off the deep end?"

"I don't know. Maybe he was always bipolar, and it took the sad event to amplify it. It's hard to say with abusive situations like you and my mom experienced. You are both whole, happy, sane people who have had crappy experiences. You might help other people. Plus, you're famous. That never hurts."

"Right. I don't know. I'll think about it."

Jesse exhaled deeply. Aliza looked at him and realized that he had taken quite a risk in speaking so frankly with her. Again, for the past two months, she might not have taken it quite so well. She smiled at his visible relief and decided not to belabor the point.

"One more and then bed, okay?" She pressed play and snuggled back up to Jesse who held her tightly, kissed her head, and whispered, "I love you, Aliza."

"I love you too, Jesse."

# FIFTEEN

*Pleased with her work, the jeweler knows she has managed to create something beautiful. The pendant has come through torture, pounding, piercing, and fire, all to become this gleaming, meaningful object. It all stems from one word, she muses, from the most important word in her new life's vocabulary. Love.*

They got down to business the next day at the shoot. Everything was just as they had left it except everyone seemed refreshed, revived, and ready to work hard. Rudy put it best during his welcome back address. "Vacation does you good. Now get back to work."

Michelle commented on Aliza's well-rested visage, going on about her perfect face and attractive eyes. Aliza was about to ask her to dial it down a notch when Rudy came in to talk to her.

"Hi, Rudy."

"Good morning, beautiful."

"Thanks for keeping me distracted last night. Sorry Jesse put you up to it."

"He was worried, was all. You've come back from your vacation looking quite well."

279

"Thanks. I think I fell in love with Marblehead. Can we move the shoot there?"

Rudy laughed. "Yeah. I can see how you'd go for a quaint Massachusetts town, all curvy roads and cobblestones. Did anyone tell you where to pahk yah cah?"

Aliza giggled. "As a matter of fact, there was some seriously outrageous accents floating around, but we didn't go local too much, if you know what I mean. Jesse's grandmother's house was great, and we mostly hung out there a lot and relaxed."

"Glad to hear it. Well, let me know if I can do anything for ya, pal, but you look like a changed woman. You do."

"Thanks, Rudy. Good to see you."

"We're all so happy to see you looking more like yourself, Aliza," Michelle added when Rudy was gone. "It was terrible to see you hurt."

"I know. I appreciate your patience and understanding. Please pass on that sentiment, if you don't mind. I am still going to pay for the mess I made before we left, by the way."

"It's all taken care of, sweetie. No worries, but that's the kind of great person you are. You are still willing to admit your faults and own up to your actions. I appreciate it."

"I felt so bad about losing it. I'm relearning to keep my emotions under control, and I'm trying to, um..." She paused, looking embarrassed. "It sounds so stupid. I'm trying to *love* myself again."

"It doesn't sound stupid at all, sweetie. There's a lot to love and don't you forget it."

Michelle embraced Aliza and patted her on the back. Then she looked her full in the face. "Go get 'em, kid."

"Thanks, Michelle. See you later."

Leaving the makeup room, Aliza's stomach reminded her that she had skipped breakfast and hadn't had time to pick something up on her way to the studio. Then she remembered the snack table. She tried to resist, but it was too hard. Smiling to herself, she went in search of donuts. *It's good to be back.*

Shooting went smoothly, because everyone was well rested and enthusiastic. Aliza shot some scenes with Jesse, and there was real chemistry between them. Their interactions felt more authentic than they had up until that point, and Aliza was grateful. She didn't want to admit it, but she had questioned for a while whether she had lost her ability to act. The vacation had done her more good than she realized. She was doubly thankful for Rudy's patience during the past months as well. Many directors wouldn't have put up with a sub-par performance from their leading actress regardless of the assault. If she couldn't live in Marblehead yet, this was good enough.

Jesse seemed enthused as well, and after the shoot they took a drive on Aliza's motorcycle. They grabbed some sandwiches for dinner and rode out to the gorge. It was a perfect afternoon. The air was still warm but not humid, and the sunlit trees stood vivid against the pure blue sky. There was no one at the gorge, which made sense since it was a Monday. They sat on the rocks and dangled their feet in the cool river, watching an occasional tiny fish flit by. Jesse and Aliza frolicked and played like children, skipping rocks and chasing each other from boulder to boulder. They hiked downstream as far as they could and found an exquisite waterfall. They took pictures of each other posing against the sky, on the rocks, and nestled against the soft green moss clinging to the ledges where the forest ended, and the gorge began. It was magical. Aliza managed to keep all negative thoughts at bay, and by the time they decided to eat their sandwiches, it was almost dusk. They finally lay down on a sun-warmed rock, in each other's arms, watching the changing colors of the sky, feeling extraordinarily content.

She had collected a pocket full of rocks, some of them were black and smooth like the one on her necklace, others were jagged with bits of exposed quartz and garnet. They were lovely, and she had a plan. Tomorrow, she was going to visit Karen McDonald the jewelry maker and beg for tutelage. She had not shared her plan with Jesse yet, although she wasn't sure why. It didn't seem necessary unless Karen said yes. Aliza decided that she had to say yes. No wasn't an option.

This is where her thoughts were when Jesse turned on his side and faced her. "Hi," he said. "You look far away with the sky reflected in your eyes."

"I'm thinking, I guess. It's such a gorgeous afternoon."

"Gorge-ous?" Jesse repeated the word, emphasizing the *gorge* part of it and raising his eyebrows in anticipation of her reaction.

"What am I going to do with you?" Aliza wondered aloud, clearly amused.

"I have some ideas," Jesse replied seductively.

Aliza shook her head and lay quietly on the rock for a while. "How are you, now that we're back?"

"So happy. I wondered if Marblehead was a dream and if we would come back to Twin Falls and forget how to be overwhelmed by happiness. Turns out, we taught ourselves something, or relearned it, or whatever. The point is, we can do it. We can be happy together anywhere. I'm so happy."

"I guess so. You said the word happy like four times in one breath." She giggled at him playfully. "I'm happy too, now that you mention it. It's been a very good day."

"I'm glad we're in agreement." He leaned down to kiss her, moving his prone body closer to hers. The sensation of Jesse pressing her against the rock was electric. His heat, the rock's solidity, her living, yearning being, all fused together in a burst of deep, thrilling, primal energy. She wanted him closer.

When she had caught her breath, she asked him in a near whisper, "Do you think anyone would notice if we made love right here on this rock?" She ran her hand under his shirt, down his bare back, letting the passion she felt transfer in pressure to his body.

Jesse, taken aback, took a moment to answer. "Um, I don't know. We're dogged by tabloid photographers sometimes, so I don't know if we should take that kind of chance. The last thing we'd want to see is our most intimate moment on the cover of every magazine in the grocery store."

She sighed. "You're probably right. It would be perfect, though." Ferocity rose in her again, however. "I'm tired of waiting. I'm ready now. I'm willing to risk it. Are you?"

Her gaze darkened as desire overrode her logic. Pulling him back on top of her, she kissed him madly. They wrapped the picnic blanket they had brought over themselves and undressed each other slowly, giggling as they fumbled with the physical logistics, taking their time with every tiny movement. It had taken them so long to get to this moment, Aliza wanted to slow down time and enjoy the experience fully.

Once they were undressed and thoroughly excited, Jesse paused to ask her again. "Are you sure?"

"I want you. Now," she replied gazing into his eyes with a look of pure, unrehearsed seduction.

They made love on the sun-warmed rock, the sound of the rushing torrent of water only inches away. Jesse was gentle and thoughtful. He knew exactly how to make Aliza's body respond. They didn't pause for breath. They didn't speak. They only stole glimpses of each other's passion in the swiftly dimming light, in the rare moment when their bodies separated enough to provide a vantage point. It was the pure joy of a long-awaited union, sweet and full of love, and they savored every second, willing it to last forever.

Later, when they got back to Aliza's apartment they repeated their performance in the living room and then in the bedroom. It was almost like an exorcism, Aliza later determined, as though they were purifying the apartment of the past and filling it with a new, pure, and ecstatic energy. She had never slept better in her life than she did that night, and when they woke, they started all over again.

After shooting was over for the day, Aliza told Jesse she had to run an errand.

"I'll meet you for dinner at my place," she said, kissing him goodbye.

"Okay, Aliza. See you later."

She set off towards Karen's jewelry store and since Twin Falls was the size of a postage stamp, she was there in no time. A bell tinkled as she entered the store, the glass cabinets glowed with warm light, showcasing the artwork within. The air smelled faintly of incense. A woman's voice called from the back, "I'll be with you in a moment."

"No problem," Aliza answered. "Please take your time."

This gave her a few minutes to look around. Aliza immediately responded to the way Karen had arranged the display cases. Interspersed with the jewelry were little natural objects like shells and sea urchins, minuscule antique statues from South America and Asia, bits of poetry from famous authors typed up on old parchment, and to Aliza's delight, there was a book about labyrinths on the counter. After admiring every case of Karen's jewelry, she returned to the book and began reading it. She found the unicursal labyrinth upon which Karen had based her necklace and read the entry.

She was almost finished when she realized Karen had been standing behind one of the counters watching her.

"I didn't want to startle you," Karen said, her husky voice subdued and her expression inscrutable.

"Thanks," Aliza replied, setting down the book. "I hope you don't mind I was reading your book."

"Of course not, that's why it's there. I can understand why you might be interested in it. I hope you're enjoying the necklace, Miss Bennett." Karen smiled warmly. "I'm glad you came by. I've kind of been expecting you for a while."

"You have? Why?"

"I don't know. I had a feeling you'd make your way here eventually."

"Well, please call me Aliza," she said, moving forward with her hand outstretched.

Rather than shake her hand, however, Karen took it gently in both of hers and turned it over, examining her palm. "May I?"

"Um, I've never had anyone ask me that before. Sure. Just spare me any bad news, if you don't mind."

Karen studied the lines on Aliza's hand for a few moments and said, "Hmm. I am glad you waited to come. You've recently had a turning point, and I wouldn't have wanted to ruin the surprise for you. You're over the hump, my dear. In the clear. Healing. I'm so glad."

Her tone was so earnest and her eyes so kind behind those dark framed glasses that Aliza exhaled a sigh of relief and let out an involuntary giggle, trying with all her might not to cry at Karen's words.

"Anything else?"

"What do you want to know?"

"Anything you can tell me, I guess."

"Well, your lifeline is long, and your love-line is strong, but jagged at the beginning. It evens out, so don't worry. I think you're going to make a great artist."

"So, you know why I'm here?" Aliza was totally mystified. How could this stranger know so much about her?

"I can guess. You want to make something beautiful, but you don't think you know how."

"You're right. I want to make jewelry, but I wanted to start by thanking you for making my necklace. It has helped me through some rough times, a constant reminder that I needed to find my way back to myself. I'm still working on it, but it's getting much better. It occurred to me recently that I want to be able to create things that can have that much meaning for someone else. I want to learn from you, if you'll teach me."

Karen didn't reply right away. She let go of Aliza's hand and studied her eyes instead. Her gaze was unrelenting, but somehow it didn't make Aliza uneasy. She returned it undaunted. "You are a strong woman. Most people would cower after what you have been through, but here you are asking for what you want. Learning metalsmithing is not a task that should be undertaken lightly, though. It is laborious and often tedious. You may not want to do it after you see how much work can go into the tiniest of things."

"I've never been afraid of hard work."

Karen smiled. "If you're serious, let's give it a trial period. After that, if you decide that metal work is not for you, then we will discuss your various other options for creative self-expression, not that acting isn't an art form, which of course, it is."

"That's fair. What kind of trial are you talking about?"

"Watching. Just watching. Have you ever seen someone make jewelry?"

"No," Aliza replied honestly.

"It's not like blowing glass, for instance. With glass, there is relatively instant gratification. The finish work takes time, but the body of the piece usually happens in a few short hours. Drawing, also. Metal work, however, and in particular jewelry, takes days to shape things. Filing, piercing, soldering, polishing. It's all done on such a small scale and in such a meticulous way that you need to have the right temperament, or you go crazy."

"Oh," Aliza said, feeling kind of silly for even being there.

"If you do have the right temperament, it can be like meditation. You focus so intently on the task that hours speed by, your mind finds an incredible calm. If that sounds good to you, come with me."

"It does sound good. It's exactly what I'm looking for."

Aliza followed Karen through a curtained doorway to the back room. Small windows at the top of the far wall let in a lot of natural light. The area held two jeweler's benches, a soldering station with two different torches, a fascinating selection of hammers and die, and some strange smelling liquids in hot pots. There was also a dorm fridge and a ratty, retro sofa with a coffee table in front of it.

"This is my studio. It took me years to get to the point where I could have my own space. It's ironic. I yearned to have a studio of my own, not to have to share with ten other people, but when I got it I was lonely for weeks. Go figure."

Karen led Aliza to her bench, upon which was a work in progress. Aliza leaned in to take a closer look and gasped. "It's incredible," she breathed earnestly. "I've never seen anything like it." Aliza examined the tiny piece of artwork before her. There was a large, round, slightly domed moonstone. The metal work setting around it was an intricate filigree done in silver resembling waves or wind. It reminded Aliza of her night on the beach with Jesse with the full moon reflected in the water, bouncing playfully on the waves. "Can I pick it up?"

"Sure. But the stone's not set yet, so don't drop it."

Aliza carefully picked up the piece, looking closely at the patterns in the metal. "How do you come up with your ideas?"

"Every stone has a story, I think. I try to listen to what they each have to say. This one wanted to be reunited with water. So, I obliged."

"How do you part with them? I mean, this is so much work, and it's so beautiful. Wouldn't you be sad to see it go?"

"You said so yourself. I make things other people will connect with. Jewelry is essential to human expression. We have always adorned ourselves with objects we find meaningful. Artists tap into the energy that links people with things. We are the conduits for that link. When the right person finds this piece, it will come full circle."

"Twin Falls is so small how do you sell enough to stay open?"

"The internet, of course. It's the only way I could do what I do. I have a following around the world. It's great. I get some major attention at galleries in New York and LA that I never would have garnered as a small-town jeweler otherwise."

"Are you from here?"

"Nope. I grew up in Chicago. I hated the city. I longed for a tiny town, so after college I drove around a while and looked for the right place. This felt right, and I've been here going on fifteen years."

"Wow. I know what you mean. Jesse took me to Marblehead, Massachusetts, where he's from, and the same thing happened. I fell in love with the place, and I think I'd like to live there eventually."

"All in good time, I'm sure."

"Yep. I've got a lot of commitments I need to follow through with right now, but someday."

"Pull up a stool and I'll show you what I do."

Aliza spent an hour watching Karen's fine, careful work. She gently tapped bits of silver into a refined shape, following some plan Aliza couldn't see until the metal was in its new position. She watched as Karen pinched and filed and tested the stone in its setting again and again. Filing the metal created silver dust that fell into a leather pouch beneath the worktable. It was like every other aspect of jewelry making, Aliza learned, to save such a small amount of precious material. In this work, small mattered.

After a while, Aliza's thoughts stopped coming in words. She just watched, curious and interested, but calm and content. She even had a little smile on her face.

Eventually Karen looked at her. "This always happens. An hour went by. It's getting late, and I have plans tonight."

Aliza looked at the clock, startled. "I was supposed to meet Jesse a half an hour ago. Can I come back tomorrow?"

"Of course. See you then."

———

"I've been worried about you," was Jesse's greeting to Aliza. She could smell that he had cooked dinner, and he looked slightly amused by her late arrival.

"Sorry, I should have called. I've been with Karen, watching her work."

"Karen McDonald?"

"Yep."

"Cool.

"Yeah, she is neat."

"What did she say?"

"She knew me the moment she saw me. Then, she read my palm."

"Really?"

"Yep, and it wasn't weird or creepy or anything. It's just her *way* if you know what I mean."

"I think I do. She is a unique person."

"She's also an amazing talent. Her work is incredible. I hadn't thought much about what her other work would be like, but when I saw it, I was floored. She is a true artist."

"Then what?"

"Then I asked her to teach me how to make jewelry, and she said she'd consider it on a trial basis and for me to watch her for a while to see if making jewelry is a good fit for me."

"What do you think?"

"I don't know. The work is extraordinary to watch, but it's so time consuming. I don't know if I have that kind of patience, and I'm sure I don't have that kind of time."

"You'd find the time if it's important to you."

"Yeah, I guess. I'll watch Karen for a few days and think about it. There's no rush. I want to create something beautiful, that's all."

"Do some sketches. See if you can get the ideas out of your head so even if you can't make them now you don't lose them."

"That is a great idea, Jesse. Thank you so much. I'll do it."

Jesse pulled her to him and kissed her. "You must be hungry."

"How did you know?"

"Because I'm hungry too."

They ate their dinner side by side at the small dining room table. There was no trace of tension or sadness in their manor. Aliza realized that this is how Christopher and Charlotte were in each other's company, perfectly at ease, meant to be together. The thought warmed her from the inside out, driving out old fears and miseries and self-doubts, transforming the vacant places they left behind in her mind into gardens by the sea.

She could finally see a clear picture in her mind of what she wanted and what she deserved. She would live on the East Coast, she would make jewelry. She would act to pay the bills, and most of all, she would be peaceful. She would love with abandon, because she had every right to do so. As joy and love nestled into her, Aliza knew, absolutely, that she would be okay.

# EPILOGUE

*Art can begin with a full-fledged idea, springing forth like Athena from Zeus' skull, glorious, brimming with meaning, the creator's delight. Other times, a concept struggles for form, a changeling in darkness, striving to be born. This creation can be a long labor, emerging through pain and sacrifice, blinding the creator for a moment when the true form finally takes hold. Still other times, the creation is a surprisingly gentle walk down a moonlit path to the sea. The artist finds her way one step at a time, and although she cannot see very far into the darkness she can hear the crash of the surf against singing sands. She puts her faith in the path itself, knowing her destination is not so far away.*

———

# ACKNOWLEDGMENTS

Thank you to my dear friend Carly and to my wonderful Dad for being my first beta readers. Your thoughtful encouragement and knowledgeable comments bolstered my courage. Thank you as well to T and E and S for your continued love and support.

# THANK YOU FOR READING

_____

Did you enjoy this book?

We invite you to leave a review at your favorite book site, such as Goodreads, Amazon, Barnes & Noble, etc.

## DID YOU KNOW THAT LEAVING A REVIEW...

- Helps other readers find books they may enjoy.
- Gives you a chance to let your voice be heard.
- Gives authors recognition for their hard work.
- Doesn't have to be long. A sentence or two about why you liked the book will do.

## ABOUT THE AUTHOR

Emma Hartley is an author and artist living in picturesque Maine. She has been writing and making art since childhood and has been insatiably curious and industrious her whole life. Emma was a double major in English and Fine Arts and holds a Masters in Art and Design Education. This devotion to art is apparent in her in her novels, manifesting itself in the work her characters enjoy. Emma's other interests include playing drums in an indie rock band, gardening, and exploring every square inch of the Maine coastline. *The Annealing of Aliza Bennett* is her second novel.

www.emmahartleyauthor.com
www.facebook.com/emmahartleyauthor

## ALSO BY EMMA HARTLEY

*The Nature of Entangled Hearts*
*The Annealing of Aliza Bennett*